Praise fo.
THE JUDGE HUNTER

"An entertaining and nicely crafted picaresque thriller with crackling dialogue and a brace of Colonial cops as appealingly mismatched as any of Hollywood's buddy efforts."

—*Kirkus Reviews*, starred review

"Christopher Buckley's style of satire has a peculiar bite: It nibbles, nibbles, nibbles—gently, even delightfully—before chomping down and leaving teeth marks as distinctive as any known to forensic science. . . . *The Judge Hunter* is a brisk adventure."

—*The Weekly Standard*

"Christopher Buckley fans and newcomers to his work will delight in this humorous historical novel."

—*Bookish*

"It's murder and mirth in Christopher Buckley's *The Judge Hunter*."

—*Vanity Fair*

"A wry, witty, enjoyable romp. . . .With an almost British, Monty Python–esque dryness, Buckley traipses through the American Colonies and skewers the foibles of the inhabitants."

—*Library Journal*

"Buckley (*The Relic Master*) has turned his quick wit and sharp writing focus on the 17th century in this 2nd book in his historical fiction series. . . . Peppered with historical characters—Peter Stuyvesant, John Winthrop II—and cleverly using Samuel Pepys' famous diaries, Buckley masterfully weaves a fictional story with historical fact . . . a rich story ripe for Buckley's humor and pointed satire on Puritan ideals, royal peccadillos, and political intrigue. *The Judge Hunter* is an absorbing mystery/thriller with humorous dialog and characters that resonate and draw in the reader. Buckley's ability to fuse fact with fiction makes this book a must for not just fans of historical fiction but anyone looking for a great read."

—*Historical Novels Review*, editor's choice

"*The Judge Hunter* is a captivating and witty new novel that combines adventure, comedy, political intrigue, and romance around real-life historical characters. Buckley has a razor-sharp wit . . . [a] brilliantly plotted historical novel that is extraordinarily entertaining. You will not stop laughing as you read it."

—*Washington Book Review*

"Wildly satisfying and funny. . . . *The Judge Hunter* is a satisfying romp through America in the 1600s."

—*Washington Independent Review of Books*

"Buckley's writing is breezy and his descriptions vivid."

—*The New York Times Book Review*

"Buckley's wry wit is on display throughout. . . . The characters and events of the period covered in *The Judge Hunter* offer a trove of material. . . . Carefully researched and constructed with a wealth of authentic details, the novel succeeds in making a sometimes distant and stodgy-seeming era feel somehow contemporary."

—*National Review*

"In these days of nasty name-calling passing as humor there is thankfully one true practitioner of the literary art of satire still standing, and Christopher Buckley's second historical novel proves it. *The Judge Hunter* is full of humor that skewers historical figures in all their self-serving political ambitions. . . . Buckley's humorous satire . . . is both revealing of painful truths and the timelessness of bad human behavior."

—*New York Journal of Books*

"[Buckley is] a roaringly funny writer of polished comic novels. It is no exaggeration to say that, today, he is one of the best American writers working the genre. . . . [He], as always, has delivered a clever literary entertainment that manages to be both warm and wry."

—*The Washington Times*

"[A] rollicking, raucous, murderous, deliciously funny historical novel. . . . The book's a rush and a sheer delight, swift and scandalous, salty and sagacious, savvy and silly. And eminently enjoyable."

—*Providence Journal*

"Might be pitched Hollywood-style as *The Princess Bride* meets *Ocean's Thirteen*."

—*Kirkus Reviews*, starred review

"There's plenty of fighting and fakery, deceit and rationalization to go around. The political posturing, religious hypocrisy, and some of that old-time self-satirizing humor should entertain everyone."

—*The Boston Globe*

"Part Monty Python and part *Ocean's Eleven* . . . filled with laugh-out-loud one-liners but, amazingly, doesn't stint on the suspense."

—*Publishers Weekly*

Also by Christopher Buckley

The
JUDGE
HUNTER

Christopher Buckley

Simon & Schuster Paperbacks

New York   London   Toronto   Sydney   New Delhi

Simon & Schuster Paperbacks
An Imprint of Simon & Schuster, Inc.
1230 Avenue of the Americas
New York, NY 10020

First Simon & Schuster trade paperback edition May 2019

SIMON & SCHUSTER PAPERBACKS and colophon are registered trademarks
of Simon & Schuster, Inc.

For information about special discounts for bulk purchases, please contact
Simon & Schuster Special Sales at 1-866-506-1949
or business@simonandschuster.com.

The Simon & Schuster Speakers Bureau can bring authors to your live event.
For more information or to book an event, contact the
Simon & Schuster Speakers Bureau at 1-866-248-3049
or visit our website at www.simonspeakers.com.

Interior design by Paul Dippolito

Illustrated map by David Atkinson
handmademaps.com

Manufactured in the United States of America

1   3   5   7   9   10   8   6   4   2

Library of Congress Cataloging-in-Publication data is available.

ISBN 978-1-5011-9251-7
ISBN 978-1-5011-9253-1 (pbk)
ISBN 978-1-5011-9252-4 (ebook)

For Katy, thankfully

Contents

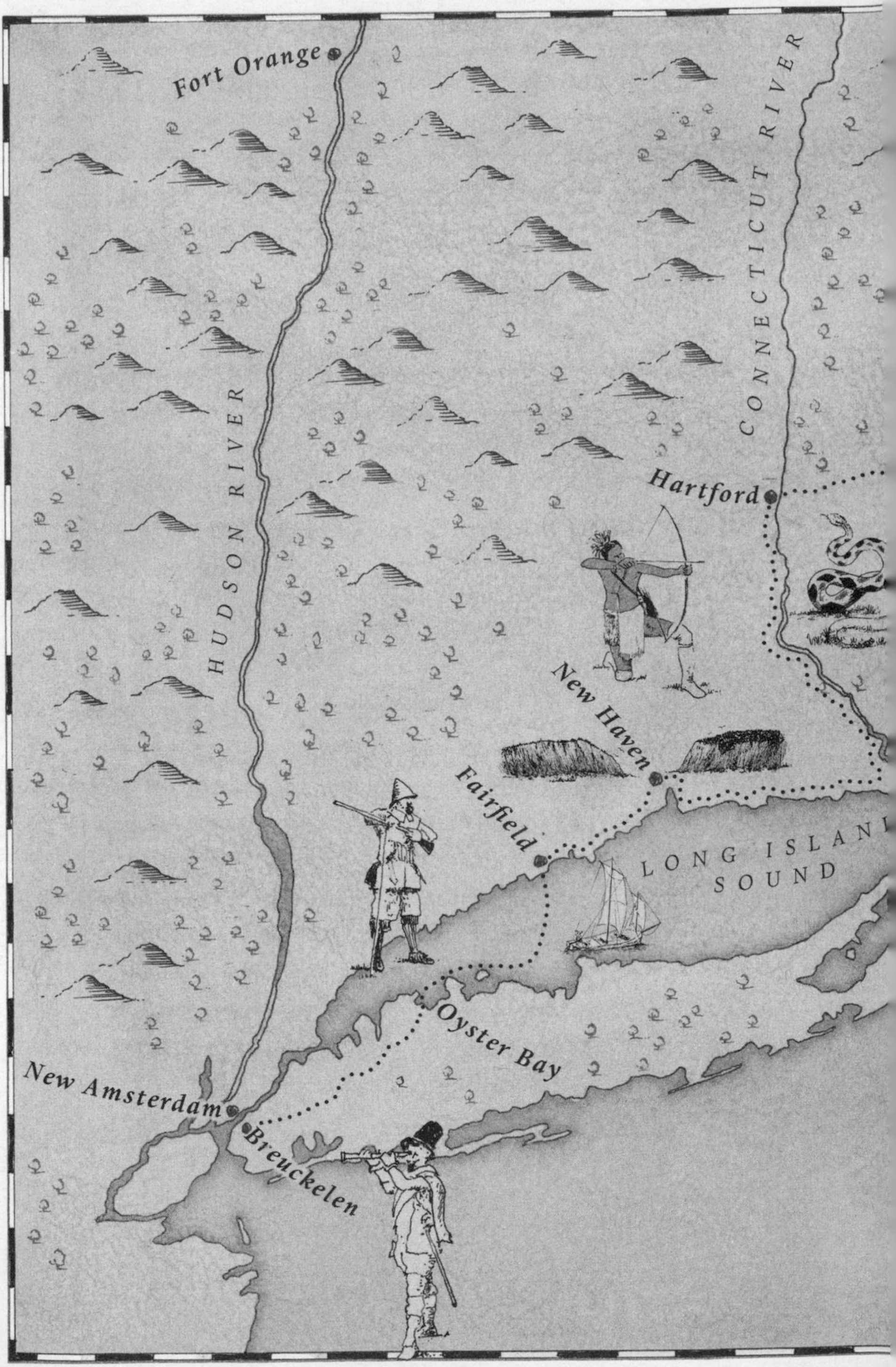

Fort Orange

CONNECTICUT RIVER

HUDSON RIVER

Hartford

New Haven

Fairfield

LONG ISLAND
SOUND

Oyster Bay

New Amsterdam

Breuckelen

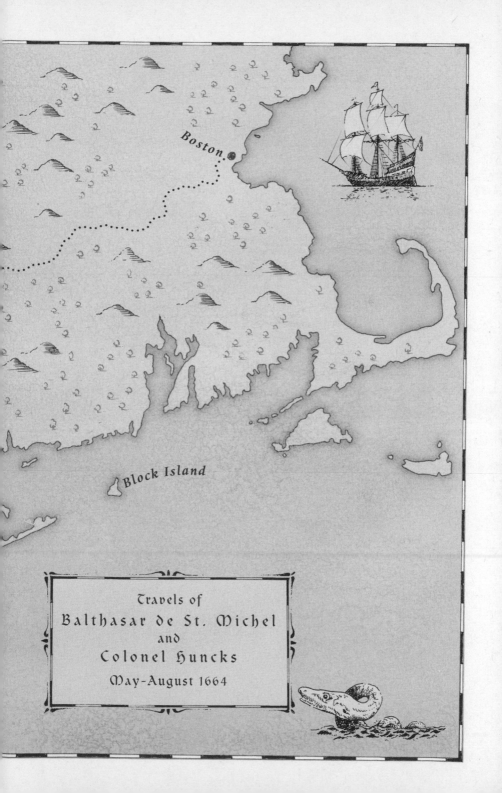

Boston

Block Island

Travels of
Balthasar de St. Michel
and
Colonel Huncks
May–August 1664

October 13th, 1660. *To my Lord's in the morning, where I met with Captain Cuttance, but my Lord not being up I went out to Charing Cross, to see Major-General Harrison hanged, drawn, and quartered, which was done there, he looking as cheerful as any man could do in that condition.*

Thus it was my chance to see the King beheaded at White Hall, and to see the first blood shed in revenge for the blood of the King at Charing Cross. From thence to my Lord's, and took Captain Cuttance and Mr. Sheply to the Sun Tavern, and did give them some oysters.

—Samuel Pepys, diary entry

CHAPTER 1

London, February 1664

Balthasar de St. Michel was contemplating his excellent good fortune at having such an influential brother-in-law as Samuel Pepys when he looked up and saw the head of Oliver Cromwell, mummifying on a pike. *Revolting*, he thought.

It had been there for—what—three years now? When the late king's son, Charles II, was restored to the throne, he ordered the moldering corpses of his father's executioners dug up, hanged, and decapitated. "Symbolic revenge." Ten of the fifty-nine men who signed the King's death warrant were rather less fortunate than Cromwell. They got hanged and butchered while alive.

Balthasar shuddered and moved briskly along to his destination, the Navy Office in Seething Lane, a busy warren near the Tower of London.

"Brother Sam!" he said with a heartiness suggesting it was a social call.

Samuel Pepys, Clerk of the Acts of the Royal Navy, looked up from his desk. His face did not convey delight. He knew from experience that this was not a social call.

"Brother Balty. I fear you find me much occupied."

"I was passing by. Thought to stick my head in. Say hello."

"Good of you," Pepys said heavily.

"What's the commotion?" Balty said, looking out the window at the bustle in the courtyard below.

"Meetings. So as you see, I *am* somewhat—"

"Say, how long are they going to leave Cromwell's head on that pike?"

Pepys sighed. "I wouldn't know. For as long as it pleases his majesty, I expect."

"Frightful thing."

"Yes, I imagine that's rather the point."

"Weren't you present when they"—Balty made a chopping motion—"lopped off the king's head?"

"Yes. I was sixteen. Played truant from school. And was well whipped for it. Now if you'll—"

"Didn't you also see the execution of the first of the regicides? What's his name . . . Harrison?"

"Yes. Well, good of you to—"

"Must have been ghastly. Hanging, disemboweling, cutting off the privy parts. Then—"

"*Yes*, Balty. It *was* horrid. So much so that I endeavor not to dwell upon it."

"People will suspect you've a *penchant* for gruesome entertainments." He pronounced the word in the French way, himself being half French. Balty and his sister, Pepys's wife, had the tendency to lapse into their father's native tongue.

"My *penchant*, Balty, is to be witness at great events. I do not attend only executions. I remind you that I was aboard the ship that brought his majesty back to England from Holland four years ago."

Pepys did not mention—to Balty or anyone, for that matter—the diary he'd been keeping since 1660. He wrote it in a shorthand decipherable only to himself, so that he could tell it all.

"Well, good to see you," Pepys said. "Do give Esther my love."

Esther was Balty's wife of two years, and the latest addition to the growing number of mouths it fell to Pepys to feed. His rise within the Navy Office had barely kept pace with the proliferation of impoverished relatives.

Balty's father, Alexandre, had been a prosperous if minor member of the French aristocracy, Gentleman Ordinary to the great King Henri IV. He was in charge of the King's Guard on that dreadful spring day in 1610 when his majesty was driven in an open carriage through the Tuileries. The guards lagged behind, preening for the ladies in the crowd. The fanatical Catholic François Ravaillac saw his opening and lunged, sinking his sword into the King. The King died quickly. Ravaillac's death was a more prolonged affair.

According to St. Michel family lore, never entirely reliable, Alexandre redeemed himself some years later when he plucked Henri's drowning son, King Louis XIII, from a pond after his horse threw him during an excited hare hunt. Thus he could claim the unique distinction of having got one king killed and another saved. A series of disastrous decisions had reduced him to his present station here in London, taking out patents for various inventions. One supposedly fixed leaky chimneys. It did not. Another was a device that rendered pond water fit for horses to drink. The horses died.

The proverbial apple did fall far from the tree. At twenty-four, Balthasar could claim no achievements, nor was there any indication of ones to come. The word "feckless" might have been coined to describe Balty. But his older sister Elizabeth, Pepys's wife, adored him and doted on him. For her, Balty could do no wrong. Pepys fumed that he could do no right. Pepys loved his wife, though fidelity was not chief among his qualities. And so it fell to Sam, again and again, to provide money and employment for his pointless, impecunious brother-in-law.

"As to Esther," Balty responded in a merry, conspiratorial tone, "we have news. We are with child."

This stung. Pepys and his wife had been trying for ten years to produce a child. Sam was more and more convinced that the hellish operation he endured to cut out his kidney stone had rendered him incapable. Elizabeth meanwhile was plagued by feminine cysts. God himself seemed against them.

"Well, Balty," Pepys said, forcing a wistful smile, "that *is* news. I am glad. Heartily glad. Bess will be very pleased to hear of it."

"That is, we *might* be with child." Balty threw up his hands to show his frustration at the impenetrable mysteries of conception. "I suppose we'll know at some point."

Pepys frowned. "Yes, I expect so. Now you really must excuse me. I've a great deal to do."

A clatter of hooves and carriage wheels came from the courtyard. Balty peered down. "A personage of significance arrives. Very lush carriage."

"Lord Downing."

Balty considered. "Downing . . ."

"Sir *George* Downing."

Balty made a disapproving face. "What, the one who lured his former comrades into a trap and got them butchered? Bloody Judas."

Pepys said sternly, "Have a care with your tongue, Balty. And for my position here."

"But surely you can't approve of such a man as that? It was monstrous, what he did. Perfidy of the lowest—"

"*Yes*, Balty. We all know what he did. For which service the King created him baronet. Those he lured were among the men who'd condemned the King's own father. Try to bear that in mind, amidst your deprecations."

"I find him despicable. *Honteux.*"

Pepys agreed with his brother-in-law. Privately. He confined his own indignation about Downing—"perfidious rogue," "ungrateful villain"—to his diary.

"Downing is Envoy at The Hague. And the King's spymaster. He's a powerful man, Balty. I'd urge you to keep that in mind before you go emptying your spleen in public houses. His lordship's not someone you want for an enemy."

"I shouldn't want him for a friend." Balty sniffed. "Not after what he did to his."

"Well, what a pity," Pepys said with a touch of pique. "I was about to suggest the three of us take tea together. Now really, Balty, I must say good day to you."

Balty took a few steps toward the door.

"Brother Sam?"

"Yes, Balty?"

"Might you have something for me? A position?"

"A position? Well, yes. I could arrange a *position* for you today. Aboard one of our ships."

"Sam. You know I'm no good on ships. They make me ill. Even when they're not moving."

"This is the Navy Office, Balty. Ships are what we are *about*."

"Couldn't I be your aide-de-camp? Or subaltern, or whatever they're called in the Navy. Here. On land."

"Balty, I say this with the deepest affection—you have no qualifications. None. You have not one scintilla of qualification for Navy work." *Or any other kind*, he thought.

Pepys regarded the specimen of aimlessness who stood before him. He knew what scene would greet him at home tonight—his wife berating him, either with icy silence or volcanic eruption. Elizabeth, being half French, was capable of both modes. It wasn't fair. Again and again, Pepys had done what he could for Balty, usually in the form of "loans."

"There might be something in Deptford, at the dockyards. Let me make some inquiries."

"Oh, bravo. Thank you." Balty added, "Nothing *too* menial."

Pepys stared.

"I'm told I've got rather a good head on my shoulders," Balty said. "No sense wasting it putting me to work hefting sacks of gunpowder and dry biscuit all day. Eh?"

Pepys inwardly groaned, but his desire to be rid of Balty was greater than his temptation to box his ears. "I'll make inquiries." Pepys rubbed his forehead in exasperation.

"Valerian," Balty said.

"What?"

"Valerian. The herb. They call it the Phew Plant. On account of the stink." Balty pinched his nose. "But there's nothing better for headache. Or the colic."

"Thank you. But I have my hare's foot for that."

"Cures flatulence, too."

Pepys sighed and pointed to the door. "Go, Balty."

"Shall I stop in tomorrow?"

"*Go.*"

– CHAPTER 2 –

Downing

Pepys waited outside the Lord High Admiral's chamber. It was a closed meeting, just the Duke and Downing, no attendants.

It was no secret that Downing had been pressing hard for another war with the Dutch. Pepys had confided to his diary: *The King is not able to set out five ships at this present without great difficulty, we neither having money, credit, nor stores.* He wanted desperately to focus the Duke's attention on this lamentable but inescapable reality. His brother, the King, was bleeding the Exchequer white with the extravagances of his merry court.

The door opened. Downing emerged: forty-one, corpulent, suspicious eyes that seemed to look at you sideways, cruel smile, blue-tinted periwig.

"Ah, the evitable Mr. Pep-iss."

Pepys fell in beside him as they walked to Downing's carriage. They'd known each other for fifteen years. Downing had been chief judge at Pepys's school examination, awarding him a scholarship to Cambridge. Downing found it witty to mispronounce Pepys's surname, instead of the correct "Peeps."

"I trust my lord's meeting with my Lord High Admiral was satisfactory?"

"Very. I am as ever impressed with his grace's grasp of affairs, naval and otherwise."

"And are we to have *another* war with Holland?"

"What, Sam—no badinage today? You know how I enjoy our chin-wags."

They reached Sir George's carriage. Downing gestured for Pepys to climb in. The carriage started on its way to Downing's house in Whitehall, abutting St. James's Park.

His lordship was in a frisky mood, which always accentuated his air of malevolence. There was no softness to Downing. Some ascribed this to his being New England born and bred. He was notoriously mean with his money, of which he possessed a great deal. He maintained his aged mother in wretched poverty.

"War," Downing said idly. "Did the Duke and I talk of war? Let me see. There may have been some mention of war. We talked about so many things."

"If I may, my lord—the Navy is simply not equipped. It would be calamitous to embark on—"

"Yes, Sam. All in good time. *In omnibus negotiis prius quam aggrediare, adhibenda est preparatio diligens.*"

Pepys couldn't be flummoxed by extracts from Cicero.

"'In all matters before beginning,'" he translated, "'a diligent preparation must be made.' From the *De Officiis*, I believe."

"A lump of sugar for my clever boy. Was I not perspicacious to promote your career? My eye for talent is peerless."

He liked a bit of groveling, Downing. Pepys was content to acquiesce if it would get him heard on the catastrophic consequences of starting a war with Holland.

"I should be shearing sheep, were it not for my lord's generous patronage."

Downing stared at his protégé, trying to decide if he was being flippant.

"You overstate. No, you'd be in your father's tailor shop. But as it happens, the Duke and I spent most of our time on another subject. New England."

New England was of no great interest to Pepys, except as a potential source of timber for the Navy's warships.

"The Duke informs me his brother the King is much vexed by his colonies there. Since his restoration, they have been conducting themselves very sourly. But then"—Downing smirked—"the Puritan saints have *always* been sour."

Downing's family had emigrated there from Ireland. Downing was in the first class of the Harvard College in Boston. His first cousin, John Winthrop, was Governor of the Connecticut Colony.

"Massachusetts has been minting its own coinage," Downing said.

"Is that not contrary to law?"

"Very contrary. They also chafe at his majesty's recent missive constraining their persecution of the Quakers."

"We persecute Quakers here." Pepys shrugged. He disapproved of it, privately. "Just yesterday I saw twenty of them being marched off to jail, clapped in chains." He stopped himself from adding, *Poor lambs.* "Why does his majesty not approve persecuting them in New England?"

"The New Englanders' zeal was somewhat extreme. When Endecott hanged the Dyer wench in Boston four years ago it apparently left a bitter residue. Three other Quaker women caused a fuss and got sentenced to be tied to the cart and whipped naked through ten towns. Ten! A bit harsh, arguably. Left a trail of bloody snow for miles. Finally, the local magistrate at the next town said enough and cut them loose. Queer lot, Quakers. But if his majesty tells his colonial governors to stop killing them, then stop killing them they must. And get on with it. At a practical level, if we want the Quakers here to emigrate, we ought to make New England more hospitable to them. Or at least less lethal."

"Quite."

"The Puritans despise them almost as much as they do papists. They are convinced his majesty and his brother the Duke are secretly Roman. That his real purpose in protecting the Quakers is to give him cover to protect Catholics. Under the guise of 'general toleration.'"

Pepys trod carefully in these matters. His wife was Huguenot, but she often remarked—in front of others, for which Pepys boxed her ears—that she intended to die in the Catholic faith.

"The New Haven Colony is the worst," Downing went on. "*They* left Massachusetts because it wasn't strict enough for them. Can you imagine? Not strict enough! I spent years in Massachusetts, and let me tell you, it was plenty strict."

"So I've heard." New England sounded very grim to Pepys.

"It was New Haven protected two of the regicide judges, Whalley and Goffe. We tried to get them in '61. But they hid them. Gave the hunters a jolly runaround. It was most brazen. His majesty has not forgotten it. I've half a mind to have another go at finding them and bringing them to justice."

"If it's been three years, surely the trail's gone cold by now?"

"Oh," Downing said, "I shouldn't expect to *catch* them. My purpose would be otherwise."

"How so?"

"To annoy them. Let them know his majesty still remembers their lack of fealty."

Pepys smiled. "Seems rather gentle. Surely better to tax them than vex them."

"Oh, no. I think it would unsettle them no end to remind them of his majesty's authority. Nothing vexes a Puritan more than *superior* authority. It's why they left England in the first place. And now, the monarch has returned. It's put them in a terrible funk. Their hopes for heaven on earth died with Cromwell." Downing seemed quite taken with his idea. "*In the name of his majesty, open up! We seek the regicides Whalley and Goffe!* I can see their long faces. It would be quite . . . sporting."

"I expect his majesty would find it so."

"The King is droll. I think it might amuse him."

Pepys suddenly found himself saying, "If you decide to proceed, I've just the man for you."

"Ah?"

Pepys had to keep from laughing. "Well, if the idea is to *annoy* them, I can't think of a better person. The one I have in mind has a genuine talent for annoyance. Genius, even."

The carriage had reached Charing Cross. Ten of the regicides had met their fate here in October 1660 after the return of the King. The stench of their burnt bowels finally became so noisome that the locals appealed to the Crown to move future executions elsewhere.

"This fellow of yours," Downing said. "Send him to me."

– CHAPTER 3 –

Our Own Brave Balty

Pepys's initial exhilaration at the prospect of getting Balty dispatched to New England was short-lived. Downing was a man of remorseless cunning. He would see in a minute that Balty was a popinjay incapable of striking fear in a butterfly. Why had he even suggested such a thing? Then he thought: no harm in seeing how far it might go.

He didn't tell Balty the real reason Downing wanted to see him. Balty would only tell Esther and Elizabeth, which would cause family mayhem. He told him Downing was considering him for some gamekeeping job on one of his estates.

"He's very tight with money," Pepys said, "so he's death on poachers."

"Oh," Balty said, "I should love to shoot poachers."

"Just say as little as possible. No prattling. Understood?"

"*Entendu, mon vieux.*"

"And no French. He hates the French."

"Why?"

"He hates everyone. Dutch, French, Spanish. Just stand there, nod, and for God's sake, try not to talk. And if it turns out to be something other than gamekeeping, well, it could only be to the good. Just nod and don't talk and when it's over, bow and say what an honor it's been. And leave. Clear?"

"Yes." Balty nodded. "You are good to have fixed this up, Brother Sam."

"Well, you're family, aren't you?"

To Pepys's astonishment, Downing was quite taken with Balty, even charmed. Pepys deciphered this as Downing thinking it would gall the New Haveners even more to be bossed about by a nincompoop.

When Downing revealed what he had in mind, Balty's mouth went agape. He looked at his brother-in-law. Pepys feigned surprise and nodded brightly as if to say, *Well done, Balty! Your ship has come in at last, old cock!*

Downing wrote out Balty's commission on the spot, signed and sealed it. He then wrote a letter that he didn't show to Balty, and sealed it, instructing Balty to give it to Downing's agent in Boston, one Plantagenet Spong. He would act as Balty's aide-de-camp and bodyguard. Pepys knew the name must be a pseudonym. He'd done a lot of ciphering for Downing, rendering his messages in code. No one in the spy business used real names.

Pepys took the stunned Balty to the Legg tavern in King Street and in a celebratory mood ordered Rhenish wine and lobsters.

"Sir George certainly went lighter on you than he did on me at my school examination. Grilled me remorselessly on Catullus."

Balty was subdued. "I . . . It is a *bit* overwhelming, Brother Sam. New England."

"Overwhelming marvelous, I should say. It's not every day one receives a Crown commission. I confess I'm a bit jealous."

"Did you know? Beforehand?"

"Well, yes. Of course."

"You might have told me. Instead of making up that jibber-jabber about gamekeeping."

"Brother Balty. You must understand—this is the King's business. It's highly confidential."

"Yes, but I'd rather be a gamekeeper. Or work at your dockyard."

"Oh, come. Testing hemp at the Ropeyard? Tallying barrels of pitch? Instead of a commission to hunt for killers of his late majesty?" Pepys sighed heavily. "I fear, dear Balty, you do not comprehend what a great honor this is."

"I don't say it's not. It's jolly lovely. But New England? I shall have to take a ship."

"That is the customary way of going. But if you can find a land route to New England, that would certainly be an achievement to eclipse finding regicides."

"But what if I *don't* find them?"

"Oh, I shouldn't worry. I suspect Lord Downing's real purpose in sending you is to remind the recalcitrant Puritan 'saints' of New Haven that a new King sits on the throne. I'm sure he's well aware that Whalley and Goffe are long gone. Probably dead of the rheumatic fever from years of hiding in dank basements. I venture to suppose that your true task is merely to stick to these New Haveners. Let them know all is not forgiven. Remind them of the King's continuing displeasure." Pepys grinned. "Make a nuisance of yourself. Shouldn't be—" He stopped himself. "Puff out your chest, bang on their doors, wave your commission in their faces. Demand to inspect the premises. That sort of thing. Sounds rather a lark. Almost wish I were going with you."

"What if they slam their doors in my face?"

"God help them if they do. Obstructing a Crown commissioner in the course of his duty? Treason! Punishable by death. That paper Downing gave you entitles you to be the biggest pain in the arse in all New England."

Balty brightened. "Oh. Well, I suppose. Yes."

"I envy you. I should love to make sour-faced Puritans dance to my tempo. I've long yearned to see the New World. I hear it is full of marvels. Who knows? You might fall in love with a beautiful Indian princess and decide to stay."

"But I love Esther."

"Yes, of course. But you might fall in love with New England. You could send for Esther to join you there."

"I . . ."

"They say a man can be anything he wants to be there. I must say, it sounds perfect heaven. Virgin land. Forests teeming with game. Rivers. Lakes. *Skies.*" Pepys leaned closer and purred. "With all respect to Esther, I am reliably informed that the native women are not only beautiful but complaisant. They hurl themselves at Englishmen. Oh, dear. Now I truly do wish I were going with you."

"But there are savages. One hears appalling stories."

"No, no, no," Pepys said emphatically. "All that's in the past. There *was* a bit of unpleasantness at the outset, but the savages have been entirely domesticated. Apparently they make very good servants. I wonder—do they put them in livery? Hm. We English have the gift of civilizing our conquered peoples. Unlike the Dutch. Hollanders are constantly at odds with their savages. Always having to put down rebellions. We give ours a nice bit of land of their own and everyone's content. We keep the peace among the various tribes so they're not at each other's throats over beaver hides and oyster shells and wampum and whatnot. You'll meet one or two, I imagine. I saw a painting of one. *Superb*-looking chap. Feathers everywhere. Marvelous cheekbones. Some say they're descended from the Trojans."

"How did they get to New England from Troy?"

"Slowly, I should think. But they are talented about boats. Some other scholars say they're the rump bit of the Lost Tribe of Israel. Take notes, Balty! I shall want to hear every detail. In the event you do decide to return."

"So it is safe?"

"Oh, far safer than London. And no plague. You'll have Downing's man, Spong, looking after you. I've met some of Downing's men. And they're not ones to tangle with. You'll be in the best of hands."

Balty considered. "I don't know how Esther's going to take the news. Or Elizabeth."

Pepys said gravely, "Balty, you must understand, this is a highly—*highly*—secret undertaking."

"I can't *not* tell Esther and Elizabeth."

Pepys shook his head. "It is *imperative* that you not tell Esther. Or my wife. It could put your mission at risk. Even your life."

"My life?" Balty squeaked.

"Dear, sweet Balty. His majesty has enemies in London. Do you think Esther and Elizabeth would be able to keep your secret? They would be so . . . proud of you, they'd be shouting it from the rooftops. *Our own brave Balty, off to New England to hunt for traitors!* Absolutely, no. Under no circumstances must they know the true nature of your business. For your own safety. Once you're in Boston, you'll be under this Spong's protection."

"But—what am I to tell them?"

"Yes. We shall need a legend for you. We shall tell them . . . we shall tell them that I managed to secure a place for you on a . . . survey. Um. Yes. Just the thing."

"Survey? Of what?"

"Forests. You will be scouting for timber. For the Navy's warships. Certainly we shall be needing no end of timber if we're to have another go at the Cheesers. New England white pine is far superior to what we get from Norway and Sweden. Taller. You can make an entire mast from a single tree. Norwegian wood requires two. And doesn't last as long."

"I don't know much about timber."

"Dear Balty, let us speak frankly. You don't *know* much about anything. Which is why at age twenty-four you are *sans* career. But no longer. Now you are employed. Gloriously employed!"

Pepys raised his glass. "A toast. His Majesty, Charles the Second. Long live the King."

Balty raised his glass solemnly. "*Vive le roi.*"

"And to Balthasar de St. Michel, judge hunter. Let New England tremble at his approach!"

Balty blushed. "Rather like the sound of that."

They clinked glasses.

Pepys was all aglow. "Another round of lobsters? And another bottle of this damnably expensive wine? I think the Navy Office owes us a celebratory dinner. What say?"

"I say, *Encore!*"

– CHAPTER 4 –

March 2nd. I cannot but think that Providence itself hath smiled on this strange undertaking, else how could it ever have come about, against all expectations? My heart full to bursting.

Despite joy at being rid of him, find myself afflicted with strange tender feelings for Bro Balty, which hitherto I have <u>never</u> entertained, as a consequence of his incessant neediness and importunings.

I pray he will not make a pig's breakfast of matters and reflect ill upon me. Yet I can foresee no reason why he should not be up to the task of making Puritans yank out their hair, since he has made me yank out mine on so many occasions.

Tomorrow shall inform my wife. Doubtless there will be a scene. In anticipation thereof, today purchased a pretty pearl necklace at a cost of £4 10s.

And so to bed.

– CHAPTER 5 –

Baltee 'ates Boats

"**N**ew England? *New* England?"

Elizabeth Pepys's round face flushed pink with outrage. Her ringlets jerked and bounced in rhythm with her outbursts. During scenes like this—not uncommon in the Pepys ménage—her French blood dominated the English. "But Baltee cannot support 'imself in *old* England. No. *Non.* It is *completement absurde.* I forbid!"

She'd been going on now for hours.

"Nonsense," Pepys said. "It'll be good for him. Don't you want him to make something of himself? Other than a beggar?"

"You are a 'orrible person, Samuel Pepys."

"Well, *there's* gratitude, I must say. Have I not been the sole support of your brother all these years? To say nothing of other members of your helpless family? And for this Christian charity I am called 'orrible. I ought to box your ears."

Elizabeth had seized one of his lutes, a particular favorite for which he paid the sum of ten pounds. She held it by the neck, brandishing it as if it were a club.

"Woman," Pepys commanded, "put that down. This instant. Or you'll be hearing church bells for a week!"

She collapsed onto a chair, sobbing. Pepys went to his wife, knelt, and held her and kissed her hand. "My love. What a silly girl you are."

"'E will never return," she whimpered.

Pepys averted his face so she would not see what unalloyed joy this prospect brought him.

"Tush. Really, what a to-do my sweet darling makes. Why, you make it sound as though he's going off to war." Pepys thought, *Hm.* "There's talk of war with Holland, you know. If you would really prefer, I could get him a billet tomorrow on one of our warships. Perhaps that would be best. Nothing turns a boy into a man like a good, raging sea battle. Cannonballs smashing through the hull, rigging crashing down on the deck, bits of wood and iron flying through the air like knives. Smoke everywhere. Fires raging. Grappling hooks, the cries of the dying . . ."

Pepys seized a poker from the fireplace and began slashing at imagined boarders. "The cut and thrust with cutlass and pistol and axe." Pepys paused in his bellicose miming and said pensively, "Perhaps in the end that *would* be better for Balty. To be blooded in battle, rather than tromping about forests, marking trees to cut down."

"No!" Elizabeth said, weeping anew.

"All right. If you say. You might be a bit happy for him. It's a *job*, darling. How long has it been since your brother had one? The reign of Charlemagne?"

"Esther is not 'appy about this."

"Perhaps. But neither, as it happens," Pepys said with a trace of acerbity, "is she pregnant. She bloody well ought to be thankful."

Elizabeth wiped her tears with her sleeve.

"Where is New England?"

"Oh, not far. Just, you know, other side of the water."

"Baltee 'ates boats. Always he is vomiting."

"Darling, in the Navy, we call them ships. And my job is to help the Navy build them. Which is how I rose to be Clerk of the Acts. Which is how we can afford such a fine home, and servants, and your petticoats, and your baubles and all the rest. As for Baltee's *mal de mer*, until I assume the powers of Neptune and am able to calm the waters with a wave of my triton, there's not bloody well much I can do about that. Maybe a sea voyage will cure him of seasickness. And of his other chronic affliction."

"What affliction?"

"Poverty."

Before she could remonstrate, Pepys leaned forward over her lap and kissed her between her breasts, inhaling sweet perfume. "Now, come, my strumpet. Put on that lovely pearl necklace I bought you and see how it hangs on this delectable neck. It was *very* expensive, you know. What an extravagant husband you have!"

– CHAPTER 6 –

March 4th. My wife at first exceeding stroppy on news of her brother's coming timber quest in Newe England. Threatened me with my lute. Eventually pacified. Exprest pleasure at gift of pearl necklace.

For dinner a dish of marrowbones, neat's tongue, a plate of anchovies, and a tart. Also a cheese.

Played "Gaze Not on Swans" for her on my lute, passingly well.

Afterward merry in bed.

And so to sleep.

CHAPTER 7

The Devil's Own Work

Balthasar de St. Michel looked out upon Boston harbor from the deck of the ship *Nymph* with a joy greater than he had ever known, having spent the previous ten weeks with his head in a bucket while being violently hurled from one bulkhead to another amidst incessant gales. He had lost so much weight that his clothes hung from him like an insufficiently stuffed scarecrow. His pallor resembled a corpse too long awaiting burial.

During the first of the Atlantic gales, Balty had crawled from below on all fours to the quarterdeck and demanded that the captain turn his ship back to England. Being somewhat occupied trying to keep his ship afloat, the captain ignored him. Balty clung to the mast so as not to be swept overboard and repeated his demand, insisting that as Crown commissioner, he outranked the captain. The captain paid no attention to his ululations. Balty contemplated letting go of the mast and allowing the waves to sweep him into the deep and end his misery. Finally he crawled back to his berth, where he spent the next weeks regretting that he had not chosen to end his life.

He stood at the head of the gangway, holding on to both stanchions for support as he gathered strength to disembark.

"Rest assured," he croaked to the captain, "his majesty shall hear of your contumacy. To say nothing of your atrocious seamanship."

"And a good day to you, sir."

Balty wobbled down the gangplank onto the New World. He would have dropped to his knees and kissed the ground beneath his feet, except that it was a mire of muck.

He stood, dizzy and weaving, and beheld Boston Town.

Elated as he was to be standing on terra firma, Balty was not impressed by what he saw. Boston seemed somewhat shabby. But it did not heave and pitch beneath his feet.

His nostrils twitched from a sour smell. A building by one of the wharves was smoking. A line of men were passing buckets, one to the next, throwing water onto it. Balty wandered toward the commotion.

It appeared that the battle was lost. The fire had consumed all but a few beams. A cluster of official-looking men stood nearby, observing the scene with grim faces and much stroking of chins. Armed constables appeared to be standing guard over the charred remains. Odd.

Balty went over to the clump of officials.

"What burned down?"

"Our mint," a man said crossly.

"Oh, dear. Bad luck."

The man scowled at Balty. He said, as if speaking from a church pulpit, "Bad luck? Be not deceived, sir. This was the devil's own work."

His tone was not inviting of theological debate.

"Could you direct me to the Blue Bell Tavern? I'm told it is somewhere in the vicinity of Oliver's Wharf."

This seemed to inflame the man further. "You seek drink, sir, on the Sabbath day?"

"Sabbath? Ah. I wasn't aware. You see, I've just landed here in Boston. I crossed on that godforsaken ship there." Balty pointed at the *Nymph*. "I do not recommend it, in case you are contemplating a passage. The captain is quite incompetent."

"We tolerate no blasphemy here. Mind your tongue, lest you want it bored through with a red-hot poker."

"Um, yes, well, I'll leave you to your mint. What's left of it."

Balty walked away, trying to think what blasphemy he'd uttered that had set the fellow to threatening him with boring a hole in his tongue with a red-hot poker. What an appalling town.

For the first time since leaving England, he felt a growl of hunger in his belly. He got directions to the Blue Bell Tavern from a more obliging local and made his way to his rendezvous with Downing's man, Spong.

The tavern keeper was an enormously fat man with a rubicund face between two bushy white side whiskers.

He greeted Balty, taking in his forlorn appearance.

"Good day to you, friend. Are you . . . well?"

"A bit tucked up. Just arrived. From London. Hellish voyage."

The tavern keeper walked to the fireplace and pulled a poker from the embers. Its tip glowed red. Balty wondered: Had he blasphemed again? What was wrong with these people?

"Now see here," Balty said. "I meant no offense."

"Sit you down."

The man filled a tankard from a jug and plunged the tip of the poker into it, causing a great bubble and hiss. He handed the tankard to Balty.

"This'll set you right."

Balty drank. It tasted like hot, sweetened beer, excellently spiced. His tormented insides glowed with delicious warmth.

"Oh," he said. "Oh, I say. This *is* good."

"Flip, it's called."

The man went off and returned with a plate of cold roast fowl, pickled onions, cheese, jam, and boiled potatoes. Balty ate with relish. It was the finest meal he'd ever had.

"I seek a Mr. Spong. A Mr. Plantagenet Spong."

"Ain't seen him lately. He comes and goes. Like the tide. In, out."

"I have business with him. Of some significance."

"What about?"

"Confidential. Crown business."

Some drinkers sitting nearby stared.

"Crown business?" the tavern keeper said. "Well, well. I'll give him a message if I see him. And you would be Mister . . . ?"

"St. Michel. Balthasar de St. Michel."

The drinkers tittered.

"You are amused?"

"Where'd ye get a name like that?"

"From my father. Where did you get yours?"

"What were 'is name? Beelzebub de Saint Michelle?"

The tavern filled with snorts and guffaws, hands thumping on tables.

"As it happens, his name is Alexandre."

"Alex-*andre*? Alex-*andre* the Great. King of—what were it?— Greece or thereabouts?"

"Since you ask, he was in service to the late Kings Henri Quatre and Louis Treize. Of France."

"Service? Did 'e service 'em well and proper?" The fellow made an obscene gesture, prompting a fresh convulsion of mirth.

"His position was one of eminence," Balty replied. "Beyond the understanding of peasants like yourselves."

Silence. Mugs slamming on tabletops.

"What'd you call us?"

"Pheasants," said a man apparently well marinated in flip.

Several men rose from their chairs, fists clenched.

"Now, now," said the tavern keeper, his right hand going below the counter. "Everyone just settle down."

"You 'eard what he called us."

"Well, John, you weren't so cordial yourself, were you? Now sit down."

John held his ground. The tavern keeper drew a club from beneath the counter.

"You all know the penalty for fighting on the Sabbath." The tavern keeper turned to Balty. "As for you, Mr. Whatever's your name, I'll say a good day to you. It's four shillings sixpence for the food and drink."

"I require a room," Balty said, "while I await Mr. Spong."

"This is a peasant establishment. Try the King's Arms. Henri *Quatre* and Louis *Treize* stay there when they're in town."

The drinkers laughed and sat down.

"It's for your own good, sir," the tavern keeper whispered to Balty. "I'll tell Mr. Spong where to find you if he calls."

Balty sniffed and counted out coins. "Less than one hour have I been in this town of yours, and already I have been threatened with mutilation, and now with a beating. For taking offense at my dear father's noble name being abused by brute inebriates. I will say good day to *you*, sir. My compliments to Mr. Spong."

Balty found the King's Arms and collapsed onto his bed, too exhausted to undress.

Next day, Spong not having materialized, Balty decided to pay a call on Endecott, Governor of the Massachusetts Bay Colony.

On being ushered into the Governor's office, Balty started. The grim, pinched-looking man behind the desk was the same person who had threatened to hole his tongue with a poker.

Endecott looked up from examining Balty's Crown commission, unfolded before him on his desk. He peered with vague recognition.

"Have we . . . met?"

"We have, yes. Yesterday morning. At your mint."

Endecott frowned and went back to examining the commission with an air of searching for evidence of forgery. He sat back in his chair and scowled at his visitor with beady eyes. He had a long black goatee. His neck protruded from a square of delicate white lace against a black doublet.

"What is it you seek from me, Mr. . . . . St. Michel?"

"I so enjoyed our first chat I thought I'd pop in and have another."

Endecott stared.

"To pay my respects, as it were," Balty added. "On behalf of his majesty."

"If you've come seeking regicides, I assure you we have none here. We are *out* of regicides."

Endecott seemed a bit nervous. Balty suddenly felt something he'd never felt before in a lifetime of being the spaniel in any situation—power. Evidently Brother Sam had spoken the truth when he told Balty that his Crown commission would entitle him to be the biggest pain in the arse in all New England. *Well, well,* he thought. *This might be fun.*

"His majesty certainly hopes there are none in Boston. Or elsewhere in your *Bay* Colony, as you call it," Balty said. "To think what dishonor that would bring. *Quelle honte!*"

Endecott stared. "Are you a French person, Mr. St. Michel?"

"Half. My pater is of the *noblesse.* He was in service to their majesties Henri Quatre and Louis Treize."

Endecott's eyes widened. He pushed backward in his chair, as if trying to increase the distance between them.

"You are a . . . papist?"

"Not at all. Huguenot. Protestant. Like yourself."

Balty's claim of coreligion didn't sit well with the Governor. "We are Puritan here, sir."

"Yes. I noticed."

"We live godly lives."

"Doesn't sound much fun. But to each his own. Judge not lest ye be . . . et cetera. Lovely book, the Bible. Wish I had more time for reading. Damned time-consuming, chasing regicides."

"As we have no regicides here," Endecott said icily, "perhaps you will find the time to study Holy Scripture."

"We have Puritans back in England. Not as many as before, mind you. Things have rather loosened up under the new king."

"So we have heard."

"The theaters have been reopened. Bear pits, too. Very exciting. We're back to celebrating Christmas again. I missed Christmas. I was only a lad of nine when Cromwell chopped off the King's head and everything got so grim." Balty laughed. "I imagine that's not quite how the 'godly' folks here view it. Toleration's not really your thing, is it?"

"Obedience is our 'thing,' Mr. St. Michel. Obedience to God."

Balty stared. Endecott looked like a man straining at a difficult stool. He added, "*And* to the King."

"I'm sure his majesty will be pleased to hear it."

"You are at Court, then?"

"I sort of skulk about the edges, you might say. But near enough to hear the laughter and the music. Very *gay*, his majesty's court. And the ladies. Such pulchritude has not been seen since the days of . . ."

"Sodom and Gomorrah?"

"I was going to say ancient Rome. But his majesty's court is very splendid. The King has set a new tone. England seems quite a bit happier now."

Endecott smiled. It seemed an unnatural expression on him, like a blemish in marble.

"Then you must be in haste to conclude your mission here in New England. So that you can return to the pleasure gardens of Old England."

"To be perfectly honest, I am." Balty added, "No offense to *New* England."

"None taken. How, then, may I expedite your return?" He glanced again at the commission on his desk. "These fugitive judges, Lieutenant General Whalley and Major General Goffe . . . you are doubtless aware that in 1661 I deputized two men to hunt them in New Haven."

"Um. After they'd spent a jolly time here in Boston. As honored guests of your Bay Colony."

"That is putting it strongly, sir. In any event, they fled. And alas, the hunters failed to find them. In New Haven."

"The New Haveners were very naughty. They did not cooperate in the least with your hunters."

"I am not responsible for the New Haven Colony, Mr. St. Michel. Massachusetts keeps me well enough occupied."

"I suppose. Lots going on. Mints burning down. I gather the devil keeps you busy."

Endecott stared, trying to decide if he was being taunted.

"Your ship," he said. "It tied up at the dock at what hour?"

"I hardly remember. I was in a coma since leaving London."

Endecott sifted some papers on his desk and peered.

"*Nymph*. Docked May 7th, just before midnight." He resumed staring at Balty. "About the hour it is reckoned the fire was set."

Balty stared. "Oh? Well, I wouldn't know. I was in my bunk, praying for death."

Endecott continued to stare. "There is some disharmony between London and here as to whether we are within our rights in minting our own coinage."

"Oh? Yes, I should imagine."

It dawned on Balty that the sour old coot was implying that he had torched his mint. Balty held a Crown commission. And he had arrived simultaneously with the burning. *Hm.*

Balty shifted uncomfortably in his chair.

"You are off to New Haven, then?" Endecott said. "In pursuit of your regicides?"

"Yes. As soon as . . ."

"As?"

"I am to rendezvous with Lord Downing's agent. But he has not shown up. And I can't seem to find him."

"Perhaps I can help." Endecott's sudden friendly tone made Balty wonder if he had volunteered too much information.

"He's to be my guide. Keep me out of trouble."

"Yes. One *can* get into trouble in New England. What is his name? Perhaps we can help you find him."

"Jolly good of you to offer. But best not."

"Oh, come, Mr. St. Michel," Endecott said silkily, "I am Governor here. And a loyal subject to his majesty, whatever differences of perspective we may have with regard to certain . . . principles."

"In that case, thank you. Let's see, what was his name? Odd name. I wrote it down. Somewhere. I think. Must be back at the inn."

Endecott stroked his foxtail goatee. He wondered: Was his visitor coy, or an imbecile? He inclined to think the latter. But how had such a blithering tosspot managed to procure a Crown commission from Sir George Downing, one of the most powerful men in the realm?

Whalley and Goffe were long gone. Governor Leete in New Haven might still be hiding them, after all this time, but was that likely?

Endecott entertained possibilities. Had Downing dispatched this bumbler all the way across the ocean to twist his nose for dragging his feet back in '61?

No. Surely. He knew Downing well enough to fear him. Downing wasn't one for games. No, there must be some other aspect here. Quite other.

Had some fresh intelligence about Whalley and Goffe reached London? After the last hunt, Endecott had made a point of not inquiring of Leete or any of the Puritan saints of New Haven as to the whereabouts of the judges. Better not to know.

But if there had been news, this stammering ninny before him seemed an unlikely choice for a Crown pursuivant. Downing's agents were steely, fierce, and no fools. Perhaps this St. Michel was only playing the fool.

"Well, lovely seeing you again," Balty said, suddenly in a hurry to be gone from the gubernatorial presence. "Good luck with your new mint."

CHAPTER 8

A Whole Different
Kettle of Nasty

Where *was* Spong? It was intolerable. Hanging about Boston, with Endecott convinced Balty had torched his precious mint, was not appealing. Should he press on to New Haven on his own?

The prospect held little appeal. Indeed, none. The very thought of boarding another ship made him break out in a cold sweat. He inquired at the waterfront and was told that sailing from Boston to New Haven could take a week or more, depending on the winds. New England was larger than Balty had thought.

At a stable he asked about going by horse. The answer was also dismal. By way of something called the Connecticut Path, via a town named Hartford, this, too, could take a week, but at least he'd be on solid ground.

The stable owner, an ostler of coarse aspect whose breath reeked of rum, told him with inappropriate jocundity that another consideration was "what type savages yer encounters."

"What do you mean by 'what *type*' savage? How do they differ?"

"Well," the ostler said, "there's yer praying savage, as we calls 'em.

Them what's been learnt the Bible and been civilized. Then there's yer nonpraying type. Them's the type yer not wanting to encounter."

Balty stammered, "But . . . but I was informed that your savages had been . . . I was told all that had been *settled*."

The ostler spat. No one in this dreadful town was capable of completing so much as a sentence without expectorating a dozen times.

"Well, it have been settled, and it haven't. If yer gets my meaning."

"I do not."

"For the most part, it have been. Yer Pequots, them's were the worst. Heathens to the bone. But Govner Endycott and Captains Underhill and Mason slartered most of 'em at Fort Mystick, back in '38. But there's some still left, here and there. And their temper weren't improved any by the slartering. Can't really blame 'em."

Balty drew himself up. "Look here. Are you saying that the road to New Haven is not *safe* to travel?"

The ostler frowned deeply and pensively, as if being asked to rule on a point of philosophy.

"It aren't the roads. It's who's sharing the roads with yer."

"Yes, *yes*," Balty said, exasperated. "I grasp that."

"Yer Nipmuck and yer Massachusett, by and large yer don't have to fret about 'em. But yer Wampanoag . . ." The ostler summoned a half pint of phlegm and expelled it. "Yer Wampanoag is a whole different kettle of nasty. Yer Narragansett? That can go either way. You say yer's going t'New Haven?"

"As I've said, yes."

"Well, then yer's almost certain t'encounter Mahican. The thing about yer Mahican—and yer not wantin' to forget it, neither—is yer Mahican hates yer Pequot. Hates 'em worse than anything. So if yer encounterin' Mahican, whatever yer do, don't be singin' no praise of yer Pequot." The ostler shook his head to emphasize this essential point. "No. T'wouldn't do. T'wouldn't do at all."

Balty ruled out traveling alone to New Haven and left the stable feeling abandoned by the universe.

In England before departing, he'd imagined being greeted in Boston by the Governor and the town elders. A dinner given in his honor. Speeches. Downing's man Spong at Balty's disposal, arranging every detail. A well-springed coach to carry them to New Haven, with periwigged postilions hanging on to the back to shoo away curious savages. An outrider in front, shouting as they went, "Make way for Balthasar de St. Michel, emissary of his majesty, King Charles!" New England had failed him in all these expectations. There was nothing else to do but continue to wait upon the elusive Mr. Spong, whose appearance seemed as likely as the Second Coming. And God knows what revenge the odious Endecott might be planning as punishment for having burnt his bloody mint.

Balty endured several more bleak days, walking aimlessly from one end of Boston to the other and back again, certain he was being watched.

One night in his room at the tavern, having nothing else to do, he decided to write Brother Sam a report.

> *Of the general character of these New Englanders, I can render no good opinion. They are without exception brutish, rude, and egregiously disrespectful. And this swinish and sullen behavior directed at one carrying a Crown commission!*
>
> *Of the character of Governor Endecott I have nothing favorable to say. At our first encounter he threatened—for no good reason—to bore a hole through my Tongue with a red-hot poker. Welcome to Massachusetts.*
>
> *At our second, he all but accused me of torching his Mint. He is a disagreeable personage of unredeemable grimness. He would be better—and, I dare to say, happier—employed administrating a prison or a torture chamber. (In many respects, his "Bay Colonie" resembles both.) I should not be surprised to learn that for divertissement he pulls the wings off butterflies. Or drowns cats.*
>
> *On my return, which pray God will be not be long retarded, I shall enumerate in detail these insolences I have suffered to my Lord Downing and to His Most Gracious Majesty, should He grant me audience thereof to do so.*
>
> *As for Mr. Plantagenet Spong, there has been no sight of him,*

nor have I expectation of <u>ever</u> seeing him. Perhaps he too found
Boston intolerable and has departed for happier precincts. I should
not blame him, tho' it was not respectful of him to abandon me so.
Your wretched but ever obedient and affectionate Brother, etc.,
I am, sir, His Majesty's Crown Commissioner,
B. de St. Michel

Balty awoke in his room at the King's Arms uncomfortably aware of light, despite having snuffed out his candle on retiring. He peered over the edge of his blanket in the direction of his toes. In the corner of the room sat a man, reading. Balty slowly pulled himself up on his pillow, bunching the covers up to his chin as a shield.

"What the devil . . . who *are* you? What do you want?"

The intruder glanced at Balty and went back to reading the sealed letter Downing had given Balty for the elusive Mr. Plantagenet Spong.

"I say. That's Crown business, and none of yours."

The man ignored him and continued reading.

He was a stout, well-muscled fellow, of thirty or so years. His hair and beard were jet, flecked with white. His cheeks bore smallpox scars. He looked unperturbed, yet there was something of the panther about him, coiled energy. Not a man to cross. Balty bunched his coverlet closer to his chest. What on earth?

The man finished reading. He put Downing's letter on the table and turned his attention to Balty.

His gaze was hard, but there was melancholy behind it. It reminded Balty of that line in the Shakespeare play about the gloomy Dane: *I have of late lost all my mirth.* Whoever this chap was, he'd misplaced his mirth somewhere along the way.

"You're awake," he said. "I see you are not a light sleeper."

"If it's money you're after, there's some in that bag."

"If I wanted your money, sir, I would have it already. And you would be sleeping for eternity with your throat cut."

The man held Downing's letter over the candle and watched it burn.

"What are you *doing*?" Balty protested.

"As you can plainly see, I am burning it." His voice was deep, plummy, with a bit of rasp.

"That letter was intended for someone."

"Indeed. For myself."

"*Spong?*"

"At your service."

Relieved that he was not about to be killed, Balty replied, "You call this service? Stealing into my room in the middle of the night? Scaring me half to death? Setting *fires*?"

He pushed aside the coverlet and rose from the bed. Spong held the flaming letter over the washbasin and dropped it in. It curled into ash.

Spong poured himself a cup of wine and drained it in a gulp.

"You made quite an impression at the Blue Bell. I take it you are new to this line of work."

"What line of work?"

"Regicide hunting. That is your purpose here, is it not?"

"It is. And since you ask, no, it has not been my life's career. It's not really something one makes a career of, is it? One doesn't study regicide hunting at university."

Spong looked faintly amused. He poured another cup of wine and handed it to Balty.

"What have you made a career of, might I ask?"

"Well, a bit of this. And that."

"A dilettante."

What a malapert, Balty thought. *Best establish the rules.*

"Let us have things clear, Mr. Spong, so that we may avoid misunderstanding."

"As you wish."

"As you are aware from the document that you did *not* burn, I carry a commission from Lord Downing."

"Indeed."

"Which carries the same force as a commission from the King himself."

"If you say."

"I *do* say. Your function is to serve as my guide. In this ghastly land."

"New England is not to your liking?"

"It is not. I have yet to meet one accommodating or respectful person. Indeed, I have been most abominably used. Especially considering my position."

"You must excuse us, Mr. St. Michel. We are a new land. New people. We lack English refinement."

"Among other things."

"How was your interview with Old Nebuchadnezzar?"

"Endecott? How'd you know about that?"

"I have been observing you, Mr. St. Michel. Since you arrived."

"What? Then why the devil didn't you identify yourself before now?"

"Because I am not the only one who has been watching you. Look outside the door."

Balty got up and opened the door. A man lay facedown on the floor, unconscious.

"Good Lord!" Balty said. "Who's that?"

"His name is Roote. One of Endecott's men."

"Is he dead?"

"No. But he'll have an achy head when he wakes. In consequence of which his mood will be foul. So let us be on our way."

"Steady on. I'm not some footpad to skulk out of town in the dark. I carry a Crown commission."

"So you do. Which also serves as your death warrant. Gather your things, sir. We depart."

"Death warrant? Are you suggesting that the Governor would dare to harm a Crown commissioner?"

"Not suggesting. Come."

"I'll have you know that in addition to carrying the King's commission, I am intimately related to Mr. Samuel Pepys."

"Whoever Mr. Peeps may be, his name isn't one to inspire fear in Boston."

"He is Clerk of the Acts of the Royal Navy. A highly influential personage."

"Like Henri Quatre and Louis Treize?"

"Oh. You heard about . . . that."

"All Boston heard about that, Mr. St. Michel."

"I was only trying to demonstrate to the rabble at that inn that—"

"Your connection to eminent persons is established, sir. As for Endecott, believe me, he would not hesitate to have your throat cut and your body sent out with the tide as shark meat. Boston is not royalist territory. Nor is most of New England. Endecott despises the King. And therefore despises you. That man on the floor there—I've seen his work. And God knows, I have seen Endecott's." Spong tossed Balty's clothes at him. "Let us go."

The tavern was empty except for a few drunken dozers. Spong led Balty through the kitchen to a back door. Balty followed, heart thumping, head spinning.

Spong peered out a window. A lantern outside the door cast a faint glow. Two horses were tethered to a tree. Spong motioned to Balty to remain and unbolted the door. He stepped out into the light.

A shape leapt at Spong from the side. Spong sidestepped the man and tripped him to the ground. His assailant went down in the dirt with a thud. Spong took him by the throat with one hand and with the other beneath his cloak drew a caliver pistol. He put the muzzle to the man's head.

"Master Markle. What, up at this ungodly hour? Doing ungodly work, I should think."

"Huncks."

"Shh. You'll wake Master Roote. He's sleeping. On your feet."

Markle stood.

"What's your business?"

Markle made no reply. Spong pressed the muzzle against his forehead and cocked the hammer.

"Him," Markle said, pointing at Balty. "And you."

"Me? I'm flattered. Why?"

"For burning the mint."

"Dear me. Always rushing to judgment, our dear Governor. Well, we must go have a chat with him. Clear the air. Come." Spong prodded with his pistol.

"You won't get away," Markle snarled. "They're watching the docks and the gates."

The streets were deserted. There was a curfew. Only the watch was abroad at this hour. They walked. Balty recognized Endecott's house. What on earth was Spong doing? Was he going to wake the Governor?

They entered through a gate into what seemed to be a vegetable garden, sparse at this early time of year. In the center was a well, with an overhanging pulley and bucket.

"In you go."

"Damn you, Huncks."

"In or die. Your choice."

Markle sat on the rim of the well and swiveled his legs to the inside.

"You're a bastard."

"So me old mum told me. Down you go."

Markle gripped the rope dangling from the pulley and let himself down. Spong drew a knife from his boot and sliced the taut rope. A splash and muffled cry came from below. From the echo, it sounded like a deep well.

"You can't just . . . ," Balty stammered.

"He was sent to murder you, sir. But if you prefer, we can haul him up and allow him to complete the task."

They returned to the King's Arms and mounted the waiting horses. In his agitated state, Balty immediately spurred his mount to a gallop. Spong caught up with him and took the reins, slowing it to a walk.

"Never leave town at a gallop. Arouses curiosity."

"That man you put into the well, why did he call you Huncks?"

"What's in a name?"

"What are you talking about?"

"You're the one doing the talking."

They made their way along the High Street toward the town gate.

The first faint glow of dawn showed in the east. Two watchmen were warming themselves by a brazier, muskets close at hand.

"Say nothing."

They reined to a stop in front of the guards.

"You're a frigid-looking pair."

"Hand over your passes."

Spong reached into his jerkin and gave papers to the guard, who unfolded them and tried to read them in the faint light of the brazier.

"Not worth ruining your eyes for. That's the Governor's signature. Meself, I'd rather be in my warm bed, rogering my missus. But I've to get this one to Punkapog. He's the new pastor."

"What happened to the last one?"

"Who knows? Maybe they et him."

A guard addressed Balty, "Going to learn Scripture to the savages? What in God's name were you thinking when you volunteered for *that*?"

"Ah, leave off. Don't be putting a fright into the lad. He's already shat himself twice."

The guards snorted.

"Someone's got to learn the savages to be Christian."

Spong pulled a leather flask from his saddlebag and tossed it to the guard. "This'll warm you better than that fire there."

"Pass on. Don't get yourself et up all in one gulp."

They rode in silence for an hour. The sun rose, making long shadows over dewy fields. Soon only the brightest stars and planets remained. They dismounted to water the horses at a stream.

Balty was all in a fog. Rousted from a warm sleep, made accomplice to murder—unless Markle was treading water at the bottom of Endecott's well, abducted by a brute named Spong—or Huncks. The guard's taunt echoed in his head: *What in God's name were you thinking when you volunteered for that?* What, indeed. What—in God's name— had he been thinking when he accepted this cursed commission from Downing?

Balty's companion handed him a piece of jerky. "Eat. You'll need your strength. We've a long ride."

It tasted like boot leather, which was a taste Balty knew. Once, in an extremis of poverty, Balty boiled old shoes into a disgusting bouillon.

"What *is* your name, then?"

"It was Spong. Lovely name, Plantagenet Spong. Took a while to come up with it."

Balty said with annoyance. "What am I to call you?"

"Whatever you like."

"Then I'll call you Beelzebub. Apt enough, as I find myself in Hell," Balty moaned. "Why am I being punished so cruelly? Were my sins so grievous?"

"Cheer up, man. Look." He pointed to a cluster of purple croci pushing up from the thawing earth. "It's a sweet spring day in New England. You won't find such pretty flowers as that in Hell."

Balty stared miserably at the croci, finding no consolation in them.

"Balthasar de St. Michel's an out-of-town name. Papist?"

"Huguenot. French, on my papa's side. He . . . But you know all about him. Don't you?"

"Only that he keeps very refined company, what between Henri Quatre and Louis—"

"*Yes.* Never mind."

"Just as well you're not a papist. They hate Catholics here almost as much as they hate Quakers. Not sure what they'll make of a Huguenot." He put out his hand. "Huncks. Hiram Huncks. At your service."

"You do work for Downing, then?"

"Why else would I be here?"

"I haven't the faintest idea. I certainly don't know what *I'm* doing here."

"Feeling sorry for yourself, it appears. *When, in disgrace with fortune and men's eyes, I all alone beweep my outcast state, and trouble deaf heaven with my bootless cries . . .*"

"What are you talking about?"

"Shakespeare. I recite it when I'm feeling low. Try it."

"I'm not in the mood for Shakespeare just now."

"*Tant pis.* Some other time. Best be moving on. Endecott'll have the watch out after us. That nonsense I gave them about taking you to teach Gospel to the Punkapog won't stick for long."

They mounted and set off. Huncks led the way off the path into a forest. Balty had never been in such a thick one. The morning sun, though strong, barely penetrated. Balty imagined painted savages behind trees. He kept close to Huncks.

They rode all day and well into the night. Huncks refused to stop other than to water the horses. Balty became so tired he nearly toppled off his horse. Huncks tied him to the saddle.

"There," he said. "You're Odysseus." An owl screeched. "That's your siren, beckoning."

How did a rough fellow like this know Shakespeare and *tant pis* and Odysseus?

"I've no feeling in my legs," Balty groaned.

"We'll rest at dawn."

"This is torture."

"I assure you, Mr. St. Michel, were you put to torture by those who inhabit these woods, you'd look on your present discomfort with longing."

"You sound like that dreadful ostler in Boston. In London I was told that the savages here had been dealt with. Was *everything* they told me a lie?"

They continued through the woods. Presently, they came to a jumble of rocks by a stream. Huncks's horse whinnied and reared. Huncks took its reins and steadied it. Balty's horse was nervous, too.

"Be still," he told Balty.

"Why?"

"Catamount."

"A what?"

"Lion."

"*Lion?* Sweet Jesus!"

"Hush."

Huncks had his caliver out. Moonlight glinted on the barrel.

The roar was close, causing panic in the horses. Balty's reared again and tried to bolt but Huncks kept it gripped. Balty clung awkwardly to his saddle.

Huncks fired the pistol into the air. A jet of yellow sparks spewed into the dark like a fountain of fire. Balty's nostrils filled with the tang of gunpowder. The horses bucked frantically. Huncks soothed them with murmurs, and they pressed on to Hartford.

CHAPTER 9

The Chelsey Trollop

Try as he might, Pepys could not grasp why the Duke of York—Lord High Admiral of England—and Downing were so blithe about the prospect of another war with Holland. Surely they knew that England's Navy was not ready. Again and again, to the point of becoming a nuisance, Pepys had sought to convince them of this inconvenient yet insistent truth.

Downing was now back in London, having come from The Hague to confer with the Duke. Pepys decided that he must confront him. He felt more comfortable presenting his case to him rather than to the King's brother. The Clerk of the Acts briskly made his way to Downing's house in Whitehall.

Lord Downing was not in. His secretary, Flott, told Pepys that his lordship would return shortly. Pepys and Flott were old acquaintances and enjoyed trading morsels of gossip, especially concerning court *amours*.

They were both fascinated by—and not a little infatuated with—Lady Castlemaine, King Charles's favorite mistress. She'd now borne him five bastards (some said six). Indeed, she was so fecund the King had installed nurseries for the litter of royal illegitimates at Whitehall Palace. This arrangement did not bring unbridled joy to the Queen,

Catherine of Braganza. And now word had it that Lady Castlemaine had secretly become a Catholic. Pepys and Flott discussed this development with greatest relish. At least *this* should please the devoutly Catholic queen!

Flott pressed Pepys to reveal what he knew about the current subject of titillation—Lord Sandwich's flagrant *delictoes* with Mrs. Becke of Chelsey.

Pepys trod carefully on this tricky ground. Sir Edward Montagu, First Earl Sandwich, Lieutenant Admiral in the Royal Navy, was Pepys's cousin and great patron. But everyone, down to the lowest charwoman and dogsbody in London, knew about Sandwich's carryings-on with Mrs. Becke. Pepys thought her entirely unsuitable as a mistress for a man as eminent as his cousin. He privately referred to her as "the Chelsey trollop." He'd remonstrated with Sandwich, not only for his infidelity to his wife, Lady Jemima, whom Pepys loved, but also for risking his reputation and career in the Navy. Pepys's concern was not entirely disinterested: if Sandwich's ship went down in a gale of scandal, Pepys could sink with it.

Sam could hardly claim any moral high ground. Marital fidelity was not among his virtues. After a bout of wenching, he would express remorse to his diary, swearing never again to succumb to temptation. And invariably would yield to the next temptation to come along. Expressing remorse to his diary at least provided a simulacrum of repentance. It was something, anyway.

Pepys was not yet aware of another element at play here. Years later, after a particularly stormy marital battle, his wife would inform him that Sandwich had asked *her* to be his mistress. One can only imagine his lordship's innermost thoughts when Pepys showed up to berate him for his carnality with Mrs. Becke.

Was it true, Flott asked Sam, that the Chelsey trollop had given his lordship the clap?

Eager to change the subject, Pepys pretended he knew nothing about that unhappy subject. Meanwhile, he remarked that he was surprised Lord Downing had not asked him to do any ciphering for him recently. Pepys enjoyed working at "character"—that is, devising private codes for confidential messages. He told Flott that he felt a bit put out at not having been asked. Had his skill at character been eclipsed by someone else?

Flott replied that he, too, was surprised that Lord Downing hadn't called on Pepys, for in recent weeks, his lordship had dispatched so many ciphered messages that, "all collected, they would surpass in number the pages of King James's Bible."

Pepys was speechless. *Why hadn't Downing called on him?*

It could only be that Downing didn't want Pepys to know about whatever it was. Which meant that whatever it was must concern the Navy. But why, Pepys asked himself, keep a Navy matter secret from the Clerk of the Acts of . . . the Navy—the person most responsible for naval preparedness?

What Navy matter could Downing be keeping from him? Pepys mentally reviewed the roster. He knew the location of every anchored or docked ship in the Navy—not that there *were* many.

There was Colonel Nicholls, commander of a British force, and his squadron of four ships at Portsmouth, preparing to sail in May for Boston. This was a peaceful undertaking, an administrative review of the New England colonies. The mission itself wasn't secret, so there would have been no need for a blizzard of ciphered messages. Downing had even alerted the West India Company in Amsterdam about it, so that there would be no misunderstanding should Nicholls's squadron wander into Dutch waters near New England. Downing even proposed to them that Nicholls pay a courtesy call at New Amsterdam. A gesture of goodwill would go far, at a time of such great tension between the two nations.

Musing on the Nicholls squadron reminded Pepys that he meant to ask Nicholls to inquire after Balty. And to give him letters for Balty from his sister and wife, who'd both been in a swivet since he'd left. How they fretted over their Balty! But how peaceful it had been without Balty barging into Pepys's office every day, sniffing about for a sinecure or another "loan."

A bustle approached: the clack of heels on parquet.

"Ah, Mr. Pep-iss."

"My lord."

"*Suivez, suivez.*"

Pepys followed Downing into his chambers.

Downing spoke with a distracted air. "Haven't seen you about, Sam. Where have you been lurking?"

"At the ropeyard, testing hemp. And Waltham Forest, supervising the hewing of timber. And dealing with cheating flag makers."

"Ah. I trust you made an example of the flag makers."

"I had them whipped."

Downing frowned. "I call that lenient. Symbolic things, flags. Sends a bad signal. I'd have had a hand taken off. At least a thumb."

"I agree. But removing their hands and thumbs would only encumber their stitching." Enough badinage, Pepys thought. "I wonder, my lord, if we might have a *tête-à-tête*, *vis-à-vis* Holland?"

"Holland," Downing groaned theatrically. "Mr. Pep-iss, I begin to think that Holland is the only thing in your *tête.*"

"I assure your lordship that it is not my intent to inflict tedium. I merely—"

"*Yes*, Sam, you merely worry that we are rushing pell-mell into a war for which we are inadequately equipped. Et cetera, et cetera. Your concern has not gone unnoticed. How could it have, it being your *only* conversation these days."

Pepys bowed. "Yet again, I marvel at my lord's ability to distill the quiddity of any matter at hand."

"As I delight, yet again, in our *tête-à-têtes.* Do come and see us again. Soon."

Pepys lingered, unwilling to quit the field. "As I find myself here, is my lord in need of any service? Ciphering?"

"Not at the moment."

Pepys knew not to press. As a spymaster, Downing would be suspicious if he did. And he must not reveal to Downing what Flott had told him about the recent torrent of ciphered messages. Still, he was reluctant to leave it at this.

"I'm to Portsmouth next week," Pepys said casually.

"Ah?"

"Um. To complete the victualing of Colonel Nicholls's squadron."

"Yes? Good."

Downing was reading, barely listening. Pepys probed for an opening: "I have letters for him to convey to our Mr. St. Michel."

"Who?"

"My brother-in-law. He whom you dispatched to New England. To arrest the regicides Whalley and Goffe."

Downing looked up from his desk. "Ah, yes. Our intrepid judge hunter. I'd forgotten him. Any word?"

"No. But it occurs to me that Colonel Nicholls's mission, his administrative review of the colonies, might intersect with Mr. St. Michel's undertaking."

"Intersect?" A flicker of interest.

"Perhaps Mr. St. Michel may have found something of interest to Colonel Nicholls."

"Oh, I shouldn't think. Anyway, your formidable brother-in-law's mission is to make a nuisance of himself in New Haven. You did avouch that being a nuisance was his great facility."

"Yes. No doubt he's vexed them to the point of making them want to move to New Netherland."

"No, no," Downing said, suddenly stern. "We can't have *that*."

"I spoke in jest. Why?"

"New Englanders forging alliances with New Netherlanders? No good could come of *that*. We've had a report that some of the New Haveners, chafing under Connecticut rule, are making plans for a new settlement. New Ark, they're calling it. Better that they remain in Connecticut, where we can keep a eye on them, rather than having them go making common cause with Peter Stuyvesant."

"In that case," Pepys said, "I shall instruct my brother-in-law not to annoy them so greatly as to drive them into the arms of the cheese makers." Pepys bowed. "To Portsmouth, then. If your lordship has any dispatches for Colonel Nicholls, I should be glad to convey them."

"We have couriers for that."

"It's no trouble. I am going there, myself." Pepys smiled. "No task in his majesty's service can be considered menial."

"Accommodating of you. Very well. Come back tomorrow morning. Flott will give you a packet for Nicholls."

CHAPTER 10

What a Dreadful Story

Balty awoke to the flutter of bat wings. He gasped, then remembered that he was in a place were bats tended to be—namely, a cave.

He sat up. Huncks was by the entrance, tending a small fire. They'd finally stopped here after riding for twenty-four hours, just as dawn was breaking. Now the sun was setting. He'd slept all day. He remembered Huncks saying that from here it was no more than a half day's ride to Hartford, which for reasons Balty had forgotten, Huncks also called "Hoop."

"I let you sleep. No need to set out in the dark. We'll leave for Hoop at first light."

"Is it Hartford we're going to, or Hoop? Not that I care."

Huncks seemed amused by Balty's pique.

"Hartford, Hoop. As you please. Hoop's the old name. Block, the Dutcher, called it that—House of Hope. Hooker renamed it after his home in England. Most places here are on their second name. Third, if you include the Indian names. Which is only fair. Local tribe around here are the Podunks. Their name for it meant place of black river dirt. Good soil. So for now it's named after a town in England. Maybe someday you Frenchies will own it and call it *Nouveau Paris*."

"I'm not a Frenchie. I'm English."

"I was going to shoot something for dinner but I fell asleep. Here." Huncks tossed Balty a small pouch of dried fruit.

It was a spacious cave with plenty of head room, about a hundred or so feet up a sharp incline. Huncks seemed quite at home, as he seemed everywhere.

Balty went and sat next to Huncks. The mouth of the cave looked over the forest, now loud with crepuscular avian chatter.

"This would make a good refuge from one of your . . . what did you call them? Catamites?"

Huncks grunted with amusement. "I suppose you could hide from a catamite here. Or a catamount."

Huncks chewed on dried fruit and looked about the cave, aglow from shafts of the dying light.

"Two lovers took refuge here," Huncks said. "Thirty years ago? Yes, thirty. There, where you were sleeping, where the rock's dark? That's where he died. The discoloring of the stone is his blood. It's all that remains of him, poor beggar."

Balty shuddered. "You might have told me."

"You went to sleep kinda sudden."

"Who was he?"

"Peter. Peter Hager. About your age. Dutcher, one of Block's crew on *Onrust*. Fell in love with a daughter of the Podunk sachem. A princess. We have princesses here, too, you know. Wunnectunah. Called Wunnee. They say she was very beautiful.

"Peter wanted to marry her, Christian like. So they went to Boston. He was arrested for failing to observe the Sabbath and put into the stocks. Somehow Wunnee freed him. They fled into the woods—as we did. One of the pursuivants who went after them fell and hit his head on a rock and died. So now Peter and Wunnee were murderers.

"They made it back to Fort Hoop. But with a price on them, they had to keep moving. One day a bounty hunter shot Peter. He managed to crawl here to this cave, where he died in her arms, there, where you slept.

"Wunnee buried him. She never said where. She returned to the Podunk, to the place by the river with the good black soil. Ended up a servant to an English family. Died just a few years ago. I knew her. By then she was no longer beautiful. She was known as Wun Hag. She's buried over at Windsor. Her gravestone says, 'One Hag.' They spelled it wrong. Like I say, the names here are always changing."

There was only the sound of the birds, exchanging the last gossip of the day.

Balty wiped his eyes. "What a dreadful story."

"Wasn't my intention to bore you."

"No. I mean . . . what a sad story. A terrible sad story."

Huncks poked at the fire. "Oh, we have lots more of those here, Mr. St. Michel."

They quit the cave at first light and by noon had fetched the east bank of the river. The ferryman greeted Huncks jovially.

Balty was relieved to be out of the woods. Huncks had told him about the Puritan belief that the devil is physically present in nature. At first Balty thought this foolish, a superstitious notion. Then trees closed around them as they made their way deeper into the forest, and scoffing gave way to chill. Balty was a city creature. Seeing the rooftops of Hartford heave into view downriver on the far bank was very welcome.

"This river, what is it called?" Balty asked the ferryman.

"Depends who's arsking."

Balty sighed. Another impudent New England peasant? Did no one in this dismal wilderness possess even rudimentary courtesy?

"*I'm* asking."

"Where be you from?"

"London. A very great city, by a great river. Called the Thames, no matter who's asking."

"Ain't heard of it. A Hollander'll tell you this is the Fresh River. But you won't be finding many Hollanders hereabouts anymore. We calls it the Great River. Which it be. Look at her, the beautiful, brown thing. Old Dildo Leg may still claim it for his. But we don't pay *him* much mind now, does we, Mr. Huncks?"

Huncks grinned.

The ferryman summoned a gobbet of tobacco-colored sputum. Balty edged away so as not to be misted.

"Who, pray, is Old Dildo Leg?"

"Stuyvesant," Huncks said. "Governor of New Netherland. Of which all this fine, rich black river soil was once part."

"Why is he called that?"

"His leg got taken off by a cannonball while he was sieging against the Spanish at Saint Martin. Stumps about on a wooden one."

"It's his head what's wooden," the ferryman said. "Like all Dutchers."

"He's a tough old bird, Stuyvesant. You may meet him."

"Why would I be meeting the Governor of New Netherland if our destination is New Haven?"

Huncks shrugged. "Perhaps in New Haven we'll learn that your regicides have legged it to New Amsterdam. They wouldn't be the first Englishmen to seek refuge there. Stuyvesant loves taking in English refugees. It's a way of sticking it to us."

"Why should he want to do that?"

"How long did you say you've been in service to the Crown?"

"I didn't."

"But you are aware that relations between England and Holland aren't what you'd call cordial."

"I had heard something about it."

"The border between New England and New Netherland isn't much of a border. Stuyvesant tends to be pettish about it. Feels encroached on. He's always sending men to nail metal signs on trees: HERE BEGINS NEW NETHERLAND. BUGGER OFF, YOU TRESPASSING ENGLISH BASTARDS. The trespassing English bastards pry them off and trade them to the Indians, who melt them into arrowheads. Which the Indians shoot into Dutch and English alike. A cycle, you might call it."

"In the event I meet Governor Stuyvesant, do I address him as your dildoship, or is there a more respectful form of address?"

"He's an educated man. He was going to be a minister. Knows his Latin and Greek. And Hebrew. His name being Peter, he signs it Petrus. Like in *Tu es Petrus.*"

"Is that Dutch?"

"Not unless Jesus and the disciples were yakking in Dutch at the Last Supper. You have heard of the Bible, Mr. St. Michel?"

"*Yes.*"

"*Tu es Petrus* is Latin for 'You are Peter.' Ring a bell? 'Upon this rock I will build my church'? Not that they were speaking in Latin. So we call him Old Petrus. It's what his friends would call him, if he had friends. He's not a bad man, Stuyvesant. In many ways, a rather good man. But temperamentally, he's more of a generalissimo than a governor. That doesn't make you many friends."

The ferryman left them at the landing, declining payment from Huncks.

They made their way up the riverbank into the marketplace. From there Huncks led the way to a neat, prosperous-looking house whose door was attended by an armed sentry. The sentry greeted Huncks as an old friend. Inside, Huncks was clasped in a tight hug by a man whose gay, playful eyes and almost comically large nose contrasted with his somber Puritan attire. Here was John Winthrop (the Younger), Governor of the Connecticut Colony.

Balty stood awkwardly, waiting to be presented as the exuberant reunion continued. Finally, Winthrop noticed Balty.

"Who's this, then?"

Balty drew himself up, preparing to announce his credentials as Crown commissioner in the service of His Majesty King Charles.

Huncks said, "He wants explaining. Me, I want a drink."

Winthrop laughed. "No surprise there! Come!"

"Mr. St. Michel could also use a good washing up," Huncks said. "We had a run-in with a catamount. He had a bit of an accident."

Balty's cheeks flushed. Winthrop nodded sympathetically. "Fearful things, catamounts, specially to newcomers. Don't worry. We'll get you cleaned up. Martha! Priscilla!"

Balty's humiliation was now compounded by finding himself captive of two stout, aproned women who tugged at him like termagant nursemaids, pulling off his hat and gloves and other articles of clothing. A door closed behind him. Balty beheld a beautiful sight: a soft, clean bed. How it beckoned.

From the other side of the door came stern female commands to disrobe and hand over his remaining garments. Shortly, he heard the sound of water splashing into a tub.

He soaked in deliciously hot, soapy water. Then, as commanded by his jailers, he returned to the bedroom, where he found a bottle of rum and a glass on a side table. A clean nightshirt was laid neatly upon the bed. He filled the glass to the brim and drained it, tumbled into the bed, and fell into a sleep as deep as the Atlantic Ocean.

Balty awoke to darkness. His clothes had been washed and fire-dried and laid out on a chair. The rips and tears had been repaired with neat stitching. Hospitality of the first order. How different from the disgraceful reception accorded him in Boston by *its* governor!

Balty dressed and ventured into the house, pleasantly filled with aromas of cookery. The rations of dried meat and fruit had left him famished for real victuals.

One of his female captors found him and prodded him into a parlor. Winthrop and Huncks were so deep in conversation that they took no notice of him. Balty stood, listening. He heard names. Pell. Underhill. Nicholls.

Winthrop saw him and grinned. "*Ecce homo!*" He clapped Balty on the shoulder and nudged him to sit by the fire.

"Come, Mr. Balthasar. Join us. Colonel Huncks has been telling me all about you."

Colonel Huncks?

"Hartford is honored by your presence. Honored, indeed. It's not every day we receive such a distinguished visitor. The fatted calf awaits.

You shall feast, sir! Meanwhile, might I force upon you a glass of Madeira?"

"Well . . ."

"Splendid!"

Balty struggled to assert a semblance of control but was overwhelmed by Winthrop's prodigal geniality. The Madeira went down warm and silky, with a bit of a kick at the end. For the second time in this house today, Balty found himself a happy captive, all at peace on the far side of the river from the roar of catamount and ghosts of poor Peter and Wunnee.

Winthrop said, "Now, sir, before we get down to business, tell me, how is my cousin? Sir George. Lord Downing. The Colonel tells me it was he who has sent you here."

"Ah. Yes. He is . . . well. Very well indeed. He asked me to convey his compliments. A superlative personage, Sir George. Lord Downing."

"Not sure I'd go *that* far," said Winthrop. He and Huncks roared with laughter.

"But I rejoice to hear he is well. He must think very highly of you, sir, to entrust you with such an important mission."

"Well, I . . . I suppose. It is a serious business. Regicide."

Winthrop seemed to be waiting for more. Balty added, "The late King Charles, God rest his soul, may not have been a perfect monarch. Still . . ."

"*Nullum argumentum est.*"

Balty had no clue what this meant. Should he nod in agreement?

Winthrop said, "Doubtless, you are aware of my father-in-law."

Balty found himself again clueless. Winthrop's father-in-law must be some other significant personage.

"Oh, indeed, yes. Splendid. Admirable."

Winthrop stared. He looked puzzled. "Generous of you to say so. Marks you as a true Christian. Especially given your purpose here in New England."

"Oh?"

"By all accounts, he met his fate like a man."

Fate?

Winthrop continued, "I've no doubt that he went to God with open hands and heart, and was so greeted in Heaven."

Balty cleared his throat. "That is . . . yes, the general view."

Winthrop fell silent. "*Beastly* way to go."

Had his father-in-law died of the plague? Been eaten by a catamount?

Balty ventured, "No. Certainly, not the way *I* should choose to, uh, go."

"Hardly *likely*," Winthrop said with a touch of asperity.

Desperate to change the subject, Balty said, "Might you indulge me another glass of this excellent Madeira?"

Winthrop refilled Balty's glass.

"It's the '38. Same year the New Haven Colony was founded. You'll be meeting the Reverend Davenport. His cofounder, Mr. Eaton, has gone on to his heavenly reward. They did not remain long in the Bay Colony. My late father was governor then. They did not get along. So Davenport and Eaton went off to create a new haven for themselves, amongst the Quiripi. I fear you may find New Haven a bit grim."

Huncks snorted in amusement.

Winthrop continued. "You will almost certainly find less Madeira there. If you do find some, don't drink it on the Sabbath. They are harsh there. Even by Puritan standards. You're not by chance Quaker?"

"Huguenot."

Winthrop smiled slyly. "Pity."

"Why?"

"I meant, that you are not Quaker."

Another amused snort from Huncks.

"I fear I don't understand," Balty said. How refreshing it felt to admit, finally, that he had not understood most of what had been discussed.

Winthrop said, "You must forgive me, Mr. St. Michel, I'm being mischievous. Your Crown commission confers immunity upon you. The New Haveners despise Quakers above all other sects. If, as Colonel Huncks says, the mission is to vex them, how better than to send a Quaker commissioner."

Huncks cleared his throat. From the look on Winthrop's face, Balty inferred that he'd said something indiscreet. Balty was again plunged into confusion.

"His majesty," Winthrop said, "has forbidden persecution of Quakers here. But New Haveners are determined. They find ways around his edict. Charge them with other things—disturbing the peace, what have you. We in Connecticut get along very well with our Quakers. They give us no trouble. Indeed, they are splendid citizens. When they flee Endecott's Massachusetts, we make them welcome. And they are grateful in return. I do not say that I approve of their ways. I, too, quake before God, but"—Winthrop laughed—"I manage to keep control of my limbs. I saw a woman once in the street, convulsed. I thought, must be Quaker. Turned out the poor thing had the palsy!" Winthrop laughed. "Do you know why Puritans—and New Haveners especially—despise Quakers?"

"Theological differences, I should imagine."

Winthrop shook his head. "No. Because they refuse to doff their hats to the magistrates."

"Well," Balty said, "I suppose it is somewhat disrespectful."

"Of course it's not about hats, is it? It's that they reject authority. They've no bishops, elders, even pastors. They commune directly with God. Every man, every woman, his or her own priest. Imagine! Drives the Puritans up the nearest elm. D'you know what else drives them fruity? That Quakers embrace persecution. They're like the early Christians in Rome. The more you fed them to the lions, the hungrier they were to *be* fed to the lions. I've seen—"

Winthrop glanced over at Huncks. He was staring morosely into the fire, a strange look on his face.

"Well," Winthrop said, "let us talk of other things."

Balty said, "You're Puritan, aren't you?"

Winthrop smiled. "Well, I rather have to be, don't I? I am Governor. Did Colonel Huncks mention that I do a bit of doctoring?"

"Oh?"

"Indeed. Yesterday, I set a broken humerus bone. What do you think of that?"

"Humerus?"

"Oh, very good, Mr. Balthasar! You're a wit. You must excuse me. I don't mean to preen, but I *was* a bit pleased with myself. Mind you, I'm not the town surgeon. Just a dabbler. Still. Nice feeling. As to Puritanism . . . you've heard of the Great Dying?"

"Was that some war, here?"

"No. A half century ago, all this land was ravaged by a great pestilence. Plague. Probably brought by Dutch sailors. I say that as a medical man, not because I am an enemy of the Dutch. My office obliges me to be so, just as it obliges me to be a Puritan. It devastated their population. Wiped out perhaps as many as eight out of every ten natives."

"We have the plague in London."

"Yes, but you see, it is an article of faith among the Puritans that the Great Dying was *not* brought by Dutch sailors. That it was the work of Divine Providence. Sent by Almighty God."

"Not very nice of God."

Winthrop smiled. "Ask yourself—why would the Almighty do such a thing? Ah, don't you see? To clear the land for us! So that we could build our New Jerusalem here. Or as my late father put it, our 'city upon a hill.' What do you make of that, Mr. Balthasar?"

"Seems a bit extreme."

"This was no virgin land, Mr. St. Michel," Winthrop said gravely. "It was a widowed one."

He refilled their glasses. "But enough of that. I was at Court in London, you know. In '61."

"Oh?"

"Sir George mentioned it, surely?"

"Indeed. Yes."

"It was very merry. His majesty and I spent hours looking through his royal tube. We observed Saturn. *And* Jupiter."

"The royal tube. Ah. Yes."

"He was most congenial. But I did not go there just to immerse myself in nectar. No, sir!" Winthrop smiled slyly. "My purpose was to obtain a royal charter for Connecticut. And, by George, I returned with one."

"Well done."

Winthrop's delight was boyish.

"You see, it puts New Haven under Connecticut rule. Imagine how warmly the Reverend Davenport and Governor Leete received *that* news! But they had only themselves to thank. His majesty was much displeased by the protection they gave to Generals Whalley and Goffe. Not only did they harbor them. They sent the hunters chasing after geese. They *say* that the whole time they were hiding in Davenport's basement. And Leete's."

"Shocking."

"Leete's great mistake was panicking after the fact. Not the steadiest of temperaments, old Leetey. He did the full grovel. Wrote his majesty an apology. Can you *imagine*, the stupidity!

"I saw my opportunity. Told Leete we must both go to London to assess the situation." Winthrop chortled. "Then snuck off and got the first ship. Left him twiddling his thumbs on the dock.

"His majesty was altogether disposed to my argument that New Haven ought to be—shall we say—*absorbed* into the Connecticut Colony. Oh, it was . . . really lovely.

"And now his majesty sends *you* to New Haven, in further search of his papa's murderers. I wonder. Can they *still* be there? It's been three years. Surely they'll have fled by now. Perhaps to New Amsterdam. I would have.

"I do not think you will have a warm reception from Davenport and Leete. You'll find them sulky, like whipped children." Winthrop smiled. "But you shall hear a fine sermon from the Reverend Davenport. He gives a cracking good homily. Perhaps you will hear some inspired invective on the subject of the Wickedness of Winthrop!"

They sat quietly for a while. Huncks was still staring into the fire.

Winthrop said, "Is it true, about Lady Castlemaine?"

"About the latest royal bastard?"

Winthrop chuckled. "What's that make now, five? She *is* prolific. But no, I meant the rumor that she's poped."

Balty said, "Well, one way or the other, she does seem to be spending a lot of time on her knees these days."

Winthrop clapped his hands. "So it *is* true! I wonder—did she do it to please his majesty?" Winthrop lowered his voice. "By all accounts, he himself has gone over to Rome." He smiled. "Well, Mr. Balthasar, none of this will make you very welcome in New Haven. If they hate anyone more than Quakers, it's Catholics." He sighed. "What a lot of hating they task themselves with, Puritans. It's a wonder they have any time left over to build the New Jerusalem."

"Governor, sir. Dinner is ready."

"At last! Thank you, Priscilla. Let us to feast. Hiram. *Hiram.*"

Huncks looked up. Winthrop put a hand on Huncks's shoulder and said gently, "Come back to us, old friend. We dine."

– CHAPTER 11 –

May 23rd. To Portsmouth to review final victualing and provisioning of Col. Nicholls's ship <u>Guinea</u>, thirty-six guns. N. sails on the 25th inst. at the head of a squadron of four ships of war, for Newe England, there to undertake an administrative review of the colonies.

In London, was entrusted by my Lord Downing with conveyance of various dispatches for Nicholls.

Prior to departing for Pmouth, made inquiries about Nicholls. By all reports, a commendable officer: age forty, devout royalist, commanded troop of horse in the Civil War. Following Restoration was made Groom of the Chamber to the Duke of York, now Lord High Admiral of England.

The Duke being keen for war with Holland—along with Downing, every grasping merchant in London and, not least, his majesty the King—my curiosity as to Col. Nicholls's appointment was naturally piqued.

Found it passing curious that my Lord Downing, as Envoy to The Hague, should have urgent dispatches for a Navy squadron embarking for New England. Told D that as was going to Portsmouth myself, I volunteered to convey said dispatches to Nicholls.

Whilst en route to Portsmouth, took the liberty of inspecting said dispatches, to ensure that the seals were unbroken and all was in good order, etc., etc.

So doing, found several seals had come loose, owing to an accumulation of moisture, there having been copious rain and humidity of late.

Whilst inspecting dispatches themselves for damage by moisture, discovered that the dispatches had been written in my own character, which I had priorly devised for Sir George. Thus I was able to decipher their contents.

Found these to be <u>extremely troubling</u>, indeed alarming, tho' not surprising, given the agitation "War Party" here for Conflict with Holland.

Diligently resealed the dispatches by means of melting new wax, to which I affixed Downing's own wax seals, namely, those loosened by moisture.

Spent rest of the journey with my mind in a state of greatest agitation and fever.

Arriving at Portsmouth, made my way to Col. Nicholls aboard his flagship <u>Guinea</u>. Duly conveyed Lord Downing's compliments, along with the dispatch box, revealing nothing of my knowledge of their contents.

Nicholls most cordial. Said he had heard "excellent reports" of my "fastidious labors" on behalf of the Navy, etc., which naturally I found gratifying.

Invited me to partake of refreshment in his cabin, so sat down to a fine meal of roast pigeons, pease and pork, an eel pie, various cheeses—which he jocosely averred were "not Dutch." Drank good quantity of Margate ale.

Complimenting him on his assignment, I apprised him of Brother Balty's current undertaking in New England, with respect to the regicide judges.

To my surprise, Nicholls indicated he was already aware of Balty's mission. Oh? said I. Yes, he said—that matter of the regicides Whalley and Goffe was included among the "various items" relevant to his "administrative review." Oh, I said.

Asked if he would kindly inquire after Balty whilst in Newe England. He happily consented to do so, whereupon I conveyed to him the letters for Balty, adding that my wife was most anxious as to her brother's well-being.

I remarked that as Clerk of the Acts, I was of course familiar with the provisioning of Col. Nicholls's ships and exprest some curiosity as to the great quantity of Munitions, viz., cannonball, powder, musketry, pistols, mines, granados, etc., etc., amongst the stores of his four ships of war. Attempting to strike a jocose tone, I said, "With such stores, sir, you will be able to conduct a most Fearsome administrative review!"

He replied blandly that these instruments of Mars were replenishments for the various forts in Newe England—Boston, New Port, Saybrook, etc.

Probing further, I remarked that four ships and 450 men-at-arms was certainly a formidable array with which to undertake an "administrative review." He replied with a blandness that now struck me as concerted, saying, "'Of course the Navy must be prepared for _any_ vicissitude.'"

I agreed and further prest him as to what manner of "vicissitude" might present itself in the course of an "administrative review."

Whereat his cordiality diminished and he excused himself, saying that he must attend the flogging of a sailor who had beshat a midshipman's boiled beef.

He invited me to attend, but I begged off, saying I had already attended two hangings this week at Tyburn and was surfeited with such entertainments.

Thanked Nicholls for his hospitality, wished him every success with his "administrative review," and thus set about returning to London, in no small turmoil of mind.

– *CHAPTER 12* –

Narragansetts Coming In

Balty awoke with sticky mouth, parched tongue, and pounding head. He stared ruefully at the ceiling beams, gathering the strength to rise and vowing that never again would Madeira or any spirituous liquor pass his lips.

He splashed his face with water, dressed, and made his way unsteadily through the house. One of the housemaids found him and, identifying his distress, led him into the kitchen. In a wooden bowl she whisked together raw eggs and various liquids and a sprinkling of dark powder from a small bottle.

Balty drank. He winced. On reaching his bowels, the sulfurous elixir ignited a rumbling that could have been mistaken for a cannonade or erupting volcano. He clutched his stomach.

"In God's name, woman, why have you poisoned me? I hold the King's . . ."

"There, there, ducks. Give it time. It's Governor's own remedy. He's also a doctor, you know. We've our own herb garden, and very fine it is."

Tsunamis contended against each other inside Balty's bowels.

"What . . . have you *given* me?" Balty moaned, holding his stomach as if it might burst open.

"There's eggs, juice of peppers, a tot of rum, and a pinch or two of gunpowder."

"Gunpowder? God's mercy, woman! You have assassinated me!"

"Tush. Governor says it's the gunpowder what makes it work."

"I shall die. Here, in this godforsaken land."

"Godforsaken, is it? I reckon Hartford's as God-fearing a town as any on this earth. It's not Hartford's fault you can't hold your liquor. Is it?"

It was misery enough to die such a wretched death, but to be hectored by a charwoman as his life ebbed . . . oh, cruel fortune!

Then in the next instant, the churning gale in Balty's bowels abated, and all was suddenly calm. Balty heard the placid cry of seagulls above now-still waters. The scrim of fog cleared from his eyes, his nostrils twitched to the pleasing aromas of breakfast, the rat-a-tat drumbeat in his skull subsided.

"Well," he said. "*Well.*"

"Told you to give it time. Now sit and eat your breakfast."

Balty went at it like a trencherman. The woman told him he would find the Governor in his chambers, across the courtyard.

Balty emerged from the house, blinking in the rebuking light of day. The sky was blue, the clouds puffy and innocently white. A breeze came in off the river. All this freshness was chastening. If he weren't still a bit shaky, he'd have complimented New England on providing such a fine spring day.

The guard let him inside. Balty found the Governor and Huncks examining papers laid out upon a table.

"Ah, Lazarus is risen!" Winthrop said.

Huncks briskly rolled up one of the papers, giving Balty an impression of furtiveness.

"Up to traveling?" Huncks asked. "We leave within the hour. The Governor's arranged a shallop."

"A what?"

"Boat. Downriver, to Fort Saybrook. New Haven's less than a day's ride from there."

"Boat?" Balty said glumly. "Is there no *road* to New Haven from here?"

"I take it you are not a sailor, sir," Winthrop said. "Have no fear. It's a river, not the raging Atlantic."

Balty comforted himself that at least there would be no encounters with catamounts, or hatchet-wielding savages and ghosts of star-crossed lovers. He decided that he must, if only for the sake of dignity, evince curiosity about the maps Winthrop and Huncks had been so intently examining, and which Huncks had been at pains to conceal from him. He pointed to an island on the map lying open on the table.

"New Haven?"

Winthrop and Huncks smiled.

"Forgive our rudeness," Winthrop said. "No, that is New Amsterdam. On the island of Manhatoes."

Balty examined it. "Um. So it is. Yes."

Winthrop's finger moved east from Manhatoes along a shoreline. "Here"—he paused—"New Netherland meets New England. The border. Such as it is." He circled a large area. "All this bit—considerable, fifty thousand acres—is the property of a Dr. Pell, of Fairfield. Bit of a no-man's-land." Winthrop chuckled. "Not that Dr. Pell regards it as such. Mrs. Hutchinson perished here. Anne Hutchinson. Are you aware of her?"

Balty didn't have the energy to pretend. He shook his head.

"As fine a woman as this land has produced. As fine a woman as *any* land has produced. As brave, if not braver, than any man I've fought alongside. Colonel Huncks will agree. She died in '43."

"What happened?"

"Long story. She was banished from the Bay Colony by Governor Endecott."

"Why?"

"Antinomian heresy."

Balty stared.

"General disdain for authority. Didn't sit well with the Puritans."

"No, shouldn't think."

"She did a bit of wandering. Ended up seeking protection from the Dutch in New Netherland. Governor at the time was Kieft. Disastrous man."

Huncks nodded.

Winthrop went on: "He provided her refuge—in the heart of Siwanoy land. The local tribe. Their headman, Wampage, warned her she should leave. She didn't. Like I said, brave. Perhaps too brave.

"The Siwanoy butchered her, six of her children, a son-in-law, half dozen servants. They spared one of her daughters, a girl of nine named Susanna. Probably because of her red hair. When she was ransomed three years later, she didn't want to return. Not uncommon. Wampage sold the land to Dr. Pell."

Balty's eyes went wide. "Do you mean to say, an Englishman—a *doctor*—bought land from someone who massacred an Englishwoman and her entire family?"

"Yes."

"But . . . it's monstrous!"

Winthrop's face tightened. "Perhaps you'll have the opportunity to express your indignation to Dr. Pell directly." He returned to the map. His finger traced the coastline.

"Here is New Haven. And there is Fort Saybrook, at the mouth of the Great River. Here endeth the lesson in geography."

"What's this?" Balty pointed to a long island designated "Sewanhacky."

"The Long Island. Sewanhacky's the aboriginal name."

Balty's eyes fastened on the body of water between Connecticut and the Long Island. The map indicated it as "The Devil's Belt."

"The early English sailors called it that, on account of the abundance of rocks. Most now call it the Sound."

"Is it noisy?"

The guard opened the door. "Governor, sir. Narragansetts coming in. Five. Bearing tribute, from the smell of it."

Winthrop sighed. "Not again. Keep them outside, James. Give

them tobacco. Have Winchell and Wheary fetch hides. Fox and beaver if we have any left. And two fathoms of wampum. The black-eye, not the white. I'll be there shortly."

"Very good, sir." The guard closed the door.

"You may prefer to remain inside, Mr. Balthasar," Winthrop said.

"Uncas?" Huncks said.

Winthrop nodded. "Second time this month. His loyalty is . . . unappeasable."

"It's a wonder there are any Pequot left. Assuming they *are* Pequot heads. Wouldn't put it past Uncas to substitute."

"I prefer not to think about that."

"Heads?" Balty said. "What's all this about?"

"We had a war here, Mr. Balthasar. Many years ago. The English allied with the Narragansett and the Mohegan against the Pequot. A fierce tribe. They allied with the Dutch. The war was concluded to our advantage. But despite the years that have gone by since, the Narragansett persist in a . . . you could call it a protocol . . . that was encouraged during the war. I have told our Narragansett brothers, again and again, that it is no longer necessary, or even appropriate, to the maintenance of harmonious relations. But they persist."

Balty stared. "Do you mean to say . . . they bring you *heads*?"

"Heads. Hands. Feet. It's their belief that the soul resides in the head. If the head is severed, the soul cannot enter into the afterlife. Without feet, the soul cannot walk to paradise."

"And you *accept* these heads? And other tokens?"

"Refusing would give insult."

"But it's barbarous!"

"Mr. St. Michel. My wife's father was dragged on a sled from the Tower of London to Charing Cross, where he was hanged, cut down alive, disemboweled, his privy parts cut off and burnt before him. His head was then cut off and his body quartered, the parts impaled on pikes around the city. What would you call that, sir? Now if you will excuse me, I must receive my guests."

Winthrop and Huncks went outside. The breeze blew through the opened door. Balty doubled over and retched. He heard voices. Winthrop's.

"*Neen womasu sagimus!*" My loving sachem!

Another voice said, "*Neemat Weentrop!*"

CHAPTER 13

A Bit of a Tit

Balty kept to himself on the bow of the shallop, or whatever the bloody boat was called. Huncks stayed by the stern with the crew and soldiers Winthrop had sent with them.

Toward dusk the wind dropped. Huncks walked forward.

"We'll stop here for the night. Tomorrow if the wind's fair, we should make Fort Saybrook by nightfall." He threw the anchor over the side. The shallop swung parallel to the sandy riverbank. Behind it a steep cliff rose above thickets.

"Have a swim." Huncks peeled off his shirt and sat to tug off his boots.

"I don't care to swim."

"You mean you can't swim. Too bad. It's refreshing."

"I didn't say I can't swim. I said I don't care to swim."

Huncks continued stripping. Balty saw how powerfully built he was. His body was covered with scars. He dove into the river, came up on his back, and spat out a plume of water like a figure in a fountain as he swam to the sandy bank. He climbed out and disappeared into the bushes. Balty went back to musing on the morning's hideous revelations.

The men in the stern began shouting and pointing in the air. Balty looked up and saw a stick twirling toward the boat. It landed on the deck with an un-sticklike sound and began to wriggle and writhe.

The men roared with laughter. Two soldiers drew their swords and poked at it. Confronted at one end of the boat by a hubbub, the snake chose to make its way to the quieter other end.

Balty cursed and jumped to his feet. Undeterred by profanity, the snake continued its advance.

"Shoo! *Shoo!*"

Balty's impression of a housemaid admonishing a cat brought fresh convulsions of laughter from the men. The snake came closer. It paused a few feet from Balty, coiled, reared it head, and made an unpleasant rattling sound with its tail.

Balty gripped the boat's forestay and pulled himself off the deck. The men found this, too, wildly amusing. The snake struck at Balty's dangling feet, tongue flicking.

"Help! For God's sake! Someone do something!"

Huncks pulled himself aboard. He stamped his foot on the deck to distract the snake. It turned to him. Huncks held out his left hand as a target, wiggling fingers. The snake went for it. As it did, Huncks's right hand shot out and seized it behind the head.

He held the snake aloft. Its body curled around his forearm in a pantomime of the Laocoön. The men cheered. Huncks bent, kissed the snake on the back of its head, pulled it free of his arm, and heaved it into the air. It landed on the sandbank, where it lay for a while, probably wondering what on earth *that* was about, then made its way back into the bushes.

Balty lowered himself onto the deck. "Damn it, Huncks!"

"Indians call them *wishchalowe*. Frighteners. But I see you need no translation."

Balty swung. Huncks sidestepped. Balty went overboard.

He came up spluttering and flailing. Another grand entertainment for the men. What a rich evening of theater!

Huncks regarded Balty thrashing at the water.

"Thought you said you could swim."

He reached down and pulled Balty onto the deck. Balty sat, wet and gasping.

Huncks handed him his flask. Balty took a long pull on it, athwart his morning vow to abstain forever from spirits.

They lay on their backs on the deck looking up at the stars. It was a clear and moonless night. Orion drew his bow to aim at Taurus and the Bear. Faithful Sirius, dog star, followed at his heels. All was calm on the Great River. Even so, Huncks had posted watches throughout the night.

"Are we expecting to be attacked?"

"Sometimes they swim out and cut the anchor line."

"Why?"

"For the rope. And to let us know they're here."

After a pause, Balty said, "I didn't mean to offend the Governor. But this business of heads . . . it's horrid. And by the way, you might have *told* me."

"What?"

"That Winthrop's father-in-law was one of the bloody regicides. Really, Huncks."

Huncks shrugged. "He's made his peace with it. You heard him talk about how matey he and the King were together in London. The same King who ordered his father-in-law's execution."

"See here. You seem a decent chap. I don't think you have a very high opinion of me. But I am doing my best, you know."

"I've not said a word."

"No, but you're always keeping things from me. You burned Downing's sealed letter back in Boston. Yesterday, you and Winthrop were huddling like conspirators. And this morning when I came in, you were in a great hurry to roll up that map or whatever it was."

"It's nothing. Habit. Tell me, is she as toothsome as they say?"

"What? Who?"

"Lady Castlemaine."

"How should I . . . well, I suppose she *must* be. His majesty certainly seems to think so. Installing her at the palace, royal bastards everywhere. Not much fun for her majesty. She probably can't even see them, what with those great Portuguese skirts, constantly tripping over them."

"I'm a bastard."

Balty sighed. "Sorry. I can't seem to put a foot right today."

"No need to apologize."

"Actually, I did know you're a bastard. Throwing that damned adder at me. Treating me like the village idiot."

"Well, you are a bit of a tit, aren't you?"

"Perhaps in these woods of yours I may be somewhat out of context. In London, where I dwell among civilized society, I assure you, I am not a *tit*."

"*Ce n'est que la verité qui blesse.*" It is only the truth that hurts.

"How it is you speak French? And Latin? And quote Scripture and Shakespeare? And why does Winthrop address you as 'Colonel'? If you insist on being mysterious, fine, but you might provide me with some information as to who you are. It would only be the decent thing," Balty added in a tone of hurt.

Huncks said nothing. Balty rolled onto his side to sleep and pulled his blanket over him.

"Good night, then," Balty said huffily.

After a while, Huncks spoke.

"I was put into training for the ministry. Not my choice. At the Harvard College. Same as where Downing went. Didn't last a year. Got sacked for being drunk on the Sabbath. Took up soldiering. Turned out I had some talent for it. As much as I had for drink, anyway.

"Served in the Bay Colony militia. Went well enough. After a spell, I left. Fetched up in Hartford. Soldiered for Winthrop. He recommended me to his cousin, Downing. Which is how I came to be burning down Endecott's mint just as you were arriving in Boston. And how I come to be escorting you through the forest and down this fine river beneath these stars."

"So it *was* you burnt the mint."

"Um."

"And what are your instructions with respect to me?"

"You're precious cargo, Mr. St. Michel. I'm to keep you un-et by catamounts and return you to London in one piece. After our business here is concluded."

"And what is our business here?"

"As your commission says—to apprehend the judges."

"Look here. I may be a tit, but I'm not a complete nincompoop. There's something else going on here."

"Is there? My instructions seemed straightforward."

"You're as straightforward as that bloody snake you assaulted me with."

"Tell me about your relative, Mr. Peeps."

"He is a personage of the very highest rank."

"Like Henri Quatre and Louis Treize."

"I wish you'd stop banging on about that. The Navy would not function without Brother Sam. His cousin—and very great patron—is Admiral Montagu, First Earl Sandwich."

"Should I be impressed?"

"Yes. It was Montagu escorted the King back to England from Holland to be restored to the monarchy. Brother Sam—Mr. Pepys—was aboard. He is on *intimate* terms with his majesty."

Huncks considered. "Why's he want to get rid of you?"

"Who?"

"Peeps."

"What can you mean?"

"No matter. Good night."

Balty sat upright.

"I ask you again, sir—what do you mean by such a contemptible assertion?"

"Good night."

"This is a calumny."

"Good night, Balty."

"How—why do you call me that?"

Huncks yawned. "It's what Mr. Peeps calls you, isn't it?" Huncks rolled to his side and pulled the blanket over him. "Dream sweetly. Wake me if Indians cut our anchor line."

Balty fumed in the evening chill beneath the unconsoling stars.

– CHAPTER 14 –

So-Big-Study-Man

"**I**s there anything I should know about *this* governor?"

Balty and Huncks were in Guilford, standing on the threshold of the house of New Haven Governor William Leete.

"Is he related to any regicides? Will a delegation of savages be interrupting us at tea with a basket of severed heads?"

Huncks ignored the taunt. "Leete obstructed the hunt for Whalley and Goffe. Probably hid them in the basement of this very house. When he got word that his majesty was displeased, he shat himself and wrote him a kowtow. What does that tell you?"

"That he's a traitor."

"No, Balty."

"Don't call me that. That name is reserved for my friends. In whose company you are not included."

"What it tells us is he's weak. And fears the King. As you bear the King's commission, the very sight of you ought to make him soil his britches again. Unless you reveal yourself to be a tit."

"Finished?"

"Yes."

William Leete, Governor of the New Haven Colony, received his visitors with smiles and punctilios befitting Balty's station. On learning the nature of their business, his face collapsed like a pudding left out in the rain.

"*Another* regicide hunt? But Whalley and Goffe have long since fled." He added lamely, "If ever they *were* here."

"Mm," Balty said in the censorious tone of a displeased schoolmaster, a tone he knew well from experience. He snapped his fingers at Huncks, who handed Leete Balty's Crown commission in all its sealed and vellum glory.

Leete examined it. A heavy man, he began to sweat. Balty took this as an encouraging sign.

"Of course," he stammered, "I shall assist you in every way. But I fear you have come very far, Mr. St. Michael, to little avail."

"*Michel.*"

"Forgive me. Yet there *is* no news of the judges Whalley and Goffe."

"I shall be the judge of that." Balty sniffed.

Balty paced the room, eyes darting about. He tapped on the wall. Stomped on the floorboards. Leete stared, wide-eyed.

Balty grinned and said enigmatically, "I congratulate you, Governor. A most . . . capacious house."

Next morning, Balty and Huncks set off on the fifteen-mile ride to New Haven, having spent the night at a tavern. Governor Leete had pointedly not invited them to stay.

"Was it necessary, looking under his infant daughter's bed?" Huncks asked. "There wasn't room enough in it to hide a rabbit, never mind two regicides."

"I was making a point."

"Looking up the chimney flue—was that also making a point?"

"During Queen Elizabeth's time, Roman priests hid in chimneys. Rather rum, this Crown commissioner business."

"I'd tread more gingerly when we call on the Reverend Davenport."

"Why? Didn't he too hide Whalley and Goffe?"

"Probably. But he's the grand pooh-bah here."

"Let the saints of New Haven tremble before the King's majesty."

"If they tremble, it'll more likely be from rage. I'm glad you're enjoying yourself, but we ride into the enemy's camp. And they'll be waiting for us. Your new friend Governor Leete will have sent a rider to alert them. As for the king's majesty, don't expect bows and curtseys. They detest the King here. Better hold on to this."

Huncks reached into his saddlebag and handed Balty one of his pistols.

"Do you know how to use it?"

"Of course."

"Is it loaded?"

Balty peered into the muzzle.

"Jesus, man." Huncks snatched the pistol back. "Tell me, Mr. St. Michel, do you possess *any* talents?"

"They're not going to shoot a Crown agent." Balty sniffed. They rode in silence for a while. Balty said, "Would they?"

"We'll find out soon enough."

The King's Highway emerged from the woods and there before them lay New Haven at the head of its great harbor.

It was a town of unusual design—nine squares, the one in the center the town common. The layout was meant to symbolize the encampment of the Israelites in the desert, also the Temple of Solomon, and the New Jerusalem of the book of Revelation. The design was to inspire its citizens, the self-called saints, to lead godly lives.

Flanking the town on the west and east like a pair of matching bookends were majestic, nearly identical cliffs, rising hundreds of feet above the trees. They were striking by virtue of their bloodred color.

"Handsome, those," Balty said admiringly. "What are they called?"

"The Dutch called them *Rodenbergh*. The Red Hills."

Balty considered. "Shame the Dutch got here first. They deserve better than the Red Hills."

"Why don't you name them, then?"

"I shall." Balty pointed to the west cliff. "*That* shall be Whalley. And *that*"— he pointed at the other— "Goffe."

"Regicide Rocks. Why not? You should inform Governor Leete, so he can update his map."

"It would serve New Haven right. Harboring such men."

They continued on. Huncks knew his way, as he seemed to everywhere, but here he was not greeted as a friend. Everyone they passed stared with hard, unmistakable looks. Leete had sent word on ahead.

Huncks led them to a mean-looking tavern near the town wharf friskily called Regicide's Rest.

Huncks left Balty in their room, saying he must go and see someone. Another of his mysteries.

"I'm going with you. Don't fancy staying here by myself."

"No. My contact will be suspicious if you're with me."

"I'm coming with you."

"No you're not."

Huncks gave Balty the pistol. "It *is* loaded, so be careful. Pull the hammer back, so. Now it's cocked. Try not to shoot yourself."

Balty sat on the edge of the bed, facing the door, pistol in hand. The hours passed slowly.

Huncks returned in late afternoon, closemouthed about his rendezvous with whoever it was. Together they set off for the house of the Reverend Davenport.

It was one of New Haven's finer ones, boasting thirteen fireplaces. Huncks said this bespoke bravery on the Reverend's part.

"Why?"

"Puritans believe fireplaces are used by demons as passageways to the nether regions."

"Rot."

"I'm sure the Reverend will be interested in your theological insights."

"Nothing to do with theology. Bloody nonsense."

They reached Davenport's. Huncks pointed to a large house on Elm Street, catty-corner to Davenport's.

"That was Eaton's. The other founder, with Davenport. He had even bigger bullocks than Davenport."

"Why?"

"Nineteen fireplaces."

The door was opened by a pretty young Indian girl of perhaps fifteen years, primly dressed in servant's attire. She led them to a finely but sparsely furnished parlor, where they found an elderly man of placid mien, his head covered in a Roundhead-style black cap, turning the pages of a large Bible.

The Reverend John Davenport greeted his visitors with a benevolent smile. His sapphire-blue eyes seemed far younger than the rest of him. This was not the grim, pursed countenance Balty had expected. He seemed devoid of malevolence, even of sternness. His features were fine, almost feminine. At a distance, he might be taken for a woman, but for the silver wisps of his neat beard.

"Mr. St. Michel, Colonel Huncks. Welcome."

He addressed the servant girl: "Me-Know-God, bring ale for our guests. And tell Necessity we shall be three at dinner."

The girl curtseyed and glided out of the parlor on bare feet. Balty stared after her.

"Me-Know-God is her Christian name," Davenport explained. "Before I instructed her in the faith, she was Me-No-Know-God. Not a name to flow trippingly from the tongue. Her brother is called Repent. From his name, you may infer that his Christian instruction is, shall we say, ongoing. Myself the Quiripi call So-Big-Study-Man. I confess that I like the name. They are very dear to us, our Quiripi. But how strange all this must seem to you, Mr. St. Michel. Less so to Colonel Huncks. You are, I think, New England born?"

"Boston."

"I have a great fondness for Boston. True, that Mr. Eaton and I had our differences with Governor Winthrop, yet I am grateful to him, for it was he who inspired us to leave the Bay Colony and make our own, here. What an irony that we now chafe under the rule of his son. I do not conceal that we in New Haven are not joyous that his majesty had enfolded us into the Connecticut Colony. But we are loyal subjects. We abide. But I prattle. Forgive me. It is a vice of old men. You came from London, Mr. St. Michel?"

"Yes."

"I came over in '37. Then here in '38. Theophilus—Mr. Eaton—was our Moses, parting the waters to take us to the Promised Land. I gather you come in search of regicides. What a pity that we have none to offer you."

Huncks said, "Mr. de St. Michel bears a commission from the Crown to apprehend the judges Whalley and Goffe." He produced the document and held it out for Davenport's inspection. Davenport gave it the merest glance.

"A brave undertaking."

"Brave?" Huncks said. "How so?"

"It is no secret that some here feel a certain sympathy for the judges."

"I'd call *that* brave," Huncks said, "considering his majesty's resolve to bring his father's murderers to justice."

Davenport smiled.

"Murderers? What a difference just a few years make. Not so long ago, the generals Whalley and Goffe were considered very great men, saviors of their country. Now they are wretched exiles, fugitives, lost to their families and loved ones, hounded to the ends of the earth. Some here find it harsh that their miseries should endure, when so many others who played roles during that epoch have been shown mercy and forgiveness. Lord Downing among them."

Davenport went on: "We here had heard that his majesty was surfeited with vengeance. Yet your presence here attests to the contrary. I can only conclude that the reports of his majesty's compassion and mercy were false rumors. But come, gentlemen, let us eat."

Davenport said a lengthy blessing over the food, a bland porridge and blander still dish of overboiled root vegetables. No wine was served, only watery ale.

"Do you seek my assistance in your mission?" Davenport said. "Or is this visit by way of a courtesy? I emphasize that I am pleased to visit with you."

Huncks smiled. "Rest assured, Reverend. We have no expectation of assistance from you."

"Will you be needing to search the premises, as you did Governor Leete's?"

"Oh, it wasn't a search," Balty said. "More of a—"

"Tour?" Davenport smiled. "Well, I should be happy to give you a *tour* of my house."

"That won't be—"

"I'd like a tour," Huncks said.

"Then you shall have one, Colonel. Who knows what we may find. Hidden treasure, perhaps. The Holy Grail. But in the event we don't find judges hiding under my bed or in my cupboard, might I suggest that you seek them in New Amsterdam?"

"Oh?" Balty said.

"I should not be in the least surprised if they were there. New Amsterdam is a proverbial bolt-hole for those who flee our godly land. A Sodom and Gomorrah of vice and corruption. But then, New Amsterdam is Dutch. The Dutch came to the New World for one end—commerce and self-enrichment. The English came to sanctify the land to the glory of God."

"And so it pleaseth God," Huncks said, "to prepare the way of the English by sending a great plague to wipe out those who inhabited the land. Selah."

"You mock, Colonel Huncks. Did God not send seven plagues into Pharaoh's land?"

"Indeed. Frogs, blood, boils, fiery hail, locusts, darkness. I'm missing one. I wonder how God kept track of them all? So much easier to send one plague of Dutch pox."

A rime of frost formed on Davenport. "You abuse my hospitality, Colonel, blaspheming at my table."

"Dreadful people, the Dutch," Balty said, trying to thaw the room. "Despite their admirable cheeses. My brother-in-law—Mr. Samuel Pepys, a significant personage in the Navy Office—says we may have another war with them."

"We have little interest here in European scuffling, Mr. St. Michel.

Though of course as loyal subjects we pray for English victories. And for the health of the King. Given what we hear about the luxuriance and pleasures of his court, his health must be sore taxed."

The Indian girl entered with the savory dish, a pinkish pudding that looked devoid of taste.

"Me-Know-God. What is the Third Commandment?"

"Not to blaspheme."

"Very good. And the sixth?"

"Not to kill."

"Off you go, child."

"Most impressive," Balty said.

"She's coming along nicely."

Huncks said, "You acquainted with Metacomet? Sachem of the Wampanoag?"

"The one called King Philip? No. I've not had the pleasure."

"You may, someday. He's got a saying: 'When the white man came, he had the Bible and we had the land. Now we have the Bible, and the white man has the land.'"

"Our Quiripi still have their land, *and* the Bible."

"Yes, you and Mr. Eaton were generous. You let them keep—what?—twelve hundred acres of their own land?"

"It's all they need. They have rights of hunting and fishing on our land."

Huncks smiled. "What more could they ask? Greed *is* one of the seven deadly sins."

"The Quiripi sought our protection against their enemies, the Pequot and the Mohegan. We gave it."

"A right tidy deal. Though since the massacre at Fort Mystick, they've no need to fear the Pequot."

"That was war, Colonel." ·

"Indeed. And sanctified by God. As Captain Underhill wrote in his pamphlet, 'We had sufficient light from the Word of God for our proceedings.' I wonder if he had sufficient light for his proceeding against the Siwanoy and Wappinger at Pound Ridge. Another seven hundred red souls, burned to death. Seems the Almighty didn't quite finish clearing the land, by way of preparing the way of the English. One might call that careless."

"You offend, sir," Davenport said, his face reddening.

"Forgive me. Being New England born, I lack English manners."

Davenport rose. "You will excuse me, Mr. St. Michel. I must prepare my sermon for tomorrow. I hope you will attend."

"Bit rough on the old boy," Balty said. "And you telling me to tread gingerly. You were about as ginger as a battering ram."

"I don't do well with certain types of pharisee."

"That dinner was appalling. And that endless blessing he gave over it! You'd think living in a house with thirteen fireplaces, he could afford a decent cook. Come, you're all aboil. Let's get a drink into you before you bubble over."

They drank rum and ale at the Regicide's Rest.

"So, the old buzzard got to you," Balty said. "Well, well. Colonel Huncks has a chink in his armor. Hiram Huncks is human after all. Well, thank God. What say to one more, and to bed?"

Huncks was lost in thought. "We'll find them. By God we will find them."

"Who?"

"The judges."

"It's why we're here, isn't it?"

"It is now," Huncks said enigmatically.

CHAPTER 15

Hide the Outcasts

Next morning, a hungover Huncks announced that he had no intention of accompanying Balty to hear Davenport's Sabbath homily; moreover, he would sooner listen to Caligula preach on virtue.

"It *is* the Sabbath," Balty said. "From the look of you, might do you a bit of good."

"Bugger the Sabbath."

"Suit yourself. But the taverns are closed. What are you going to do?"

"Hunt."

"I'm certain that's not allowed on the Sabbath. Nothing is. While you were snoring, I went downstairs to fetch some hot water for shaving. Do you know what that slattern of an innkeeper told me? You're not allowed to shave on the Sabbath. Or go for a walk. And God help you if you're caught running—unless it's to church. She was quick to point out that you can't cook, either. So no warm supper for us tonight. Oh, and no sweeping the floor or making the bed. I said to her, 'What about dying of boredom? Is *that* allowed on the Sabbath?' She scowled at me. What joy, Sundays in New Haven. What were you going to hunt?"

"Judges."

"Oh, I'm sure that's forbidden, and not just on the Sabbath. By the way, what did you mean last night, when I said that's what we came here for, and you said, 'It is now'?"

"Don't remember. I was drunk."

"I was drunk, too. And I *do* remember. Another of your bloody mysteries, I suppose."

"No profanity on the Sabbath."

Balty went alone to the meetinghouse on the New Haven common, drawing cold stares from passersby. People pointed at him as if he was a plague carrier. Had Leete and Davenport put up posters during the night with Balty's and Huncks's faces, to warn the populace? It was a fine spring day, but there was a distinct chill in the air.

The meetinghouse was packed. Balty stood in the back by the door like a pauper who couldn't afford a seat.

The Reverend Davenport entered and climbed the pulpit. He carried the same Bible he'd been reading at home.

This was Balty's first time in a New England Puritan worship house. Having been brought up in the Huguenot faith, he was accustomed to unadorned churches. But this one he found aggressively plain, not so much as a vase of cut flowers to add a note of warmth, or to remind people that outside these drab walls, life was bursting forth from the awakening earth in joyful bloom. Were flowers also prohibited on the Sabbath? Where in the Bible was it ordained that the Sabbath should be joyless and grim? Wasn't there something about God liking flowers? Lilies of the valley? The only warmth here would be references to hellfire.

Davenport spotted Balty and nodded in welcome. He turned to his congregation and spoke, but not in flames or brimstone. The old boy sounded like the genial host he'd been until Huncks taunted.

He announced that his homily today had two themes, the first from Hebrews 13:2, wherein it sayeth: "Be not forgetful to entertain strangers: for thereby some have entertained angels unawares."

Pleasant surprise, Balty thought. Davenport extolled the virtues of giving hospitality, especially to those we don't know. He urged his congregation—which seemed to consist of the entire population of New Haven—to throw open their doors and share their bounty. Nice touch, that, about how strangers might be "angels in disguise." Here was true Christian spirit. Huncks had been a bit hard on the old boy.

Davenport's voice was like music, swelling and filling the meetinghouse. It no longer felt chill and stern and forbidding. The pulpit was a hearth—welcoming, a refuge from the outside world, which was filled not with blossoming flowers but evil incarnate in the person of the devil. Davenport barely glanced at his Bible. He knew it by heart. The words rose from its pages into the air like wisps of incense from a brazier, sweetening and sanctifying. Balty was very impressed.

Davenport came to the end of his first theme and fell silent. No one stirred. He turned the pages to Isaiah 16:3, wherein it sayeth: "Take counsel, execute judgment; make thy shadow as the night in the midst of the noonday . . ."

Balty again surrendered to the preacher's mellifluous voice. He closed his eyes, imagining the words as musical notes from flute, viola da gamba, lute. Lute—he thought of Brother Sam and his beloved lute, how he'd take it out after dinner and . . .

". . . hide the outcasts; betray not him that wandereth."

Balty opened his eyes. *Hide the outcasts?* The congregation shouted "Amen."

This was no homily—he was issuing instructions from the pulpit: *Hide the regicides.* Why, the sly old buzzard, inviting Balty to come hear him.

His pulse quickened. Here—surely—was confirmation that Whalley and Goffe were still in New Haven. He must rush—Sabbath be damned—to tell Huncks.

As Balty made to leave, a gasp went through the congregation. In the next instant, Balty, too, gasped. He froze.

Could it be real or some fata morgana?

Real or not, it was only few feet away. Everyone in the church was staring at it, mouth open in shock. Gasps became moans; moans cries. Mothers covered their children's eyes.

The apparition glided down the aisle toward Davenport.

It was a young woman, naked—entirely naked. The sight of her back made Balty wince. It was crisscrossed with stripes, raw wounds. She'd been horribly whipped.

She continued toward Davenport. No one moved. People began to shout.

Harlot! Witch! Satan seed! Save us, Reverend!

She reached the end of the aisle and stood, looking up at Davenport. The congregation was roaring, bellowing. Davenport raised his hands. The place instantly quieted.

"Woman, *again* you profane this house of God?"

Again? Balty thought.

Two men wearing the uniform of the watch rushed up the aisle. Each took an arm. The girl went limp. They began to drag her out. Balty saw her face. She couldn't be more than twenty. Her loveliness took him aback. Her expression was weirdly serene, as if she were strolling through an orchard on a summer's day, not being dragged by two brutish men, her back flayed bloody to ribbons.

Her glance fell on Balty as she passed. She smiled at him and was gone.

Balty ran back to the inn, drawing shouts of Sabbatarian rebuke from various New Haven saints.

Huncks was still in bed. Balty had to pause to catch his breath.

"Must have been quite a sermon," Huncks said.

Balty told what he'd seen. "It was the face of an angel, Huncks. I was this far from her. She looked at me as they hauled her off and smiled. Smiled!"

Huncks said nothing.

Balty babbled on: "She must be a lunatic. Distempered in the head. But to flog such a creature. It's monstrous. You've never seen such a thing."

"She's not lunatical," Huncks said. "She's a Quaker."

"Quaker? How do you know?"

"It's what they do."

"What?"

"The women. It's their way of protesting."

"Walking into a church, starkers?"

"Or through town."

Balty considered. "Well, *I'd* call it lunatical. At the very least, fruity."

"Religions are fruity."

"Jesus didn't go parading about naked."

"He went looking for trouble, didn't he? Same with Quakers. They embrace persecution. Fulfills them."

Balty weighed this. "Damn strange bit of business, however you slice it. The sight would have broken your heart. A constable who bellowed at me for running said she's to be tried tomorrow. Probably because they don't have trials on the Sabbath. What will they do to her?"

"The King's missive forbids them to persecute Quakers. No more hangings, floggings, cutting off ears, branding. What *shall* they do for entertainment?"

"She's already been flogged. His majesty's missive seems not to have been communicated to the New Haven saints."

"They won't try her for being a Quaker. They'll charge her with indecency. Profaning the Lord's Day. Blasphemy." Huncks considered. "What's she protesting, I wonder."

"We have to do something. Send word to Winthrop. He's a decent chap. He'll stop it."

"It's within their right to charge her with indecency and blasphemy. Hartford and back is a two-, three-day ride. Whatever they do to her, they'll do tomorrow. Puritans like their justice speedy."

"If you'd seen her, you wouldn't be so blithe."

"We're here to hunt regicides. Not get embroiled in local civic matters."

"*You're* a chivalrous one."

Balty found himself thrown against the wall, Huncks's hand squeezing his windpipe.

"What the devil's got into you?" Balty gasped.

Huncks released Balty. He went and stood by the window looking out onto the wharf. Balty rubbed his neck.

"Since you know nothing," Huncks said, "I won't ask if you know the name Dyer. Mary Dyer. Fine lady. Quaker. Friend of Anne Hutchinson.

"Endecott put her on trial with two other Quakers. Men. The men were hanged. Their executions sat ill with the people, so Endecott commuted her sentence to banishment.

"She left Massachusetts but then came back. He had her whipped. She wouldn't recant. Endecott tried her again, this time sentenced her to hang.

"It was a fine summer morning. The whole town turned out. She had admirers, Mrs. Dyer. Even among the Puritan saints of Boston. As I say, an admirable woman.

"Endecott and the magistrates feared there'd be trouble. They ordered out the militia. Hundred strong, fully armed.

"It was quiet. You could hear the birds in the trees. Even in the elm she was to hang from. Then the drumming started and you couldn't hear them.

"The Reverend Wilson was there. He'd been her pastor before she went over to the Quakers. An old man, all eaten up with hatred. Had given a sermon the day before saying he'd carry fire in one hand and faggots in the other, to burn all the Quakers in the world.

"She mounted the ladder, with Wilson hectoring her, demanding she repent. She showed no fear. Said she had nothing to repent of.

"The sentence was read and she was swung off the ladder. The drumming stopped. Then you could hear the birds again."

Huncks turned away from the window, to Balty.

"I was in command of the militia. The soldiers were my men. It was *my* hanging, you see. Whatever claim I ever had to chivalry I forfeited that day on Boston Common. Resigned my commission the next day."

They were silent for a while. Balty said, "My father was in charge of the guard the day Henri Quatre made a progress through the

Tuileries. A Catholic fanatic leapt onto the carriage and mortally stabbed the King. Papa wasn't held to account for it, but . . . I don't think he's ever got over it."

"Is this supposed to console me?"

"Well, it's all I have. By way of consolation."

Huncks sighed. "Very well, Mr. St. Michel. Let us see what's to be done about this Quaker wench of yours."

CHAPTER 16

What, Only *Five* Pounds?

"Let the prisoner be brought."

The magistrate was a well-fed man named Feake, whom Governor Leete addressed as "Dependable." Balty and Huncks were left to infer whether it was his given name or an adjective.

The room was crowded with saints come to see New Haven justice.

The prisoner entered, clothed, hands bound in front and flanked by the same guards who'd hauled her from the meetinghouse. Balty studied her face. It was, as before, composed and unafraid. She looked even younger, dressed.

"State your name."

"My name is well known to thee."

"It will not go well for you, Mistress, if you trifle with this court."

"I have little expectation that it will go well, whether I trifle or not, sir."

"Let the prisoner's name be entered as Thankful Mott, Quaker, of New Haven, in the colony thereof. Mistress Mott, you are charged with indecency and profaning the Lord's Day. Moreover, you are charged with repeating these offenses. How do you plead?"

"I make no plea."

"You must."

"How can I, when I do not recognize thy authority?"

"You *shall* know my authority, Mistress!"

"I hold every day to be the Lord's Day. As to indecency, we are all made in God's image. How, therefore, can our bodies be indecent?"

"You compound your crime with yet more blasphemy. This is no defense."

"If I do not admit of a crime, how can I compound it?"

"Repent your sins and your sentence may be mitigated. If you do not, you shall be judged severely."

"I have but one judge, sir, who is also judge of thee."

"Enough. Your obstinacy convicts you. Thankful Mott, you shall be taken from here directly and tied at a cart's tail, with your body naked downward to the waist. And from New Haven, you shall be severely whipped through every town—Milford, Fairfield, Stratford, Fivemiles, Norwalk, Stamford, and Greenwich. In addition to which, you shall pay a fine of five pounds."

The room hushed. Came a loud, mocking laugh.

"What, only *five*? That's letting her off easy."

All eyes turned on Huncks.

Magistrate Feake glared.

"You mock these proceedings? How dare you, sir? Hold your tongue, lest you find yourself brought on charges. This is no place for jesting."

"I agree with you there, Dependable Feake. Since I arrived in New Haven two days past, I've yet to hear a single jest. Even from the village idiots, who seem in abundant supply."

"Bailiff, seize that man!"

The bailiff moved toward Huncks. Huncks drew back his cloak, revealing his short sword. The bailiff hesitated.

"You come *armed* into our court?" Feake said. "You profane our laws!"

"Not nearly so well as you do."

"Seize him!"

The guards came at Huncks. He drew back the other side of his cloak to reveal the pistol tucked into his belt. The guards, unarmed, halted.

Governor Leete stood, his face florid.

"Mr. St. Michel, sir, curb your dog!"

Balty stood. "May I approach, Magistrate Feake?"

Feake stared. He looked at Leete, who looked at the Reverend Davenport. Davenport gave a nod. "Very well. Yes."

Balty approached. He laid his commission in front of Feake.

"In the name of our Sovereign Lord, his majesty, Charles the Second, King of England, Scotland, France, and Ireland, and of this New England colony, I arrest this woman."

"*What?*"

Balty pointed to the bottom of his commission.

"You'll find Lord Downing's signature here. He has a fine hand, do you not think?"

Feake, Leete, and Davenport examined the document.

"This commission gives you no power to arrest this woman," Feake said.

"Oh, I disagree with you there, Dependable."

"This is outrageous! *You*, sir, are outrageous!"

Davenport raised a silencing finger and spoke.

"Mr. St. Michel, we are all the King's good subjects. Your commission is to apprehend the judges Whalley and Goffe. It invests no authority upon you in the present matter, which anyway has no bearing upon your charge."

"Ah. With respect, Reverend, it does."

Davenport leaned back in his chair.

"How, sir? What does this harlot have to do with the King's matter?"

"I have reason to believe she has information pertaining to the whereabouts of the judges."

The court burst out in murmurs.

"I therefore ask the court to remand her into my custody, so that I may examine her. But I thank you for warning me that she is a harlot.

Colonel Huncks and I will remain vigilant, lest she try to lead us into temptation."

Davenport leaned forward, all business. "You bluff, Mr. St. Michel. And sorely try our goodwill. I will ask you again to desist. Or face grave consequences."

"Are you threatening an agent of the Crown, Reverend?"

"I merely point out that you are two. *We* are a town."

"So, you defy a Crown agent. Dear, dear. That is grave, Reverend."

"London is many miles from here."

"Indeed. And wretched, watery miles, at that. But Hartford is not so far."

"What has *Hartford* to do with this, sir?"

"Hartford has expressed the keenest interest in my mission. We came through Hartford on my way here. Governor Winthrop was a delightful host. He spoke warmly of his intimacy with his majesty. He spent months at court, in the course of obtaining the royal charter that gives him authority over New Haven. Indeed, it was he who seconded me Colonel Huncks, of his Connecticut militia. To assist me. In every way."

Davenport pointed at Leete.

"New Haven's governor is here, not in Hartford! Under the terms of the charter, Winthrop's authority does not fully vest until—"

Balty held up his hand.

"Reverend. Magistrate Feake. Governor Leete. Here is the issue before this court. You have now openly threatened us"—Balty swept the courtroom with his hand—"in front of all these witnesses here assembled."

The words took effect. The spectators' faces showed hesitation, fear.

"Ask yourselves: Is this girl's death—or mine, and Colonel Huncks's—worth bringing down upon your saintly heads the wrath of the King? It seems to me a heavy price to pay just for the pleasure of flogging a young woman to death. Not forgetting the five-pound fine. Are there no other entertainments to be had in New Haven? Perhaps you'd enjoy such spectacles as London offers. As when traitors who defy the king's majesty are dragged through the streets to be hanged, disemboweled, and quartered."

Color drained from Feake's and Leete's faces. They turned to Davenport. He stared without expression at Balty, then, with a bare nod, gave the signal. Thankful Mott was remanded to the custody of the Crown.

Balty and Huncks led her from the court, past gelid stares of New Haveners.

Thankful whispered to Balty, "Sir, I know nothing of these judges of whom thou—"

Balty squeezed her arm. "*Later*, miss, please."

The horses were saddled and ready at the stable on the far side of East Creek at the outskirts of town. Thankful rode on Balty's horse behind him. They went north, toward the red cliff Balty had named after Goffe.

"Nicely done, Mr. St. Michel," Huncks said.

"Did a bit of theater acting in my youth. Always got the girl parts."

"You were no girl today."

Balty turned to Thankful. He held out his hand, which shook in an exaggerated way. "See? I'm one of you."

"How so?"

"I quake."

Huncks tossed Balty a flask. Balty took a long pull and handed it over his shoulder to Thankful. She shook her head.

"Where shall we take you?" Huncks asked.

She pointed to the cliff. "My place is near there."

"It won't be safe for you at home. Do you have friends we can take you to?"

"I would not imperil them by asking refuge of them."

"We can't take you with us."

"I do not ask thee to."

"Look, Miss—"

"Mistress, if thou please."

"Where's your husband, then?"

"Dead."

Balty said, "What were you protesting about?"

"I would not involve thee in my affairs, sir. For thy own good."

"Bit late for that."

"Even so."

"Is it some Quaker thing?"

Huncks snorted. "Of *course* it's some Quaker thing. Did you think she was reenacting Lady Godiva's ride?"

"I was asking *her.*"

"What I did, I did for my own reasons."

"Twice? After what they did to you the first time?"

"My cause is greater than any tribulation in their power to inflict. However many times."

"It must be a very great cause indeed, if you're willing to let them flog you to death."

She asked, "Did thou really come from London?"

"Yes."

"What is it like?"

"Well, it's . . . very grand. His majesty's court is the finest in all Europe."

Huncks grunted. "Spent a lot of time there, have you?"

"Thou've come to arrest the judges?"

"Yes. You don't happen to know where they are, do you?"

"If I knew, I shouldn't tell thee."

"There's gratitude."

"Pray stop. I'll dismount here."

Balty reined his horse. Thankful slid off.

"Where will you go?"

"I'll make my way. I know these woods well."

A fringe of golden hair protruded from beneath her white cap. It was a milkmaid's face: wide, soft, fresh, rosy. She smiled at Balty. Her dimples gave a hint of impudence but for which her countenance was vestal.

"Why do thou look at me so, sir?"

"I'm trying to fathom you, Mistress Mott."

"Goodbye, Mr. St. Michel. Goodbye, Colonel Huncks. Thou were kind to do what thou did."

She turned and walked away. Her wounds had seeped through the muslin of her dress. The sight was discordant beside the fairy lightness of her step. Balty stared after her until she disappeared.

"Oh, God." Huncks groaned. "Smitten."

"Not in the least. I feel sorry for her. You will admit she's rather fair."

"Avoid Quaker women, Mr. St. Michel," Huncks said. "They're only trouble."

"That's a bit strong, after what you told me last night."

Huncks turned his horse back toward New Haven.

"Hold on," Balty said. "We're going back? We didn't make ourselves popular today."

"Isn't that your mission? To vex the New Haveners? So far, you're succeeding admirably."

"What do you mean, my mission?"

"I misspoke."

"My *mission*—stated clearly in my *commission*—is to apprehend the judges."

"So it is. Shall we go about it, then?"

"I'll tell you what's vexing," Balty said hotly. "Your damned secrets."

"Yes, I imagine. Coming?"

"They'll tear us to pieces."

"I think not. Didn't you tell them, one snap of your fingers and Winthrop's militia will howl down on them like the Four Horsemen of the Apocalypse?"

"I was bluffing."

"They don't know that. Want to find your judges or not?"

"Yes, but . . ."

"They're still in New Haven. And we're going to find them. But first, a drink. Thirsty work, vexing Puritans."

– CHAPTER 17 –

Mr. Fish

They sat in a corner at a wharfside tavern called the Prickly Pig. Business was brisk. New Haven might be a godly town, but its saints were thirsty.

Huncks knew someone in Milford, next town over. Tomorrow he'd go find him.

"I'm going with you. I'm not staying here by myself. That man by the window, he's been staring at us."

"I saw."

He was stout, forty or so, bushy eyebrows, cheeks florid from burst blood vessels. A drinker. Seeing Balty and Huncks return his stare, he nodded and touched the brim of his hat. He approached. His manner was deferential, obsequious.

"Greetings to thee, sirs. It would be my great honor to buy thee a drink."

"Why not?" Huncks said.

The man went off and returned with two large mugs of ale.

"May I join thee?" He sat and spoke in a whisper. "I was present this morning at the court, when thee saved Mistress Mott. God bless thou, sirs. God bless and save thee. Thou are angels, sure, heaven-sent."

"Well, couldn't just sit there." Balty shrugged.

"Simeon Fish, at thy service. A Friend of the Truth, like her whom thou saved."

"Friend of who?" Balty said.

"Quaker. We call each other 'friend.'"

"Ah. Quite."

Huncks raised his mug. "To friendship, then."

Fish leaned in closer. "You seek the regicides Whalley and Goffe?"

"We do."

"It might be something. Or might not."

"Go on."

"My farm is just beyond the East Hill. The red cliff. Small farm. Nothing much. Corn, squash, beets. Bit of tobacco. Orchard. Apples, peaches. Last year, we had a splendid peach crop. Chickens. A few pigs. After tobacco, eggs are my most profitable—"

"Mr. Fish," Huncks said. "Are you here to tell us about regicides or agriculture?"

"Forgive me. To the point, then. One of my farmhands—a boy, not the smartest lad, but a good lad, not the sort to make up tales, you know . . . We've had eggs go missing. Our hens are regular, but if there's thunder and lightning—"

"Mr. Fish."

"Forgive me, forgive me. The boy—he says he's seen two men. Lurking, like. In the woods near the coop. Twice, he's seen them. Again, it may be nothing."

"Did he describe these men?"

"He did. He did. What struck me was he said they were old. And carried themselves like soldiers."

"How does an old soldier carry himself?"

"Well, Colonel, you'd be the expert there. I suppose he meant straight-spined. Neat. That's it. He said they looked neat like. Beards trimmed. Point is, they didn't look like tramps."

"Well, Mr. Fish. Thank you for this. You say your place is beyond the cliff?"

"I could take thee there, if you like. I was on my way home when I saw you through the window. My horse is outside."

"Then we'll finish our drinks and join you outside."

Fish left.

"Then well, there's a bit of luck," Balty said.

"Anything strike you as queer about our new Quaker friend?"

"The eyebrows?"

"His Quaker pronouns weren't consistent. Mixed up his 'thees' and 'thous' and 'yous.' Quakers don't say *you*. His boots were a bit shiny for a farmer. And Quakers don't go in for vengeance. Or violence. Your inamorata Mistress Mott, who owes us her life, wouldn't even help us. Why should he?"

"Oh, hell. So it's a trap?"

"Without doubt, I'd say."

Balty peered out the window. "Swine. Fawning all over us in that disgusting fashion. *God bless thee. Thou must be angels.* I say we heave him off the wharf. Feed him to the lobsters. The size of the lobsters here—bloody sea monsters."

"Gratifying as that would be, it's possible Mr. Fish *is* sincere. Perhaps a recent convert to quaking who's not got his 'thees' and 'thous' straight yet. There are farmers who give their boots a polish when they go into town, so's not to look like bumpkins. But I've yet to meet the Quaker who'd abet at manhunting."

"Well, where does that leave us?"

"If it is a trap, he's going to a lot of trouble. And risk."

"Oh, Huncks, *do* get to the point."

"If he's going to the trouble, he may have a personal stake in protecting the judges."

"Yes? And?"

"In which case, he might know where they are."

"Ah." Balty considered. "So . . . what? Are you proposing that we walk into his trap?"

"Do you have other plans for the evening? Bible study with the Reverend Davenport? Here, take this."

Huncks handed Balty one of his pistols under the table.

Balty stared at the thing in his lap.

"It's loaded," Huncks said. "Draw the hammer back with your thumb—"

"*Yes.*"

"Try not to shoot me. Think how lonely you'd be without me."

"I still don't grasp the wisdom of walking into a trap."

"The wisdom is in knowing it's a trap."

"Is it not a sight?" Mr. Fish said as they came into view of the cliff. The late-afternoon sun bathed it in a fiery red glow. "It's the iron in the rock gives it that blood color. In all my years here, I've never tired of it."

It was a sight, Balty thought. Huncks gave it only a glance.

Twilight turned the air cool and the light purple. They rode along a stream that skirted the base of the cliff. It grew darker. Hawk screech echoed off the rock face.

"Raptors," Fish observed. "Great falconers, Quiripi."

They stopped to let the horses drink.

"How far?" Huncks said.

"Less than a mile. My land starts at the foot of the slope that goes up to the cliff. Goes all the way."

"It's getting dark."

"I know the way well."

"Strange place for a farm, isn't it?"

"How so, Colonel?"

"No water."

"Oh, there are springs," Fish said. "I shouldn't want to haul my water up a hill every day. It's good land, you'll see. And none in New Haven have a view like mine."

A half mile on, they turned up the slope. It was almost dark now.

"I've got the boy watching in the coop. If you like, you can watch with him. Or from the house. Whatever suits thee."

"Very obliging of you. Tell me, Mr. Fish, how long have you been a Quaker?"

"All my life. From the cradle."

"You're fortunate. Living as we do in a time of so much shifting of religions."

"It is a comfort, yes."

"How old are you, might I ask?"

"Forty-two this November. And still in possession of my teeth. Most of them, anyway."

"I congratulate you. Yet one thing perplexes me."

"Oh?"

"Mr. Fox established the Quaker faith—what?—fifteen years ago. Yet you say you've been quaking since you were in the cradle. Which makes you either a prophet or a liar."

Fish reined his horse to a halt and turned to face Huncks. Huncks had his pistol out.

"What say *thee* to *that*, Mr. Fish?"

Fish spurred his horse.

"Tricky subject, religion," Huncks said, charging after him.

Balty watched Huncks disappear into the dark.

"Did I not *say* this was a bad idea?" But no one was present to affirm the truth of Balty's remark.

Swish. Thwack.

Balty's horse whinnied fiercely and bucked, kicking backward. Balty was pitched forward hard onto its neck, abrading his face, filling his mouth with mane. He lost his grip on the reins.

"What's got into you! *Hold!* Damn you, horse! Hold, I say!"

The horse continued bucking and craning its head back toward its hindquarters. Balty looked and saw something—a stick of some sort, protruding from its flank. He glanced again and saw that the tip of the stick was feathered.

Oh, hell, he thought.

Another *swish* and *thwack.* The horse bellowed in fresh agony and bolted forward up the slope.

Balty clenched the mane in a death grip. His feet came free of the stirrups. His chest and stomach thumped against the saddle, bruising and knocking the air out of him.

His instinct was to arrest the frenzied animal. But his brain, violently shaken along with his other bodily organs, cautioned that stopping was not desirable. Whoever was firing feathered missiles into his horse might be in pursuit. Unless the saints of New Haven had adopted the bow and arrow, the likelihood was that his assailants were of aboriginal persuasion, a disagreeable prospect. What had Balthasar de St. Michel done to give offense to the New Haven indigenes?

Balty did not linger over this rhetorical inquiry. He clung like a desperate limpet to his pain-maddened horse, which continued its headlong charge in darkness toward the edge—somewhere ahead—of a four-hundred-foot cliff. He was not an accomplished horseman. He wondered, hopefully: Could the beasts see in darkness? Surely they possessed some primordial instinct that would alert them before they leapt, pell-mell, off a cliff into a yawning abyss. Surely? Pray.

What if they didn't? Should he hurl himself off now? He dismissed this option on the grounds that it would likely result in breaking a dozen bones, including his skull. Even if he landed without injury, there remained the—pressing—question of pursuivant savages.

Balty closed his eyes. If he was going to sail off a cliff, he didn't want to watch. There was nothing he desired to see. No, that wasn't true. England—*oh*, to see England again! And Esther. And sister Bess. And Brother Sam. Oh, yes, he would very much like to see Brother Sam again, if only to wring his damned—

Bang.

A pistol shot, directly ahead.

Balty's horse burst from the woods into a wide clearing. Silhouetted against the night sky were two horses, riderless, standing near a tree. He made out other shapes, structures. Beyond he saw lights, twinkling, as if a portion of the stars had fallen to earth. New Haven. He saw the edge of the cliff toward which his horse continued its mad, headlong charge.

"Huncks!" Balty shrieked. "For the love of— Help!"

Huncks leapt in front of the horse, arms outstretched. It tried to veer around him, then jerked to a halt.

"Hoah! *Hoah* . . ." Huncks got a rein. The horse snorted. Huncks gentled it.

Balty saw the body sprawled facedown on the ground.

"Did you kill him?"

"He turned to fire at me and ran into the tree." Huncks pulled the arrow from Balty's horse and felt its head.

"I told you this was a terrible idea!"

"Quiet."

Huncks listened. Balty looked. What were these strange forms? Looked like platforms of some kind.

"What are those—"

"Keep your voice down. Burial ground."

"Doesn't look like a cemetery."

"Quiripi burial ground. Get down."

"Gladly." Balty dismounted with a groan. His body was one entire bruise. He spat strands of mane.

Huncks slapped the horses. They ran off.

"Come. Keep low."

They crouched behind a large rock near the cliff edge.

"Wait here."

"Where are you going?"

"To look for a way down."

"Down what?"

"The cliff."

"No. No. Absolutely not."

"Do you know what they do to grave violators?"

"I'm not violating their damned graves!"

"They start with your fingers. After a day or two, they get to your torso. Cut holes, put in hot coals and sew them in. It can last three or four days."

"But I'm not violating their—"

"Then stay and explain to them. While they cut."

"Huncks. I'm . . . I'm not good at heights. I went up the tower of Westminster Abbey once and fainted."

An arrow splintered against the boulder.

"Coming?"

Arrows hissed through the air above the boulder. Balty pressed himself against it. His heart pounded.

"Can't you *speak* to them? Explain?"

Huncks had his pistol out. "When I fire, follow. Stay close."

"I thought they'd been *domesticated*."

"Shut your eyes."

"Why?"

"So you won't be night-blinded. Ready?"

"God. Yes."

Huncks cocked the pistol and raised it above the boulder, drawing a hail of arrows. He fired. A jet of yellow and orange flamed from the muzzle.

They crawled along the edge of the cliff.

"Here," Huncks whispered. He let himself over the edge. Balty followed.

The cliff was sheer but fractured and jagged, providing hand- and footholds. Red cedar trees rooted everywhere in cracks, making a series of ladders. They made their way down slowly, groping, holding on to cedar limbs, pressing themselves against the still-sun-warm rock.

A rain of arrows descended.

"Hug the rock," Huncks hissed.

"If I hug it closer it'll be indecent."

Rocks rained down.

"Huncks, this is no good at all."

"Keep moving, unless you fancy spending the night here."

They came to an outcropping and maneuvered beneath it, finding some shelter from the hail of arrows and rocks. They clung to cedars, breathing hard.

"Huncks."

"What?"

"I shall die here."

"No you won't."

"I shall. I know it. I have a sense about these things."

"You've no sense at all. About anything."

"Don't let me die in ignorance. You owe me *that* much."

"For God's sake, man."

"When you said my mission was to vex the New Haveners, what did you mean?"

"I was being jocund."

"Don't lie to me. Not now. Was I sent here to find the bloody judges, or for some other reason? I shan't continue down until you answer."

Huncks sighed. "The judges aren't the principal objective."

"So all along you *have* been keeping things from me."

"Shall we discuss this once we get off this cliff?"

"Why are we here? Why am *I* here?"

"Your Mr. Pepys wanted to be rid of you. And having spent these last weeks with you, I fully understand why."

"No. It can't be. Brother Sam and I are devoted to each other."

"It was in Downing's letter. The one I burned. Your Brother Sam thinks you're a pest."

"Lies. Foul lies."

"There's a larger scheme. Your part in it is not without value."

"Oh, well, bloody marvelous. So now I can plunge to my death, pierced through by heathen barbs, in the consolation that my death is not 'without value'! How *very* gratifying!"

Arrows swished past like lethal sleet.

"Mr. St. Michel. Pray, cease blubbering and *listen*. It doesn't matter *why* you are here. You are here. I am here. I assure you our mission is vital to the Crown. Critically vital. If we succeed, you'll return to England wreathed in so many laurels you'll resemble a damned topiary. And your Brother Pepys will spend the balance of his life choking on crow and addressing you as *Sir* Balthasar de St. Michel. But if we're to succeed, we must first get down off this rock. Shall we proceed?"

Balty nodded miserably.

"Good. Careful, now."

They lowered themselves. They'd only gone a few feet when a rock struck Huncks on the head. He toppled backward, lost his grip, and fell.

"Huncks!"

From below came the sound of crashing branches.

Balty called again. No reply.

Balty shouted up the cliff: "The King of England will hear of this! He'll have your red guts for garters!"

His jeremiad was interrupted by another cascade of rocks, one of which caught him on the head, causing sparks in his eyes. Balty clung desperately to a cedar. Rivulets of blood streamed into his eyes. He blinked to clear his vision, what little there was.

A surge of something else new rose in Balty—rage. He heard a voice, his own, commanding him not to succumb—to live, if only to deny the heathen brutes the satisfaction of sending him to his death, along with Huncks. Poor Huncks!

He continued down the cliff, head pounding, gasping for breath, blinking blood. An eternity passed, then suddenly he felt sturdier footing. He'd reached the bottom, a jumble of scree, the detritus of millennia. He clambered down until finally his feet touched earth. He sat, breathing, face sticky with warm blood. His hands and fingers were shredded, throbbing and raw.

Huncks—where was Huncks? He called his name. No answer.

The forest was thick around the base of the cliff. He called again and listened. In the silence, he heard only the babble of the stream they'd followed on their way up.

"Huncks! Huncks—are you *there*?"

A groan.

"Huncks! Oh, thank God!"

Balty threw himself on Huncks, hugging him.

"I thought you were dead!"

"Let go. Can't breathe."

"You're alive! Good. Good. All right. We'll . . . rest. Then we'll . . . do something."

"Can't move legs."

"I'll carry you."

Balty tried to lift Huncks. It was useless.

"No matter. We'll rest here. I'll get you some water. There's a stream. Somewhere."

Balty saw light through the trees.

"Huncks! Someone's coming! We're saved!"

Huncks gripped Balty's ankle.

"*Quiet.*"

The lights grew more distinct. Torches.

Huncks whispered, "Quiripi."

"How can you—"

"Go. Quickly."

"No."

"For Christ's sake, man, I'm done. *Go.*"

Balty felt for his pistol. It wasn't there.

"For once, don't be a fool."

Balty took hold of Huncks's jacket and dragged him toward the scree at the foot of the cliff.

"What are you doing?"

"Shh."

There was a recess created by large fallen shards. It was a tight space, but he succeeded in stuffing Huncks in, then squeezed in himself. He sat, bent over, breathing hard and listening.

The torches drew closer.

"Go."

"Quiet, Huncks."

Balty took Huncks's pistol from its holster and drew back the hammer.

Huncks whispered, "Balty, listen to me."

"*What?*"

"Get to Fairfield. Find Dr. Pell. Tell Pell . . . squadron of Navy ships coming. Mid-August. Commanded by Nicholls. Colonel Nicholls."

"Shh."

"Tell him . . ."

The torches were close. Their light fell across the threshold of their bolt-hole.

Balty held the pistol. He heard a voice say, "*Owanux.*"

"Stay here," Balty whispered.

He emerged from the hiding place, pistol in hand.

There were a half dozen. Their skin, greasy with raccoon and eagle fat, gleamed in the torchlight. Some held hatchets; others, bows, arrows nocked. Balty saw no muskets or pistols.

White man and red men beheld each other. Balty was light-headed from blood loss. He tried to stand upright so as not to show fear. He held the pistol at his side, pointed at the ground.

Should he smile? He'd tried that once on London roughs, and it got him nothing but contempt. He waited for one of them to reveal himself as head man.

The one closest had some design on his forehead. Balty blinked blood from his eyes and stared. It looked to be some kind of face, with wings. He was a tall man, strongly built, who might have looked handsome were it not for the thing on his forehead.

He spoke. The two Quiripi with bows drew back the strings.

"Now, *now*," Balty said in the matey, scolding tone of the gaming table when someone deals out of turn. "No need for *that*. We're all good fellows here. My friend and I were only taking the night air. I assure you we had no designs on your graves."

The bowmen took aim. Balty raised his pistol and aimed at the man in front.

"Look here, old chap, I'd rather it not come to this. *Do* get it into your head we didn't come here to rummage in your tombs."

A voice from the woods. "Coming in. Steady, all. Steady."

A man and boy stepped into the torchlight. Both had muskets shouldered.

"We heard a gunshot. That you, Repent? What are you on about?"

The Indian with the decorated forehead replied, "Hunt."

"Bit late, isn't it?"

"Cat."

"Ah. Then I'll wish you good hunting. The catamounts have been at our chickens. I'll say good night to you."

Repent hesitated, then spoke to his men. The Quiripi turned and walked away, taking the light with them.

The three white men stood in the silence, eyes adjusting to darkness.

"What passed here?" the man asked Balty.

"My friend . . . in the rocks, there. Wounded. Please . . ."

Balty's legs wobbled. He felt cold. He lowered himself to the ground and lay, looking up the cliff. It seemed beautiful now, with the stars glimmering above.

– CHAPTER 18 –

Pepys in a Pickle

Pepys had little liking for the country road from London to Chelsey on any day; even less today.

Once while traveling this way his coach was stopped by three masked highwaymen. One put a pistol to the coachman's breast, another to Pepys's. They relieved him of a silver ruler (value: 30 shillings), his beloved gold pencil (8 pounds), five mathematical instruments (3 pounds), a magnifying glass (20 shillings), gold and silver purse (10 shillings), and 2 guineas and 20 shillings in money. Pepys was so cooperative handing it all over that the chief thief chivalrously offered him a rebate.

"You are a gentleman," he said, "and so are we. If you will send to the Rummer Tavern at Charing Cross tomorrow, you shall have one of your mathematical instruments there."

Pepys called at the Rummer the next day; no mathematical instrument. So much for the probity of varlets. Two of the "gentlemen" were arrested and hanged at Tyburn, and good riddance.

Today, trying to distract himself from the unpleasant errand ahead, Pepys wondered what had become of the third thief. Was he in prison somewhere? Writing a farewell letter to his doxy on the eve of his hanging—with Pepys's much-missed gold pencil? It pleased him to think so. He'd written some saucy *billets-doux* with that pencil, and not to Mrs. Pepys.

This reverie ended as his carriage drew up to his destination, lurching him harshly back into the present.

Pepys hadn't seen much of Edward Montagu, First Earl Sandwich, since confronting him over his scandalous *ménage* with Mrs. Becke. He regretted the coolness that had settled like a frost between them, for he loved Montagu.

They were related by blood. Montagu's father had married Pepys's great-aunt. Montagu recognized his young cousin's talents early and lifted Sam from what might otherwise have been a life of drab obscurity—notwithstanding the Cambridge degree Sam's other patron, Downing, had helped him gain.

As admiral, Montagu promoted Sam up the civilian ranks of the Navy. In 1660 he took him along on his flagship when he brought King Charles II back to England from his exile in Holland. Restored to the throne, the King rewarded Montagu for his services, creating him Baron Montagu of St. Neots, Viscount Hinchinbrooke, Earl of Sandwich, Knight of the Garter and Admiral of the Narrow Seas (otherwise known as the English Channel). Later, the King entrusted Montagu with another great mission: fetching his future queen, Catherine of Braganza, to England from Portugal.

The King's confidence in Edward Montagu was all the more remarkable for Montagu's having been an ardent antiroyalist. He'd served Cromwell and the protectorate valorously. But after Cromwell died and the parliamentary cause faltered, Montagu was among the first to reach out across the Narrow Seas to the King in exile. Stalwart monarchists chafed at what they viewed as unseemly adaptability. But in time they conceded that Montagu had acted out of patriotism, not opportunism. Montagu was a hard man to dislike, harder still to hate. He was honorable, charming—a "good fellow."

But his dalliance with the unsuitable Mrs. Becke was a disaster! His standing at Court and in the Lords had sunk like a rock, a rock that had yet to hit bottom. People no longer expressed their contempt in whispers. Mrs. Becke was now openly referred to as "that courtesan." Most wrenching of all to Pepys was the hurt and shame Montagu's affair inflicted on a woman for whom his devotion verged on adoration: Montagu's wife, Jemima, mother of their *ten* children.

Pepys stood on the doorstep of the rather mean Chelsey house, summoning his strength. He took a deep breath, fortifying himself with the knowledge that he had not come to this shabby place to beg personal favor of his lordship. No. His mission was a noble one. He had come to persuade the Admiral to intercede with the King *not* to start a war with Holland.

Pepys was in a pickle. He couldn't reveal that he'd read Downing's confidential dispatch to Nicholls. Nor could he go to his superior at the Navy—the Duke of York, Lord High Admiral, brother to the King. *He* was the leader of the "war party."

But as Clerk of the Acts, Pepys knew better than anyone else that the Navy was in no way ready to conduct the war that Nicholls's mission would surely trigger.

Pepys had yet another pressing reason for wanting to avoid a war between England and Holland: Brother Balty.

If war broke out, New England would be a battleground. And somewhere wandering about New England was his feckless brother-in-law. How long would the innocent dolt survive, amidst the clash of steel and boom of gun? About ten minutes, Pepys reckoned. And what *then?* Pepys winced to think of it. The prospect of his wife's wrath—unquenchable, unappeasable, unyielding, eternal. (She was, after all, half French.) She'd lay the blame for Balty's death squarely at her husband's feet. Recrimination and blame would be his marital portion unto the last syllable of recorded time. He could hear her lamentations, the crockery smashing against the walls of their house. *Monstre! Fiend! You 'ave murdered my beloved Balty! Hell will be a paradise to you, next to the suffering I shall give you in* this *life!*

Balty's demise would be the death knell of the domestic life that Pepys cherished, athwart his frequent infidelities. He might make merry with strumpets and tarts, but despite the peccant part of his anatomy, his heart remained true to the dowry-less fifteen-year-old he'd married a decade ago. Their marriage sometimes made Atlantic hurricanoes seem like balmy zephyrs, but his devotion to Elizabeth had never faltered.

In this desperate hour, there was no one to whom Pepys could turn but his fornicating cousin, the Admiral of the Narrow Seas.

CHAPTER 19

How Clever of God

Balty opened his eyes and saw that he'd died. His sadness was mitigated by the loveliness of the angel ministering to him. She was of heart-stopping beauty, not that hearts stopped in Heaven. How lovely to find, after all the promises of Scripture and pulpit, that Heaven *was* real.

Then he thought: How had *he* earned Heaven? He hadn't led a very wicked life; but neither had he been a paragon of Christian virtue.

He gazed at the angel's face. She had golden hair. How clever of God to make his angels blond. She reminded him of someone. Who? Ah, the Quaker girl. Yes, the resemblance was striking.

Balty lifted his head from the pillow. He felt a sharp stab of pain, like a nail being driven through his skull.

Pain—in Heaven?

The angel spoke. "Lie still. Thou've had a bad knock on thy noggin."

He blinked and looked about. Shouldn't there be clouds? And other angels? Heaven seemed rather drab: walls of logs and wattle; beams, a small window.

"Thou've lost much blood."

"Where . . . what is this place?"

"Hush, now."

"Huncks? Is he . . . ?"

"In the other room. Bartholomew and his son found thee last night, by the cliff. Micah, the boy, has gone to fetch a surgeon. Bartholomew thought it best not to seek one in New Haven, so he sent him to Milford."

"We were . . . attacked."

"Don't speak. Rest. Thou will be safe here. Bartholomew has taken measures, in case they return."

The door opened. It was a stout woman of commanding aspect.

"Awake, is he? Praise God." She addressed herself to Balty: "You've *her* prayers to thank for that. You bled through three of my best pillows."

Amity Cobb lifted the bandage on Balty's head and peered beneath.

"Clean through to the skull."

"I shall recompense you for your pillows, madame."

"Never mind my pillows. What were you up to out there? Don't you know better than to go trespassing on Indian burial ground?"

Balty groaned. "Why must *everyone* insist we were robbing graves?"

"Then what were you doing?"

"Hunting."

"Hunting? Ha! Either that hole in your head made you daft, or the truth isn't in you."

"Hunting regicides."

"Daft. Stay with him, love," she said. "Try to keep him awake until Micah returns with the surgeon. I'll be with the other one."

Mrs. Cobb took Balty's hand in hers and patted it.

"What you did for her. Bless you for that." She left.

"Who was that termagant?"

"Mrs. Cobb. Amity."

"Amity? Ha. Mistress Dragon. What are *you* doing here?"

"My cabin is not far. My husband and I were employed here. When I came this morning, here thou were, with Colonel Huncks. Shall I read to thee from the Bible?"

"Why would you do that?"

"Mr. St. Michel, what a question." Thankful smiled.

"Call me Balty. Read to me if I start to die. Which I may at any moment, given the intense pain in my head. Why do Quakers say *thou* and *thee?*"

"If thou knew the Bible, Mr. Balty, thou would know why."

"Wouldn't it be simpler just to tell me?"

"I'll give thee a clue. '*Thou* shalt honor *thy* father and mother'?"

"Ah. Sermon on the Mount."

"Oh, Mr. Balty. *Shame.*"

"D'you really think Moses and Jesus and all that lot went about saying 'thou' and 'thee'?"

"I should not speak so impiously," she said, "if *I* were gravely injured and flirting with death."

"I'm not flirting with death. I'm flirting with thee."

"What were thou doing out there last night?"

"What his majesty sent us here to do. Which doesn't include robbing bloody Indian tombs. How's Huncks? Is he all right?"

"He cannot move his legs. He has no feeling in them."

"Christ."

"I see thou are not familiar with *any* of the commandments, Mr. Balty."

"I wasn't taking his bloody— I wasn't taking his name in vain. I was praying."

"One doesn't address our Lord as if he were in a tavern, Mr. Balty."

"Very well. Teach me how to address him."

"Don't be impious."

"I'm perfectly serious. Show me."

"All right. Let us be silent together."

"Silent? That's a dull way of praying."

"It is in silence that we see the inward light. And hear the Holy Spirit."

"Does he moan and rattle his chains, like other spirits?"

"He spoke to me just this morning. While I was praying for thee."

"Oh? What'd he say?"

"He said, 'I shouldn't bother praying for Mr. St. Michel. He's thoroughly wicked and beyond redemption.' I replied that he might be right, but that thou and Mr. Huncks had been kind to me. It took a bit of convincing. But here thou are. Alive."

Toward evening, Balty got out of bed, despite Thankful's protests. Standing made him dizzy, but he wanted to see Huncks.

Bartholomew Cobb sat by the open door. His clothes seemed very dirty, not that this was unusual in a farmer. His musket lay across his lap. On a table nearby, Balty recognized two items: Huncks's pistol and Balty's own clock-watch. The watch was a going-away present from his sister. What was *it* doing there?

Seeing him, Bartholomew rose and shut the door.

"I wanted to thank you," Balty said, "for last night."

"Thank Providence. You were lucky we heard the gunshot. What were you doing?"

"Not robbing graves. Did Thankful tell you about us?"

"Only that you'd saved her from the magistrate. And about looking for the regicide judges. What made you think they're hiding in the cliff?"

"This chap in a tavern said he'd lead us to them. Colonel Huncks— my companion—knew it was a trap. So we—"

"Walked into it. May I ask, is manhunting your profession?"

"It is at present. Colonel Huncks is the one who knows what he's doing. I'm just . . . may *I* ask, why is my clock-watch on that table with the Colonel's pistol?"

"Might come in useful. Why'd you walk into what you knew to be a trap?"

"It was Huncks's idea. He's not one to hold back. He tricked the fellow into revealing himself. But he bolted. Huncks gave chase. Then your local savages assaulted us. Rudely. I had been under the impression that the local red folk were better mannered."

"They're touchy about their graves."

"We had no intention of . . . oh, never mind. Where's Huncks? I must see him."

"In there. Keep away from the windows. And keep your voice down."

Huncks lay on the bed, eyes closed, arm cradled around an earthenware whisky jug.

Balty sat on the edge of the bed. Huncks opened his eyes.

"What, gone over to Mahomet?"

Was he delirious, or drunk?

"How are you feeling, old man?" Balty asked.

"You'll have to pray five times a day. Make a pilgrimage. Give alms."

"Huncks, what *are* you going on about?"

"Your turban."

Balty felt his head. It was wrapped in bandages.

"Oh. How do you feel?"

"I don't. From the waist down."

"The boy's gone to fetch a surgeon. To Milford. Our host, Mr. Cobb, didn't want to alert the saints. A New Haven surgeon would only finish us off."

Huncks took a pull on the jug.

"Easy, old man," Balty said. "You'll be too drunk to tell the surgeon where it hurts."

"Wish it did hurt. Can't feel my bollocks."

"Well, they say Milford surgeons are brilliant with bollocks."

"Balty."

"Yes, old man?"

Huncks struggled to get it out. "Thanks."

"What for?"

"Oh, don't be a tit."

"Thankful's praying for you. For thee. Quaking like a jelly pudding. Oughtn't we send for your Dr. Pell?"

Huncks stared. "How do you know about Pell?"

"You told me about him last night. When you thought you were done for. Told me to get to Fairhaven and find Dr. Pell. To tell him some Colonel Nickel is coming. With a fleet."

"The fall seems to have loosened my tongue."

"Yes, you were quite chatty. Rather a nice change."

"What else did I say?"

"It was just getting interesting when that appalling Indian, Repentance, or whatever he's called, arrived with his cannibal entourage."

"They don't eat each other. You mean Repent? Davenport's Indian?"

"I assume. He's got a ghastly face with wings carved into his forehead. Frightful looking. I was trying to establish an understanding with him. I didn't get very far. Thank God Mr. Cobb arrived when he did."

Huncks mused. "Davenport . . ."

He said he must write a message to Dr. Pell. Balty went to see about writing material. Mr. Cobb was at his vigil by the door. It was dark now.

"I say, you wouldn't have some paper and—"

Cobb stood up. He whispered, "Get back. Quiet."

Balty retreated. Cobb stood in the doorway. Balty saw the panes in the window glow orange. Torches.

Cobb raised a hand, cradling the musket in the crook of his arm.

"Greetings, friends."

Balty couldn't make out the response but recognized the voice. He listened and made out the word "Owanux."

Cobb pointed. "There. Dead. Of their wounds."

He leaned his musket against the doorway and picked up Huncks's pistol and Balty's clock-watch and stepped out of the house, disappearing from view.

Balty listened.

"Take these as tokens of respect, for the spirits of your dead."

Cobb reappeared in the doorway. The glow on the windowpanes faded. Cobb closed the door, looked at Balty, put a finger to his lips.

"Sorry about the pistol and your watch. But they were gifts well to your advantage."

"What does 'Owanux' mean?"

"English."

"What were you pointing at?"

"Your graves."

"Oh. I say. Well done."

"The pistol's a great prize. They've no reason now to come back. But keep away from the windows. Great skulkers, Quiripi."

Mrs. Cobb and Thankful emerged. Balty saw something unfamiliar in Thankful's face. Fear.

"It's all right, girl," Cobb said. "He's gone." Mrs. Cobb took Thankful with her into the kitchen.

"I could use a nip of that whisky," Cobb said. "Imagine you could, too."

"She was frightened."

"Weren't you?"

"Yes, but at the church and in the courtroom, she didn't so much as blink. Serene as a swan."

They went into Huncks's room and passed the jug around. Balty told Huncks what had just passed. Huncks seemed downcast hearing of the loss of his pistol.

Cobb said, "I melted lead into the barrel. It's useless."

"D'you have another?" Huncks asked.

"Only the muskets."

Cobb left.

"You might have thanked him," Balty said. "That's twice he's saved us."

"I'll express my gratitude to Mr. Cobb in the fullness of time."

He asked again for writing material. Balty got some from Mrs. Cobb. Huncks sat up and scribbled.

"What are you writing?" Balty asked.

"Message to Pell. In Fair*field*, not Fairhaven. Try to remember, as you'll be the one delivering this if I don't get my damned legs back."

"Is it about Colonel Nickel and his fleet?"

Huncks finished. He unscrewed his signet ring from his finger.

"Get me some sealing wax."

"*Another* letter I'm not to read?"

"It's for your own protection. You're safer not knowing the contents."

"So it's back to Huncks the Sphinx."

Huncks signed. "Very well. You've earned the right. Our mission's to gather information."

"What's so secretive about that? These *are* his majesty's colonies. Surely his agents are entitled to gather information."

"Gathering information is another term for spying, Balty. Spies get hanged."

"Who's going to hang us? The Indians?"

"Dutch."

"We're in New England. There are no Dutch here."

"We might be going to New Amsterdam."

"In connection with the regicides?"

"Yes. And no."

"Huncks."

"The judge hunt is a cover."

"Well, bloody good of you to share it. What's the actual mission?"

"Bit of scouting. In advance of Colonel Nicholls's visit."

Balty stared. "He's visiting? With a squadron of warships?"

"Nothing belligerent. Conducting an administrative review. Of the New England colonies."

"Then why's he going to the Dutch colony?"

"Courtesy. The West India Company in Amsterdam have been informed about it by Downing. Matter of protocol."

"Then why all this effort to keep me in ignorance? And why should Hollanders hang us for helping to arrange an official visit?"

"Perhaps you're right. I'm being overcautious."

"Well," Balty sniffed, "sometimes a fresh perspective helps."

"Agreed. I see the thing in a new light."

"Good. There it is."

"There it is," Huncks said. "Now go ask our good hosts for some sealing wax."

"Is that necessary, now you've vouchsafed me your great secret?"

"Pell would take it suspicious if it didn't bear my seal. It's only by way of establishing your bona fides."

"Protocol?"

"Quite."

Presently, the boy Micah arrived from Milford with the surgeon, a rotund, wheezing, bewhiskered, and bespectacled Dutchman named DeVrootje. Like all Dutch in New England, he felt vastly superior to the English by virtue of having gotten here first. By the time he opened his medicine case and laid out his instruments, he'd established that his great-grandfather, one Linus DeVrootje of Rotterdam, dealer in beaver pelts, had arrived with Block in 1614 aboard *Onrust*. He explained (without having been asked) that his Dutch accent was due to Dutch having remained the lingua franca of the DeVrootje household in the New World. Before turning to his patient, he desired confirmation of Micah's promise of a half sovereign for his services. Twice his usual fee, in consideration of the great distance he'd had to travel here and back, twenty-four miles. Was this still the understanding? Yes? Good.

He asked the particulars of Huncks's injury. A fall, from a horse.

He pursed his lips dubiously and instructed that Huncks be turned over onto his stomach. Surgeon DeVrootje walked his fingers up and down his spine like a militant spider. He paused at various vertebrae, prodding, frowning, making little humming sounds and grunts.

Now, he said, he must do something the patient would not find pleasant, but it was necessary. With that, he inserted one hand between Huncks's legs, and with the other grasped Huncks's virile member. Huncks's eyes went wide. In the next instant he had DeVrootje by the neck and was throttling him. DeVrootje squeaked, face reddening, *as he* continued with his ministration. Bartholomew and Balty pried Huncks's hands from the surgeon's throat.

"Do that again," Huncks snarled, "and you'll be the one needing a damn surgeon!"

DeVrootje took it all in calm, professional stride and explained that the finger he'd embedded inside Huncks was in hope of feeling a contraction caused by squeezing Huncks's *membrum virile.* The good news was there had been a contraction. If there hadn't . . . but never mind. He now produced a needle and made pinpricks up and down Huncks's lower torso, legs, and feet. He seemed encouraged that the soles of Huncks's feet and one or two of his toes reacted to the pricks.

Surgeon DeVrootje removed his spectacles which, in the excitement of Huncks trying to choke him, had fogged. He wiped them and said Huncks had suffered a "paraplegia consequenting from a dislocation or compression of the lumbar vertebra." A mouthful. It was possible, he continued, there had been a fracture of something called the transverse process. Here DeVrootje paused, then said Huncks might walk again. Or might not. The next three to six days would tell. If there was no improvement, no return of feeling, mobility, control of bodily functions, these would be not good signs.

Addressing himself to Thankful and Mrs. Cobb, he gave instructions. Huncks was to be fed great quantities of milk, clams, and fish. He must "eat and eat and eat."

They asked why. DeVrootje shrugged. He said it could not be explained, but over many years of practice, he had found that people who lived by the shore and ate a diet of clams and fish and milk tended to heal from such injuries more than people who lived inland. His explanation left everyone staring.

He now turned his attention to his other patient. He cleaned Balty's head wound and stitched it up. Had *he* also been thrown by a horse? he asked skeptically. Hmph. He shook his head and said they should learn to ride better, or not ride at all. Balty was to rest for at least a week. Turning again to Mrs. Cobb, DeVrootje instructed that he be fed as much red meat as was available, to stimulate a replenishment of the blood.

His ministrations done, Surgeon DeVrootje accepted his half sovereign, made a little bow to Mrs. Cobb, and departed, tsk-tsking that it would be well past midnight until he reached Milford.

Balty remained in the room with Huncks.

"Well, old boy."

"Bloody Dutch," Huncks grumbled.

"Seemed to know his business."

"I can't move my legs, and he tells me to eat chowder? Quack."

"He seemed encouraged when he gave your Master John Good-fellow a squeeze and you . . . contracted."

Huncks gave the letter to Balty. "Looks like you'll be delivering this to Pell."

"How far *is* Fairhaven?"

"Fair*field*. Try not to make a muck of it."

"I can't go. I'm to stay in bed and eat Bartholomew's cows. While you gorge on clams. Are we pressed for time?"

Huncks considered. "Nicholls was to sail by late May. Eight, nine weeks to Boston . . . Gravesend by late August. It's midsummer now. We've time."

"Then we'll heal up together, and both go to Fairhaven."

Huncks stared forlornly at his legs. "We'll see."

- CHAPTER 20 -

May 28th. *To Chelsey to plead with my Lord Montagu and beg his intercession in the matter of Col. Nicholls's "administrative review" of the New England colonies.*

Arrived much apprehensive, owing to the coolness he has shewn me since my remonstration with him for his lubricity with the trollop Becke.

Found him in an agreeable mood and pinkish flush, doubtless from carnal exertion. The strumpet was "at market." Was sore tempted to ask my lord if she was there to buy or sell but did not.

Informed my lord about Nicholls, begging him to keep confidential the manner of my learning of it.

My lord readily agreed that the Navy is not at present equipt to fight another war with the Hollanders. But he said, "What would you have me do? If 'tis the will of the King, and his brother, and Downing, and Lady Castlemaine, Africa House, the Admiralty, Navy Office, every d——d merchant in London, and the rest of the War Party?"

I replied, "If Nicholls causes a war with Holland, our Navy will be sunk to the bottom of your Narrow Seas—and every other sea. Where will England be then? And where will you be? At the bottom, with the ships."

He admitted this not the most desirous of outcomes. But pacing the floor with no little agitation, said the thing was beyond his ability to influence or repair.

I remonstrated anew that he must not so blithely abrogate

responsibility, being the Admiral in whom the King himself once reposed more trust and confidence than any other.

He retorted, "What do you mean, sir, by 'once'?"

I suggested, perhaps too candidly, that his ability to influence great matters might be ameliorated if he spent more time at Court than in Mrs. Becke.

My lord, not pleased, called me a "flippant fellow" and said I had "the tongue of a moray."

Exprest my continued affection for him (etc.), averring that my concern sprang only from love for country and himself. But pointed out—pointedly—that war with Holland would propel him posthaste from his present bower of pudendal bliss to the quarterdeck of a warship, facing a fleet far more numerous and better equipt than his.

This prospect did much sober my lord, as indeed the prospect of death tends to.

He said he would approach his majesty but must mull how best to do this.

Took my leave, begging him to be discreet as to how he came by knowledge of Nicholls's true mission.

– CHAPTER 21 –

The Razor's Edge

Thankful remained at the Cobb farmhouse to help Mrs. Cobb tend to Balty and Huncks.

Balty's dizzy spells from blood loss kept him in bed for days. One afternoon he got up and wobbled about the house. He took care to stay away from windows and doorways, but one day glimpsed Thankful arranging flowers over the two false graves Bartholomew had dug to deceive Repent.

"Very thoughtful," he said, when she came in.

She seemed embarrassed. "The Quiripi know that we put flowers on our graves. If there were none on these, they might wonder."

"You seemed to recognize the one with the thing on his face."

Thankful blushed and left the room without responding.

Later that same day, Balty sat at the kitchen table, gnawing on yet another serving of raw meat. He and Mrs. Cobb were alone.

"Bit of a mystery, isn't she?" Balty said.

Mrs. Cobb's back was to him. She went on with her washing. "How so, Mr. Balty?"

"She won't explain why she was there in the worship house, naked as Eve. Never mind why she was there a *second* time. This morning I asked her if she recognized the Indian who came to finish us off, and she went pale as milk. Can't make sense of her."

"Why must you?"

"I only want to understand her. I realize this is *New* England. But in old England, people don't swan into church stark naked. Certainly not if they've been whipped within an inch of their lives for doing it before. It's a bit fruity. But maybe that's it. Is she . . . all right?"

"How do you mean?"

"In the head."

"She'd have every right not to be, after what she's been through."

"I don't mean to pry."

"Then why *are* you prying?"

"I don't know. Perhaps I feel responsible for her. Aren't you supposed to feel responsible if you've rescued someone?"

Mrs. Cobb went on with her scrubbing, her back to Balty.

"She and her husband, Gideon, they came from Barbadoes. They never thought to stay in New Haven. It's sure no place for Quakers. But they'd no money. Sweet pair. Always a good word.

"They managed. Built a little cabin not far from here. Repent, the one who came for you, he took a fancy to her. Began skulking about. Being Quaker, they didn't do nothing. Went on about their own business. But after a time, his skulking worked on her nerves.

"Gideon asked him not to hang about. Polite like. But he went on hanging about. Gideon went to the magistrate. Mr. Dependable Feake, him who you've met. He asked him to speak to the Reverend Davenport, Repent being Davenport's Indian godson, or whatever you'd call him. Don't know if Feake ever did speak to Davenport. Repent kept on with his skulking. Gideon and Thankful tried to make their peace with it and get on.

"One day Gideon went out to hunt and didn't come back. There was a search. He was found, dead. Snakebit. Terrible. They counted over twenty bites on him."

"Good Lord," Balty said. "So many?"

"It was reckoned he'd stepped in a nest. But when the body was given to Thankful to prepare for burial, she saw marks on his wrists and ankles. Rope marks. And the bites, they were all on one side of him. His front. If you go stepping into a snake nest, you'll be bitten front, back, every part of you. Even so, how were the rope marks to be explained?

"She went to Feake. He said they could have been from anything. Anything! Far as he were concerned, it were no tragedy there was one less Quaker in New Haven. He told her to get the body into the ground quick like, or he'd fine her. That was the justice she got from our magistrate.

"She buried him. The next day Repent appeared at her door and asked her to marry him. That was when she knew it was him had killed Gideon. She refused. Then . . ."

Mrs. Cobb paused in her scrubbing. ". . . he done worse to her. Had his way. She went to Davenport. And what did he tell her? That he'd never permit no godson of his, white or red, to marry a Quaker.

"So she made her protest in the worship house, in the Quaker way. You saw her back, what they done to her.

"I nursed her back to health. It was days until she healed enough to walk. Then on the Sabbath day, she was gone, without telling us. To make another protest. Knowing full well it would be at the cost of her life. That was the day you first saw her."

Mrs. Cobb finished her washing and left Balty alone in the kitchen.

Ten days after Surgeon DeVrootje's visit, Huncks had regained only slight feeling in his toes. Thankful and Mrs. Cobb did what they could to lift his spirits. Thankful cut fresh flowers every morning for his bedside; Mrs. Cobb varied the seasonings in the relentless servings of chowder. Huncks finally announced that he would eat not one more clam, not one more spoonful of chowder, and lapsed into a silence from which no entreaty or pleasantry could beguile him.

One afternoon when Balty went to look in on him, Huncks surprised him by asking for a razor.

"A shave." Balty said. "*Just* the thing. I'll have Mrs. Cobb heat some water."

"Just the razor will do."

"No need to dry-shave. Mrs. Cobb would be happy to—"

"Damn it, man. I want a razor. Nothing more."

Balty sat down on the edge of the bed. "Is that why you were so anxious about your pistol?"

"I've no intention to spend the rest of my life in Mrs. Cobb's bed."

"She'll be cross if you ruin another of her pillows. Look here, old man. Let's not give up just yet."

"I'm done, Balty."

"I won't have your death on my conscience."

"Then bugger off."

"There's gratitude. Should have left you at the cliff."

"Get out."

"As you're in no mood for company, I shall leave."

Balty went to the kitchen. Thankful asked, "What ails thee, Mr. Balty?"

"He asked me for a razor. Not for shaving. He's given up."

"Poor man."

"I don't know what to do."

"Thou cannot do that. Life is God's to take, not ours."

"Yes." Balty sighed. "I *know* all that."

"Supper's on the table. I'll stay with him awhile."

Balty sat glumly at the table. Bartholomew had been to market in New Haven and had overheard people talking about two English grave robbers who'd been killed falling off East Hill.

Balty groaned. "This is how I'm to be remembered. For scavenging Indian tombs."

"The fellow what led you into the trap. Called himself Mr. Fish, were it?"

"Simeon Fish. Bastard."

"We don't talk that way at table, Mr. Balty," Mrs. Cobb said. "Nor anywhere else."

"Sorry."

"What'd he look like?" Bartholomew asked.

"Biggish fellow. Fat. Great bushy eyebrows and rum-blossom cheeks."

"What's rum-blossom?" Micah asked.

"When blood vessels burst under the skin. Leaves red spider-webby marks."

"From excess of *drink*," Mrs. Cobb added.

Micah said, "That's Mr. William Jones."

Bartholomew and Mrs. Cobb glanced at each other.

"We don't know that, boy," his father said.

"He's got eyebrows like bushes. *And* rum-blossoms all over his face."

"That's enough, boy. Eat your food."

Balty said, "Who's William Jones?"

"Prominent citizen. And I much doubt someone of his station would be up to such mischief as luring people into traps at night."

"Why *did* you walk into his trap, Mr. Balty?" Micah asked. "Weren't it foolish to do so?"

"Micah," his father rebuked, "don't be disrespectful."

"You were the one called them fools."

"You'll feel the back of my hand."

"Now, now," Balty said. "No disrespect taken. Yes, Micah, it was foolish. But, you see, Colonel Huncks knew it was a trap, so . . ."

"You walked into it?"

"You sound remarkably like your father. We'd just turned the tables on this Mr. Fish when things, well, got away from us, you might say. Tell me more about this William Jones."

"It wouldn't have been him," Bartholomew said.

"All the same."

"No good comes came of idle talk."

After dinner Balty took Bartholomew aside.

"This afternoon my friend asked me for a razor to cut his own throat. Now, maybe it wasn't this prominent citizen who crippled him. But maybe it was. Either way, it's not idle talk, is it? So please—tell me about this William Jones."

"Did you bring it?"

"No. But I've had a think on it. And I'll fetch you a razor, if it's what you truly want."

"It is."

"Very well. I see Thankful brought you more whisky. Give us a taste."

Huncks handed Balty the jug.

"She stayed an hour. Kneading my legs. Sweet girl."

"She is, yes. By the way, Bartholomew was at the market in town today. People are talking about the two Englishmen who fell to their deaths trying to rob Indian graves."

"Nice to be talked about."

"Yes, I thought you'd be pleased. I learned something else. Who our Mr. Fish is. One William Jones."

Huncks considered. "William Jones who married Eaton's daughter?"

"The same."

"John Jones served under Cromwell. Colonel of Cavalry. Distinguished himself. Married Cromwell's sister. A widow. Jones was one of the commissioners of the High Court in '49. He was one of the judges. With Whalley and Goffe."

"Ah."

"He was among the first to be arrested and executed. Conducted himself well at the end, by all accounts. His son William arrived in Boston in '60, aboard *Prudent Mary*. In the company of Whalley and Goffe."

"So he's *that* William Jones?"

"It would provide a motive."

"Is everyone in New England related to a regicide?"

"Who told about you about Jones?"

"Micah. I was describing our Mr. Fish. The eyebrows and rummy cheeks. He piped up and said, 'Oh, that's Mr. Jones.' His mum and dad weren't pleased."

"No, I shouldn't think. We've caused them enough trouble as it is. Jones is Deputy Governor here."

"That would qualify him as a prominent citizen."

Huncks stared at his legs. "Shame these sticks don't work. What I'd give to pay a call on Deputy Governor Jones."

"There are a number of people here I should like to call on. Including Davenport and his murderer godson."

Balty related what Mrs. Cobb had told him. "That's why she was there in the church that day."

"Sweet Jesus," Huncks said. "Poor girl."

"That's what she said about you when I told her you wanted a razor. She said, 'Poor man.' Then came in and rubbed your legs to cheer you up. She who's not said a word to either of us about what she's been through. If you're still feeling sorry for yourself, I'll get your razor."

"No. Not just yet."

CHAPTER 22

Integendeel

Pepys's legs ached. He'd stood on the wheel of a cart for over an hour, waiting to watch Turner the highwayman hang, for stealing £4,500 in jewels. He'd paid the owner of the cart a shilling for the privilege.

It was a popular hanging. Crowds poured into St. Mary Axe. Later it was said fourteen thousand had watched the handsome robber flung off the ladder. Pepys hoped it was Turner who'd robbed him on the Chelsey road that day.

After the execution, Pepys visited with a pretty young merchant, a seller of ribands and gloves. Things got so exceeding merry he forgot the pain in his legs.

Then to the Sun Tavern, to meet with Mr. Warren, timber merchant of Wapping and Rotherhithe. Warren presented Pepys with a fine pair of gloves. Sam wondered if Warren had purchased them from the same pretty merchant.

Warren said the gloves were a gift for Pepys's wife. They were neatly wrapped in paper, and weighed very heavy, being stuffed with forty pieces of gold. A gesture of gratitude, for his continuing good relationship with the Navy's chief purchaser of timber.

And so home to Seething Lane.

Pepys waited anxiously for Elizabeth to go see about supper so he could admire his gold in privacy. He dumped the coins onto the table, purring at the sight of them, all lambent in candlelight. He congratulated himself on his good fortune and gave thanks to God Almighty for his blessings. He felt surpassingly happy, which always made him want to take wine and play his lute.

This pleasant idyll was interrupted by knocking on the door. His servant entered with a message. Pepys recognized Downing's seal. A summons to Whitehall, a matter of "some urgency." The wine and the lute would have to wait.

On his way out, Pepys's nostrils filled with the aroma of roasting marrowbones. It was a particular favorite dish of his. He hoped Downing's matter wouldn't keep him long.

He reflected anew on the happiness he felt here. How blessed he was! Sated as his exertions with the riband merchant had left him, he felt a surge of concupiscence in his loins. He thought of the wenches he'd recently seen at Ludgate Hill. It wouldn't be too much of a detour on his way back from Whitehall.

But no, he told himself sternly. One dalliance a day was enough. He would return straight home. He'd go by water, so as to avoid temptation. There were no sirens on the Thames! Then he and his wife would drink wine and suck on marrowbones and he would play his lute for her. His "Gaze Not on Swans" was coming along nicely. The lute often put Elizabeth in the mood for bed—and not for sleep. Pepys's heart was burstingly full.

"My lord."

"Ah. You arrive. I trust this is not too great an inconvenience?"

"Being of service to my lord is never an inconvenience."

Downing rang a small silver bell on his desk. His scrivener, Fell, entered. Pepys nodded a greeting. They knew each other. Fell sat, dipped a quill in ink, and looked on with the expectant but patient face of one awaiting dictation. Odd, Pepys thought. Downing rarely made a record of their meetings.

"Perhaps you can illuminate a matter for me."

The scratch of Fell's quill filled the silence.

"Yes?"

"When did you last see the Earl of Sandwich?"

Pepys's buttock cheeks clenched. "Sandwich?"

"Your cousin. And patron."

"Distant cousin. Well . . . let's see. My Lord Sandwich has not of late been much at Court."

"No," Downing said, not looking up from the papers on his desk. "He has been much occupied in Chelsey. What *can* be keeping him there? I wonder. Perhaps he prefers the tranquility of village life to the cut and thrust of Court."

Pepys squirmed. "He does, yes, have an affinity for the rustic."

"Get out there much yourself, do you?"

"Chelsey holds nothing to attract me. The road is a horror. Highwaymen and cutpurses at every turn."

"Then you have *not* visited with the Earl of Sandwich in Chelsey?"

The scratch of Fell's quill sounded like the fire-etched writing on the wall at Belshazzar's Feast: *Mene, mene, tekel: You have been weighed on the scales and found wanting.*

Pepys spurred his brain. Better to offer Downing something.

"As a matter of fact, I have."

Downing leaned back in his chair and cocked his head to the side, resting temple on a finger.

"A most unhappy undertaking," Pepys said. "But I deemed it my duty."

"Yes?"

"I had arrived at the melancholy conclusion that my lord's comportment there was doing him no good at Court. Or with his majesty."

"Yes. Family relations can be such a burden."

"I have a great affection for my Lord Sandwich."

"As you should. After all, look how high his patronage has lifted you."

"I am indeed fortunate."

"No wonder, then, you should risk the horrors of the Chelsey road to entreat with him to give up the pastoral life and return to Court. How gallant you are, Pepys."

"My lord exaggerates my heroism. It was no more than my duty."

"'*Non nobis solum nati sumus*.' Eh?"

"'Not for ourselves alone are we born.'" Pepys cleared his throat. "How well the imperishable Cicero puts it."

"And when *did* you visit with Lord Sandwich in Chelsey?"

"Well . . . Let's see. Was it . . . ?"

"Tuesday, perchance?"

"Tuesday? Well, I would have to consult my calendar . . ."

"In the absence of your calendar, let us, *arguendo*, say it was Tuesday." Downing's tempo quickened to a trot. "In which case, your mission to Chelsey must be adjudged a success. You are to be congratulated, Pepys."

"I am?"

"Yes. It shows you dispose of great powers of persuasion. I must keep you in mind for some embassy in the future. Clearly, the Crown has not availed itself of your full talents."

"My lord is too kind. Yet I do not know quite why I deserve such . . . garlands."

"Then I shall explain. Only two days after your . . . let us call it your Chelsey remonstrance, your prodigal cousin sought an audience with his majesty."

"Ah? Oh."

"And not merely just to show his face. Far from it! Indeed, from the specificity of his business with the King, one would think Lord Sandwich had spent the previous months immersed in military matters. Instead of Mrs. Becke's crinkum-crankum."

"I . . ." —Pepys's mouth had gone dry—"rejoice to hear that my Lord Sandwich has stayed . . . on top of things."

"His majesty was most impressed. Not only that the Earl was so well-informed. But that a matter of such great confidentiality had somehow"—Downing walked two fingers across the surface of his desk—"found its way to *Chelsey*."

Pepys swallowed. "Did my Lord Sandwich vouchsafe to his majesty how he had come by this intelligence? Whatever it was."

He braced to hear Downing utter that most dismal of sentences: "Take him to the Tower!"

But Downing said, "No. His majesty did not think it polite to ask."

Pepys stifled a sigh of relief. "How very gracious is his majesty."

"Yes," Downing said. "And how fortunate for whoever provided the information to Sandwich. But no matter. Secrecy is a chrysalis inevitably shed in the fullness of time. The matter will reveal itself soon enough. Out of the shadows, into the sunlight. Nothing like sunlight, eh, Pepys?"

"Quite, my lord." Pepys was sweating.

"You look pale, Sam. I think you must get some sunlight."

Downing returned to his papers. Pepys rose and walked to the door.

"Pepys."

"My lord?"

"Did I ever thank you for delivering those dispatches to Colonel Nicholls in Portsmouth?"

"I . . ."

"I don't believe I did. Thank you."

"It was nothing, my lord."

"*Integendeel.*"

"My lord?"

"Good night, Sam."

Pepys went directly home, with no thought of the lusty wenches of Ludgate Hill. Nor was he in the mood for wine or marrowbones or strumming bars of "Gaze Not on Swans" nor for making merry in bed with his wife.

He tossed and turned until three, when, giving up on sleep or breakfast, he dressed and went down Seething Lane to the Navy Office. He found what he sought in the library, in an English-Dutch dictionary and phrase book.

Integendeel meant "on the contrary." But what did *that* mean?

CHAPTER 23

Promise?

Balty woke to the sound of shouting. He bolted from bed. Thankful and the Cobbs were standing outside Huncks's door.

"What on earth?" Mrs. Cobb said.

"Another of his nightmares," Balty said.

"Doesn't sound like a nightmare."

A yelp came from the other side—a demented whoop.

"Told you he was drinking too much whisky," Mrs. Cobb said.

"I'll deal with it." Balty opened the door. Huncks was standing, propped against the wall. He was looking down at his feet, lifting one, then the other in turn. He looked up at Balty, grinning, and resumed his foot raising, as if in awe of a newly invented mechanical marvel.

"Look, Balty! *Look!*"

Mrs. Cobb and Thankful came in.

"My legs!"

"It's your knees you should be on," Mrs. Cobb said. "Giving thanks."

Huncks continued his foot lifting.

"I was dreaming I had to piss. Reached for the pot. Couldn't find it. Next thing, I'm standing. Standing!"

Over the next few days, Huncks regained full use of his legs.

Mrs. Cobb and Thankful competed with each other for the credit. Mrs. Cobb asserted it was her clam chowders. Thankful said it was her prayers and rubbing his legs. Balty offered his own opinion that the credit must go to God for a miracle, not a miracle of healing, but mercy—liberating the Cobbs from further burden of hospitality. Micah took to calling Huncks "Mr. Lazarus."

Thankful, who throughout had been attentive and gay, now grew distant and withdrawn. Balty noticed it more than the others. As Bartholemew urged Balty and Huncks to remain inside out of sight, it was difficult finding a chance to speak with her alone. Finally he did, the day before their departure.

"Is all well?" Balty said. "You seem a bit sad."

"Perhaps." She went on with her housework as she spoke. "Where will thou go?"

"I'm not supposed to say. New Amsterdam. Don't let on to Huncks I told you."

"Thou'll not linger in New Haven?"

"Not sure what Huncks has in mind. He's pretty hot about Mr. Fish. Huncks isn't one to let bygones be bygones. Not that *I* wouldn't mind dangling him from the cliff. Or that damned Quiripi—"

Balty paused. "Amity told me. About Gideon. And . . ."

"Vengeance is mine, saith the Lord. I shall repay."

"That from the Book of Quaker?"

"There is no Book of Quaker, Mr. Balty. Paul's letter to the Romans."

Balty harrumphed. "From the sound of it, Paul never made it to New Haven."

"God has spared thee and Mr. Huncks. Thou might repay *him*."

"I'll propose it to Huncks. But I don't think he and Paul are of the same mind."

"Then for me?"

"You are a puzzle, all right. After what these *saints* have done to you?"

"Leave justice to God, Balty. Promise?"

"I will if you'll promise not to go parading in their worship house without clothing." Balty pressed. "Forgive me for saying, but I wonder if your mind's jiggled loose from all that quaking. You know what they'll do to you. Do you *want* to die like that?"

Thankful smiled. Their lips came together. Larks sang hymns at Heaven's Gate. Then the door banged open and Mrs. Cobb came in swinging a beheaded chicken in each hand.

"*Well*," she said. "Didn't mean to interrupt."

Balty and Huncks left the next morning. Thankful accompanied them as far as her cabin. Huncks said his goodbye and waited at a distance.

Balty said, "I didn't know Gideon, but I can't think he'd want you to throw away your life like that. I'm sure of it. I do know he was lucky to have you."

She put her hand to his cheek. "I thank thee, Mr. Balty, for all thou did for me. Whatever lies ahead, I pray I shall be worthy of your good heart."

She kissed him on the forehead, then turned and went into the little cabin by the pond and closed the door.

CHAPTER 24

A Fish for Mr. Fish

"**B**ut I promised."

"I didn't."

"Well, it was rather a promise from *both* of us."

Huncks sighed. "Quiet, man. You natter like geese."

It was going on sunset. Balty and Huncks, posing as fishmongers selling from a cart, had positioned themselves up the street from William Jones's house.

"I don't believe you were thrown out of Harvard for drinking on the Sabbath."

"What are you talking about?"

"It's obvious you didn't pay the least attention to your Bible studies. Certainly not to Paul's letter to the Romans."

"Do you want to find the regicides? It's why you're here, isn't it?"

"I thought so. Until you told me my brother-in-law's only trying to be rid of me."

"*I'd* like to be rid of you."

"I thought our mission was to assist Colonel Nicholls with his visit."

"It is. It's all of a piece. But if the New Haveners are protecting the regicides, they may also be conspiring with the Dutch. We'll find that out from Jones too. *If* you cease nattering."

The front door opened. Out stepped the familiar stout figure.

"Look lively," Huncks said.

Huncks led the horse down the street toward the approaching Jones.

"Oysters! Mussels! Lobsters and cod!" His neckerchief was pulled up around his face.

"You there!" Jones said. "What are you about? I'll see your license!"

"Got it right here, yer worship," Huncks said. He drew a truncheon and clubbed Jones on the back of the head, dropping him like a slab.

"Quick—into the cart."

Balty tried to lift his end of Jones. "Weighs more than a bloody horse."

"Come on, man."

Balty dropped his portion of Jones onto the street with a fleshy thud.

"Can't we tie him to the cart and drag him?"

"D'you want the whole town after us? Get his legs. One, two, three."

With Herculean grunting they got the carcass onto the cart and shoved Jones in among the ice, slime, and rotting fish. Outside the town, Huncks bound Jones's hands and feet and stuffed a gag in his mouth.

An hour later they reached a clearing in the woods north of the town.

It was dark and moonless. Getting William Jones out of the cart was easier than putting him in. He fell to the ground and moaned.

Huncks worked quickly, spread-eagling him, driving wooden stakes into the ground, tying him hand and foot. He opened Jones's waistcoat and shirt, exposing his cetacean belly and chest. He scooped the most putrefying of the fish into a bucket and dumped the rank contents onto Jones and removed his gag.

Jones sputtered and spat. He couldn't make out his captors' faces in the dark. He demanded to know the meaning of this outrage.

Balty lit a torch. Jones's eyes went wide. Huncks squatted beside him, dangling a mackerel over his face.

"A fish, for Mr. Fish."

Jones sputtered, "But you . . ."

"Died. So we did. We must be ghosts, then."

"What do you want?"

"It's not what we want. It's what *they* want. The ones out there, in the dark. The creatures. Once this fine"—Huncks sniffed and made a face—"scent reaches their nostrils, oh, they'll be hungry. There's nothing better to water their mouths than rotten fish. Eh, Mr. Fish?"

"I've got money."

"Indeed you do, sir. And a splendid house. Clever of you to marry Eaton's daughter. How many chimneys you got? Nineteen? More than the Reverend Davenport! More than enough to keep your fat carcass warm on a winter night. But on a summer night such as this? Give me the outdoors."

Huncks inhaled.

"What *is* that smell? Normally it's nice and piney. Not tonight. Imagine all those noses out there, twitching. A smell like this is a dinner bell. Who'll come to table first, I wonder? I'd wager on the catamounts. Though foxes and wolves are quick to a feast. Then there's the smaller creatures. Weasels. Raccoons. Rats. Not forgetting the creatures of the air. Hawks and vultures and such. Say, Balty?"

"Yes?"

"That chap in Greek mythology who made the gods angry and got himself chained to the rock and his liver et every day by the eagle. What was his name?"

The story sounded vaguely familiar to Balty, but he couldn't put a name to the fellow.

"Prometheus, was it?" Huncks prompted.

"That's him," Balty said. "Damned unpleasant business."

"Um. Wouldn't want *my* liver et every day. Nasty enough a thing to endure once, never mind every day for all eternity. But Mr. Fish here, being a mere mortal, he'll only have to endure it once. But then, there's lots of him to eat. Might take a while."

"What do you want?" Jones said, struggling. "I'll give you anything."

"You're accommodating tonight. Anything? Hardly know where to start. Where shall we start, Balty?"

"I should like an apology."

"Just the thing. Me, too."

"I apologize," Jones said.

"Hear that, Balty? Mr. Fish says he's sorry."

"I heard. But is he sincere?"

"I'll ask him. Sincere, Mr. Fish?"

"I swear!"

"Well, Balty? You heard the man."

"Do you know, Huncks, I think I believe him."

Huncks patted Jones's belly. "You're doing very well, Mr. Fish. Very well. Balty, what was the next thing we wanted to hear?"

"I forget."

"Me, too. Why don't we go back to town and have a nice supper. Maybe that'll help us remember."

"No! Don't leave me like this!"

"Oh, I shouldn't raise my voice like that were I you. Might attract animals."

"Don't leave me like this!"

"Hold on," Balty said. "I remember now. We were going to ask Mr. Fish the whereabouts of Whalley and Goffe."

"That's it," Huncks said. "Bravo, old cock."

Huncks said, tone earnest, "They say your father was brave at the end."

"He was."

"Terrible way to die. Not that this is much better. Tell me what I want to know, Mr. Jones."

"You wouldn't do this. I hear it in your voice."

"Then your ears do you mischief, sir. You left us to die at the hands of Quiripi. Next to that, being eaten by beasts is a mercy. Tell me what I want to know. I shan't ask again."

"They've left."

Huncks sighed. "Don't trifle with me, Jones."

"Some say the Indies."

"No, no, no. 'Some say' will not do."

"Have a heart!"

"I did, once. Come, Balty. Let us wish Mr. Jones a good evening and be on our way."

"New Amsterdam," Jones said. "They're in New Amsterdam. Under Stuyvesant's protection."

Huncks crouched again over Jones. His interrogation came rapid-fire: *When? Where in New Amsterdam? Why hasn't Stuyvesant said anything publicly? He's never been one to shy from trumpeting about protecting English fugitives. Is there a* quid pro quo? *An arrangement between the Hollanders and the New Haveners? Are Whalley and Goffe advising the Dutch on military matters? Is New Haven supplying materiel to New Amsterdam? Have any ships carrying Dutch troops put in at New Haven?* Bang, bang, bang, on and on it went.

Balty could barely keep up. It struck him that Huncks's interrogatories had less to do with regicide judges than with New Haven and Dutch alliances and New Amsterdam's defenses.

Finally, Huncks stood, satisfied with his extractions.

Balty crouched beside Jones.

"I've no questions for you, Mr. Jones. Only a word of caution. The Quaker girl, Thankful. In my capacity as his majesty's agent, I place her safety in your hands. If she's harmed—for any reason, in any way—I swear by God Almighty you'll find yourself back here in this field watching every animal in the forest gorge on your guts."

They untied him and put him on the cart horse.

"Ride north until dawn," Huncks commanded. "And quickly. Cats can outrun a horse when they're on the scent."

Jones spurred the horse to a gallop and disappeared into the night.

Balty sniffed at his sleeve. "We reek. And these woods teem with beasts. Why'd we give Jones the bloody horse?"

"Because we have these." Huncks patted the brace of pistols in his belt.

They walked through the woods to New Haven, keeping their thoughts to themselves.

"Think they'll leave her alone?" Balty asked.

"Jones seemed attentive enough when you threatened him with disemboweling."

"I care for her safety."

"Was it her safety you were seeing to when Mrs. Cobb found you both in the kitchen?"

"I was trying to talk her out of— I'm a married man, Huncks."

"Did you tell her about your wife?"

"I didn't get the chance."

Huncks snorted.

"The subject didn't come up."

"Something else came up."

"Don't be crude."

"Crudity's one of my talents. Smitten."

"I am *not smitten*."

"Course you are. Otherwise, you'd have told her about Ethel."

"Esther."

They walked on.

"Very well," Balty said. "I do have feelings for her."

"Where are these feelings located, exactly?"

"Huncks."

"You've done all you can for her. If she's bent on martyrdom, there's nothing you can do. We're not here to rescue Quaker girls. There are larger matters at stake."

They walked on, the silence interrupted by bat-squeak and the hoot of owls.

"There's one last thing we can do for her."

"All right. But then we're done here. Agreed?"

"Agreed," Balty said.

CHAPTER 25

Ghosts

The door to the Reverend Davenport's house opened. The Indian servant girl Me-Know-God stared at Balty and Huncks. She gasped and put a hand to her mouth. Her eyes rolled up into her head and she collapsed to the floor.

"Good Lord," Balty said. He bent to help her up. Huncks stopped him.

"No. Don't make it worse."

"We can't just . . ."

"Don't you see? She's Repent's sister. He told her we're dead. She's just seen two ghosts. If she comes to with you cradling her in your arms, her heart'll stop. Leave her."

Huncks and Balty stepped over the prostrate girl and proceeded into Davenport's house. They found him in his study.

The Reverend absorbed the shock of seeing them better than his servant had. An intake of breath, a patrician gasp.

"*You . . . ?*"

"In the flesh, as it were," Balty said. "Do we intrude?"

Davenport rang a small silver bell. No one came. He rang it again more forcefully.

"I'm afraid your servant girl is indisposed."

"What you done to her?" Davenport sniffed at their fishy smell and put a handkerchief to his nose.

"Fainted. She's unharmed."

Davenport stared, sapphire-blue eyes gleaming hatred.

"What do you want?"

"We've come to say goodbye," Balty said. "To thank you for your hospitality. Rest assured his majesty shall hear how graciously we were treated by his loyal subjects in New Haven."

Davenport regarded them in silence, the gifted homilist at a loss for words.

"There is one other matter. The Colonel and I have examined the Quaker girl Thankful as to the regicides Whalley and Goffe. We're satisfied that she knows nothing of them. However, as his majesty's commissioner, I reserve the right to reexamine her. To that end, I shall be returning to this . . . happy corner of New England. At which time I shall expect to find her as I left her. Which is to say, unharmed."

"Why do you tell me this?"

"Because, Reverend, you are New Haven's first citizen. Its most esteemed and beloved figure. I leave her under your protection."

"I have no authority over that woman. Nor do I want any."

"You sell yourself cheap, Reverend. But if you truly feel you lack authority . . . may I?" Balty took paper and quill from Davenport's desk, dipped the quill in ink, and began scribbling. He handed it to Davenport.

I, John Davenport, burgess and pastor of New Haven, in the colony thereof, hereby avouch that I undertake as my personal responsibility the safekeeping and welfare of the Quaker woman called Thankful, resident of New Haven, hereto sworn this 28th June, Year of Our Lord 1664.

Witnesseth Balthasar de St. Michel, His Majesty's Commissioner, and Colonel Hiram Huncks, late of the Connecticut militia. Long live Charles II, King of England.

Davenport's hand balled into a fist. He looked at Balty with contempt.

"I will not sign this," he said, flinging the piece of paper at Balty.

"You're sure?"

"Entirely."

"I had hoped to avoid unpleasantness. But as you wish. Colonel, place the Reverend under arrest."

"For what?" Davenport said.

"Contempt of the Crown."

Davenport seemed about to erupt, then cooled. He smiled. "You overplay your hand, sir. Do you propose to march me off to jail? You wouldn't get ten feet from my front door."

"No, shouldn't think so. Colonel Huncks and I would be overwhelmed by your constables and thrown into jail. Or killed.

"But what then? You don't think we came here without telling Governor Winthrop? Should we fail to report, it will not go well for you. Or New Haven."

Balty leaned over the desk and put his face in Davenport's.

"Look around you, you horrid old man. The walls of your New Jerusalem are crumbling. The city will live on. But how will the history of John Davenport end? Arrested for treason? Brought back to England in irons? Take the pen. Write your own ending."

Balty and Huncks left the house, document in hand, signed and witnessed. Me-Know-God was nowhere to be seen.

It was a still, muggy summer morning. Stepping into the street, their nostrils were assailed by the reek of spoiled fish. Jones's horse was tethered outside his house across the street, flanks slick and foamy with sweat.

- CHAPTER 26 -

June 30th. *Summoned to White Hall by my Lord Downing,
and there interrogated as to my recent visit to Chelsey. Downing
full of innuendo as to how a matter of such great secrecy
should have "walked itself" all the way to Chelsey, etc. A most
uncomfortable interview.*

*His majesty—may God keep and bless him with long life
and health—did not ask my Lord Sandwich <u>how</u> he learnt of
Nicholls's mission. But my Lord Downing left me in little doubt
as to his suspicions thereunto.*

*He bid me adieu in Dutch, causing me no small agitation of
mind. I entertained no lustful thoughts for Ludgate sluts on my
way home, being very fretful.*

*On the morrow, I examined more closely the forty pieces of gold
gifted me by Mr. Warren and was surprised to find not crowns or
sovereigns but ducats bearing the image of Ferdinand III.*

*Gold is gold whatever the specie, and am heartily glad to
have them but am left puzzled as to why Mr. Warren exprest his
gratitude to me in Dutch coinage rather than our own.*

– *CHAPTER 27* –

Vengeance Is Mine

Balty and Huncks were exhausted. They decided to stop at an inn on the King's Highway west of New Haven, at the foot of the other red cliff. Looking up at the towering wall of rock face gave Balty a frisson. It was nearly identical to its counterpart, where they'd met with great grief.

The innkeeper wrinkled his nose.

"You don't look like fishermen, but you stinks like fishermen."

Huncks was too tired to cuff the fellow for insolence. They did stink, for a fact. Five shillings bought them a hot bath in tubs out back, and their clothes washed. They ate a hearty breakfast of cheese, sausage, pickled onions, bread, and ale, and fell into sepulchral sleep. They awoke to long, blue twilight shadows outside the window.

Huncks mulled whether to proceed the twenty-five miles to Fairfield now, or to wait until morning. As a rule, he preferred to travel at night, but setting off now would mean arriving at Dr. Pell's at an indecent hour. And he and Balty were still weary, despite having slept. So it was decided to spend the night here and push on in the morning.

They sat in the tavern with mugs of ale, discussing their confrontations with Jones and Davenport. They laughed at the image of Jones lumbering in to see Davenport, furious and covered with fish slime.

What would they do?

Jones would know they were on their way to New Amsterdam. Would he send out the constables to intercept them? What would Davenport advise? If he believed Balty's threat about Winthrop poised to descend on New Haven with his Connecticut militia, he'd likely urge caution. Why risk bringing down the thunder?

"Turn the other cheek?" Balty asked.

Huncks considered. "No. It's gone too far for that."

"What, then?"

"I imagine they're discussing extrajudicial courses of action."

"You mean . . ."

"Killing us. In such a way as not to have to explain our deaths to Governor Winthrop."

"I'm a Crown commissioner. You can't just kill me. Can you?"

"Who'd know? I doubt they'd publish news of our demise in their gazette. They tried once. Or have you forgotten our night on the cliff?"

"All we did was tell them hands off Thankful."

"Yes, but Jones told us where the regicides are hiding."

"So?"

"He and Davenport might be willing to forgo the satisfaction of killing us for cheeking them. But protecting the regicides is another matter. Jones's father was a regicide. For Davenport, it's a matter of faith, isn't it? 'Hide the outcasts. Betray not him that wandereth.'"

Balty sighed. "Where does that leave us? Marked for assassination by a fanatical minister and the deputy governor of this hellish colony. And God knows what the Indian's up to at this point. Sharpening his hatchet, I should think."

"Christ," Huncks said.

"What?"

"We have to go back."

"Back? But you just said that they're—"

"Davenport's servant girl—Repent's sister. She'll have told him she saw us. I doubt he'll believe she saw ghosts. We must warn the Cobbs."

*   *   *

It was deep night by the time they reached the edge of the farm. They stopped and looked across the field at the house. No lights. They approached silently, pistols at the ready.

Huncks opened the back door. He gestured for Balty to remain. Balty's heart pounded as he listened to the creak of floorboards beneath Huncks's feet.

"Bartholomew? Amity? Micah?"

They lit the oil lamps and searched the house. Huncks cast his eyes on every surface, put his hand to the ashes in the kitchen chimney. Nothing was missing. No signs of struggle—blood, overturned furniture, smashed crockery. Huncks picked up the whisky jug from which he'd drunk a hundred times, jiggled it, and felt the heavy centrifugal swirl within. He went into the Cobbs' bedroom and emerged.

"The muskets are gone."

"Maybe they went to visit someone," Balty said.

"They're farmers. Cows and goats need milking. Pigs and chickens need to be fed. Christ, how could I have been so stupid?"

"It's not your fault, old man."

Huncks sat on a stool by the cold fireplace and put his head in his hands.

"What will they do to them?" Balty asked.

"Kill the men. Women and children they ransom. Sometimes."

"We'll find them. We'll find them and we'll ransom them."

Huncks stood and went to the front door. "Can't track in the dark. First light. I'll stand first watch."

"We'll both watch."

Stars were out, revealing the outline of the cliff.

The hours passed slowly. The eastern sky turned blue. Huncks stood and began to pace back and forth in front of the house, impatient for the sun to get on with rising. The bird-chirp began. The field turned pearly with dew. The sky lightened, blotting the lesser stars one by one, until only the brightest remained. Huncks continued pacing. Balty's gaze wandered across the field, and saw.

"*Huncks.*" He pointed.

Beside the two sham graves Bartholomew had dug weeks ago was a third one. Huncks ran to it. He fell to his knees and began to claw at the earth. Balty remained where he was, frozen.

Huncks let out an animal wail and fell forward onto the mound, moaning and clenching fistfuls of dirt, drenching the earth with tears.

Their arms and legs had been tightly bound. Their faces revealed what they'd suffered. Their mouths were full of the earth that had choked and suffocated them. Amity's face—formidable, blusterous, defiant—suggested that at the end she had drawn some strength from knowing that at least she was going to her death in the company of her two men, husband Bartholomew and son Micah.

Huncks refused to leave them where they'd died so wretchedly. He found a spot some distance from the house by the stream, a peaceful place bowered by willows. They were digging the new graves when they heard Thankful's wails.

She'd come to start the day's work. They found her, Micah clasped to her breast, rocking back and forth on her knees as she brushed dirt from his hair and face. Balty and Huncks kept their distance, leaving her to her grief, sunk anew in their own.

When she had no more tears, Thankful stood and wiped her face with her apron. She told Balty and Huncks to bring the bodies into the house so that she could attend to them. She washed them, removing every particle and speck from eyelids, ears, nostrils, determined to erase every trace of their ordeal and send them to God unsullied as the day they entered into life. She washed and combed their hair. Balty and Huncks helped get them into their Sabbath clothes and sew them into burial shrouds improvised from bed linen. Searching for these in a closet, Balty came across the three pillows he'd ruined, and wept. It was late afternoon by the time all this was finished.

They laid the bodies on a cart and pulled it, making a kind of procession, to the place by the stream. There they lowered them gently into the welcoming earth. Thankful stood between Balty and Huncks. She took each by hand. They stood in silence, the only sound the burble of water on mossy stones and the evening coo of mourning doves.

That night they sat at the kitchen table in the farmhouse, saying little. Huncks cradled the whisky jug on his lap but didn't raise it to his lips, badly wanting a drink.

"You can't stay," Balty said.

"No," she said.

"Is there somewhere you can go?"

"There's a settlement of friends in New Netherland. Vlissingen."

"I know it," Huncks said. "On the Long Island."

"If thou go to New Amsterdam to find thy judges, then take me that far, if it is not inconvenient."

Thankful stood. "I'm tired." She went into the bedroom and closed the door. Balty and Huncks listened to her sobs though the wall.

– CHAPTER 28 –

Mrs. Cobb's Flower Beds

Balty woke to the sound of hooves.

He leapt from bed. Huncks was already up, at the front door, shirtless, pistol in each hand. Four constables. They reined to a halt at the graves. One dismounted, picked up a stick, and began poking at them.

Huncks put his finger to his lips and whispered, "Get the girl."

Balty went to the bedroom and touched Thankful's shoulder. She started awake with a gasp.

"Soldiers."

Balty returned to Huncks. Huncks handed him one of the pistols.

"Go behind the house. If things happen, go. Leave the horses. Too easy to track. Stay low, make for the woods. The field where we took Jones—can you find it?"

"Past the boulder and the big dead tree?"

"Wait for me. If I'm not there by nightfall, I won't be coming. Get to Fairfield. Stay off the King's Highway. Dr. Pell will look after you. Do you have the letter?"

"Yes. I think."

"*Balty.*"

"Yes, somewhere."

"Fair*field*. Remember. Pell."

"*Yes.*"

All the constables had dismounted by now and were poking at the graves.

"What are they doing?" Balty asked.

"Looking for bodies. Unless they've come to plant potatoes."

"Why?"

"My guess is the good Reverend sent them. Doubtless leaving out mention of his Quiripi godson. Very neat."

The constables now turned their attention to the farmhouse.

"Go, now," Huncks said. "Balty?"

"Yes?"

"Take care of yourself, eh? Use the pistol if you must. Get close to your man."

Balty led Thankful out the back. They crouched and watched.

Huncks presented himself to the constables, framed in the doorway, pistol tucked into the back of his trousers.

"Morning. How may I help you gentlemen?"

The sleeve of the youngest-looking constable bore the insignia of sergeant.

"Identify yourself," he said.

"Huncks. Colonel, late of the Connecticut militia. What's your business here?"

"The law is our business."

"I see that from your uniform, sergeant. But what law in particular?"

"There's been a report of murder. Three murders."

"Grave business."

"This place yours?"

"No. Belongs to friends. I'm looking after it for them."

"Where would they be, these friends?"

"Saybrook."

"What takes them to Saybrook?"

"They've gone to fish. The shad are running."

"What are their names?"

"Cobb. Bartholomew, Amity, Micah. Husband, wife, son."

The sergeant and his men exchanged glances.

"It's them we seek."

"Who reported these murders, might I ask?"

"That's our business."

"Come, sergeant. If my friends have been murdered, surely you'd not begrudge telling me who reported it?"

"What do you know about these graves here?"

"Graves? Those are Mrs. Cobb's flower beds."

The sergeant took off his hat and wiped the sweat from his forehead. "I see no *flowers*."

"Come back in August. She likes the late bloomers. Bishop's weed, hyssop, and such. Now you mention it, I remember she said something about gathering seeds in Saybrook. Will that be all, then?"

"We need to search the house."

"For what?"

"Look here, Colonel, I'll thank you not to interfere with our business."

"I would never interfere with the law, sergeant. Show me your warrant and I'll welcome you in."

One of the men muttered contemptuously at the sergeant, "Going to let him push you around?"

The sergeant said to Huncks, "I ask you again. Step aside and let us about our business."

"I say again show me a warrant and the house is yours."

"We don't have a warrant."

"Then I respectfully suggest you go back to New Haven and obtain one from the magistrate. That's how we do it in Connecticut."

Another of the men said to the sergeant, "Get on with it. We'll be here all day."

"You try my patience, Colonel."

"Tell me what you're looking for, and I'll tell you if it's here."

Another of the men said, "Enough of this."

The sergeant said, "A Quaker woman. Name of Thankful."

"Haven't seen her."

"If you'll stand aside, we'll see for ourselves."

"Why do you seek her?"

"She's wanted for *questioning*," the sergeant said in a pleading tone.

"About what?"

"The murders. Look, I won't ask you again."

Huncks shook his head. "Not without a warrant."

One of the men raised his musket and aimed at Huncks. "Here's our warrant. Go on, lads."

The sergeant ordered the man, "Smith, lower that!"

Smith kept his musket shouldered. "Go *on*," he ordered his companions.

"Smith! I gave you an order!"

The two other constables approached Huncks. He reached behind for his pistol as he stepped aside to admit the first man. He brought the barrel down on his head, dropping him. He yanked the second constable forward by his chest strap and butted his nose with his forehead. The man staggered back, nose broken, spurting blood. Smith fired. The shot went through the constable and into Huncks's shoulder.

Huncks bounded toward Smith as he tried to reload. He swung his pistol at the side of the man's head, crushing his skull. Smith fell to the ground, dead.

The sergeant ran to his horse and was half onto the saddle when Huncks caught him and jerked him down to the ground. He straddled him with his legs, cocked the pistol, and put the muzzle to his forehead.

"Please! I've a family!"

"Who sent you? Answer, boy, or by God, I'll put a ball between your eyes."

"Jones! The Deputy Governor!"

"Where did he give you the order?"

"At his house."

"Was he alone? Answer fast, or you're dead."

"No."

"Who else?"

"The pastor. Davenport."

"What were you told?"

"That the Quaker girl, the one who's been causing all the trouble . . . she went mad and killed the family she worked for."

"What else?"

"That she buried them. In front of the house."

"Davenport's Indian, the one called Repent, with the markings on his face. Was *he* there?"

The sergeant said, "Outside. On the street."

"Get up."

The sergeant got to his feet. He was trembling. His trousers were soaked at the crotch.

"You've been deceived, sergeant," Huncks said wearily, uncocking his gun and stuffing it into his waistband. "And now two of your men are dead. You should have controlled them better. How old are you?"

"Twenty, sir."

"Sergeant, at twenty?"

"I've been constable three years."

"I didn't ask for your life history. How is it you're sergeant?"

"My father's cousin is married to the magistrate. So when Sergeant Wilcox fell ill—"

"Enough. What's your name?"

"Bartlett. Amos Bartlett."

Balty and Thankful were watching now from the front room. They couldn't hear what was being said. Seeing Huncks's shoulder drenched with blood, Thankful said, "He's wounded. We must—"

"No," Balty whispered.

Huncks went over to the graves.

"The Indian, Repent, *he* killed them. Buried them alive. Vengeance. The boy was thirteen. We found them yesterday and gave them better graves. You've been played, sergeant. What will you do now?"

"I must make a . . . report."

"To whom?"

"Captain Thripp. Chief constable. He's visiting a sick aunt in Guilford. That's why I was called . . . But it's the magistrate who decides . . ."

"Feake."

Bartlett nodded.

"Tell me, sergeant. Will justice will be done?"

"Mr. Feake is a person of integrity."

"I've witnessed his integrity. When he sentenced the Quaker girl to be flogged to death for showing her titties in church. She whom Jones and Davenport seek to hang for these murders. If you act on what I've told you, you'll be doing your future no good. But that's up to you. Come, let's get your dead and wounded into the cart."

Huncks and Bartlett put them in. Huncks hitched the dead men's horses to the cart.

"I'll say goodbye to you, sergeant. I wore a uniform at your age. I ride for Hartford."

"Why do you tell me this?"

"Because I'm hoping that's what you'll report."

Bartlett stared.

Huncks smiled. "As a professional courtesy. Soldier to soldier."

Sergeant Bartlett nodded.

Huncks and Balty and Thankful left the Cobb farm. Only Thankful looked back. If Sergeant Bartlett was true to his word, the constables wouldn't be watching the King's Highway. Still, taking no chances, Huncks led by a circuitous way: north for seven miles, then southwest along an old Indian trail through deep woods. Twenty miles later they emerged from the woods at the northern edge of Fairfield, a small, neat town whose lights were just starting to go on as they rode in, slumped forward in their saddles from weariness.

CHAPTER 29

Doctor Pell

Mrs. Pell answered the door. She stared at the three bedraggled people before her. Then, squinting at Huncks, his shirt caked stiff with blood, she said, "*Hiram!* Good Lord—come in, come in!" She shouted, "Thomas! *Thomas!*" The woman's got bellows for lungs, Balty thought.

Dr. Pell hove into view, a trim, elegant man in his early fifties with a long nose, spectacles at the end of it, lips pursed in reproof at his wife for summoning him so brusquely from his Madeira. Seeing Huncks, his eyebrows shot up.

"Hiram!" He barked at Mrs. Pell, "Why didn't you *tell* me it was him, foolish woman? Don't stand there gawking. Hot water. Get my instruments ready!"

He led Huncks into his surgery, in a building attached to the main house. Balty started at the arms and legs hanging on the walls, then saw they were prostheses. They gave the room a macabre aspect.

Pell slid his spectacles back up the bridge of his nose and examined the entry wound.

"Musket?"

Huncks nodded.

"And these?"

"Friends," Huncks said.

"Lucy!" Dr. Pell bellowed.

"What?" she shouted from another room.

"Are you seeing to the *water*?"

"What did you suppose I was doing? Needlepoint?"

"Wouldn't surprise me in the least," her husband muttered.

Mrs. Pell arrived, toting a kettle.

"What's your name, love?"

"Thankful."

"What a sweet name. I'd be thankful if you'd reach me that copper bowl there." She poured steaming water into it and went about sorting her husband's instruments.

"Do you want something for the pain?" Pell asked.

"Wouldn't refuse a brandy."

"Brandy! Quickly, woman! Stop fussing with the water. Can't you see the man's in agony?"

Balty sensed this marital *opera bouffa* between the Pells was contrived.

"*Yes.* Coming." Mrs. Pell took a bottle off a shelf, poured a large measure into a glass, and gave it to Huncks.

"Here you are, my dear. Who did this to you? Never mind. Let the butcher have at you first. If you survive his ministrations, you can tell us all about it then."

She took Thankful by the hand. "Come, love. Let's get you out of those clothes and into a hot bath." She said over her shoulder, "If Hippocrates can spare us."

"*Hippocrates* will manage," Dr. Pell said, scissoring Huncks's shirtsleeve. "As he always does."

"I see you and Lucy are as domestic as ever," Huncks said, wincing as Pell began probing the wound.

"Marry a rich widow and reap the whirlwind. Ah, *there* you are." He nudged the tip of the probe against the ball. Huncks gasped.

"What range?"

"Fifteen paces."

"Fifteen? Should've smashed right through the bone."

"Went through someone else first."

Dr. Pell chortled. "Lucky you. Unlucky him. *Lucy!* Oh, that woman."

Balty said, "Could I help?"

"That bit of wood there. Give it to Hiram."

It was indented with tooth marks. Balty handed it to Huncks. Huncks regarded it dubiously. "Who's been chewing on this?"

"If you die of infection, it won't be from that."

Huncks tossed the bite stick over his shoulder. "I'll take my chances."

Pell inserted the extractor. Huncks sucked in his breath and bared his teeth.

"Should've taken laudanum."

"I know you prefer your victims to be drugged," Huncks grunted. "So they won't realize you've no idea what you're doing. *Jesus Christ!*"

Pell pushed the extractor deeper.

"I prefer my victims, as you call them, drugged so that I don't have to listen to them whinge. Steady."

He withdrew the musket ball and held it up to the candlelight, then dropped it into a metal pan with a *plunk*. "Laudanum has the added virtue of rendering my victims pliant when I present my bill."

He poured brandy into the wound, which made Huncks hiss, then smeared ointment on it and bandaged the shoulder.

"You've lost a lot of blood. You'll need to stay off your feet a few days. Eat plenty of red meat."

Balty groaned.

"How about a proper drink?" Huncks said.

"Indeed," said Dr. Pell. He turned to Balty. "We've not been introduced."

"Balthasar de St. Michel."

Dr. Pell looked amused. "Well, there's a name. *Vous parlez français?*"

"*Bien sûr. Depuis enfant. Mon père était en service au roi Henri Quatre. Et après, au roi Louis Treize.*" Of course. Since I was a child. My father was in service to King Henri IV. After, to King Louis XIII.

Pell's eyes widened. "Bless me. *De mon part, quand j'était jeune homme, j'était en service au roi Anglais Charles le Premier. Comme gentilhomme du cabinet. A ce temps, j'ai poursuivi une dame d'honneur dans la cour de sa reine française, Marie-Henriette. Une dame vraiment ravissante. Malheureusement, il a fini mal quand . . .*" Myself, as a young man, I was in service to the English king Charles I. As a gentleman of the chamber. I conducted an affair with a lady-in-waiting to his French queen, Marie-Henriette. A ravishing girl! Alas, it ended badly when . . .

Huncks groaned. "If you two are going to croak at each other like frogs on a lily pad, I will need laudanum."

"Hiram, you bring me a *chevalier.*"

"Is that what he is?"

"Clearly, we have much to discuss. Much!"

Which they did, over a restorative dinner of lobsters and oysters and commendable wine. Out of respect for Thankful, Huncks didn't tell the Pells her story but confined his narrative to the hunt for the regicide judges: the events at the cliff, their rescue by Bartholomew but not the rest. The Pells listened, rapt. They knew the terrain and the players well.

After Pell was forced to leave the court of Charles I as a result of his unwise pursuit of one of Queen Marie-Henrietta's ladies-in-waiting, he went off to campaign in the Netherlands during what was now being called the Thirty Years War. It was the fashion at the time among young men of good birth. Pell served under Baron Vere of Tilbury and was present at the siege and capture of Bois-le-Duc.

In 1635, after surgical training, he enlisted for service in New England, at Fort Saybrook, as lieutenant and surgeon. He was at nearby Fort Mystick in 1637 for the final engagement of the Pequot War, when Captains Mason and Underhill surrounded the Pequot village there and killed seven hundred Pequot men, women, and children with musket, sword, and fire.

Underhill denounced Pell for lingering aboard ship before coming ashore to see to the wounded. Pell countered that this was unfair. He'd waited to debark until the beach was secured and then did everything he could. Even now, almost thirty years on, he still had nightmares of the carnage, the piles of amputated limbs, the stench of hundreds of Indians broiled to death.

He left military service and migrated down the Connecticut coast, settling in the new colony at New Haven founded by Eaton and Davenport. He made a good living as a surgeon, but his irrepressible cheer and ardent royalism set him apart from the dour saints. He in turn grew to despair of their long, drawn faces and implacable grimness. In all his years there, he said, he could count on a single hand the number of times he had heard laughter. He scoffed at their credo that the New England Indians were the remnant of the Lost Tribe of Israel. This tenet was central to Puritan cosmology, for if the Indians themselves were descendants of immigrants, then the English were merely more recent immigrants, with equal—if not superior—rights to the land. Pell held in equal contempt the other Puritan belief that God had sent a plague to clear the land for English settlement. These contrarian views did not endear him to the New Haveners. He and Davenport finally fell out in 1650 when Pell refused to take an oath of loyalty to Oliver Cromwell. His already strained relations with the saints were exacerbated when he married Lucy Brewster, a formidable, peppery-tongued widow of a wealthy merchant. Lucy despised Puritans and defiantly refused to pay New Haven death taxes on her deceased husband.

"Good, my hen," Pell applauded. "Spend it on me, not the saints!" Iron willed and unyielding, they fought constantly and adored each other.

They left New Haven without regret and moved twenty miles down the coast, settling in the place named for its fair field. Pell had first been here during the Pequot War, accompanying Underhill's men as they ran fleeing Pequots to earth. Few of that tribe remained now. Those captured were put in chains and shipped to Barbadoes as plantation slaves. Sachem's Head, a promontory on the shore, was named for a Pequot chieftain killed and decapitated there, his head mounted in a tree.

Financed by Lucy's widow money, Pell prospered, not from doctoring but land speculation. He purchased the fifty thousand problem-
atic acres between Connecticut and New Netherland from Wampage,
chieftain of the Siwanoy. The land became known as No-Man's-Land.
The label amused Pell, who took to calling himself "Dr. No Man."

But it was a buyer's market. Between murderous Indians and skir-
mishing Dutch and English, the marsh and woodland weren't especially congenial to settlement. The Restoration, along with increased
religious tolerance in England, had curtailed emigration. As one pamphlet noted sardonically, "New England is Old Newes, and Old England New Newes."

Rumor was, Dr. Pell's real purpose in buying the land from Wampage was to provoke the war between England and Holland that everyone knew must come sooner or later. This in turn fueled speculation
that Pell, a conspicuous royalist for having served in the household of
the present king's father, was an agent of the Crown. His private militia,
headquartered on City Island, enjoyed a robust enrollment. It was well
armed, trained regularly, and maintained a vigilant patrol of Pell's acres.

Thankful, grieving over the Cobbs, barely spoke a word at dinner.
Mrs. Pell noticed her distress and fussed over her like a mother, gently
scolding, urging her to eat for strength and asking questions to draw
her away from the increasingly loud, wine-fueled talk among the men
about the regicide judges.

When Balty described Dr. DeVrootje, the Dutch surgeon of Milford, Pell let out a groan and declared that DeVrootje was the worst
bandit in all New England and, into the bargain, incompetent—like
all Dutch surgeons, he added, who knew nothing of medicine other
than how to cut off limbs, along with their owners' purse strings.

Balty told about DeVrootje's odd prescription of clam chowder.
But instead of letting loose a fresh torrent of ridicule, Pell fell silent.
He sat pensively, then said that this in fact was *his* experience, too.
Shore dwellers seemed to recover from what he called "traumatic pa-
ralysis" at a greater rate than inlanders.

Pell shrugged off his epiphany and poured another round of wine, eager to resume the evening's conviviality and disparagement of Dutch surgeons.

How much did DeVrootje charge? A half sovereign? Larcenous! Did Balty and Huncks know *why* Dutch doctors charged so much? he asked. They're saving money to buy tulip bulbs. Bulbs! One bulb—one single bulb—had sold in Amsterdam for 4,200 florins—the price of a fine house. Tipsy now, Pell muttered that perhaps God should send a plague to cause a "Great Dying" of *Dutch* in the New World.

This brought a sharp rebuke from Mrs. Pell, who pointed out that the Dutch tulip craze had ended years ago—about the time, she said acidulously, "that you and Underhill were causing a 'Great Dying' of natives."

Pell fell into a sulk.

"Come, pet," Mrs. Pell said, taking Thankful by the hand and tugging her off into the kitchen. "There's no conversation fit for listening at *this* table."

Alone with Balty and Huncks, Pell said, "Tell me the rest of it."

Balty told of Repent's murder of Thankful's husband, her attempt to get justice, her naked protest, and flogging. Huncks told what befell the Cobbs and the constables sent by Jones and Davenport to arrest Thankful for Repent's crime.

Pell listened without expression. Balty thought him indifferent. Perhaps he'd witnessed too much cruelty and misery here himself. Then he saw the tear leak from his eye, which Pell brushed away with annoyance, as he might a mosquito, and poured another round.

- CHAPTER 30 -

Underhill Is Critical

Next morning Balty awoke with a throbbing head and gummy eyes. Huncks's bed was empty. Balty shuffled into the kitchen and found Mrs. Pell rolling pastry.

"Where is everyone?"

"Thankful's in the garden. The others are in the surgery. And how are *we* feeling this morning, Mr. Balty?"

"Bit baggy, actually."

Mrs. Pell wiped her hands on her apron. She went to a cupboard, took down a small bottle, and poured some dreadful-looking thick, dark liquid into a small glass and gave it to him. "Drink it all down in one gulp."

Balty stared at it. "Does it contain gunpowder?"

"Gunpowder? I should say not. Go on. It won't kill you. Hippocrates and Hiram have already had theirs."

Balty closed his eyes, uttered a quick prayer, and tossed it back. It was tarry and vile. Indeed, he had never tasted anything so tarry and vile. His esophagus constricted like a boa. He gasped and squeaked, thinking he might suffocate. Then the boa unconstricted and he could breathe and suddenly all was well. Quite well, considering.

"I won't ask what's in it," he said, handing her back the glass.

"No, don't." She went back to her pastry. Not looking up, she said, "She told me everything."

"I rather hoped she would."

"I don't like to think evil thoughts, Mr. Balty. Evil makes evil. But I'll say, with God listening: if the earth opened and swallowed all New Haven and all its saints, I wouldn't cheer, but neither would I weep."

She stopped rolling and tucked an errant lock of hair back into her cap. "She's a darling. She can stay here as long she wants. And if Jones or the Reverend Davenport's Indian godson comes looking for her, I'll shoot them myself."

"They think we've gone to Hartford."

"Then I've half a mind to go to *Hartford* and shoot them there. And don't think I wouldn't." She had the rolling pin by the handle, shaking it like a club. She went back to her rolling. "Go on. They're in the surgery."

Balty went to the door.

"Mr. Balty?"

"Yes, Mrs. Pell?"

"What you and Hiram done for her. It was good of you."

"Well . . ."

"She's sweet on you."

"Oh?"

"Come, Mr. Balty." Mrs. Pell laughed. "Surely you can do better than 'Oh?' "

"She is . . . a fine person."

Mrs. Pell shook her head. "You can't be half French."

"I only meant . . ."

"Do you love her or not?"

"Mrs. Pell. Really. This is most awkward."

"Life's short, Mr. Balty. Why waste time? You can stay here with her, if you like."

"Colonel Huncks and I have pressing business in New Amsterdam. Which I really must discuss with him. If you'll excuse me."

"Then come back after you're done *pressing* in New Amsterdam."

Balty made his way to Pell's surgery through a passageway between the buildings. There was a window. He saw Thankful outside, in Mrs. Pell's flower garden. He paused, watching. The sunlight made her hair radiantly golden. She was examining flowers, sniffing them. Balty reflected it was the first time, since he'd seen her that day in church, that he'd seen her at peace—not defying a courtroom of furious Puritans, or lurking in fear of the Indian who'd murdered her husband and violated her, or tending to wounded Huncks, or weeping at graves, or preparing the bodies of loved ones for burial, or hiding from constables.

He watched. The scene was of such loveliness and placidity it might be a rendering of Eden, divinely ordained. Any minute now, a lion and lamb would appear and lie down together. Vines would sprout from the earth and climb Thankful's legs, entwining. A pair of doves would alight, one on each shoulder, and coo. Balty sighed and leaned against the wall. He felt light-headed.

Voices from the surgery on the other side of the door jerked him back into the present. He paused to compose himself, hand on the doorknob. From the other side he heard Huncks, emphatic: "No. Underhill is critical. *Critical.*"

Balty opened the door.

"Am I interrupting?"

"Ah, you're alive," Huncks said.

"Barely. What's going on?"

"Dr. Pell and I were just . . . discussing."

"I heard. Why is Captain Underhill critical? Will we be slaughtering an Indian tribe?"

"You misheard," Huncks said. "Underhill is critical. Of Stuyvesant."

"Oh? Why?"

"He disapproves of his administration of New Netherland."

"I see that I *did* interrupt," Balty said huffily. "So why don't I just bugger off and leave you two to discuss Captain Underhill's *critique* of Dutch administration? God forbid you should share confidential matters with the King's own commissioner. I'd only blurt it out to everyone at the nearest tavern. Indeed, I think I shall repair to a tavern. Tell me, Doctor, does Fair-*field* possess such an establishment?"

"If it's drink you're wanting, you're more than welcome to my cellar, Monsieur Balty."

"*Trop gentil. Mais ce n'est pas une question de boire, mais de compaignie.*" You are too kind. It's not a question of drinking, but the company. "Never mind, I shall find it myself. Good day, gentlemen. I leave you to your *hatchings.*"

Balty left by the door onto the main street, the King's Highway, giving it a good slam behind him. He looked up and down the street.

Fairfield wasn't very big. He walked toward what seemed to be the center of town and indeed, a block later, arrived at it. The village green was bisected by the King's Highway. Here were the four pillars of a New England village: courthouse, schoolhouse, meetinghouse, and whipping post. Where was the fifth—the tavern?

A passing Fairfielder informed Balty that the public house was on Concord Street, by Burial Hill, adding that it was closed, the hour being somewhat early for spirituous refreshment. Balty plunked himself down on a bench by the whipping post. Thoughtful of Fairfield to provide seats for the entertainment.

He pondered, stewing: Why did Huncks persist in being so damned secretive? Hadn't he demonstrated his mettle? It was insulting. But at least it had taken his mind off Thankful. Thankful. He thought of her, standing there amidst the flowers, looking so . . .

Balty rebuked himself. He must write a letter to Esther. Yes. Telling her . . . well, something. How much he missed her. How much he loved her. He would certainly write perfidious Brother Sam and give him a large piece of his mind. He'd write *that* letter first.

How should he begin it? *My very dear Brother Sam.*

No.

Pepys, you treacherous ———.

He went on, mentally composing his *J'accuse* as the traffic came and went. Rather busy, the road. But it was the King's Highway, connecting Boston and New Amsterdam; England and Holland.

In the distance, on the eastern edge of town, Balty spotted a pair of riders approaching. His gaze settled on them as he went on composing his letter to Brother Sam, enumerating the countless in-dignities he had condemned him to in this awful land.

The two riders drew closer.

Balty leapt from the bench and ran to a nearby alley between two houses. He poked his head out from behind the corner and peered.

Repent and Jones dismounted by the pond on the green and stood while their horses watered.

Balty's heart pounded. He reached for his absent pistol.

Presently, Repent and Jones remounted and continued west on the highway through the town. Balty followed at a distance, leaping like an ungainly frog from house to house and tree to tree. At the western edge of town he ran out of things to hide behind as they continued out of sight. He ran to Dr. Pell's and breathlessly told what he'd seen.

"Balty," Huncks said, "we have more urgent business."

"But they'll lead us to the regicides."

"The regicides are not the mission. Nicholls is."

Balty threw up his hands. "What, making sure some colonel gets a nice welcome from Old Dildo? How's *that* more important than settling up with him who buried the Cobbs alive? Or have you already forgotten about them?"

Huncks's eyes narrowed.

Pell spoke up. "For God's sake, Hiram, *tell* him."

"Nicholls isn't paying a courtesy call on Stuyvesant. He's seizing his colony."

Balty stared. "Oh."

"Yes, 'Oh.' And try to keep it to yourself when they pull out your fingernails."

− CHAPTER 31 −

August 2nd. Grievous days.

Returning to my house after dining on a veal choppe with my brother at the Black Spread Eagle in Bride Lane, found two men of coarse aspect awaiting.

One identified himself as Mr. Whelk, saying he was on "business pertaining to his majesty's exchequer" and I must show him where I kept my money box.

I replied hotly that this was d——d irregular, cheek of the highest sort, and under no circumstances would I shew him where I kept my house money. And begone.

He said in that case they must make a search of the house.

I demanded by what presumed authority he should accost me, Clerk of the Acts of the Navy. Whereat he waved at me a document purporting to authorize the search "of such places as are of interest to his majesty."

I told him this would not do at all. Moreover, that I took grave exception to being harassed so bumptiously in my own home.

Upon which he said to his fellow ruffian, "Place Mr. Pipes under arrest that I may conduct our business." Whereat his fellow caitiff produced hand shackles and made as if to put me into irons.

Perceiving that further protest would bring only diminishing returns, I yielded, saying, "If you would only tell me _what_ you seek, I will tell you if I have it."

But no, this would not do. They must needs _see_ my money box.

In greatest agitation, and now suspecting they were enterprizing varlets come to rob me, I shewed them, expecting to be clubbed or have my throat slit.

Whelk reached in and raked up the topmost layer of coins. He held one gold piece to the light, examining it, asking how was it I should be in possession of Dutch specie.

Not desiring to explain the provenance of the ducat he beheld—or its thirty-nine brethren ducats in my money box— namely, that they were a gift from one of the Navy's timber suppliers—I temporized, saying it amused me to keep coins from various countries, as curio items. And such.

This did not satisfy Whelk. Stroking his chin like a schoolmaster prior to wielding the cane, he said I must needs now accompany him and "explain the matter more fully in a less congenial setting."

I riposted, "Explain what? To whom? And in what less congenial setting, pray?" To which he replied, "As to the first, possessing a quantity of enemy coinage. As to the second, Lord Downing. As to the third, the Tower, which as it happens is convenient, being not more than one furlong from here."

At this, an evil feeling overcame me and I was violently ill upon the persons of Whelk and his manacle bearer, which did nothing to improve their temper.

– CHAPTER 32 –

The Belt

Dr. Pell arranged for a shallop to take Balty, Huncks, and Thankful to Oyster Bay, where they would rendezvous with Captain Underhill.

Underhill, Pell told them, had recently married a Quaker woman. She would see that Thankful got settled among the Quakers of Vlissingen—Flushing, as the English called it. Stuyvesant had tried to ban the Quakers there from holding meetings. They sent a petition—now known as the Flushing Remonstrance—to Stuyvesant's superiors at the Dutch West India Company. Amsterdam overruled Stuyvesant, much consternating him.

Pell was greatly amused at the rumor that Underhill himself had converted to Quakerism.

"The hero of Fort Mystick and Pound Ridge—a *Quaker!*" he chortled. "New England'll do queer things to a man, and that's no lie."

He warned them it was far from certain Underhill would lend his support to Nicholls's seizure of New Netherland. The old warrior was sixty-seven now. The "Cincinnatus of Long Island" had laid down his musket and taken up the plow (Tobacco). Age, farming, and Quakerism mellow a warrior.

On the other hand, Pell said, Underhill loathed the Dutch and "Old Petrus"—Stuyvesant—in particular. Underhill knew him well, having lived in New Netherland for years. Underhill had been sheriff of Flushing. But in 1653, he broke with Stuyvesant over his autocratic ways, denouncing him as a "tyrant." That earned him a spell in Stuyvesant's jail. A year later, at the end of the Anglo-Dutch War, Underhill moved away to the edge of New Netherland, to put distance between himself and his nemesis.

Like most New England eminentoes, Underhill was born in England, in Warwickshire. His grandfather Thomas was Keeper of the Wardrobe for Queen Elizabeth's favorite, Robert Dudley, First Earl of Leicester. Dudley was imprisoned in the Tower of London over the plot to install Lady Jane Grey on the throne. He was eventually released, unlike his less fortunate brother Guildford, Lady Jane's husband. A half century later, the Underhill family got itself mucked up in another plot, this one the Earl of Essex's attempt to dethrone Queen Elizabeth. The Underhills fled to the Netherlands.

The future Captain Underhill was then four. He grew up among the Dutch, married a Dutch girl, had a Dutch son, then emigrated to New England aboard *Arabella*, flagship of John Winthrop, founder of the "city upon a hill," the Massachusetts Bay Colony. Underhill became a soldier and Indian fighter in the Bay Colony militia, rising to rank of captain. The Bay Colony elders dispatched him to Salem to arrest Roger Williams for promulgating his heretical view that the English should pay Indians for land rather than seize it. So began his disenchantment with Puritan theocracy.

Two years later, he got himself banished from the Bay Colony for anticonformism, along with his friend Anne Hutchinson. He became a soldier for hire, privateer, sheriff, and general dissenter. Along the way, he forged a bond with Winthrop the Younger, Governor of the Connecticut Colony, providing him with intelligence on Dutch schemes to foment Indian trouble in English territories.

Following the massacre of Anne Hutchinson and her family on what was now Dr. Pell's land, Underhill played a role in the ensuing Indian war. Receiving a report that a large number of Siwanoy and

Wappinger were encamped at Pound Ridge, Underhill marched his men from Stamford through a bitter winter night. They surprised the Indians and encircled their palisaded village and put it to the torch. Those who tried to flee were shot down. The Indians resigned themselves to the fire, man, woman, and child dying in silence. Veterans of Pound Ridge, whose butcher bill of seven hundred was eerily identical to that at Fort Mystick, were haunted to the end of their lives by the memory of that terrible silence, the only sound the crackle of flames and hiss of melting snow.

Now, in the winter of his life, Underhill distrusted and deplored all authority, Dutch and Puritan. Planting himself in Oyster Bay on the Long Island put water between him and Stuyvesant, and between him and the Puritans. He was moated, finally at peace.

Dr. Pell said the best hope of getting Underhill to join the fight would be simultaneously to play on his loathing of the Dutch *and* Puritans: losing New Netherland would stick it to the Dutch, while Puritan New Englanders would shudder at the brazen action by the new English king they despised. What might he do to *them*? If Charles II would seize New Netherlands, what would he do to his own functioning colonists? Dr. Pell chortled. *That* would that put a chill into their already cold spines!

Balty stood on the Fairfield wharf, forlornly regarding the shallop. It resembled a bobbing coffin. The prospect of another sea voyage—and this across a body of water called the Devil's Belt—made his innards wormy. Thankful, ever attentive, tried to jolly him. What could be more invigorating than a brisk sail on a moonlit night?

He was having none of it. Brisk their journey would certainly be, for the wind was increasing to a howl. The shallop's halyards and stays slapped against the mast. The wind was northwesterly, which— apparently—would make for a good "reach" southwest across the Belt to Oyster Bay, a "mere" (as Thankful cheerily put it) thirty miles. God willing, she said, they should fetch their destination at first light, "with a pretty dawn at our backs." Balty was having none of that, either. An invocation of "God willing" invariably prefigured disaster. Thankful told him to hush and bundled him into the boat.

Dr. and Mrs. Pell were there to see them off. Pell gave Huncks a letter for Underhill sealed with his signet, whose emblem was a pelican. He hadn't seen Underhill since Fort Mystick, over a quarter century ago. Bygones *should* be bygones. There were bigger matters at stake than holding an ancient grudge. That said, Pell warned, Underhill was a stubborn old bastard.

"You'll have no trouble finding him," he said as the shallop's skipper cast off lines. "His is the largest estate on the Long Island. Named Kenilworth. Or Killingworth. Worth *killing* for! Ha!"

As the boat pulled away from the dock, sails snapping full with wind, the doctor shouted, "It's a clever man who weds a rich widow!"

Mrs. Pell boxed her husband's ear. Then, arm in arm, they waved as the boat sailed into the gusty night.

The skipper was an incessant talker who delighted in regaling his passengers with lurid accounts of terrible wrecks along the Belt. Another favorite theme was harrowing accounts of painted savages paddling long wooden war boats called *canows* carved from tree trunks.

"You're not wanting to see one of *them* coming up on yer arse, let me tell you. Oh, no!"

Woozy, Balty nestled his head on Thankful's lap and murmured, "Offer him money to stop talking."

Huncks enjoyed the old salt's palaver and stoked the conversation with his own memories of the diabolical Belt. The two prattled happily away, exchanging stories of skirmishes with Indians along the shore and of people being eaten by large fishes with triangular fins that cut the surface like axes. Balty groaned and nuzzled on Thankful's lap. She giggled and cupped her hands over his ears to spare him the more gruesome snatches.

The wind increased. The shallop bucked, waves slapping against the sides and slurping over the gunwales. Thankful recited from memory the Gospel story of Jesus calming the storm on the Sea of Galilee as his disciples huddled, whimpering, in the lees.

Irritated at being compared to timorous Judean fishermen, Balty moaned, "Why don't you ask Jesus to calm *this* bloody sea?"

Thankful shook her head. "I thought thee fearful. But now I see thou *are* brave."

"Brave? How?"

"To blaspheme on such a sea as this. No timid soul would tempt our Lord so to sink his vessel."

Balty groaned and closed his eyes, and burrowed deeper into Thankful's lap. It was the loveliest pillow he'd ever had. He opened his eyes and looked up. She was looking down at him a certain way. She bent closer. Their lips came together. For a moment the wind ceased to roar in Balty's ears and his stomach calmed. Indeed, the boat itself seemed to hover, still, above the menacing waves. Then came a tremendous bang and shudder as a cataract of seawater roared over the side, drenching them to the skin. They sputtered and coughed. Huncks and Thankful and the skipper roared. Without understanding why, Balty found himself laughing.

Huncks rummaged in a bag and produced a bottle of Barbadoes rum and passed it around.

The skipper pointed to a low, white spit of sand on the Long Island shore.

"Eaton's Neck. Good harbor in a nor'easter. Belonged to Eaton, him who founded New Haven, with the minister, Davenport. Bought it from the local savages, Matinnecocks." He took another long pull on the rum bottle. "He sold it to his son-in-law, Jones, under-governor of New Haven. Then Jones, he sold it to Cap'n Seeley. That is, Cap'n Seeley *thinks* he owns it." He laughed. "The Matinnecocks sell the same land to different folks. Keeps the courts busy!"

They dropped anchor in Oyster Bay at first light. As Thankful had also predicted, the dawn at their backs was pretty.

– *CHAPTER 33* –

The Cincinnatus
of Long Island

They found Killingworth without difficulty: a fine, bustling manse on a hundred acres of good farmland looking out over Oyster Bay and the diabolical Belt. After an introductory volley of *thees* and *thous*, Mrs. Underhill whisked her fellow Quaker Thankful off to get dry clothes, leaving the men in the forecourt.

Captain Underhill, the "Cincinnatus of Long Island," was dressed for farming, but even in this attire and old age he cut an imposing, even dashing figure. He was tall, with lively eyes, neatly trimmed mustache, and small triangle of beard under the lip. His posture was military: erect and commanding. Balty could imagine him standing at the head of a troop, sword drawn, ordering cannonades amid explosions of smoke.

At the moment, however, Captain Underhill was staring with distaste at the unsealed letter from Pell, as if Huncks had just handed him a turd.

"*Pell* sent you?"

Balty, exhilarated at no longer being in a boat, chirruped enthusiastically, "If I may, Captain, *I* am sent by his most gracious majesty, Charles, King of England, Ireland, and . . . and . . ." Balty's wave-pummeled brain went blank on whatever it was his most gracious majesty was also king of.

Underhill and Huncks stared. Finally it came to Balty: "Scotland. Allow me to present my . . ."

Balty rummaged in his satchel for his commission. He couldn't find it. He began tossing various items to the ground.

"Bear with me. I have it . . . here . . . somewhere . . ."

In frustration, he turned the satchel upside down, emptying its contents at the Captain's feet.

"Ah—*here.*"

Balty retrieved his damp commission, unrolled it, cleared his throat, and began to read from it aloud, in the stentorian tone of the Lord Chamberlain announcing the opening of Parliament.

By now the Cincinnatus of Long Island had concluded that he was in the company of either a lunatic or an imbecile and anyway had no interest in his visitor's credentials. He conversed with Huncks. The two began to stroll toward the house, leaving Balty unaware, declaiming his commission to geese and piglets. Looking up from the scroll and finding that his audience was avian and porcine, Balty refurled his commission and scurried after them.

Captain Underhill knew the reputation of Hiram Huncks, late colonel in the Connecticut Colony militia, boon companion to his own great friend Winthrop. He and Huncks spoke in the language of soldiers. Huncks discreetly persuaded Cincinnatus that Mr. de St. Michel was not the flibbertigibbet he seemed, but, like the fool of the proverb, was adept at the art of concealing his skill behind a mask of imbecility. Captain Underhill accepted Huncks's representation, and the three proceeded into his study, where the Captain poured glasses of Madeira, a furtive pleasure in the Quaker Underhill household.

"In my youth, I hid from Queen Elizabeth," he said. "In old age, I hide from Wife Elizabeth. To your health, gentlemen. You are welcome at Killingworth."

Underhill's conversion to his wife's Quakerism had apparently not yet extended to abstinence from beverages improved by fermentation. Nor, he said, did he incline at his age to reform his pronouns, pausing in every midsentence to substitute *thou* and *thee* and *thine* for *you* and *yours*.

"Even if," he said, "this was how our Lord spake whilst he was on earth."

He poured a second round and told his visitors that despite the inconveniences and its absurd-sounding name, "this Quaker business" was rather agreeable.

"Harmless, anyway, which is a damn sight more than can be said for the *other* religions. Who wants to sit in a frigid worship house while some ass prattles on about the fires of Hell, or Deuteronomy, or the multiplication of the bloody loaves and fishes?" (The Captain's vocabulary bespoke his years in the barracks.) "If a Quaker wants to commune with the Almighty or whoever the hell's up there, he just plops his arse down wherever he is and closes his eyes and *communes*. And if the Almighty ain't in the mood for communing, you get a fine snooze. Tell me if *that* ain't an improvement on Sunday worship."

This called for a third glass of Madeira. Huncks steered the conversation to his subject—gingerly, since it was one to give pause to even the most *laissez-faire* practitioner of Quakerism. Namely, war.

He presented the situation crisply and concisely, as if briefing a senior officer: Colonel Nicholls's squadron of four ships would be entering New Netherland's waters any day now, under the guise of paying a courtesy visit. Its actual purpose was to seize New Amsterdam and New Netherland in the name of the King.

Dr. Pell would render support with his militia. Winthrop was standing by with his. Would the Cincinnatus of Long Island join in the fight?

Huncks laid it on thick as clotted cream: Would the *legendary* Captain John Underhill, hero of Fort Mystick and Pound Ridge, the most renowned fighter in New England, lend his name, his prestige—and his devoted followers—to King Charles's great endeavor?

Underhill began to chuckle.

Odd response, Balty thought. Weren't soldiers—even old ones—always champing at the bit to grab their muskets and strap on the armor?

"Once more onto the beach, eh?" Underhill said, pouring another round.

"Beg pardon?" Balty said.

"Don't you know your Shakespeare?"

"Ah. Isn't it 'Once more *unto* the *breach*'?"

Underhill shook his head. "I see you do *not* know your Shakespeare, sir. Henry the Fifth, on the eve of Agincourt. The English outnumbered by the French ten to one. *Twenty* to one. Then victory, snatched from the jaws of defeat! By English longbowmen. *There* was a battle. *There* was a fight!"

The old man's eyes were aglow with martial fever.

Underhill continued in a melancholy tone, "Different kind of fighting here. Skulkers, the savages. Can't blame the beggars, really, lacking guns and armor. Tell you one thing—their bows are no match for English longbows cut from yew. Still, effective enough. Always popping out from behind a tree or rock. *Ssssupp . . . Ssssup . . . Ssssup . . .*"

Balty, having himself experienced the sound of arrows, was tempted to remark that Quiripi arrows made more of a *swish* sound. Wisely, he didn't.

Underhill turned to Huncks. "Familiar with my pamphlet on Fort Mystick, Colonel?"

Huncks recited from memory: "'We had sufficient light from the Word of God for our proceedings.'"

Underhill smiled, pleased by this recital of his claim of divine justification for slaughtering seven hundred Pequots.

"Would you like to have a copy?" the old man asked.

"I should be honored, Captain."

Underhill rose, a bit wobbly, went to a shelf, and pulled one out. Its cover proclaimed:

NEVVES FROM

AMERICA;

OR,

A NEW AND EXPERIMENTALL

DISCOVERIE OF

NEW ENGLAND;

CONTAINING,

A TRVE RELATION OF THEIR

War-like proceedings the*fe* two yeares la*f*t
pa*f*t, with a Figure of the Indian Fort,
or Palizado.
By Captaine IOHN UNDERHILL, a Commander
in the Warres there.

"It was well received, you know," Underhill said. "Very well. Numerous printings. All sold out."

Underhill sat at his desk, dipped his quill, and scribbled an inscription for Huncks, who seized on the moment to remark that it would lend Colonel Nicholls's assault on New Netherland great luster to have the support of the Hero of Fort Mystick.

Underhill grunted.

"Tempting, having a go at Old Petrus. Pompous old ass. Still, formidable. No lack of grit there. I wonder, will his people fight for him? They don't like him. Nobody does. Could go either way. Tell you this—Stuyvesant'll never surrender. Even if it means defending the damned place by himself. If his men do stand with him, it'll be a fight to the end. A bitter end. He'll bring it all down around him."

"Are you with us, Captain?" Huncks pressed.

"Certainly not." Underhill poured another round.

"Why?"

"What do you think of this Madeira?"

"It's very good. Excellent."

"Winthrop sent me a few casks, from Hartford. Damned thoughtful."

"A token of his esteem."

"So," Underhill said, "*Pell* has signed on for this, eh? No surprise. He wants that tract of land he bought from Wampage under an English flag. Never search for noble motives where *Pell* is concerned."

"Is that why you won't join?" Huncks asked.

"Not at all. How is Winthrop? Haven't seen him in over a year."

"He's well."

Underhill smiled wryly. "Do you think me a coward, Colonel? An old, soft man?"

"Certainly not, sir."

"My Quakerism may strike you as lacking in rigor. But I assure you, my wife's is very strict. I've stomach enough for war with Holland. Not for one with *her*. Speaking of my beloved, let's have one more glass before we join the ladies."

Huncks looked at Balty and shrugged. The Cincinnatus of Long Island could not be budged.

"Why you hate Dr. Pell?" Balty asked. "Won't you even open his letter to you?"

"I would open it, sir, only to wipe my arse with it."

"Pity. He wrote it on his very best paper."

Underhill seemed amused. "Who *are* you, sir?"

"Balthasar de St. Michel, at your service."

"That's a frilly name. *Are* you French?"

"Half. But no—English. Every inch. And the King's good servant. As we are all, here."

"We are in New Netherland here, sir."

"For the time being."

"How do you mean?"

"When Colonel Nicholls accomplishes his mission—even if he must without the support of the legendary Captain Underhill—where we sit will *become* England."

Underhill shrugged. "I've lived under more flags than I can count."

"Why do you so disesteem Pell? Because of Fort Mystick? Surely that was many years ago."

A flash of steel came into Underhill's eyes. "Anne Hutchinson was the best woman I have ever known."

"Yes," Balty said. "I hear she was . . . marvelous."

"Pell transacted business with her murderer."

"I gather buying land from the Indians is rather tricky. On our way here, the boat person explained how the Mannie-tockies or whatever they're called sell the same parcel of land to different buyers."

"I was called on to avenge Anne's death."

"Yes, I hear that was a great success. Pound Ridge?"

Underhill stared into the distance.

Balty soldiered on. "Dr. Pell himself speaks admiringly of how you—"

Huncks nudged Balty. *Stop talking.*

Underhill seemed to have gone into a trance. Either that, or was drunk—a distinct possibility, the Madeira being Winthrop's.

"Captain?" Balty asked.

"Mm? Where were we?"

"There was one other matter we rather hoped you might be able to help us with . . ."

Next morning, Mrs. Underhill gave them a fine breakfast. Before they tucked into it, she asked Balty and Huncks to join her in a Quaker moment of silence. Balty and Huncks stood awkwardly, hats in hand, staring at the ground. The Cincinnatus of Long Island was still abed, nursing "a cold" that had come over him the day before. Thankful stood off at a distance beneath a large chestnut tree.

Soon the horses were saddled. Time to go. Mrs. Underhill hugged Balty and Huncks and told them to take care in New Amsterdam, whatever their business there was. Evidently, Thankful hadn't told her about the regicide hunt. She said not to worry about Thankful. She could remain at Killingworth for her *accouchement*. After that, she'd see to it that she and her child found a good home in Vlissingen among the Friends there.

Balty and Huncks stared. *Accouchement? Child?*

Balty walked through the field to where Thankful stood under the large tree. Huncks kept back.

"Another pretty dawn," he said.

"Yes." Her back was to him. She lifted the hem of her apron and dabbed at her eyes.

"Well you've made a good impression on Mrs. Underhill."

"She is very kind."

"She says she'll get you squared away in Vlissingen or Flushing or whatever it's called. So many names, here. It'll be nice for you there. Among your own people."

She nodded.

"Thankful . . . you should have *said*."

She turned to him. Her eyes were wet. "I wanted to tell thee. But I could not find the words. Forgive me."

"Dear Thankful, there is nothing to forgive."

She turned away from him and forced a laugh. "I am very silly this morning."

"There's something I've been trying to tell you. But . . ."

"About your wife."

"Ah. So. You know."

She turned to him, smiling. "How could a handsome, charming man like thyself not have a wife? What is her name?"

"Her name? Ah. Her name . . ." His mind went blank.

Thankful laughed. "*Balty*. Thou cannot have forgotten her name!"

"Esther," he said triumphantly.

"Queen of the Persians. Wife of Ahasuerus. Is she pretty?"

"I . . . suppose."

Thankful reached and adjusted Balty's collar. "She will be happy to have thee back. I should, were I she."

Balty moved closer. "Thankful, I—"

She put a finger to his lips. "No." She stood on tiptoes and kissed him on the forehead, then inspected his attire as a wife might, brushing away flecks of dirt and straightening his belt. "Stay close to Huncks. He will keep thee safe."

"The child," Balty said. "Whose is it?"

"Mine, Balty. The child is mine."

"Well, none of my business."

Thankful looked over at Huncks, who stood watching them, holding the horses.

"Go on, or the Colonel will be cross with both of us."

Balty turned and walked away. She called after him, "God keep thee, Mr. Balty."

Balty and Huncks mounted their horses in silence and set off for Breuckelen.

– CHAPTER 34 –

August 4th. *Escorted from my house in Seething Lane by Downing's dogsbody Whelk and his fellow meazel. Not, God be thanked, to the Tower, however "convenient." But instead to my Lord Downing's residence, and there left in a dank and ill-furnished room for three hours, and no refreshment.*

Finally brought before my Lord Downing, who greeted me most sourly, uttering my name as if the saying of it was distasteful to the tongue.

"Oh, Mr. Pepys. Alas." And so forth, etc, with great sighings and shakings of the head.

I expostulated at my rendition hither, and with some asperity asked to know why I was being treated in such a rude manner.

My lord exprest not one scintilla of miff on my behalf and what's more said I should be glad that our interview was not taking place in the Tower, that being "the customary venue for the interrogation of traitors."

Blenching and gathering my wits as best I could, I asked why he, who could surely attest to my love of King and country, should apply this odious word to myself.

He said in the labored, impatient tone of one explaining the ordering of celestial orbs to a mental defecktive that the word denoted one who "sells his country's secrets to his country's enemies."

Feeling as though I had been cuffed full in the face was at pains to formulate some coherent reply.

My lord now rehearsed the particulars of my purported treachery, to wit, first, that I had undone the seal on his confidential dispatch to Colonel Nicholls whilst in the process of delivering it to him in Portsmouth.

"It seems, Pepys, that you are well named. You are Mr. Peeping Pepys," he said, pleased with this facile japery.

He continued, accusing me of selling the "Nicholls intelligence" to the West India Company at Amsterdam, "for the sum of forty gold ducats." Adding, by way of twisting the blade already deep in my bowels, "Even Judas settled for thirty pieces. And of silver!"

By now I was having difficulty breathing and felt pains in my cheste, I stammered that yes, perhaps I had accidentally seen the contents of his Nicholls dispatch, the seal having come detached owing to moisture. But stoutly averred that I had not bartered my knowledge of Col. Nicholls's business to the Hollanders for gold; nor discussed it with anyone save my Lord Sandwich. (It seeming time to come clean on that much.)

Upon this he became tigerish and pounced: "Aha! So now you admit it was yourself who bruited the King's secret in a Chelsey bordello!"

So exercised was he, I feared he might any moment summon the executioner to have my head off there and then.

I croaked that yes, I had vouchsafed my concerns to my Lord Sandwich, he being the King's most trusted admiral, and I being the Navy's Clerk of the Acts. But wherein was the treachery?

Feeling myself on steadier ground, I prest him to tell me why I stood accused of mongering secrets to Holland.

"Are you not in possession of forty Dutch ducats? How came you by those?"

I said that a debt had been recently repaid to me but that I had not noticed that the gold pieces were of Dutch coining. Gold is gold, is't not?

My lord gave a wave of his lace kerchief and said, "'Tis not

for me, Mr. Peeping Pepys, to decide your guilt or innocence. That
shall be for judge and jury to decide at your tryal."

"Tryal?" I said, feeling my knees now very weak.

"Meanwhiles, you are remanded to the Tower and shall
remain there at his majesty's pleasure."

Whereat he rang his dreadful little silver bell. Never has such
a wee tinkling chime sounded like the very bells of hell. Whelk
and his fellow brute entered, each seizing an arm, whereat my
gullet again emptied propulsively upon their persons, much
disconcerting them.

CHAPTER 35

Being English

Balty and Huncks stood on the Breuckelen side of the East River and looked across to the island of Manhatoes.

Its outline was dominated by a signal tower, fort, two windmills, an ornate gabled house, and the inevitable gallows. Balty had seen many gallows, but none as forbidding as this one. As if reading his thoughts, Huncks said, "Let's try not to end up on *that*."

Before they left Killingworth, Captain Underhill had told them "Don't skulk, or lurk about in the shadows like a pair of cutpurses or wharf rats. Make a show of being English."

Balty asked, "How does one make a show of being English?"

"Act superior. Imperious. Look down on everyone. The moment you get off the ferry, demand to be taken to the Governor. Wave your commission at him." (Underhill had not bothered to read it himself, nor the letter from Dr. Pell.) "Puff out your chest like a bantam cock. Tell him, 'Look here, my good man—you hiding these rascals Whalley and Goffe? If you are, hand 'em over or you shall taste his majesty's wrath!'"

Underhill may have declined to join in the Battle for New Amsterdam, but a regicide hunt seemed to warm the cockles of his monarchist heart.

"Never had much liking for the first King Charles. He made a bit too much show of being English. Still, bad business, regicide. And even worse manners." He added, "Here's something to keep in mind about Old Petrus—he's a dreadful *snob*. Drop a lot of flossy names. Spent much time at Court?"

"Well . . ."

"No matter. Put on airs. *As his majesty said to me just the other day—* that sort of thing. He'll slurp it up like soup. Thing is, Old Petrus actually *likes* the English. When he was a young officer in Curaçao, he had this English chum, John Ferret or Farret. They were inseparable. Don't know if it extended to buggery. Rather not speculate. When Farret or Ferret went home, they wrote each other endlessly. In *verse*! Heroic couplets by the furlong. The old boy's got a soft spot for us in that hard Hollander heart of his. God knows why. Mind, he won't hesitate to swing you from his gibbet if he learns you're scouting for an invasion force. But if you convince him you're there to sniff out regicides, like as not he'll treat you cordial enough."

Huncks said, "Whalley and Goffe would be under his protection, surely."

"Not much happens in New Amsterdam without Old Petrus knows of it. But he's not just going to hand them over to you. When that English squadron sails into his harbor, he'll have himself two fine hostages for the negotiating." Underhill grinned. "Or four."

They crossed by the Breuckelen ferry. Huncks nudged Balty as it approached the Manhatoes landing. He pointed—soldiers, rather a lot of them.

"Seems they're expecting someone. Let's hope it's not us."

Balty felt a queasiness that for once had nothing to do with the motion of the boat.

The ferry docked. Huncks said, "*Be English.*"

Balty took a deep breath and picked out the soldier with the most metal and braid on his uniform and addressed him as a duke would one of his tenant farmers.

"I say? Hoy! You, there! Yes, you. Do? You? Speak? *English*?"

The soldier regarded him sternly. "*Ja.*"

"Good. Then conduct me to your Governor, Peter Stuyvesant. I have business with him. Urgent. You understand *urgent*?"

The soldier stared.

"Come, man. I don't have all day."

Soldiers gathered round.

"What business you have?" said the one Balty had addressed. "For the Heneral?"

Balty reached into his satchel for his commission. Three bayonets pricked at his chest.

"If you please. I only wish to show you my papers. Don't you *want* to see my papers? *Papers?* Look here, *do* you speak English or not?"

A bayonet lifted Balty's satchel by the strap. The soldier opened it. Balty's commission, looking the worse for wear, was located and unrolled. The soldiers peered.

One with even more metal and braid arrived. He read the commission, looked at Balty, scowled. Looked at Huncks, scowled.

"Come."

Balty and Huncks followed. Four soldiers fell in behind. They proceeded through the crowded waterfront, drawing stares.

New Amsterdam was tidy in the Dutch way. They crossed a bridge over a canal that, in another city, would have been a miasmic stew of detritus and offal.

On their left loomed the elegant gabled house they'd seen from the Breuckelen shore. To their right, they saw the fort, square with bastions at the corners. Inside was a hive of activity: soldiers and workers everywhere, barrels rumbling over cobbles, baskets of cannonballs being hoisted to the ramparts, soldiers drilling, stacks of muskets being carried here and there.

Huncks murmured, "*Definitely* expecting someone."

Inside the fort grounds stood a large building—the Governor's House. They went in not by the front door but one on the side. Not auspicious.

Huncks looked about, taking in everything. Presently, they found themselves in an airy, sparsely furnished room, walls hung with official documents, charts, and maps.

"Here sit."

Balty looked about disapprovingly. "I say. I asked to be taken to Governor Stuyvesant, not some barracks."

"Sit."

"My good man, I'm not sure I like your tone. May I point out that you are speaking to—"

A bayonet jabbed Balty between the shoulder blades.

"*Sit.*"

"Very well. But this is no way to greet an emissary of the King of England."

The officer disappeared into an adjoining room. They heard voices from within. The conversation went on for some time.

Presently, a thickly built, florid-faced man emerged, with more metal and braid than any of the others. In his hand was Balty's commission.

"Which of you iss"—he glanced at the commission—"Balthasar Sint Mykkal?"

"Myself, sir."

The officer looked Balty up and down with the air of a customs inspector about to demand that he open his luggage.

"I am Koontz. Deputy-Heneral."

"I am very pleased to make your acquaintance, Deputy-*General* Koontz. But with respect, my business is with his excellency, *Director*-General Stuyvesant. My reception here has been less than ideal. I had been under the impression that Dutch hospitality was second to none. I regret to say that this has not, thus far, been my experience."

Deputy-General Koontz stared, hovering between indignation and amusement at this popinjay before him. He reexamined Balty's tattered commission.

"You are seeking . . . these persons . . . Whalley and Hoffe?"

"*Goffe,*" Balty corrected. "Indeed we are."

"For why?"

"The murder of his late majesty King Charles the First. God rest his royal soul."

"What makes you to think such persons are situate in New Amsterdam?"

"Oh, I assure you, sir, I have it on the very best intelligence."

Huncks cleared his throat.

"*Intellihence?*" Deputy-General Koontz's eyes brightened, as if candles had been lit behind them. "Yes? From who you are acquiring this intellihence?"

Huncks spoke up, in a voice not his own, some mongrel blend of Irish and Yorkshire.

"Beggin' yer pardon, yer warship, it warn't intelligence but more, ye might say, a *rumor* like."

Koontz stared. "Rumor?"

"Exactly so, yer warship. See, we was in Boston—up in Massahoositts. Very grim place, I calls it. Full of grim folk with long faces. So we was in this tavern, see. A groggerie, ye might call it. And well, I reckon everyone had had more than his share of grog *that* night. Didn't they, Balto? So this bugger, this feller, I mean, he said he were a beaver dealer. Skins, that is. Balto here were tellin' him how he wrangled his commission to hunt for these blokes Whalley and Goffe. Hoffe, as you calls him. You see, we're manhoonters."

"Manhoonters?"

"Indeed so. Which is to say we catches folk what are sought for by the law. And collects the reward for it."

"For bounty?"

"Exactly so. So this beaver dealer, see, he tells us, 'It's Whalley and Hoffe yer after? Don't yer know they've fled to New Hamsterdam? Them Dootch—the 'ollanders—oh, fine folk. You won't meet finer, anywares.' So here we are, come to New Hamsterdam. *That* were the intellihence what my colleague 'ere, Mr. Balthasar, were speakin' of."

The candles behind Koontz's eyes went out.

"You are . . . ?"

"Ayrum Uncks, at yer service, yer warship. Manhoonter, Indian fighter, and general doer of whatever needs doing. Mr. Balthasar here kindly hoyared me in Boston as his ad-jootant, him being new to this part of the world. Mind you, I prefers the toytle aide-de-camp."

Koontz shook his head. "These people you seek . . . I think they are not here. No. They are not. I would know."

"Then we'll be thanking you for your time and your cartesy, and we'll be on our way. Seems a bit busy here, so we musn't take up any more of yer time. Come, Mr. Balthasar, let us leave these good Dootch folk to go about their business."

Koontz shook his head. "You cannot leave. The town is shut."

"Shut?"

"Sealed. Under orders of the Heneral. No one to enter or leaf."

"Beggin' yer warship's pardon, but we just *did* enter. Plain as day."

"The sealing was being accomplish when you came. Now you must remain."

"Well," Huncks said with an air of mild inconvenience, "I suppose, then, stay we must. And experience the delights of New Hamsterdam. Very tidy it is. Very tidy indeed." Huncks turned to Balty. "Did I not tell ye, Mr. Balthasar, how *tidy* are the Dootch?"

"You must stay here, in the fort. You will be our hests."

"Well isn't that kind of you, sir? Bless your heart."

The quarters into which they were shortly ushered by a four-soldier guard suggested latitude in the Dutch concept of "hests." Or that their hosts were convinced they were spies. It wasn't so much the sparseness of the furnishings—straw on the floor, two stools, a small table, and a slops bucket—but the bars on the windows and door. Only a determined optimist would think himself a hest here rather than prisoner.

"*Intelligence*," Huncks muttered as he bunched straw to sit on. "Lack of intelligence, you mean."

"I only meant—"

"No. Don't talk."

"What was that village-idiot performance of yours?"

"I was trying to make the Deputy-*Heneral* think we're a pair of blundering fools, rather than intelligencers." Huncks looked about their cell. "It appears I did not succeed."

Balty went to the window and peered out. Troops were drilling on the fort grounds.

"What's all this activity about?"

"Bad timing."

"How do you mean?"

"Appears Colonel Nicholls had good weather on his way from Portsmouth. He's here."

"*What?*"

"Koontz and his aide were jib-jabbering about it before you went spouting off."

"You speak Dutch?"

"A squadron of four ships under English flag was sighted off Block's Island. That's three, four days' sail, depending on the wind. Our hosts are therefore a bit on edge. It's why they were buttoning up the town when we so felicitously arrived. They seem to think we might have something to do with the English ships."

"Oh, hell."

"Certainly not heaven."

"What now?"

Huncks looked about the cell. "Might try to catch a rat for our supper. If nothing else, it would help pass the time."

"What about Stuyvesant? Why aren't we seeing him?"

"There's a lot going on. On top of the English ships, they're having Mohawk trouble upriver at Fort Orange."

"Where does that leave us?"

Huncks considered. "One, they hang us upside down and beat us with iron rods until we talk. Two, hang us right side up, and be done with us. Three, ship us off to the Dutch Indies to work the plantations. Not the pleasantest prospect, that."

"God."

"Four, keep us as hostages." Huncks laughed. "Along with Whalley and Goffe. As Captain Underhill predicted. Ironic, don't you think? Finally meeting them that way? Depends what happens when Nicholls gets here. And what sort of mood Old Petrus is in. Sour, I should think. Calvinists tend to be, even on good days."

They sat in gloomy silence.

"Balty?"

"What?"

"If they put us to the torture, just tell them everything. Straight off. Don't wait."

"Certainly not. I wouldn't let the side down. That's no way to be English."

"Trust me, old boy. You'll talk. Everyone does. The only ones who don't are the Indians. There's no glory in going to the gallows minus a hand or eye. Or your bollocks."

Balty blanched. "They *wouldn't*. Surely?"

"They bloody well surely would. Be a smart fellow. Tell them everything. If it does come to that, I intend to deny them the pleasure."

"How?"

Huncks removed his boot and twisted off the heel. Inside was a stubby razor. He drew it across his throat.

"Oh, *no*," Balty said. "No. Huncks. Please. I'd feel very . . . alone here without you."

"I could see you off first. If you like."

Balty sighed. "I hardly know what to say. No one's ever offered to cut my throat for me. As a favor."

Huncks winked. "What are friends for, eh?"

They sat in silence.

"You know, Huncks. Before I embarked on this catastrophe, my life hadn't really amounted to much."

"Look at yourself now. What a success you've made."

They began to laugh. The guards, unused to such behavior in prisoners, gathered and stared through the bars. So strange, English.

Later Huncks said, "You looked a bit rough around the edges when you said goodbye to the girl."

"Well, it's all rather sad. Wouldn't you say?"

"Who's the father? Gideon or Repent?"

"I tried to ask. I'm not sure *she* knows. Poor girl."

"She will soon enough. Mrs. Underhill will look after her. But the lass hasn't had much to be *thankful* for."

"No. She hasn't."

"D'you tell her about Edith?"

"Esther. She already knew. I suppose *you* told her."

"No. They always know, women."

They sat with their backs against the wall, listening to the sounds of the fort preparing for war.

Presently, the door opened. Koontz and an adjutant entered. The adjutant carried a tray with paper, ink, quills, and a thick leather-bound book.

"What's this?" Balty said.

"I bring for you paper. For which to compose your confessioning. Also a Bible. In English. For the consolating."

"See here, Koontz," Balty said. "We have no confessions to make. And we certainly do not require the consolation of the Word of God."

"Suit to yourself."

"I *demand* to speak to Governor Stuyvesant."

"He is occupied. He instructs to me if you are not making confessionings, you should write farwell letters. To your luff ones in England."

"*Farewell* letters?"

"Meantimes I will have to you sent food and drink. Are you wishing for person of cloth?"

"A tailor? Why on earth should we require a *tailor?*"

"Priest."

"Certainly not! This is outrageous!"

Koontz shrugged apologetically. "It's for the Heneral to decide. Perhaps he will commutate and send you to the plantations. Very *hot* there. I beg you a good evening."

Shortly arrived a reputable roast capon, bread, wine, sausage, and an assortment of Dutch cheeses (naturally), including a wedge of rather decent aged Gouda. Huncks pronounced it a feast and tucked in with relish. Balty had no appetite. He inked a quill and began a letter to Esther but got only as far as "Dearest Esther."

"Oh, hell," he said for the one hundredth time that day.

"Eat somefing," Huncks said through a mouthful of capon. "Don't want to faint on the gallows. Think of King Charles on the scaffold."

"What are you talking about?"

Huncks bit off another mouthful of capon. "It wuff cold. Late January. Fweezing. Wore an extra shirt so the crowd wouldn't think he was shaking with fear. Rather noble."

"Must you talk about that now?"

"Seemf apropos," Huncks said, through bread and Gouda.

"Can't you swallow your food before speaking?"

"If you're going to be grumpy, maybe we should send for a man of the cloth. Meself, I'd rather have a couple of Dutch tarts than a priest. And not the kind made of jam and pastry."

Balty stared forlornly at the blank paper. Why couldn't he pour out his heart to Esther? Dearest Esther. What was she doing at this moment? Missing her Balty, surely. But hard as Balty tried to think about her, all he could think about—other than his rapidly diminishing mortality, either on the gallows or the plantations—was Thankful.

"I had this Dutch girl in Hartford."

"Huncks, I don't want to hear about it."

"Fine piece of pudding. Gretchen. Fetchin' Gretchen. Sweetest titties in God's creation. Absolutely perfect, like—"

"Huncks. I'm trying to compose a farewell letter to my wife. I don't want to hear about some Dutch *putain*."

"Gretchen was no whore. And I'll thank you not to call her one. Her da was the Dutch man of the cloth in Hartford. Minister. There were still lots of Dutch there then. She'd sneak out of church soon as he started his sermon. He was long-winded, thank God." Huncks chortled. "There was this bluff above the river under a great elm. We'd spread the blanket and . . ." Huncks drank some wine and sighed. "Well, it was a paradise finer than any her father limned from his pulpit, I'll tell you." He tore off another drumstick. "How's your letter to whosis coming?"

"Esther. It's *not*."

"Pretend you're writing to Thankful, then."

"That hardly seems seem right."

"Seems to me you've more to say to her than your missus. Mind you, the first person to read it will be our gracious host, the Deputy-Heneral. Write this: *Mijn beste Koontz, zuig mijn lul.*"

"What's that mean?"

"My dear Koontz, suck my cock."

"I'll be sent to hell, for adultery."

"What, for having Koontz blow on your flute?"

"No. Damn it, Huncks."

Huncks sat up. "Why you sly old thing. It's *your* child she's carrying?"

"What an appalling thing to suggest! Certainly not!"

"Then how are you committing adultery?"

"It would be *adultery* to write Thankful and not Ethel."

"Thought her name was Esther?"

"*Esther.* It's possible to commit adultery with your heart. A priest told me."

Huncks grunted. "Well, I'm no priest, but it's a hell of lot more fun commiting it with a different part of the anatomy." He bunched together more straw and stretched out.

"What are you doing?" Balty said.

"Going to sleep."

"Sleep? Damn it, Huncks, they may hang us in the morning."

"All the more reason. Bad form, nodding off at your own hanging. Must make a show of being English."

"I don't see how you can sleep."

"Well, I shuts me eyes, so. And says me prayers, like me old mum taught me. *Our Father which art in dum de dum de dum de dum amen.* And before you knows it . . ."

Huncks began to snore, leaving Balty alone with his blank page and visions of Thankful.

– CHAPTER 36 –

August 15th. De Profundis clamavi. *Truly now I am one with the writers of Lamentations and Psalms. Hear my cry, O Israel.*

Was welcomed into captivity with fulsome politesse by the Constable of the Tower, Sir John Robinson, 1st Baronet of London, a talking, bragging bufflehead and as vile a coxcomb as any in all London, lacking brains to outwit any ordinary tradesman, and he a former member of the Worshipful Company of Clothworkers.

Greeted me smirkingly: "Mr. Pepys, what an honor to have you as our guest! 'Tis not every day we receive such illustrious—" Etc., etc.

Turning to his lieutenant, he asked, "Have we a vacancy in the Beauchamp Tower for Mr. Pepys?"

Then to me: "Or would you prefer something with a view of the River?"

I replied through gritted teeth that I was as indifferent to my accommodation as I was innocent.

"The Beauchamp Tower, then, for it hath an admirable view of Tower Green and the scaffold site. Enjoy your stay, Mr. Pepys!"

Was shewn to my "lodgings." Walls festooned with dolorous graffitoes scratched by previous "guests," including the five Dudley brothers. One of these, Lord Guildford Dudley, was the unfortunate husband of the unfortunate Lady Jane Grey, whose head was removed on Tower Green, below—part of my

*"admirable view." His head was separated from him on Tower
Hill.*

*Gave my gaoler Tom a half crown and sent him to Seething
Lane to fetch me my lute, diary, fresh shirt, veal pies, some pickled
onions, ale, and my Bible. Not wanting to alarm my wife, I
instructed him to tell her I was detained at Deptford Docks
owing to a problematical victualing.*

*Practiced "Gaze Not on Swans" on my lute, substituting
"ravens" for "swans," there being many of these hideous birds
hereabouts, screeching discordantly and copiously crapulent. His
majesty refuses to have them removed or killed, even though they
regularly beshit his royal tubes at the astronomical observatory
in the White Tower. He remains convinced by the legend that the
Kingdom will not outlive the last raven killed. Nonsense, but I
have more pressing things to ponder. God grant that I may again
see his majesty and offer him my own insight on the subject of
these satanic avians.*

*On the second day of captivity, I considered scratching
graffitoes of my own into the walls, alongside the ones carved
by those who spent decades within these walls. But thinking it
might be presumptuous, resolved to wait at least one week before
inscribing my own mementoes. But let it be stipulated that one
day here seemeth a year, and a d———d long year at that.*

CHAPTER 37

Old Petrus

They awoke to the rasp of iron, the door of their cell opening. Koontz. Alone.

"Gentlemen, forgive for the disturbing. If you will be so kind to accompany with me?"

Balty and Huncks stood, bits of straw clinging to them. The sight seemed to amuse Koontz. He picked a few bits off, saying they looked like the "person-things farmers make for which to frighten birds."

They set off across the wide fort grounds. It was still dark, with a faint glow of pinkish dawn in the east. The fort that had been so busy before was quiet now. Sentries walked the ramparts; otherwise all was still.

Balty told himself this couldn't be a walk to the gallows. Surely there would be more people, soldiers and drumming and all the rest. Then the dreadful thought came: Was Koontz escorting them to a prisoner ship to deliver them to penal servitude? Very *hot* there.

But no—God be thanked—he led them into the Governor's House, and this time by the front door, past saluting sentries.

They passed through a series of anterooms into a large, finely decorated room where behind a desk Balty and Huncks beheld the unmistakable person of Peter Stuyvesant, Director-General of New

Netherland, Curaçao, Bonaire, and Aruba. Old Petrus, in the flesh. And what a lot of flesh.

Koontz extended the courtesy of introducing the visitors in their native tongue.

"Heneral. I present you the English persons."

Old Petrus looked up from his desk. Balty was struck by the immensity of Stuyvesant's forehead. It was like the side of a mountain. It went on forever, the summit disappearing beneath a skullcap. His nose, too, was outsized. It drooped, as if made of clay that hadn't hardened. The eyes were small and beady, the lips sensual and unpleasantly moist. Cascades of hair descended on each side past the shoulders, giving him a spaniel aspect. He seemed to have been assembled from various materials. His chest swelled like a great bellows.

The General—as he was called by his subjects (his term for *them*)—was in his mid-fifties. For nine of those years he had endured agonies that would have driven lesser men to put a gun to their temple. His right leg, amputated after a Spanish cannonball reduced it to a jam of gore and splinters, never fully healed in the sweltering tropics. After nearly a decade of torment, stoically borne, Stuyvesant finally returned to Holland, to be nursed to health by his family in a more temperate clime. The ordeal of those years was visible in palimpsest beneath the bland features, a stern, Calvinist face that dared you to question its dignity or authority; there was also the unmistakable air of the *isolato*, the man apart, standing atop a parapet, directing cannon fire. Not a man you'd find at the center of jollity and camaraderie in a tavern. Balty remembered what Captain Underhill had told them: no one likes Old Petrus, even his own people.

The Governor of New Netherland addressed them in flowery but wooden English, as if his vocabulary was stored inside his leg.

They must forgive. But there was a reason that their reception in New Amsterdam had not been, shall we declare, more felicitous. The reason? Recently was viewed, in the waters surrounding Block's Island, four English warships. What could portend *this*?

It was no secret that relations between Holland and England

were—alas—disharmonious. In London, people shouting in the street, "War! We must have *another* war with Holland!"

Was one war not enough? And what did *it* accomplish, in the end? Now pamphlets everywhere, to inflame the populace into hating of the Dutch. Sad! Amidst this deplorableness and mutual distrusting, how *else* could be viewed by New Amsterdam the approach of four English ships of war?

A wry smile came over the features, a beam of sunshine on the glacier, melting ice.

But now—this very night—is arriving from Amsterdam a message. From the West India Company that administrates New Amsterdam. Welcome news! These English vessels are not intenting belligerence. For Amsterdam has received assurings from the English ambassador at The Hague, Downing, the same whose signature is on your commission. About which we shall, yes, discuss more. The English ships are making a reviewing of the New England colonies. They will come to New Amsterdam for to make a gesture of goodwill. They are important, gestures. The last war between us was commenced because our Admiral Tromp did not lower his colors to one of your ships in the Narrow Seas. And look what followed!

The sun continued to beat down on the glacier as Old Petrus went on. He was most regretful of how they had been received. Perhaps they will understand. And forgive. When two such great countries as ours make unpleasantness against each other, of necessity will frictions come, yes? But with wisdom perhaps in the end we shall see that the world is commodious enough for two great nations. Yes?

An elegant—if windy—speech. Balty was impressed. To say nothing of relieved.

Silence settled on the room. Old Petrus stared, opaque, unreadable. Balty felt panic rising. Was the old boy awaiting a reciprocal oration? Oh, dear, but all right . . .

Of *course* he understood, Balty said. Such things happen. Holland's reputation for hospitality was well known throughout the world. How gratifying that all this was . . . a misunderstanding.

How good. How marvelous. And now *that* was settled. How good to . . . bask in the radiance of the gubernatorial presence. And such an *august* presence . . .

Huncks stifled a groan.

Balty pressed on.

How good that he could now return—he stressed the words *now* and *return*—to England and report to his majesty Charles the Second, King of England, Ireland (etc., etc.), that New Netherland was truly, indeedly, ruled by a wise and good man who . . . who desired harmony between our two great nations (etc., etc.).

Balty finished his oration with a bow and a flourish of hands so elaborate it gave the impression of a man fending off a symmetrical assault by bats.

Silence again descended. Time stopped, as in one of Mijnheer Vermeer's paintings of light angling in through a window.

Old Petrus stared, in bewilderment or contempt; possibly both. Balty, rising from his genuflection, stared back. Did the old boy want *more* kowtowing? Lord. He tried to summon another torrent of verbiage, but nothing came. It was like trying to write Esther.

He cleared his throat.

"Well, jolly lovely to have met you, your excellency. We won't take up any more of your time. Come, Huncks, we're off."

Huncks spoke up. "Er, beggin' yer pardon, Marster St. Michel, but waren't there something *else* you was wanting to ask his excellency?"

"There was? Ah. Yes. There was." Balty stared blankly.

"Pertaining to our reason for being here in New Hamsterdam?"

"Ah. Yes. Forgive me, your excellency. The radiance of your gubernatorialness has quite overwhelmed me. We were by way of wondering if your excellency might be able to render some assistance to us in the matter of, well, locating a pair of fugitive regicides. That is, specifically, two of the knaves who signed the death warrant of the late King Charles. We thought perhaps they might be here. In New Amsterdam. Might I compliment your excellency on how very tidy your town is. If only our English towns were so . . . neat."

Old Petrus put on his spectacles and peered at Balty's commission. "Whalley . . . Hoffe . . ."

"Goffe, yer honor," Huncks corrected. "We pronounces our *g*'s hard. Like in 'governor.'"

Old Petrus looked at Koontz. Koontz shrugged. Stuyvesant removed his spectacles and leaned back in his chair with a creak of old leather.

"Your rehicides, they are not here."

"Well," Balty said, feeling a pressing urge to be somewhere else, "then that's that. Thank you *very* much, your excellency. Come, Huncks. We depart."

Old Petrus held up a hand. "No."

Time stopped again.

"You have come a big distance. If you must leave with hands empty, you will not leave with stomachs empty."

"Well, a spot of breakfast would be lovely. Thank you."

Old Petrus shook his head. "No. You shall be my hests. This evening."

"It's kind of your excellency. But really, if these caitiffs aren't here, then seek them elsewhere we must. Without delay. His majesty doesn't pay his manhunters to lollygag. Oh, no. He's very . . . strict, his majesty."

Huncks cleared his throat.

"But if you insist," Balty said, "by all means."

Stuyvesant said, "I will make interrogatings about these persons. But I am doubting they are here. I would know."

"Don't go to any trouble."

"It is no twrabble. Only courtesy. And tonight *you* will do to me a courtesy of partaking of the dinner. In my house, in the country. And together we will welcome your English ships when they come. It's synchronous, no?"

"Beg pardon?"

"That you and the ships are arriving"—Old Petrus made a conjoining gesture with his fingers—"simul . . ."

"Ah," Balty said. "Ourselves and Colonel Nicholls, you mean?"

Huncks winced.

Again, time stopped. Old Petrus put on his specs again and picked up another document, squinting.

"Nicholls . . . Yes. Here is the name. Richard Nicholls. Colonel. It's him who will make the reviewing of your colonies. So you *know* of him?"

Balty's mind went blank. Huncks leapt in.

"With yer warship's permission, *everyone* knows of Colonel Nicholls. A personage of the first reputation. The finest administrative reviewer in all England. Top-drawer. And a gentleman down to his boots. Yer excellency and he will get along like peas in a pod. Not to impute any vegetal connoting, mind. Turn of phrase. As it war."

Old Petrus said, "What a lot of English visitors we are having in these days." He and Koontz spoke in Dutch.

"Deputy Koontz shall attend to you. I regret we cannot make you hests here, but since the unpleasantness of the last war, the West India Company have made the rule that not-Dutch people cannot reside within the fort. Unless they are awaiting execution.

"So. Have a rest. Have a wash. Assume fresh clothing and we shall make our departure from here at"—he glanced at a pendulum clock, a fine specimen from the workshop of Salomon Coster at The Hague— "five of the clock. It's not so far, my house. Two miles only. Bouwerie Number One. As we make our progress, I will show you some small portion of Manatus. You will find it caressful to the eye. You will understand why we are so proud of our colony."

Koontz installed them in what he said was the "most finest tavern" in New Amsterdam—De Hoorn des Overvloeds, on the street by the East River. The tavern's name, Koontz explained, meant the Horn Plenty-Full. He added with a wink that its amenities included two of the cleanest prostitutes in all New Amsterdam—Derkje and Jutta.

"Jesus, man," Huncks snorted when they were alone in their room. "You got your tongue so embedded up his arse you forget to mention Whalley and *Hoffe*. Then you go blurting Nicholls's name. *Then* you tell him, 'Ooh, look at the time! Must run! Ta-ta!' I ought to take needle and twine and sew your yap shut."

"Don't you see—he's onto us. I was trying to create an exit. Then *you* started blibbering in that appalling accent."

Balty looked out the window. He could see Breuckelen on the far shore. Its farms looked so tranquil in contrast to the bustle below along the waterfront. Balty yearned to be on the Breuckelen side. Farther still—in Oyster Bay. With Thankful.

Huncks was stretched out on the bed, about to commence snoring.

"Don't you think he's onto us?" Balty said. "That business about synchronous."

"Maybe."

"What about the judges? Did you believe him that they're not here?"

"Don't know."

"Maybe. Don't know. Thank you, Erasmus of Rotterdam."

Huncks spoke with eyes closed.

"Let's review. One, we're not swinging from his gallows. Two, he sprung us from his jail. Three, I'm lying on a fine goose feather bed at the best joint in town. On his guilders. Four, we're invited to sup at his country house. On balance, I'd say no, I don't think he's onto us."

"What about the judges?"

"I incline to believe a man who thinks he's about to get et alive by wild beasts. You yourself saw Jones and Repent in Fairfield, headed this way. So I incline to think they are here. But I remind you that the regicides aren't the mission. Nicholls is. And what's *your* analysis?"

"That I never should have left England."

"Um. And you were doing so well there."

Balty lay down on the bed. He felt tired.

Huncks said, "I didn't mean that."

"No, you're right. *Ce n'est que la verité qui blesse.*"

"Cheer up. If it goes well, you'll end up Sir Balthasar de St. Michel." Huncks yawned. He began to snore, leaving Balty to his thoughts.

A knighthood. Six months ago, the thought made Balty's heart pound. But now he felt no quickening of pulse, only the dull, dutiful pump of blood. He had no thought other than for a Quaker girl with golden hair, her belly swelling with a child begot by her dead husband or the man who'd murdered him.

Balty awoke. Midday. Huncks was at the table, writing. Balty got up and looked over his shoulder: a diagram of the fort with annotations: how many cannon on this bastion and that bastion, estimates of troop strength, sentry positions, numbers of gunships in the harbor—items of interest to an invader.

"What are you going to do with *that*?"

Huncks went on scribbling. "Thought I'd nail it to the door of the fort. Like Luther and his theses."

"Shouldn't it be in cipher? It is somewhat incriminating."

"You can't cipher a diagram. And ciphers require keys. There wasn't time to arrange all that with Underhill's man here."

Underhill had given Huncks the name of someone who could get a message to him. Huncks wouldn't tell Balty the man's name, in the event of capture and torture. Underhill would relay the message to Nicholls by small boat as the squadron sailed along the Long Island shore toward New Amsterdam.

Huncks finished. He pulled on his boots and threw on his jacket. "Wait here. Won't be long."

"I'm coming with you."

"Best not be seen together. Back within the hour."

"What if you're not?"

Huncks pointed at the window. "Watch from there. You can be my guardian angel."

Balty sniffed. "I've better things to do than sit by a window like some wharfside doxy drumming up business."

Huncks left. Balty went to the window. He watched Huncks emerge below and wade into the waterfront throng.

A man stepped out from a nearby doorway and followed him. Something about him seemed familiar.

Balty rummaged in his satchel for his tube, a going-away gift from Brother Sam. It made things far off look closer. He peered. The man turned his head. Balty saw the eyebrows.

He jimmied on his boots and flew down the two flights of stairs and out the door into the crowd of sailors, merchants, butchers, fishmongers, slavers, chandlers, ropers, cartwrights, whores, pewterers, soldiers, cobblers, clockmakers, poulterers, beaver trappers, factors, masons, brewers, carpenters, flower sellers, jewelers, bakers—all sweaty humanity was abroad this warm August noon. He pushed through, drawing sharp looks and rebukes.

Reaching the water's edge, he looked this way and that. In heaven's name, *why* hadn't Huncks told him where he was going? He conjured terrible images of Jones running Huncks through with a dagger from behind. Calm down, he told himself. Huncks is no babe in the woods.

Balty turned to make his way through the crowd back to the Horn of Plenty and found himself looking at Repent. The Indian was coming straight at him. He was dressed in white man's clothes, a broad-rimmed hat pulled down to his eyebrows to conceal the winged face carved into his forehead.

Repent paused. He and Balty stared at each other, motionless amidst the swarm. The Indian grinned. Balty felt a surge of fury in him and lunged. Repent disappeared into the crowd.

Balty shoved his way through. A fist caught him in the face. Balty went down.

He opened his eyes and put his hand to his nose. It came away wet with blood. No one bent to extend a hand. New Amsterdam kept moving along. No Samaritans here. He stumbled to his feet and staggered to the inn.

The Horn of Plenty's innkeeper regarded his bleeding guest with mild curiosity.

"Fighting?"

"Fell."

The innkeeper nodded. "Too much *drink*."

Balty clutched his oozing nose, gobbets of blood dripping onto his shirt. He conjured four stout English warships and commanded them to deliver a withering, *synchronous* broadside at De Hoorn des Overvloeds: plumes of smoke, ball, grape, and chain whistling lethally, hissingly through the air, reducing the most finest establishment in New Amsterdam to wrubble.

The innkeeper, suddenly remembering that this sanguinary Englishman was a guest of the General, gave Balty a wet cloth and asked if he would like "more *hjin*." The word sounded like a summoning of phlegm.

"More what?"

"*Hjin*." He produced an earthenware bottle and pulled out the cork. Balty sniffed the astringent tang of juniper. Gin.

Balty waved away the bottle and went up the stairs, cloth pressed to his face, tormented by visions of Huncks floating facedown in the river.

Sometime later he heard the recognizable clump of boots on the stairs. The door opened and in Huncks came, hand pressed to the back of his head. He saw Balty's swollen, bloody nose, uttered a groan, and sat on the edge of the bed.

"I see you took my advice and stayed in the room."

Someone had slugged him on the back of his head. When he came to, his attacker was going through his pockets. Huncks tried to grab him, but he fled.

"Port towns. A wonder I didn't wake up pressed inside a Dutch warship."

"Jones."

"How do you know?"

"I saw him. Tried to warn you. Ran smack into Repent. I went for him and someone clomped me for shoving. Bloody Dutch."

"Well, it appears our regicides are here, after all. Why else would Mr. Fish and Repent be lurking about? The question is: Are they under Stuyvesant's protection? And what will Jones do with my fine drawing?"

"Oughtn't we to be leaving?"

"That would be the prudent thing. But what if they aren't here as Stuyvesant's hests?"

Huncks sat up, rubbing the back of his head. "I must get a message to Levy."

"Who?"

"Underhill's man. Local butcher. Jew."

Huncks went to the table and began making another diagram. Balty paced nervously, stopping to listen at the door for the thundering footsteps of soldiers.

"I've never met a Jew," he said. "What do they look like?"

"Like Jesus."

Huncks finished his drawing and got up from his chair. He staggered.

"You all right, old man?"

Huncks nodded. "This time listen to me. Stay here."

"I'm coming with you. Besides, I should like to meet a Jew."

"Wait two minutes. D'you remember the canal? Meet you there."

Balty and Huncks were back in their room at the Horn of Plenty within the hour.

"He didn't look at all like Jesus," Balty said.

"How do you know what Jesus looked like?"

"You were the one said he did."

"Balty. Please. My head's coming off."

"Seemed a decent chap. Strange, that kosher business. Why's he helping us?"

"He hates Stuyvesant."

"Why?"

"Stuyvesant hates Jews. Hates everyone. Jews, Quakers, Catholics, Lutherans. We'll find out soon enough if he hates us as well."

They lay in silence on the bed.

"Huncks?"

"Balty. I'm trying to rest. My head's on fire."

"What if this invitation to din-dins is just a way of luring us into the woods, where we'll be quietly murdered and buried in some Dutch dunghill?"

"It's a possibility."

"*That's* a bit rum."

"I don't see Old Petrus killing us and putting us in his vegetable garden. Skullduggery's not his thing. He's a soldier. And remember what Underhill told us—he likes the English, though God knows why."

"You're bleeding into the pillow."

"Please will you let me rest?"

"How am I supposed to rest?"

"We've no choice but to see it through. If we flee now, we give ourselves away. Worse, we give Nicholls away. Old Petrus will go back to a war footing and open fire on Nicholls the moment he sails in. And the blame will be ours. Think Downing will be pleased? Or his majesty?"

Balty reflected. "No. Shouldn't think."

"D'you see Breuckelen through the window?"

"Yes."

"Pell's militia are arraying themselves along the shore. And four fine English warships are on their way. Old Petrus'll realize he's been outfoxed by Downing, king of foxes."

"Then what?"

"Stuyvesant's got four hundred men to Pell's five hundred. Nicholls has another five hundred. Stuyvesant's got six canons. Nicholls has twenty times that. The numbers are against Old Petrus."

"So he'll surrender?"

"No. We shall have another war with Holland. Inevitable. But you and I will leave that to the contestants on the field of battle. And attend to our own matter."

"The judges?"

"Regicide's for God to judge. The murder of the Cobbs, what was done to the girl, those I do judge. Now rest. We must be good company at dinner. Make a show of being English."

- *CHAPTER 38* -

Chez Bouwerie
Number One

Balty went downstairs while Huncks got dressed, to tip the inn-keeper three shillings to change their blood-soaked bed linen. The prospect of sleeping in it tonight was less than appealing. Huncks descended and they made their way to the Governor's House at the fort.

Old Petrus stumped down the steps and greeted them cordially. He evinced concern at Balty's battered face. Balty said he'd had a tumble in the street. Best not to reveal their eventful perambulations, in the event the regicides were under his protection.

They climbed aboard the carriage. Stuyvesant took the reins. The gate of the fort gave out onto a broad way that narrowed as they proceeded north. Stuyvesant pointed out various houses of prominent citizens, as well as a vast garden and greenhouse—his own—the latter filled with medicinal herbs brought from Dutch possessions in the tropics where he'd served. Old Petrus's pride was evident, even touching.

The urban density thinned as they continued toward the town gate, where they arrived at a wall: an impressive palisade of twelve-foot-high oak logs, tips sharpened to dragon teeth. Stuyvesant halted the carriage so his passengers could marvel at its extent. It bisected the island, stretching all the way from the North River to the East River, with seven bastions spaced at intervals. It had been there now fifteen years. He himself had contributed 150 gold guilders to its building. The contractor was an Englishman, one Baxter. Would they like to know what this Baxter *now* was doing? He has taken up a new career—stealing the horses of Dutch settlers on the Long Island! Stuyvesant made a reproving *tuk-tuk* sound with his tongue.

Balty praised his host's admirable wall and asked if it kept out the savages.

Stuyvesant smiled. "But the wall is not for keeping out Indians. It's for keeping out English!"

"Oh," Balty said, unsure how to respond. "Has it . . . worked?"

Stuyvesant chortled. "It seems not. After all, here are *you*." He added diplomatically, "But you are welcome in New Amsterdam."

"Too kind."

"People now are saying we must have a bigger wall."

"Not on our account, I hope."

Stuyvesant shrugged. "If to this it comes, maybe I will ask your King Charles to pay for it."

"A most amusing idea. Is it not, Huncks?"

"Sartainly, his majesty would find it so."

Stuyvesant flicked his whip and they proceeded out New Amsterdam's gate, to a salute from the guards that Huncks thought a tad slovenly. Dutch.

The highway was on an ancient Indian footpath that went the length of Manhatoes, through a forest Stuyvesant called Greenwych, which he translated as "place of pines."

Shortly he veered east off the main highway onto a more narrow path through marshland alive with bird chatter and the flutter of bats. Balty thought it looked a bit malarial, though it had a kind of damp serenity. It was understandable that the old boy would look forward to ending the day here, after the thrum and bustle of New Amsterdam. They passed through squish onto more firma terra and presently arrived at Bouwerie Number One.

The address struck them as somewhat grandiose, there being no Bouwerie Number Two, Three, or Four. But it was handsome: two stories of stone and wood, with a small chapel, plain in the Calvinist fashion. The surprise was the conservatory, inhabited by a number of tropical birds. Stuyvesant had acquired a fondness for the exotically plumed creatures during his years in the Indies.

Mevrouw (Madame) Stuyvesant—Judith—was introduced. Balty thought her on the grim side. She was already a long-in-the-tooth spinster of thirty-seven when she met Stuyvesant two decades ago. She helped to nurse him back to health in Holland after his nine-year-long ordeal of the unhealing leg. Her father, like Stuyvesant's, was a minister, a Huguenot who'd fled the horrors of persecution in Catholic France. Balty was about to try a few *bons mots* on the old girl in their shared native tongue, but the Governor tugged at them to follow him to the conservatory. He was impatient to preen over his menagerie. Mevrouw Stuyvesant retreated to the kitchen to supervise supper while Balty and Huncks were introduced to various birds.

Chief among equals in this feathery multitude was Johann, a Brazilian parrot of blazing colors. The gruff and imposing Governor-General of New Netherland became a boy of seven. He nuzzled, murmured, cooed. Johann requited his affection with squawkings and purrings and screeches. Here truly, as the saying had it, were two birds of one feather. Balty thought it rather touching.

Johann hopped from his perch onto Stuyvesant's forearm and squinted in bliss as his master stroked his head with a forefinger. Old Petrus put a slice of apple in his teeth and offered it. Johann clamped his beak on it and pulled it out. A look of pure adoration came over Stuyvesant. Underhill was wrong when he said no one liked Old Petrus. And so in to dinner.

A splendid one at that: three varieties of fish, admirably poached; lobsters; roast fowl; veal and pigeon pie with a commendably flaky crust; tarts; puddings; apples, pears, peaches; a gallimaufry of cheeses— Balty tallied seven kinds—from various regions of the Netherlands. Old Petrus descanted in scholarly fashion on each, giving its pedigree as if describing lineages going back to Charlemagne. All of this washed down with an array of wines, including a standout Rhenish that had survived the tossings of the Atlantic passage without surrendering itself to vinegar. Stuyvesant barely touched his but attentively refilled his guests' glasses. A model host. Contentment and geniality settled on the table as the last rays of the sun streamed through the windows. Old Petrus seemed in every way "at home." But then, he was.

He spoke of the English with fondness, and what seemed genuine regret that the two greatest countries on earth should be at each other's throat.

Prompted by a get-on-with-it glance from Huncks, Balty gently introduced the subject of the regicides. Stuyvesant frowned pensively.

He would pay his hests the compliment of candor. Himself he was no monarchist. Sure. Anteriorly, his sympathies were with Cromwell. Yes, he would admit to this. But all that was the past. They must understand that decades of terrible wars—with Spain, with France, atrocities about which one could not even speak—had made the thought of rule by kings a thing odious to the Dutch people.

Here Old Petrus paused—for effect, perhaps.

But *rehicide* . . . The moist lips pursed. A *grave* business.

Balty wondered: Was the old boy essaying a pun?

Stuyvesant's voice lowered to the timbre of a bassoon as he embarked on an interminable story, the gist of which Balty was at pains to follow. Stuyvesant's ornate, wooden English didn't help.

So far as Balty could make out it had to do with some Old Testament king named Ahab. And another king, with far too many syllables in his name. Jehoshaphat or somesuch. Then yet *another* king was added, this one calling himself by the more modest name of Aram.

Jehosowhat and Aram didn't get on with Ahab. There was a huge to-do over . . . by now Balty had completely lost track . . . some great to-do, anyway, with much shouting and banging.

Ahab declared he would *not* put on kingly clothing. This Stuyvesant related as if it contained a clue to the Apocalypse. It seemed to Balty that a king ought to be able to decide whatever kind of clothing he wanted. What was the point of being king? But never mind.

Then it was into the chariots and tallyho and once more onto the beach. The battle was joined against the enemy, whoever *they* were. Ahab got an arrow in his armpit and out the chest. No joy there.

Whereupon Ahab announced—nay, demanded—that he be taken home to Samaria. Why Samaria? Never mind.

On the way, he bled profusely into his chariot, making a nasty mess. But good news for the dogs, who lapped up the royal blood.

Now the chariot was so disgusting the only thing to do was to immerse it entire in a pool. Not just any pool, mind—one that prostitutes bathed in. Why? Was no other pool available? Never mind.

Balty wondered if the innkeeper had seen to changing the bed linen. He certainly didn't relish sleeping in bloody sheets after this grisly story.

Stuyvesant was now in a rapture of narration. He looked like an Old Testament prophet, eyes glowing with holy fire.

Suddenly he broke off the story and went into a kind of trance.

"And so Ahab *died*," he said, as if chiseling each word into stone, "and his son Ahaziah became king in his place!"

Not another *king*, Balty thought.

Stuyvesant went back into his trance. Balty had to pee. He glanced at Huncks. Stuyvesant roused himself from holy stupor and intoned: ". . . in the palace of *ifry*."

Balty waited. "Ifry?"

Stuyvesant nodded.

"Ivory," Huncks explained. "First Kings, twenty-two. Oh, a grand tale, yer excellency. And may I say, beautifully rendered." Huncks thumped the table. "Bravo, sir. Bravo."

The air was rent with yet another shriek from the conservatory—*Akkkkkkkkhhh!* Johann had been issuing clamorous interjections throughout the story, like a beadle banging the floor with his rod to wake dozing parishioners during the homily.

More food arrived. Balty, bloated and stuperous, bladder near to bursting, let Huncks hold up the English side while he concentrated on tightening his sphincter. Old Petrus was content to do all the talking, Huncks interjecting anodyne comments here and there.

Balty squirmed, dreaming of a pisspot. Someone had told him

that Hollanders were a taciturn lot. Really? Old Petrus's capacity for monologue was Homeric. Loquacity born of loneliness? Hard to imagine him and the Mevrouw jabbering away at each other.

Passing behind Huncks's chair with yet another dish, the serving girl stopped and stared at the back of Huncks's head, eyes wide.

The attentive Mevrouw, who'd so far uttered barely a word, spoke to the girl in Dutch. The girl replied; Mevrouw Stuyvesant passed whatever it was along to her husband.

"You are bleeding," Old Petrus said to Huncks.

"Apologies, sir. I 'ope I've not ruint yer rug."

"It's not my concern, the rug. Are you wanting a doctor?"

"Not at t'all, your honor. 'Tis nothing. Had a tumble in the street. This arternoon, boulevarding in yer lovely town."

Stuyvesant looked from Huncks to Balty and back at Huncks.

"*Both* of you fell?"

Huncks laughed. "We've been in New England all this time. Where they've only dirt roads. None so handsomely cobbled as your own. You must take our injuries as a compliment."

Stuyvesant shrugged. "Our streets are good, yes. But if our English visitors are falling upon the copples . . . perhaps we must put down straw. To make soft your fallings."

"Ha. Entirely our own cloomsiness, sar. My own, rather. Marster Balthasar is himself a very deft person."

"He cannot hear?"

"No, sir, I meant—but never mind. But speaking of doctors . . ."

Huncks began to probe. On their way here, he said, they had passed through land said to belong to a certain Dr. Pell. Was it true that this Pell had purchased the land from a savage named Wampage?

Stuyvesant scowled at the mention of Pell. Yes, he said. This was so.

Huncks asked if it was also true that there was some dispute as to whether Pell's land was in New Netherland.

Out came the lion in Stuyvesant, roaring. Absolutely not! This Englishman, this Pell—he spat the word—owned the land, yes, but the land was Dutch. Every acre, Dutch! Never mind what Pell is always claiming! All the maps, all the documents to this would attest!

Huncks nodded sympathetically. "Yes, that were the impression Marster Balthasar and meself had formed. That the land is indeed part of New Netherland."

Stuyvesant nodded, ire assuaged.

"The reason I brings it up," Huncks continued, "is that whilst passing through this *Pell* land—in New Netherland, as your honor correctly points out—we occasioned to meet with some folk. We explained our parpose here—namely, that we're by way of hoonting for Whalley and Goffe, the regicide judges. We gave a description. And these folk told us that they'd seen them. A number of times. Lurking about. On *Pell's* land."

Stuyvesant roused, eyes narrowing. "Is this for sure?"

"Oh," Huncks said, "they were *quite* sure it were the dastard regicides they saw. Marster Balthasar and meself would have made a search of the woods ourselves, but it's considerable large for the two of us to cover, what with so many wild savages about. So we thought it best to continue on to New Amsterdam and pay our respects to yer warship and ask *yer* advice."

Stuyvesant fell into silent thought.

Huncks now went in for the kill. "I were only thinking, sir, that if these caitiffs—criminals, that is—*are* hiding there . . . well, as you yourself have made aboondantly clear, it *is* Netherlander land. When Colonel Nicholls comes to pay his respects to yer honor, I shouldn't be surprised if he were to ask if yer honor has knowledge as to the whereabouts of the murderers of his majesty's father. And, well, it might be somewhat *arwkward* for your honor if it turned out they was hiding in yer own backyard. So to speak. Might be taken the wrong way, I mean. I'm only looking out here for yer honor's best interests."

Stuyvesant had gone into another of his trances. He brightened. A look of mischief came over him.

He smiled. "If these persons have been seen there, then we must make a good searching of Pell's land."

"Just the thing." Huncks nodded.

A look of dreamy pleasure came over Stuyvesant as he pondered swarming Pell's land with his soldiers. "And if they are found there, it must be that *Pell* has been hiding them."

"Well," Huncks said, "sartainly *that* question will have to be asked. Oh, yes."

"In that case, then Pell must forfeit the land," Stuyvesant said. "As punishment, for hiding these men."

"Well," Huncks said, "I cannot speak for his majesty. But I believe yer honor may be onto something there. Sartainly his majesty would not be pleased to hear that one of his own soobjects has been sheltering his own dear father's murderers."

"Yes." Stuyvesant nodded. "Yes."

An expensive clock chimed the hour, prompting another ear-splitting shriek from Johann.

Stuyvesant apologized to his guests. How thoughtless of him to keep them so long. Forgive! But it was not so often that the opportunity presented to converse so pleasantly with English visitors. He pushed back from the table and, leaning on his cane, rose to flesh-and-wood feet.

His guests must bid good night to Johann. Johann would be very cross if they did not.

Good night, Johann. Johann was rewarded with a crumble of cheese. Was it not wonderful that he enjoyed cheese? Indeed, yes, it was. *Johann likes many cheeses.* Oh? *But he does not like Gouda.* Ah? Well. Fascinating. Brazilian parrots do not like Gouda. Who knew?

The carriage was sent for. Balty left Huncks and Stuyvesant talking on the stoop while he dashed around the side of Bouwerie Number One, unbuttoning as he went. With the expression of one transfigured, he *aah*ed as his undammed bladder released a cataract into the soil of New Netherland. Here was a micturition to inspire a ballad. Nothing would grow here for years. Decades.

The carriage pulled up, driven by servant Willem, who would take them back to town. Tomorrow, they must come to see him, Stuyvesant said. To discuss how to make eventful and welcome the arriving of

Colonel Nicholls. Meanwhile, he would immediately issue the orders for a complete searching of Pell's land, however many soldiers were of necessity for this.

Balty and Huncks thanked the Governor for his hospitality. If only all Dutch and English could come together in such fraternity and good feelings.

Good night. God's blessings.

Johann rent the night with a final valedictory screech.

"*Ghastly* bird," Balty said when the carriage was a safe distance from the house.

Huncks put a finger to his lips and pointed at the driver. Balty said in a louder voice, "*Glorious* bird. *Marvelous* dinner. *Splendid* host, the Governor."

The carriage rumbled along the path through the marshland. Pockets of water shimmered silver in moonlight. The chill damp and the silhouettes of dead trees gave the place an eerie air. Balty shuddered and pulled his jacket collar about his neck. They spoke in whispers.

"What was all that mumbo jumbo about Whalley and Goffe lurking in Dr. Pell's woods?" Balty asked. "Sounds like he's going to send his whole army in there."

"Let's hope he does. The more soldiers he sends there, the fewer there'll be in New Amsterdam when Nicholls arrives."

"Oh. I say. Clever you."

"Now he's got an excuse to occupy Pell's land. To make a good show of being Dutch."

"What was the point of that revolting—and very tedious—Bible story?"

"Which part of it confused you?"

"Every part."

"Ahab was a wicked king who led Israel into idolatry. I suspect that was the point."

"What's idolatry got to do with the price of eggs?"

"It's an allegory."

"Might you explain the allegory for those of us who didn't attend Harvard. However briefly."

"The idolater is King Charles."

"His majesty? He doesn't go about worshipping golden calves. Nonsense."

"Balty, by now you've gathered that many people think his majesty's a closet Catholic."

"What's that got to do with dogs lapping up blood? Chariots immersed in prostitutes' bathwater? Charming dinner conversation."

"I gather the significance of King Ahab's queen also eluded you. Jezebel?"

"It's a tart's name."

"Jezebel was the original tart. The ur-tart, if you will."

"The what?"

"The allegory there is to his majesty's mistress. Lady Castlemaine."

"Daft. All of it."

"It didn't end well for old Jez. Got chucked out the palace window. The palace of *ifry*. And et by dogs."

Balty winced. "The dogs in that household certainly didn't lack for refreshment. Horrible."

"All they could find of her to bury was her skull and the palms of her hands."

"Huncks, please. It's marvelous, this abundant erudition of yours, but my meal's going to come up if you continue."

"It was to fulfill the prophecy of Elijah. Second Kings, chapter nine."

"So endeth the bloody lesson. Amen."

Servant Willem had the horse going at a brisk trot. The lights of the town loomed.

"I'm exhausted," Balty said. "Thank God we don't have to sleep in bloody sheets, or I'd be dreaming of dogs licking at me."

"What do you mean?"

"I tipped the innkeep to change our bed linen."

Huncks groaned.

"What on earth's wrong? Did you *want* to sleep in blood-soaked sheets? Very well. I'll have him put them back on the bed. Really, Huncks, sometimes I simply don't understand you."

"You gave them a pretext to go into our room."

"It's an *inn*, for God's sake, not some inner sanctum Holy of Holies."

Huncks drew a small pistol from inside his jacket.

Balty stared. "Where did you get *that*?"

"Levy. If things happen, stay close."

"Things? We've just come from a sumptuous dinner with the Governor, for God's sake."

"Just keep your wits about you. If the word 'wits' applies in your case."

They passed through the town gate. No salutes this time, only sullen stares from guards. New Amsterdam was quiet. Even the silence seemed tidy and Dutch.

The carriage continued past the fort and turned onto Pearl Street. Huncks's eyes darted about, surveilling. Across the street from the Horn of Plenty stood six soldiers, milling about in a way that struck Huncks as contrived. They watched the carriage approach, then looked away in unison.

Huncks murmured, "Look sharp."

They went in. The innkeeper looked at them, nodded curtly, then glanced into the tavern room. Four soldiers sat at the table nearest the entrance. They looked at Balty and Huncks as their comrades outside had, and turned away. There were no drinks on their table.

They started up the stairs. On the landing below their room, Huncks motioned to Balty to stop. There was a window facing the back. Huncks opened it and peered out. The yard was deep, extending twenty-five or so yards to the back wall. Sheds, a bird coop, crates, barrels, oddments, all neatly arrayed in the Dutch way. Six feet below the window, a slanted roof protruded. Huncks motioned to Balty and pointed. "There's our way out. Can you swim the river?"

"Certainly not," Balty said, as though the question was not only outlandish but in bad taste.

"D'you remember the garden he showed us on the way out?"

"Yes. I think so."

"If we're separated, look for me there. But let's stay together." Huncks drew a dagger from his boot and gave it to Balty.

"What's *that* for?"

"To pare your nails." Seeing the look on Balty's face, Huncks put his hand on his shoulder. "It'll be all right, old boy." He winked. "Be English."

They climbed the stairs to their room. Huncks inserted the key and opened the door.

Deputy Koontz sat at the table, Huncks's fort diagram spread out in front of him. A guard in the far corner pointed his pistol.

"Finally, you arrive," Koontz said with weary heartiness, as if greeting tardy mates.

"A good evening to you, sar," Huncks said. "To what do we owe this pleasure?"

"Your dinner with the Heneral was good?"

"Very good indeed. Have you come to tuck us in?"

Koontz held up the drawing. "The servant girl is finding this, here in your room." Koontz held it to the candlelight and regarded it. "My compliments. It's good. So many informations. Cannons, troops, ships."

"May I arsk, what is it?" Huncks said.

Koontz smiled. "It's late in the night for games."

"Whatever it is, sar, it weren't in this room when we left to dine with your Governor."

Koontz folded it and tucked it away. He stood and looked about the room.

"What a pity you must change from this room to the one before, in the fort. It's not so nice."

"If the item in question was indeed found in our room, it were put here. So as to create an unfavorable impression."

Koontz said to the guard, "*Hij liegt.*" He's lying. The guard nodded.

"So now we go," Koontz said.

"As yer honor commands." Huncks made a little bow of courtesy and stood back to allow Koontz a path to the door. "If yer honor will lead the way."

Koontz passed. The guard paused and gestured at Huncks to walk ahead of him. Huncks made another bow, this one deeper. As he came up, he yanked the pistol from the guard's hand. The guard lurched forward. Huncks brought the butt down on his head, dropping him. Koontz wheeled to find himself staring at the muzzle.

"*Ik spreek nederlands*," Huncks said, adding, "*Helaas voor jou.* You shouldn't have told him I was lying, or I'd have come along peaceable like. And we'd have got all this sorted out with your General. But now it's late for that. Sit."

"You cannot get away. I have men everywhere."

"So we saw, coming in. But being innocent of this farce of yours, we thought nothing of it. Now, if you please, *sit.*"

Koontz sat.

"Marster Balthasar. Take yer knife and cut that nice clean bed linen into strips with which to tie the feller lying on the floor. Nice and tight. Not forgetting to gag him. Good thing you arsked the innkeeper to change the sheets or what a narsty taste he'd have in his mouth."

Balty went about it.

"Now then, my dear Deputy, if you'd kindly hand over the item, so that I might have a look at it."

Koontz gave Huncks the drawing. Huncks examined it as if it were unfamiliar, frowning.

"It *is* good, I must say. A most commendable rendering. Who's the artist? Was it yourself?"

"It was found in *this* room," Koontz said.

"Not so loud, if you please. Where in the room exactly were it found?"

"On the floor."

"The floor? How careless. Where on the floor?"

Koontz pointed.

Huncks smiled and shook his head.

"Darlin' Deputy Koontz. It's one thing to accuse us of being spies. But to accuse us of leaving an incriminating diagram of yer fort on the *floor* like a tossed hankie—it's insoolting."

Koontz made no reply.

"Come," Huncks said. "Surely you see what's going on, sar. It were planted. Someone shoved it under the door. Didn't even need to fuss with the lock. What time did the servant girl bring your attention to this miraculous discovery?"

"Six. Maybe after."

"Six. Well, now, aren't that convenient? Inasmooch as we departed to sup with the General at five. Whoever slid it under the door would've known we was gone. And the only people who knew that were the innkeep. And yerself."

"You are accusing that *I* am putting this?"

Huncks wondered: Might *Koontz* be protecting the regicides without Stuyvesant's knowledge? Why would he? Hatred of King Charles I? Or that most prosaic but reliable of motives—money?

Balty looked up from trussing the guard and saw Huncks holding the pistol behind his back, casually. His fingers fiddled with the pistol's mechanism.

"No," Huncks said, "I can't believe it were yerself who done it."

Huncks turned to show Koontz the back of his head, clotted with blood.

"Marster Balthasar and I were assaulted this arternoon. Down there, in the street. It weren't no robbery. I recognized the fellow, y'see. We encountered him in New Haven. Him and his Indian accomplice. They're protecting the men we seek. The regicides, that is."

"We know nothing of your rehicides," Koontz said petulantly.

Huncks nodded.

"Indeed, sar, I'm beginning to believe that you don't. But don't it interest you that we was assaulted, on your own streets, by these men? Do it not suggest to you that the regicides *are* here?"

Koontz held up his hands in frustration.

"We are many people here! Almost two thousands! We are a port. All the time, people coming, going."

"Point taken. Point taken. Well then, Deputy Koontz, where does this leave us? Friends or foes?"

"Friends do not point guns to each other."

"Point taken again. So were I to return this pistol to you, would you accept what I've told you and call it quits? And sit down and have a drink?"

Koontz stared. "Yes. I accept what you say."

"Well then," Huncks said, "friends it is."

He handed Koontz the pistol. Koontz took it, cocked the hammer, and pointed it at Huncks.

"Oh, Deputy Koontz. You disappoint me."

Huncks reached inside his jacket, as if for a weapon.

Koontz pulled the trigger. The hammer snapped against the frizzen and into the pan, sparkless.

"You disappoint me again, sir," Huncks said, dropping the accent. "An officer of your experience, not noticing that the flint's been removed. Tsk."

Huncks took the useless weapon from the blushing Deputy.

"It seems we must proceed as foes. I'd have preferred otherwise."

A clump of boots came up the stairs and stopped on the landing.

Huncks put a finger to his lips and pressed the muzzle of his own pistol, flint intact, to Koontz's forehead.

A voice called out. "*Plaatsvervanger?*" Deputy?

Huncks whispered, "Answer him. Remember, *Ik spreek nederlands.*"

"*Wat?*" Koontz said.

"*Allemaal goed?*" All good?

Huncks nodded.

Koontz said, "*Ja.*"

Huncks whispered, "It was a mistake."

"*Het was een vergissing.*"

Silence. The voice called, "*Smit! Bent u er?*" Smit! Are you there?

"You sent him to the fort. To fetch some papers."

"*Ik stuurde hem naar het fort. Voor sommige documenten.*"

"Tell them to wait for you downstairs."

"*Wacht op mij beneden.*"

"You'll buy drinks."

Koontz grinned strangely.

"*Ik koop drankjes voor ons.*"

Silence. Boots descending stairs. Huncks kept the gun to Koontz's head until the footfall ceased. He and Balty tied Koontz to his chair. Huncks balled a fistful of bedsheet.

"Who's protecting them? Stuyvesant? Or you?"

"This is all a nonsense," Koontz said sullenly.

Huncks smiled. "I wonder what we'd find if *your* room was searched? Eh? English guineas? Well, it's been lovely."

Huncks stuffed the gag in his mouth and secured it with a strip of bedsheet. He tipped Koontz and the chair backward onto the floor. He replaced the flint in Koontz's pistol and gave the smaller one to Balty.

"Now what?" Balty asked.

"Where there are no alternatives, there are no problems."

"What?"

Huncks slowly opened the door. The landing was empty. They exited the room with the two trussed Dutchmen, and crept slowly down the stairs. On the bottom step, Huncks held up a hand and listened. Voices, from the far end of the landing, murmuring. Huncks tucked his pistol into his jacket and indicated to Balty to do the same. He whispered, "Laugh."

Huncks laughed. Loudly, bellowingly. On his happiest, drunkest day, Falstaff had never laughed so hard. Balty followed.

They stepped out onto the landing. The two soldiers stood before them with drawn swords.

Huncks addressed them as though delighted. "Ah, *there* you are! Good!"

The soldiers stared.

"Speak English?"

One of them replied, "I speak."

"Good. Deputy Koontz sent us to get more gin." Huncks mimed a bottle to the lips. "Gin?" He pointed downstairs. "Drink? Gin, to take upstairs."

The soldiers advanced.

Huncks drew his pistol. "*Wie wil eerst sterven?*" Who wants to die first?

He motioned to the floor.

"*Lie down.*" The soldiers lay down on their stomachs. Balty took their swords.

"Now what?"

"Stop saying that."

"Should I get more linen to tie them up?"

"No time."

Huncks stood between the men. "Sorry about this, chaps." He clubbed each on the back of the head and pointed at the window.

Balty clambered over the sill and dropped to the slanted roof below. The tiles were slimy. His feet went out from under him. He slid on his back, feet first, flailing, and sailed off the edge. On the way down, his foot caught on something. He felt a fierce wrench in his ankle, and landed on a slumbering pig.

The pig, unaccustomed to serving as a nocturnal cushion for defenestrated humans, squealed vehemently. Balty lay facedown in pig muck, dazed, ankle aflame in pain, trying, as Huncks had so often urged him, to gather his wits.

From above he heard a torrent of curses as a second Icarus fell from the sky. Huncks was heavier than Balty, so his trajectory was shorter, but his landing—on a recumbent sow—was no less porcine. Her ululations joined the squealing in progress.

Balty felt his arm being yanked. Huncks was growling at him to get up.

Balty stood on one foot. When he put weight on the other, he collapsed.

He tried again but fell back into pig muck. Huncks bent and grabbed him by the wrist, then slung him over his shoulder and staggered off.

The back door of the inn flew open. The night filled with Dutch curses. Weaving under his burden, Huncks stumbled toward the far end of the yard. It seemed very far away. The shouting behind them grew louder and was joined by the barking of dogs.

Huncks trudged on, tilting to and fro. Summoning all his reserves of strength, he made it to the end of the yard, to a wall about the height of a man. Huncks backed away and then lumbered toward it. He pitched Balty over the wall like a sack of potatoes. In the next instant, with fangs snapping at his ankles, he heaved himself over.

They lay, gasping and aching, on the deserted street. Huncks looked in both directions. At the southern end, he saw one of the fort's bastions. At the other end, what looked to be the canal.

"That way," Huncks said, pointing at the canal.

"It's no good, Huncks. Go."

Huncks staggered to his feet and tried to lift Balty, but his epic zigzag across the swine- and dog-infested yard had sapped his reserves of strength.

From the other side of the wall came shouting and barking, louder now.

"*Go*," Balty said. "Don't be a tit."

There was a door at the far end of the wall. They heard a jangle of keys and the door rattling in its jamb.

"*Go*, Huncks."

The door swung open. Soldiers tumbled out, looking up and down the street. Huncks aimed his pistol. The soldiers ducked back through the door.

"Shooting them isn't going to help," Balty said. "For God's sake, just *go*."

"I'll be back. With the English Navy."

Huncks ran toward the canal and disappeared into the darkness. The soldiers emerged with muskets and bayonets. Balty raised his arms in surrender and was swarmed by captors.

– *CHAPTER 39* –

August 20th. My Lord Downing called late in the afternoon.
He looked about and inspected my cell, making a face at the
smell, holding his pomander to his nose and peering through the
window onto Tower Green, making little noises. "Hm! Um!
Umm!" etc., etc.

"Well, a fine view, Mr. Peeping Pepys. Perfect for peeping,
eh?" Etc.

Made no response, being in no frame for persiflage.

My lord sat himself upon a stool—the only stool—and said
in a solemn tone that he had much weighed my "matter," and
had come to the conclusion that a publick tryal would only bring
infamy and shame. Not only upon my own person, but also
upon the Navy itself and my Lord Sandwich, who despite his
"whoreing" was still held in his majesty's affections. Etc.

He continued, saying that as the hour of "the King's Great
Endeavor" was fast approaching, he had concluded that my
scandal could only hamper England's prospeckts with respeckt to
New Netherland, and then suggested that he may have resolved
upon a possible "solution."

Keenly interested in any "solution" that would spare me
living the balance of my life scratching lamentable graffitoes into
walls, or having my head separated from the rest of me and made
food for ravens, I indicated to my lord great eagerness to hear it.

"To deploy a naval term," he said, "were you to 'come about' as

to the matter of war with Holland, his majesty might incline to forgive your—let us call it out of charity—'lapse.'"

"And how would I accomplish this 'coming about'?" I asked.

"By publishing to his majesty and the Duke of York, Lord High Admiral, that you have changed your opinion and are now fully satisfied that the Navy is ready to engage Holland upon the seas. What say you, Mr. Peeping Pepys?"

Whereat Mr. Peeping Pepys gave his immediate and wholehearted assent to this solution and furthermore complimented his Lord Downing on devising such an elegant— let us call it—scaffold upon which to support his zeal for war with Odious Holland.

And lo, within the hour, Mr. Pepys made his exit across the drawbridge and under the portcullis of the Middle Tower; and never had he experienced ambulation more joyous.

– *CHAPTER 40* –

Too Kind

B alty woke to the sound of his cell door opening. He'd only just dozed off. It was early, judging from the faint light coming through the barred window. The blaze of pain in his ankle had dwindled to a small fire. Luckily, no bones protruded from the skin.

Deputy Koontz entered. He looked unslept.

"How is your angle?"

"Bit throbby. Thank you for asking."

"The Heneral has been informed."

"I should bloody well hope so."

"Can you walk?"

"No."

"I will arrange for a chair to carry you."

"A sedan chair? I've always wanted to have a ride in one of those. My mother—never mind. I must say, you're being very civilized, considering what a night we've all had."

Koontz sat on the stool by Balty's pallet bed. He looked haggard.

"The Heneral must go up the river. To Fort Oranje."

"Oh? What's in Fort Oranje?"

"There is another trwabble with the Mohawks. Always they are making slaughters."

"Doesn't sound at all pleasant. I don't envy the General, having to cope with all that."

"Let us speak about last night. Your accomplice, Mr. Uncks—"

"Associate, if you please."

"He speaks very well Dutch. And what variety, his accenting of English."

"Yes. He's quite versatile, Huncks. You rather have to be, in his line of business." Balty quickly added, "Manhunting, that is."

Koontz grinned slyly. "Do you know what was his mistake? What made alerted my men? When he made me to say that I would buy them drinks. *Never* would my men beleef that I would buy them drinks."

"Alas for me you're not nicer to your men. It wasn't very sporting of you, pulling the trigger on Huncks. You're lucky he wasn't more severe with you. He doesn't take kindly to people trying to kill him."

Koontz took a piece of paper from his pocket and unfolded it.

Balty groaned. "Not *another* drawing. Who's this by? Rembrandt?"

"No, no. It's a . . . declaring."

"What?"

"A stating of . . . *schuldgevoelens* . . . confessioning . . ."

"Is 'confession' the word you're groping for?"

"Yes. Thank you. Concerning about the true reason for you coming to New Amsterdam."

"Koontz, really, you're being a bore. We'll discuss all that with the General."

"Mr. Balthasar. I am tired. You are tired. And you are injured. And the Heneral is going up the river. So please."

"I'll discuss it *with your General*."

Koontz sighed. He stood and put the confession on the table.

"You must sign. When the Heneral returns, then will come the meeting with him." He turned to leave.

"I say, Koontz?"

"Yes?"

"Since you've introduced the subject of confession, tell me: You and Jones, *are* you doing business together? That the General doesn't know about?"

"What a question, Mr. Balthasar."

"You Dutch do have the reputation of being rather eager when it comes to commerce."

"I will ask for the surgeon to come. To see about your angle."

"Too kind."

Huncks sat wrapped in a blanket by the stove in the Breuckelen farmhouse serving as headquarters for Dr. Pell and his Westchester Trained Band of four hundred men. His swim across the East River had left him shaking from exhaustion.

Captain Underhill was present. The Cincinnatus of Long Island had finally been unable to resist the drumbeat of Mars. Mrs. Underhill had done everything in her power to bar his way: lecturing him on his obligations as a Quaker, hiding his boots, even physically barring the door. After a dialogue that would have exhausted Socrates, Underhill wore her down, swearing that he had no intention, himself, of bearing arms, or of playing any "direct role"—as he put it—in the coming engagement. His sole intention, he averred, was to be present in Breuckclen—to *observe*. To offer such advice as he might in order to mitigate the spillage of blood. And bring about peace as quickly as possible. What was Quakerism, if not *that*?

Mrs. Underhill finally capitulated to her husband's dissembling and trundled off to her bed, muttering darkly about the all-observing eye of God. The Cincinnatus of Long Island was out the door in a shot, making for the barn—by the long way, to avoid being seen from their bedroom window. He dug out his old war chest from its hiding place and got his pistols, helmet, sword, and cuirass. Thus equipped, he mounted his horse and made his way once more onto the beach.

The old warrior's departure was observed by another member of the household, who threw a shawl over her shoulders and quietly slipped out of the house and followed.

In Breuckelen, Underhill found himself all these years later face-to-face with his ancient nemesis, Dr. Pell. Theirs was a shaky truce.

But as the atmosphere in the farmhouse grew more martial by the hour, old animosities fell away.

Winthrop was on his way from Hartford. Underhill had received a communication from him. He said they would find the Governor in "no good humor."

After landing at Boston, Colonel Nicholls dispatched word to New England's governors, informing them of his majesty's intention to wrest New Netherland from the Dutch. His majesty's further intention was a dagger between Winthrop's shoulder blades.

In 1661, Winthrop returned from London with a royal charter giving him authority over the New Haven colony. His majesty had confided in him his future intention to seize New Netherland. Moreover, the king promised Winthrop rule of the former Dutch possessions, including all land south of the Massachusetts border, extending west all the way to—the Pacific!

For three years, Winthrop had smacked his lips in anticipation of becoming lord of such a vast tract of land. All the way to the Pacific—wherever *that* might be.

Now came word from Nicholls that his majesty would grant this immensity of territory not to Winthrop, but to the king's own brother, the Duke of York.

Perfide Albion! Winthrop was left to curse and mutter. How unhappy those who entrust their faith to the promises of kings! Viewed less moralistically, it was a case of the fox being outfoxed. At any rate, there it was.

Winthrop's fury was justified. But holding a grudge against one's king is usually bootless and always risky. Fortunately, Winthrop's cunning was stronger than his pride. He swallowed the latter and deployed the former, sending his compliments to Nicholls and offering his services to him and his majesty in the forthcoming action in New Amsterdam. Smart move.

All this Winthrop relayed to Underhill in his letter, which Underhill now relayed to the assembled parties in Breuckelen. Underhill strongly suggested that under the circumstances, when Winthrop arrived, japery on the theme of the empty promises of princes would be "inappropriate."

Huncks had done his job. He had only one concern now—Balty. From the moment he staggered into the Breuckelen farmhouse, drenched, shivering, half dead, he agitated with Pell and Underhill to secure Balty's release.

Pell and Underhill were adamant that nothing must be done that would give away the game. Any attempt to get Balty released, even a request framed diplomatically, might make Stuyvesant suspicious and put New Amsterdam back on a war footing. That could only result in greater casualties when hostilities commenced. Huncks must understand. Anyway, they told him, why would Stuyvesant hang an Englishman, a Crown agent, knowing that a squadron of English warships was approaching? If he was truly convinced Balty was a spy, he'd hold him as a surety.

"Surety?" Huncks said. "Speak plain. Hostage."

"What would you have us do, Huncks? Start the war *now*? Patience, man."

"So your position," Huncks shot back, "is Stuyvesant won't hang him now. He'll wait until Nicholls arrives and then hang him."

Pell and Underhill looked at each other. *Huncks served under Winthrop. He'll listen to him.*

"Hiram. Winthrop will be here any moment. Hold fast. Let's hear what he has to say. There's a good fellow."

CHAPTER 41

Very Good Surgeon

Balty's cell door opened to admit a small, weedy-looking man with a leather bag that made a metallic clank when he set it on the table. With him were two other men, stout fellows. Deputy Koontz brought up the rear.

"Here is surgeon," he announced.

"And these other chaps?"

"Assistants."

"For an ankle? Is that . . . necessary?"

The surgeon pulled the stool to the foot of Balty's bed and sat and rolled up Balty's trouser leg.

"Jolly nice of you," Balty said.

The surgeon poked at the ankle with his finger. Balty let out a yelp. "I say! Do you mind being a bit more ginger?"

Koontz spoke to the surgeon in Dutch. The surgeon seemed oddly amused. Koontz picked up the confession he'd left on the table and examined it.

"You have not signed."

"Of course not."

The surgeon squeezed Balty's ankle. Balty gasped.

"You, sir! What are you doing?" Balty said to Koontz, "I say, is this person a surgeon, or the local butcher? In the event, kindly inform him that my ankle is not a joint of mutton."

Koontz and the surgeon spoke.

"He says your angle is very bad."

"Well it's certainly no better for his ministrations."

"He says the foot must come off."

Balty stared. "I *beg* your pardon?"

Koontz made a sawing motion with his hand. "Or you will extinguish. From infecting."

The surgeon went to his bag and opened it and took out a surgical saw.

"No, no, no," Balty said, sitting up, drawing back his ankle. He laughed nervously. "I think there's some mistake here. Look." Balty wiggled his ankle. "See? Perfectly good. Just a bit sore."

Koontz shook his head. "No mistake. He's very good surgeon."

The two "assistants" produced a long leather strap and, pressing down on Balty's shoulders, cinched him tightly around the chest to the pallet bed.

"Now see here, Koontz . . ."

The Deputy seemed to find it all rather entertaining.

"Like last night, eh? When you and Mr. Uncks was tying me to the chair. Makes difficult, the breathing, no?"

The surgeon spoke to Koontz.

"He asks do you want a piece of wood for your teeth? So you are not biting off tongue."

"No! I bloody well do not! Look here, this is no way to treat a commissioner of the King of England!"

The surgeon was now tying some other kind of strap above Balty's ankle and cinching it tight. The assistants each held down a leg.

"How else should we treat his majesty's commissioner, but to give him the best of medical attentioning?"

"You can't just go sawing off people's feet because their ankles hurt!"

Koontz shrugged. "We must do what the surgeon recommends. For your *own* benefiting."

The "surgeon" finished with his tourniquet and reached into his bag and brought forth a frightful-looking implement: a long, sharp knife.

Koontz said, "First he must cut into the flesh to make . . . how do you say? . . . the flap. Then must come the—" He mimed sawing. "Do you want gin? The Heneral says they gave him gin before they amp— what's the word?"

"'Amputate'! See here, Koontz—"

Two soldiers walking the fort grounds heard the scream. They stopped, looked at each other, then as soldiers must, shrugged and walked on.

Late that afternoon, a short man with a skullcap, his face framed by neat matching ringlets of hair, arrived at the Breuckelen farmhouse. Here was Asser Levy, kosher butcher of New Amsterdam, come to relay intelligence to his patron and friend Captain Underhill: Stuyvesant was headed upriver to Fort Orange. Mohawk trouble.

This news was joyously if skeptically received. *Stuyvesant's left New Amsterdam? To go to Orange, 150 miles upriver?*

Pell and Underhill and their war captains could scarcely believe it. Could it be some feint?

They decided no. The West India Company must have fallen for Downing's deception and assured Stuyvesant that the English squadron had no belligerent intent.

Huncks pulled Levy to a corner. Did he know anything of his companion, the Englishman who'd been taken prisoner?

Levy looked away. Huncks pressed.

"Yes," Levy said. "There was a report. Screams."

"Can you get me back on the island?"

Levy said he had a boat, but he would have to inform Captain Underhill.

"No," Huncks said.

Levy hesitated. Huncks took his arm. "The man they're torturing, he's my friend. Do you understand? He's my friend and it's my fault he's there. Help me."

Levy looked over at Underhill, deep in discussion with the others. He nodded.

Huncks gathered some things—a pistol, powder, a knife. Underhill noticed, but his attention was held by the war planning. Huncks slipped out the back door.

Two people on one horse approached, a man and woman. The rider halted. The woman slipped off. Huncks heard the word "thee."

He ducked behind a shed. Thankful presented herself to the two sentries. Was this where Captain Underhill was? The sentries refused to say, or to let her pass. She looked exhausted and defeated. Huncks stepped out of the shadows.

She ran to him and hugged him.

He asked sternly: Why had she come? This was no place for a woman.

She was breathless with news, which she conveyed in a tone of schoolgirl amusement. She giggled, telling how Mrs. Underhill had hidden the Captain's boots and even physically barred the door. How he'd sworn he only wanted to be an observer. A force for peace! How she'd seen him creep into the barn, looking over his shoulder, and come out the other side on his horse looking like a Spanish *conquistadore* off to do battle with Moctezuma.

Huncks listened impassively. Yes, but why had she come? In her condition.

She looked away. Huncks said, "I meant only—why are you here, Thankful? Don't you see what's going on?"

She said with an air of defiance that if there was going to be war, which there likely would, men *being* men and therefore *fools*, she would be more use here than at Killingworth, spinning wool and listening to Mrs. Underhill grumble about her pigheaded husband. She could help with the wounded. Anyway, she was here and she wasn't leaving, and that was that.

Where's Balty? she asked.

Huncks told her. Thankful turned away, took a few steps, and stumbled. Huncks caught her and helped her to a tree stump, where she sat. He took her hand

"I'm going to get him back." Under no circumstances must she tell anyone, especially Underhill. He'd only try to stop him.

The back door opened. Underhill emerged.

Huncks whispered, "If you want to be useful, here's your chance."

He walked away. Behind him he heard, "Captain Underhill! The devil himself! But looking more like Mars!"

Underhill stammered and spluttered. He tried to reproach her for coming, but *that* went nowhere. The old warrior was up against superior odds. Thankful was Leonidas at Thermopylae, yielding not an inch of ground. She'd come, she said, at Mrs. Underhill's bidding, to see that he abided by his pledge.

Underhill withered under the barrage of castigation, reduced to pouty silence.

Huncks made his way to the creek, where Levy waited with his shallop.

The tide was flooding, the current rushing north. All favorable. Huncks pointed: "That way."

Levy, confused, pointed instead directly across the river. "But your friend is *there*."

Huncks told him what he intended. Levy's eyes went wide. He smiled. Huncks said if he wanted no part, he understood. But either way Huncks would have his boat.

Levy laughed. No, he said, by all *means* he wanted a part in this! Indeed, nothing would prevent him. Stuyvesant had tried again and again to evict Levy and his fellow Jews from Manhatoes. But like the Quakers of Vlissingen, they went over his head and appealed to the West India Company, which, in accordance with the Dutch practice of tolerance, ordered Stuyvesant to cease and desist. This, Levy said, would be a pleasure.

The wind, too, was favorable. They hoisted sail and eased into the current. The shallop made its way briskly north, into the gloaming.

*   *   *

Balty sat on his bed with his back to the wall, trying to convince himself he wasn't a coward. Then why did he feel so like one?

Hadn't Huncks told him to just tell them? There's no disgrace. Everyone gives in under torture.

Why, then, did he feel ashamed?

When they start sawing off your leg, does honor require that you hold your nose and think of England?

What would Huncks have done? Good, brave Huncks. Huncks never would have let it go that far. He'd have snatched the knife from that weasel "surgeon" and sliced off his head. All their heads. There'd have been four heads on the floor, like so many skittles balls.

He asked himself: What if Huncks *hadn't* got the knife away? Would he have talked? Never. He'd have gritted his teeth and told them to saw off *both* feet and go to hell.

At least he hadn't capitulated immediately. How long had he lasted? He remembered the knife reaching bone. The sound it made. Then everything went black and he came to with the hideous Koontz looming over him saying, "Shall we then continue?"

"No," Balty said, "we shall bloody well not continue. I'll sign your damned confession. And damn you."

The "surgeon" turned from Torquemada into Hippocrates, pulling out needle and thread and bandages from his Pandora's satchel of horrors, sprinkling the wound with powder. Would Mr. Balthasar like some laudanum for pain? Yes, Mr. Balthasar would fucking well like some fucking laudanum for the fucking pain. And fuck you. Balty wished he knew how to say "fuck" in fucking Dutch.

And Koontz, duplicitous, double-dealing Koontz—what a transformation *there*! From Grand Inquisitor to Genie of the Lamp. He would have food sent in. And wine. Would Mr. Balthasar prefer white wine or red wine? Had he actually said that?

The laudanum had made Balty's head fuzzy. Another nice touch, leaving the bottle of laudanum with him. Clever, Dutchers. Swine.

Balty tried to remember what it was he'd confessed to. Presumably, to being an English spy. To deflect suspicion away from Koontz, whose pockets were probably jingling with English gold, earned under the table, without Stuyvesant's knowledge, for hiding fugitive English regicides in the Heneral's own backyard.

Balty took another slug of laudanum. He wished Huncks were here, so he could ask him, "What now?" It made Balty smile. Huncks hated it when he asked that.

– CHAPTER 42 –

Parley

Stuyvesant rarely returned to New Amsterdam in a good mood after dealing with Mohawk trouble. There was nothing about Mohawk trouble to put anyone in a good mood.

But to return to . . . to *this* calamity! To discover his best beloved friend, the only creature on earth he truly loved and who truly loved him in return . . . to find Johann was gone. It was unthinkable. Old Petrus plunged into a gloom so cold that ice seemed to form on the walls around him.

Mevrouw Stuyvesant and the household servants cringed and tried to keep out of his sight as he stormed about the house looking for his bird. Imbeciles! Fools! *How* could they have allowed such a thing to happen? Finally he stomped out the door of Bouwerie Number One, cratering the ground with every step.

Koontz saw from a hundred paces that something was very wrong. He was accustomed to Stuyvesant's black dog moods, but he'd never seen the General look *this* furious. Had the Mohawks slaughtered everyone at Fort Oranje? Strange that no word had been received here about it.

"Welcome back, General!"

Stuyvesant returned the salutation with a grunt that a bear might make on awaking from hibernation to find that smaller beasts had consumed his entire store of food. He clomped to his desk, shaking the timbers as he went. He hurled himself into his chair and sat glowering, as if trying to remember which drawer in the desk contained the blank death warrants.

His gaze turned to the mound of paperwork awaiting him—correspondence, dispatches, reports, the quotidian stuff of administration. His eyes fastened on something odd, out of place—a long, blue, iridescent feather.

He picked it up. A ribbon was tied around the feather, at the other end a small scroll of paper.

Koontz looked on. Where had *this* come from?

Despite his laudanum bliss, Balty started as the door to his cell clanged open and several men marched in. He pulled his blanket up against him protectively and peered. Not a reprise amputation? Hands lifted him into a chair and carted him out the door.

Koontz waited on the parade ground, pacing. His face was crimson. Had he fallen asleep in the sun? Should he offer him some laudanum?

Koontz led the procession across the parade ground to the Governor's House. Balty found being carried in a chair very pleasant.

Up the steps and through the various doors and into Old Petrus's den. His bearers deposited him brusquely and departed with alacrity suggesting eagerness to be gone. Koontz remained, Adam's apple bobbing up and down.

Old Petrus looked like the volcano that destroyed Pompeii. Any moment now lava would bubble out his nose and ears and mouth. What on earth had made him scowl so? Balty's confession?

Then it dawned—Nicholls must have arrived! Well, thank God for *that*. Balty imagined the scene: Nicholls hoisting his colors, gunports opening. The English Navy, here at last. And surely its first order of business would be to demand the release of his majesty's commissioner, wrongly seized and abominably treated.

Old Petrus was holding something up. A feather? Bright blue. Odd. Was this some Dutch protocol, a blue feather to sign the instrument of surrender? Balty felt a lovely warm surge of satisfaction. Lovely stuff, laudanum.

The old boy continued to glare. What fearful looks. Probably furious over being tricked by Downing. Serves the old buzzard right.

Balty could make no sense of what Stuyvesant said next. It came out in a torrent of rage. Then beefy jailers were summoned and dragged him off. No sedan chair for the return trip to the cell. Balty's foot going *clump clump clump* down the front steps. They hauled him across the parade ground and threw him back into his cell. The bottle of laudanum snatched from his hands.

What was *that* about?

"Heneral, the Englishman has arrived."

Huncks was admitted. He respectfully removed his hat and stood, waiting for the Governor to commence the parley.

Asser Levy had bribed one of the fort maids to put the feathered ransom note on Stuyvesant's desk. If Stuyvesant consented to parley, four pennants would be run up the fort's signal tower: blue, yellow, and red (Johann's predominant colors), and a white one, guaranteeing safe passage.

Old Petrus sat back in his chair, affecting imperturbability, but inside the lava was all abubble. On his desk before him was the Englishman St. Michel's signed confession.

Was he tortured? Huncks asked.

Certainly not! He wounded himself during the escape attempt. The fort surgeon tended to him. More than a spy deserved. Stuyvesant sniffed.

He cared not a penning for the Englishman. English spies were a ducat a dozen. This one was notable only by virtue of his manifest stupidity. This story of theirs about searching for regicides—it was an insult to his intelligence. There *were* no English regicides in New Amsterdam. He would know. This was just another campaign to stir up mischief and foment more anti-Dutch hysteria back in London.

He wanted his parrot back.

He would exchange a dozen English spies for Johann. But here Old Petrus found himself in a difficulty. What would his superiors at the West India Company say if they learned he'd exchanged an English spy for a bird? And word *would* reach Amsterdam. Koontz would see to that. Koontz had been maneuvering behind his back with Amsterdam for his job. What a neat way to get it, this.

Old Petrus had no illusions. No one here liked him. He wasn't likable. He was autocratic, disciplinarian, gruff, stern, dogmatic, unyielding, temperamental, and humorless. But these were traits he viewed as assets essential to managing a colony an ocean away from home, surrounded on every side by enemies, many of them actual savages, as opposed to the Christian variety in Europe.

Thus the Governor of New Netherland found himself hobbled as he stared across his desk at the man who had abducted his one true friend. Who'd plucked one of his beautiful feathers. Who now threatened to pluck another every day that his accomplice remained in custody. And when no feathers remained, he said, he would start removing other parts of Johann. *Liefhebber!* Fiend!

Koontz looked on with an air of studied *froideur.* But he, too, was churning inside—not with rage, but fear.

Since the arrival of the ransom note, Koontz had desperately tried to persuade the Heneral to make an example of St. Michel and hang him immediately. How else to deal with English spies?

Koontz knew St. Michel wasn't a spy. And Huncks knew Koontz's dirty little secret. If Koontz could get Stuyvesant to hang St. Michel, then his friend would retaliate and kill the bird, and that would be the end of parleying.

"So?" Stuyvesant began.

"You have my terms," Huncks said.

"What makes you to think that I would exchange a spy for some bird?"

"The fact you agreed to this meeting."

"Perhaps you should consider that maybe my only intentioning was to lure you to come. Hm? So to put you in my jail along with your fellow spy."

"You wouldn't violate a white flag. And even if you were willing to forfeit your honor, you wouldn't forfeit Johann along with it, just for the satisfaction of adding me to your long list of English guests here in New Amsterdam."

"What hests?" Stuyvesant said.

"Whalley and Goffe. And their minions, Jones and the Indian."

Stuyvesant slammed his fist on the desk. "You continue these accusatings! *There are no rehicides in New Amsterdam!*"

"I believe that *you* believe that."

Stuyvesant stared, confused.

Huncks said, "Perhaps you should ask your Deputy if he has made some private arrangement."

Koontz drew his sword. "How dare you!"

"Koontz!" Stuyvesant growled. *"Onthoud waar u bent!"* Remember where you are!

"He has insulted me, Heneral!"

Huncks said, "If a duel would settle the matter, I am amenable."

"There will be no *dueling*!" Stuyvesant growled.

The seed of doubt was planted. Huncks said, "If there is nothing further to discuss, I'll take my leave. In the meantime, may I have your assurance Mr. Balthasar is being well treated?"

"*Yes*," Stuyvesant said.

"I should like to take you at your word, sir, but there's been a report, you see."

"What report?"

"Of torture."

"We do not do torture here."

Koontz was sweating. Looking at him, Huncks thought: *He*

Balty without Stuyvesant's permission. While the old boy was up-
ling with his Mohawk trwabble.

uyvesant meanwhile was wondering why it had been necessary
ring the Englishman before him in a chair.

Koontz blurted, "He injured *himself.* In the escaping."

Huncks said, "That doesn't account for screams heard from his
cell."

Stuyvesant asked Koontz, "*Klopt dit?*" Is this true?

Koontz replied, "*Hij had nachtmerries.*" He was having nightmares.

Huncks said, "*Ik denk, mijnheer, dat u binnenkort met nachtmerries.*"
I think, sir, that *you* will soon be the one having nightmares.

Huncks reached into his vest and drew out a feather. This one
was smaller, brilliantly yellow. He placed it on Stuyvesant's desk next
to the other, then stepped back, made a nod of courtesy, and turned,
leaving the two Dutchmen, one florid, the other pale.

– CHAPTER 43 –

Cincinnatus Agonistes

The atmosphere at the Breuckelen farmhouse had changed, martial camaraderie giving way to the quiet that precedes engagement. Braggadocio and tankards of ale were put aside. It was time now for inspecting weapons and writing farewell letters.

Winthrop had arrived.

As Underhill had warned, the Governor of Connecticut was in no good humor but his self-control was admirable. Not a word of denunciation of his majesty or the Duke of York for reneging on their promise. He'd drunk his bitter cup in silence and put himself at the disposal of the Crown.

Winthrop and Stuyvesant had a long history. When it came to the negotiation, Winthrop would be the one to conduct it. If it succeeded, Winthrop would be at the table to catch the crumbs, if not all the land to the Pacific.

Underhill was in a foul frame. No strutting and backslapping and declaiming the dawn of a new St. Crispin's Day. No once more-ing onto the beach. The Cincinnatus of Long Island was reduced to muttering at his wife for sending a Quaker chaperone—a *girl*, a girl in a damned apron!—to see that he abided by his pledge of nonviolence.

Thankful followed him everywhere. She wouldn't leave his side.

she asked if the Captain would care to join her in silent worship. *No!* The Captain would bloody well *not* care to join silent bloody Quaker worship! Captain John Underhill, hero ort Mystick, hero of Pound Ridge, the Achilles of New England, ampered after and tsk-tsked at by this . . . this *child*, wagging a finger at him in full view of the men. Intolerable!

To add a further note of humiliation, the girl had somehow acquired a parrot. It perched on her shoulder and screeched. Where, in God's name, had *it* come from? And what, in God's name, was it doing here, amidst a council of war?

It had taken to mimickry: "Wheyyyyrrrr's Cappunnn Nunnnnderrrrr-illllll! *Oaccck!*" Underhill tried to have it banished from the farmhouse, but no, the men wouldn't hear of it. They'd adopted the bloody thing. It must stay! They vied with each other for the honor of feeding it. Underhill issued an ultimatum. Choose: himself or the bird. The vote went to the bird.

Why didn't Huncks do something about it? He and that imbecile, St. Michel, were responsible. It was they who'd brought the wench to Killingworth, providing his wife with a deputy to harass him.

Where *was* Huncks?

The answer was: a few hundred yards away, peering through an eyeglass trained on Stuyvesant's signal post.

Afternoon was getting on toward evening, shadows lengthening over the fields. Huncks had been here since returning from the parley. He tried to conjure the scene in the Governor's House. Had he convinced Stuyvesant of Koontz's complicity with the regicides? Had Stuyvesant thrown Koontz into jail? Or had Koontz persuaded Stuyvesant he was innocent? Was Stuyvesant reconciled to forfeiting his precious bird and keeping his English prisoner? And had all this aroused suspicion about the impending visit by the English naval squadron?

Huncks heard something behind him. Thankful approached. Johann perched on her forearm. The bird had taken to her. She seemed to have some gift.

Johann's eyes narrowed, seeing the man who'd plucked two of his feathers. He lowered his head and hissed.

"*Shh*, Johann," Thankful said, stroking its forehead. "It's all right. The Colonel won't hurt thee."

Johann wasn't convinced. Thankful held her forearm to the branch of a tree. Johann hopped on. She tethered his leg to the limb and sat on the ground beside Huncks, who resumed his eyeglass invigilation.

"Anything?"

"No. What's going on in the farmhouse?"

"One of Captain Underhill's scouts came. Four ships were seen, off a place called Moriches."

"He's close. If the wind holds, he could be here tomorrow."

They sat silently. The sun was low over Manhatoes, silhouetting the taller buildings, the fort, windmill, gallows.

"What will happen to Balty if he's still prisoner when the English ships come?"

Huncks put down his tube and rubbed his eye.

"Difficult to say. Stuyvesant won't be pleased when he learns Nicholls isn't here to kiss his—when he realizes he's here to seize the colony. Whether his anger will extend to . . ." Huncks checked himself again. He smiled. "Well, he's got himself a prize hostage, doesn't he? A Crown commissioner. Brother-in-law of an important Navy person. Makes him a valuable commodity. No harm will come to him."

"But the English Colonel, he would not give up his mission for one English hostage."

"No."

"What then?"

"You sound just like Balty. Always asking, 'What now?' "

"How badly did they torture him?"

"I doubt it went far. Our Balty's not one to play the hero."

"But he did. For both of us." Thankful began to cry.

Huncks put an arm around her. "How am I to keep watch with you like this?"

"Sorry. It seems I am always crying now."

"How's Cincinnatus? Communing with the Holy Spirit?"

Thankful laughed. "It's why I left with Johann. He was threatening to cook him for the supper."

They looked over at Johann, gnawing on a pinecone.

"He'd be tough eating."

Thankful pointed. "Look."

Huncks raised the eyeglass and saw the four pennants.

Koontz's defiance was gone now. He looked like a whipped dog. Stuyvesant was on edge: hands fidgeting, eyes darting about, avoiding contact.

They'd made their agreement. Stuyvesant would overlook Koontz's treachery, and Koontz would keep quiet about Stuyvesant's exchanging an English spy for a parrot.

Stuyvesant asked if Huncks cared for a schnapps. Huncks saw the old boy wanted one himself, so he accepted. Stuyvesant did not offer a schnapps to Koontz.

"So," Old Petrus said, "after discussings with Deputy Koontz, it seems there has been a misunderstanding. From which has consequented this unfortunateness between us. I propose that together we make an overcoming."

"I salute your excellency's wise judgment."

"Are you desiring first to discuss the matter of these English persons who, it seems"—Stuyvesant shot a sharp glance at Koontz—"*have* made a refuging here?"

"My immediate concern is for the release of Mr. Balthasar. And of course, the return to you of your property."

"This, too, is my wishing."

"How does your excellency propose to proceed?"

"Well, here is a difficulty. We are a fort."

"So I have observed."

"A fort with many persons. And these many persons now cognize that Mr. Balthasar has confessed to be a spy. Here is the difficulty." Stuyvesant continued, removing his skullcap and mopping sweat from his bald dome. "The other difficulty is that these many persons are also cognizing about the disappearing of . . ."

"Johann."

"Yes. So we have two difficulties. Which together are making one big difficulty. But there is a solving for this."

"I am eager to hear it."

"Of course this must be only among ourselves."

"Agreed."

"Sometimes prisoners escape. This happens."

"Yes," Huncks said cautiously. "And sometimes prisoners are shot while escaping. That would make a very big difficulty."

"This will not happen."

"No. The consequences for Johann would be unfortunate. I insist the escape take place tonight."

"And the return of my property also."

"Agreed."

Stuyvesant said, "At four of the clock comes the change of the watch. This will be the time. Koontz will make the arrangings."

"And the exchange?"

"We are both men of honor, Mr. Huncks."

"You flatter me, sir. But we're exchanging hostages, not compliments. What do you propose?"

"The Deputy and your Mr. Balthasar will be at the Pearl Street dock. Some minutes after four of the clock."

"A dock? On your island? Hardly neutral ground. No. Midriver, due east of the dock. I'll be in a small boat, with one other person to handle the oars. I'll expect to see Koontz and Mr. Balthasar. No one else. *Afgesproken?*"

Stuyvesant nodded. "*Afgesproken.*" Agreed.

CHAPTER 44

Well Done, Koontzy

Balty awoke with a gasp. The guttering candle cast a flickery, spectral light. What now? The hangman, with some sourpuss Dutch pastor in tow, mumbling quotes from the Book of Lamentations?

No. Koontz and the night-duty guard. Koontz spoke to him in Dutch. Whatever he said seemed to confuse the guard. Koontz's voice rose, insistent. The guard, shaking his head in perplexity, began to undress.

"I say, what's all this?"

"You are making an escape."

"What?"

"Don't you want to be free? Get up."

"Why is he taking off his clothes?"

"For you to put."

"Look here—"

Balty found himself staring into the muzzle of Koontz's pistol.

"All right, steady on." Balty threw off the blanket and got up. His ankle hurt but he was able to stand.

Koontz handed Balty the guard's uniform piece by piece. Balty dressed.

Koontz pointed and said to the guard, "*Wat is dat?*" The guard turned to look. As he did, Koontz drew a knife and slit his throat. The guard fell forward onto the floor, gurgling and gasping. Balty stared in horror.

"You . . . killed him!"

"*Yes*," Koontz said with an air of mild annoyance. He knelt and wiped his knife on the dying man's undershirt.

"But . . . why?"

"To make look good your escape. Come."

Balty backed against the wall.

"Come."

"No," Balty said. "I think not."

"If you stay, you will hang for his murder."

"I didn't kill him. *You* killed him."

"But who will believe? Come. We will meet with your friend. To make the trade. You for the bird."

Balty pointed at the dead guard. "Huncks would never have agreed to *that*."

"Do you want to be free, or to hang?" Koontz put the gun to Balty's chest.

Balty followed him out of the cell, stepping around the widening pool of blood. Koontz paused at the door to the parade ground, pale in the moonlight. He took off his white scarf and wrapped it around Balty's neck and lower face and pulled down the brim of his hat.

"Don't speak. Stay behind close."

They made their way toward the gate of the fort, Balty fighting the urge to cry out and run.

The gate was open. Sentries slumped against the wall. They straightened on seeing Koontz. He and Balty walked out onto the broad way.

Koontz turned left toward the fort's north bastion, protruding from the rampart like a giant arrowhead.

The street was deserted at this hour, but for two men sitting on the ground across the way, backs to a wall. One was asleep. The other stood and watched. He and his companion had been there for days,

waiting with mounting impatience for a rendezvous now much over-
due. The man nudged his sleeping companion, who got to his feet.
They set off, following.

Koontz and Balty rounded the corner of the bastion. There was a
field between the fort and the water, with two windmills, blades at rest in
the windless night. Waves lapped gently against the shore. Koontz kept
close to the fort wall as they made their way toward the west bastion.
Above on the parapet Balty saw the glint of moonlight on bayonets.

"Where are you taking me?" Balty whispered.

"Quiet. To boat."

They heard a sound behind them. They turned and saw the two
men. Koontz's hand went to his pistol. The men came closer.

"Koontz."

So this was Koontz's trap, Balty thought. The sight of Repent
filled him not with fear but regret at his lack of a weapon.

"*Jones?*" Koontz whispered. "What you do here?"

"What I've doing these past two days. Waiting."

"Now is not good time." Koontz gestured at the parapet.

"Why didn't you come? I've been waiting."

"It's not the *time*, Jones!" Koontz hissed. "Later we talk."

Repent's gaze was fixed on Balty. He came closer. Balty smelled
rancid raccoon and eagle fat.

Koontz put up a hand. "No." The Indian kept coming. He said to
Jones, "Owanux."

Jones peered at Balty and grinned. "Well, now. This *was* worth the
waiting. Well done, Koontzy."

"No, no, no," Koontz said. "He's not for you."

Repent walked behind Koontz and Balty.

"Don't worry, Koontzy," Jones said. "There'll be more money."

Koontz drew his pistol. "No! There is an arranging."

"What about our arranging?"

"Not for this."

"How much do you want for him, then?"

"Look, the soldiers. If I give order, they shoot."

"I shouldn't worry. You Dutch fuckers can't shoot for shit."

Koontz cocked the hammer of the pistol and aimed at Jones. Repent plunged his knife into the small of his back with such force Koontz was propelled forward.

"*Bewakers!*" Guards!

Two soldiers appeared above.

"*Wie is er?*" Who's there?

Repent yanked his knife out of Koontz and turned and lunged at Balty. Balty dodged the thrust and leapt toward the staggering Koontz.

The sentries opened fire. Musket balls thumped into the ground around them, kicking up dirt. Reevaluating his opinion of Dutch sharpshooters, Jones lumbered off as the soldiers reloaded.

Balty grabbed for Koontz's pistol as the wounded Dutchman fell to the ground. He rolled over. Repent stood over him. Balty fired.

Orange and yellow flamed from the muzzle, blinding him. The air filled with smoke. Repent was gone. On the ground beside Balty, Koontz groaned and went still. Balty saw the glint of more bayonets on the rampart above.

"*Wie is er?*"

"*Wat is het wachtwoord?*" What's the password?

Balty was still on his back. The windmill was fifty feet away.

"*Wat is het wachtwoord?*"

He rolled onto his stomach and got to his feet. A musket ball ripped through his left ear. Balty stood still, one hand to his ear, the other raised in surrender.

A quarter mile away in the middle of the East River, Huncks, Thankful, and Johann bobbed in the current, listening to the sound of gunfire.

Captain Underhill had intercepted them on their way to the boat. There was a scene: words exchanged, voices raised, pistols drawn. Tragedy was averted by the intervention of Winthrop, who gave his reluctant assent for them to proceed. Underhill stormed off, muttering about the appalling lack of discipline.

An hour after the last gunshots, they knew Balty would not make the rendezvous. Huncks slumped in his seat and put his head in his hands.

The bird, perched on Thankful's arm, put his beak to her cheek, glistening wet in the moonlight.

CHAPTER 45

This Englishman, Not Gone

Peter Stuyvesant stared mumpishly across his desk at the bandaged and manacled man surrounded by four scowling soldiers. He'd been rousted from his bed at five o'clock by a banging on the door.

How, Old Petrus wondered, could it have gone so calamitously wrong as *this*?

A guard dead, his throat slashed. Koontz dead, killed by some unknown attacker. Johann, now surely gone forever. And this Englishman, not gone.

At least Koontz—the duplicitous bastard—was no longer alive to tell everyone that the Governor-General of New Netherland had tried to exchange a confessed English spy for his parrot.

But this was thin consolation beside the loss of Johann. What fate awaited him at the hands of the Englishman's confederate? Old Petrus shuddered at the image of Johann, plucked bald and shivering beside a pile of his beautiful feathers, waiting for the axe stroke.

He must speak with the Englishman alone. Find out what he knew.

"*Laat ons.*" Leave us.

The sergeant protested that the prisoner was dangerous. *He cut Jan's throat!* Stuyvesant glared. The soldiers withdrew.

"So," Stuyvesant sighed. "Now I must hang you."

"What? Why?"

"A guard is dead."

"Koontz killed him."

"Koontz is not here to say yes or no. Anyway, for killing a guard while making escape, the penalty is death."

"See here. Koontz cut his throat, then threatened to shoot me if I didn't go with him."

"You were forced to escape? Well, it's original, such a defense."

"It is not a defense! It's the bloody truth! One minute, I'm asleep, the next, Koontz is cutting the man's throat and waving his pistol at me. Then out of nowhere Jones and the Indian—bodyguards of the regicides you insist *aren't* here—appear and demand Koontz hand me over. He refused and the Indian ran him through his kidneys. And your fusiliers opened fire and managed to miss them and shoot off my damned ear. So I fail to find anything in this deplorable sequence of events to justify hanging *me.*"

Stuyvesant believed the Englishman. He wasn't the type to slash a man's throat. Damn Koontz! Why didn't he just knock the guard unconscious? He'd fatally complicated things by killing the man. Now he had no choice but to hang St. Michel. The men would mutiny if he didn't. But Johann . . .

Stuyvesant suddenly saw the solution: sentence him to hang, but defer the execution. Explain that he must consult with Amsterdam. If the Englishman was, as he claimed to be, a Crown commissioner, there was a diplomatic dimension. Let six months pass. By then no one would care. And announce Amsterdam was commuting his sentence to servitude for life in the plantations. Ship him off and be done with him. Rather elegant.

But what about these regicides and this Jones and the assassin Indian? He couldn't have them roaming his streets. He would make inquiries. Order a search.

Stuyvesant was mulling all this when Balty said, "Koontz told me I was being exchanged for your parrot. I can only assume this whole business had your approval."

Stuyvesant groaned. This Englishman was no simple fool. He was the Platonic ideal of the Fool. He'd just signed his own death warrant. How could he commute his sentence now? He'd spend the rest of his life telling *everyone* that the Governor-General of New Netherland had connived to exchange him for his pet bird.

The Englishman continued prattling. It was like listening to fistfuls of pebbles hurled against windows.

"You may rest assured, sir," Balty was saying, "that I shall be taking this matter up directly with Colonel Nicholls, when he arrives—with his *fleet*."

Stuyvesant looked at the clock. It was just after six in the morning.

"I think you will not have this opportunity."

"Why not?"

"Unless he arrives before nine."

"I don't follow."

"Nine is when we do the hangings. It's the custom. But I will tell Colonel Nicholls about your concerns when he comes."

"Look"—Balty smiled—"let's start over, shall we?"

Stuyvesant put on his spectacles, dipped a quill in ink, and began to scribble.

Balty said huffily, "You might pay me the courtesy of not doing paperwork while we're discussing my hanging!"

"It's the warrant for your hanging. Do you wish a priest?"

"Certainly not!"

"I will have sent to you some food and wine. Do you want laudanum? It makes calm."

Balty had only one card left to play, but it felt like treason to tell Stuyvesant Colonel Nicholls's real purpose. And how would that help?

Old Petrus would only be further enraged. Downing's own signature was on Balty's commission.

"Well, what about your *bird*?" Balty said. "You'll be getting feathers until Christmas—enough to stuff a pillow."

Stuyvesant finished scribbling. He reached for the silver bell on his desk. Soldiers hauled Balty off, manacles jangling.

CHAPTER 46

A Fine Summer Day

By nine o'clock in the morning, the 27th of August, Anno Domini 1664, had blossomed into a glorious late summer day of sunlight sparkling on water, clouds scudding across a cerulean sky, and a breeze to snap and flap the Dutch flag above the fort.

Even the gulls seemed aware that this was a day to soar in the zephyrs above rather than scavenge for wharfside orts. A day all residents of New Amsterdam could congratulate themselves on their excellent good fortune to be here, specifically *here*, on their island amid such a lush and providing new world.

The breeze, from the west, carried the sound of drums across the East River to the Breuckelen shore, where Huncks and Thankful had been keeping watch.

Through his spyglass, Huncks saw the procession emerge around the corner of the fort and make its way toward the gallows at the tip of the island. Thankful, watching through her own glass, was first to spot Balty, hands tied, walking between the two lines of soldiers.

Balty's head was covered in white. Bandages. Huncks lowered his spyglass.

"It didn't work," she said.

"No," Huncks said. "Appears not."

They heard shouting behind them. Men were running out of the farmhouse, pointing.

"There!"

Stuyvesant stood on the rampart of the fort watching the procession below. Reaching the gallows, the two columns of soldiers formed a square around it. The Englishman didn't falter. His bearing was dignified. Stuyvesant wondered if it was the laudanum.

The hangman led the Englishman by the arm to the foot of the ladder. The drumming ceased.

Stuyvesant heard shouting. The crowd below had turned from the gallows toward the harbor. He saw the four ships. He raised his eyeglass, saw the English colors.

The Englishman was mounting the ladder. The captain of the guard looked up at Stuyvesant, waiting for his signal.

What to do? He had authority to execute a spy. Not only a spy, but one whose attempt to escape had resulted in the death of a guard. This Colonel Nicholls had no right to intervene in a lawful execution.

Stuyvesant sighed. But there was the question of manners.

Greeting a foreign dignitary by hanging one of his countrymen—within view—was not, however one might justify the thing, particularly good manners. And greeting a foreign dignitary with four warships of thirty-six guns each and five hundred men-at-arms was not particularly wise.

Old Petrus stood on the rampart and considered. The Englishman had now reached the top rung of the ladder. The noose was around his neck. The hangman awaited the Captain's order; the Captain awaited the General's order.

Stuyvesant said to his adjutant, "*Stoppen.*"

The adjutant relayed the order to the Captain, who conveyed it to the hangman. The hangman said something to the Englishman, who collapsed. A frantic scene ensued as the hangman and soldiers tried to lift the Englishman, the noose still around his neck.

They put him on the ground. Was he dead? Stuyvesant groaned.

The hangman slapped the Englishman on his cheeks. The Englishman's eyes opened.

Stuyvesant gave the order to get him out of sight. When Colonel Nicholls weighed anchor and sailed for New England to conduct his review, *then* the execution would proceed.

Stuyvesant handed his spyglass to the adjutant and stumped off to see about welcoming his latest English hests.

As he descended the ramp, a solider ran up. He handed him a piece of paper.

"Heneral," he said, "urgent message, from your Mevrouw."

Stuyvesant growled, "*Urgent?*" This was no time for domestic messages. He stumped on, clutching it in his fist. Halfway across the parade ground he considered: Judith had never sent him a message marked "Urgent."

He unfolded it and read.

"*Johann is terug!*"

Mevrouw Stuyvesant's message that Johann had returned was to be the Governor-General's sole happy moment on August 27th and all the days to follow, for the next message he received was from Colonel Nicholls, commander of the squadron of warships now anchored within cannon range of his town.

Nicholls was not inquiring what time dinner was served, or what dress was appropriate. Neither was he complimenting the Governor on the tidiness of New Amsterdam. No. The message informed Stuyvesant that "in his Maj.^ties Name, I do demand the Towne, Scituate upon the Island commonly knowne by the Name of Manhatoes wth all the forts there unto belonging, to be rendered unto his Maj.^ties obedience, and Protection into my hands."

It stressed that the King had no desire for an "effusion of Christian blood," but made clear that failure to comply would result in "all the miseryes of a War." He signed it, "*Your very humble Servant.*"

While Stuyvesant fumed about the perfidy of Ambassador Downing and the credulity of the West India Company, a boat set off from the Breuckelen shore, where a thousand men could be observed mustering: Pell's Westchester Trained Band and various associates of Captain Underhill's. Cincinnatus had put aside his plow.

The boat flew a white flag. In its bow was a man Stuyvesant knew well: Winthrop of Connecticut. Accompanying him was a man Stuyvesant also knew—the Englishman who had been his dinner guest at Bouwerie Number One, who'd come to his chambers at the fort to present terms for an exchange of prisoners.

England's terms were unusually, indeed astonishingly, generous. Nothing would change for the inhabitants of New Amsterdam other than their flag. The town's name would now be New York, in honor of the King's brother, James, Duke of York and Albany, Lord High Admiral. All that had been New Netherland was now his.

Stuyvesant tore up the letter. This precipitated an uproar among the people he called his "subjects." *They* desired no miseryes of a war or effusion of blood, Christian or otherwise. *They* felt no fealty toward the West India Company. What had it done for them? Even Stuyvesant's own son declared against him. The fifteen hundred inhabitants of New Amsterdam confronted the prospect of English rule with a collective shrug.

In a rage at this betrayal, Stuyvesant stumped back up to the rampart of his fort, where cannons were loaded and aimed at Nicholls's flagship, fuses hissing.

Old Petrus had no fear of death. If another war with England was to be inaugurated, then why not here, why not now? He looked out on the harbor, *his* harbor, and contemplated his next move.

Time stopped. The citizens of New Amsterdam held their breath as their leader decided whether to let slip the dogs of war.

Stuyvesant wondered—a war for what? For a people who had now openly declared against him? The consequences of firing the first shot would be dire. Horrific. An English siege against the town would succeed, inevitably. The cobbles of New Amsterdam would run red with blood. How would history judge a governor who brought about sack and carnage for . . . nothing other than his own pride?

If these people of New Amsterdam, this rabble, were not, after all, his subjects, why subject himself to infamy, for their sake? This was no band of brothers, only a congeries of mixed races and religions. *This is what came of Holland's policy of tolerance: weakness and irresolution. They were not worthy of death on the field of Mars. To hell with them. To hell with the West India Company. It was over.

The negotiations would continue for weeks, but for now the moment of maximum danger had passed. There would be no war.

New Amsterdam exhaled. Cheers went up. The taverns did brisk business the night of August 27th, 1664.

Reaching home that evening, Stuyvesant was greeted by Judith. She'd heard nothing of the events in town. She told him of her strange encounter that morning, shortly after he'd stormed off. She heard a screech in the conservatory, and going in to see, had a fright. It was the Englishman who'd come to dinner, and a woman, Johann perched on her arm.

She didn't recognize the woman, who was young and fair, with golden hair, just like a Dutch girl. Knowing her husband's views, Judith did not mention her apron and cap, typical of Quakers.

The man's manner was courteous. He said they'd found Johann on the Breuckelen side of the river, and having seen him here at the dinner, recognized him. And brought him home.

When the man and woman went to leave, Judith said, Johann made a terrible screeching and tried to fly to the woman but was thwarted by his tether.

What kind of day had her husband had? Was it not a glorious day the Lord had given them? Such weather!

– *CHAPTER 47* –

No Quaker Nonsense

A meeting was convened the next day at Stuyvesant's farm—a dozen Dutch and English to discuss the details of the handing-over.

Colonel Nicholls was present, also Winthrop, and Huncks, acting as his adjutant. Huncks said nothing. When in late afternoon the meeting adjourned and the parties dispersed, Stuyvesant motioned to Huncks to remain.

They went into the conservatory. Seeing Huncks, Johann's feathers flared as he hissed. Stuyvesant calmed him with a juicy bit of peach.

"Why did not Nicholls or Winthrop mention about your friend?" Stuyvesant asked as he fed his bird.

"I asked Governor Winthrop not to raise the matter. Or to bring it to the attention of Colonel Nicholls."

"And the rehicides?"

"I asked Winthrop not to mention that, either."

"Why?"

"Thought it might complicate matters for you."

Stuyvesant considered. "Nicholls knows *nothing* of these people?"

"Only that they're hiding somewhere in New England. They're of interest to him, certainly, but for now are not his primary concern. He is occupied with other matters."

Stuyvesant nodded. "Yes. Seizing my land."

"I thought your excellency had enough on your plate without having to answer to accusations of harboring English regicides. As we both know, you weren't. Your deputy was."

Stuyvesant offered Johann another bit of peach.

"What have I done to deserve such consideration from you, Colonel?"

"To be frank, it's more a question of what you can do for me."

"Ah. Mr. Balthasar."

"Indeed."

"He is a very talky fellow, your friend."

"Well, he's half French."

"Would he be talky with Colonel Nicholls?"

"Under the circumstances, I'm confident I might persuade him of the virtue of silence."

Stuyvesant stroked Johann's head.

"After the killing of Koontz, I ordered a searching. Every house. Every room in every house. There was found no rehicides."

"I believe you. Still, the King might take it hard if he suspected you'd protected his father's executioners."

Stuyvesant smiled. "And how would he punish me for this? By taking New Netherland?"

"Fair point."

"This afternoon during the discussing, you saw when the soldier arrived to give me a message?"

"I did."

"Do you know what was this message? That two men had just departed the town through the gate. An Indian, with some strange markings on the face. The other a man with big . . . these"—Stuyvesant touched an eyebrow. "Mr. Balthasar gave us the description of them after Koontz was killed. So we were looking for these very fellows."

"Yet you say they've—left?"

"Yes."

"May I ask why they weren't arrested? They killed your deputy."

"Koontz was very naughty to be making arrangements with such men. And he should not have killed one of my soldiers, in such a way. He was a good boy, Jan, the one who died. What shall I tell his mother and father when I write to them? I must make a prevaricating. So I have no quarrel with the men who killed Koontz. I am glad to be rid of them."

Stuyvesant patted his bird. "Your friend is waiting for you at the gate. I think it would be best if you both leave New Amsterdam. New *York*. I must accustom to say it. New *York*."

Old Petrus turned to leave. He said over his shoulder, "My wife tells me there was a woman with you when you brought back Johann."

"Yes."

"It seems she was kind to Johann. Tell her I am grateful. Goodbye, Colonel Huncks. I hope never again to see you."

Balty was there at the main gate, pale, bandaged, glassy-eyed. Seeing Huncks, he brightened a bit.

He knew little of what had happened. He remembered reciting the Lord's Prayer as he mounted the steps of the ladder, and taking a deep breath on reaching the top, closing his eyes, and waiting for the hangman to shove him off. Then the hangman grabbing at him, and shouting from below. Then opening his eyes and lying on the ground looking *up* at the gallows. Odd. Hands lifting him and carrying him off. He remembered terror of being buried. It must mean he'd been sent to Hell for his sins and this was the first of the punishments. If only he'd lived a better life!

But they weren't carrying him off to be buried. They took him back to his cell and made him drink a large glass of wine that tasted powerfully of laudanum. Then everything went rather pleasantly black.

"What's going on, old man?"

Huncks told him. When he finished, Balty said mildly, "Oh," as if Huncks had related a not very interesting anecdote.

"You're foggy with laudanum. Come, we must hurry."

They set off at a gallop, Huncks leading Balty's horse by the reins.

They rode east along the town wall to the river, then turned north to the ferry.

Arriving on the Breuckelen shore, they went to the farmhouse, now swarming with English soldiers and sailors.

Thankful ran to Balty and hugged him. Huncks left them in each other's arms and went to find Dr. Pell.

Pell was in fine fettle, already brimming with plans to sell plots on his land—now indisputably *Crown* land—to the waves of immigrants who'd surely now be arriving in droves to settle in Greater New England, or whatever it was to be called.

Huncks told Pell he needed a boat. The wind was still from the west, the tide flooding. He could fetch Fairfield by dawn.

The doctor had enjoyed more than a few celebratory cups of punch. Why did Huncks want to leave? Surely he didn't want to miss the celebrations. There was to be a huge feast tonight, with a great bonfire and—

Huncks got Pell by the shoulders. "I need a boat. *Now.*"

Dr. Pell summoned one of his captains. It would be arranged. But what a pity, to miss the celebrations.

Balty and Thankful were sitting where she and Huncks had watched Balty climb the scaffold. He told them what Stuyvesant had said: that the regicides weren't in New Amsterdam, that Jones and Repent had fled the town only hours ago, by the main road. Pell was arranging a boat. If he and Balty left now, they had a chance of reaching Fairfield by morning and intercepting Jones and Repent on the King's Highway.

"Do you mean to say Whalley and Goffe were *never* here?" Balty said.

"Stuyvesant swears. I believe him."

"Then why were Jones and Repent here?"

"To kill us. Or get us hanged for spies. Deputy Koontz's integrity was conveniently for sale."

Balty considered. "Then where *are* the regicides?"

"I don't know. They're not my concern. My business is with the Indian."

Balty nodded. "Yes."

"I'm going with thee," Thankful announced.

"No," Huncks said.

"Why?"

"This is no business for a Quaker."

"I too would see justice done."

"I think we differ in our conceptions of justice."

"I would have him pay for what he did."

"With what coin, lady?"

"There are laws, even here."

"Whose laws? Magistrate Feake's? Jones's? Davenport's?"

"Vengeance is mine, sayeth the Lord. *I* shall repay."

"Don't fling Scripture in my face, madame."

"Now, now," Balty said. "No need for that." He said to Thankful, "It's not a journey to make in your condition."

"I will go to New Haven with or without thee."

Balty looked at Huncks. Huncks sighed.

"Give me your word. No Quaker nonsense."

"Not even take off her clothes?" Balty said. They laughed. Pell's man arrived to say the boat was ready.

CHAPTER 48

Oh, *Do* Get Up

he wind held from the west. They reached Hell Gate as the last
light was fading. Seeing the boiling churn of water, Balty wished
for two things: darkness, to render the froth invisible; and the bottle
of laudanum, so that he wouldn't care.

Ably steered by Pell's crew, the shallop negotiated the passage
without wrecking or capsizing. The water quieted and widened as
they entered into the Sound, a name Balty found preferable to the
Devil's Belt. As he had on their prior crossing, Balty laid his head on
Thankful's lap, now feeling the bulge in her belly where Gideon's—or
Repent's—child was growing.

Toward dawn the wind freshened. By midmorning they fetched
Fairfield harbor.

Mrs. Pell welcomed them and gave them a good breakfast and
three horses for their journey. Huncks went about the town asking if
a large white man and strange-looking Indian had been seen passing
through. No. It appeared they'd beat them to Fairfield. As was his
wont, Balty asked, "What now?"

Huncks weighed. What if Jones and Repent were avoiding the
King's Highway? They might be. The King had just dramatically re-
asserted his authority in these parts. Jones and Repent may have

reckoned the safer way to New Haven was a parallel one through the forest north of the highway. The rivers there were narrower, easier to ford.

"Do you remember the way we took when we left New Haven?" Huncks said.

"I remember that it took forever."

"That's how we'll go. But we must leave now."

They said their farewells to Mrs. Pell and left Fairfield by the way they'd come two months ago. Again Balty found himself embosomed by the New England forest, conjuring visions of slavering catamounts behind every rock. They crossed a river Huncks called Howsatunnuck, which he said in the Mohican language meant "River of the Mountain Place," though Balty could see no mountain. They rode without stopping.

Toward late afternoon they arrived at a fork in the path and dismounted and stretched. Balty vaguely recognized it. The more trodden path continued straight, toward New Haven. A less-traveled one veered right, up what looked like a long, ascending slope.

"Where does that go?" Balty asked.

"To the cliff," Thankful said.

"The cliff? Then we've passed New Haven."

"No. The west cliff."

"No more cliffs for me," Balty said. "East, west, north, or south."

Huncks said, "If they avoided the highway, they'll pass through here." He went about scouting a place to make an ambush.

The afternoon heat brought a rumble of thunderclouds and a brief, drenching rainstorm. Balty and Thankful sheltered under some elms.

Huncks found a spot that satisfied him, a hundred yards beyond the fork on the New Haven path.

They tied the horses at a distance downwind and took up their position behind some rocks. Huncks and Balty inspected their pistols and powder.

"I'll take the Indian," Huncks said. "Jones is fat. Even you couldn't miss him."

Thankful said, "Thou aren't just going to *shoot* them, surely?"

"What would you have us do? Invite them to prayer?"

"This is murder, Colonel."

"You gave your word. No nonsense."

"Condoning murder, nonsense?"

Huncks muttered, "God, give me strength."

"If thou ask God for strength, Colonel, he will give it thee. Come, let us pray together." She took Huncks and Balty by the hand and closed her eyes.

They heard sounds. Thankful was deep in communion with the Holy Spirit. Balty and Huncks saw two men emerge from the woods. Jones and Repent.

With his free hand, Huncks brought the butt of his pistol down on Thankful's head. She went limp. Huncks caught her and laid her gently on the ground.

"Huncks! What have you done?"

"What the Holy Spirit *told* me to."

"Jesus, man!"

"We should never have brought her. I told you Quaker women are trouble."

Jones and the Indian dismounted at the fork. Balty patted Thankful's limp hand in his.

"She's alive."

"Of course she's *alive*," Huncks snarled. "*We* won't be if you don't look sharp."

Jones and the Indian remounted. Instead of continuing on the path to New Haven, toward Huncks and Balty, they took the one that went up the long slope.

"Come."

"What about her?"

"Leave her."

"She'll be *eaten*."

Huncks took the small pistol from his boot and laid it on Thankful's stomach.

"Unless the Quaker aversion of violence extends to not shooting lions trying to eat you. Coming or not?"

Balty was all at sea. What kind of man would abandon an unconscious woman in the forest? A woman with child. A woman for whom he had the most tender of feelings. A woman—

"Stay, then," Huncks said.

Balty thought of Micah's face, his mouth full of earth.

"I'm coming."

They went on foot. Jones and Repent's horses were tired. They were moving slowly. Huncks and Balty were able to keep pace.

"Please tell me there's not another bloody Indian graveyard on this cliff."

"I doubt they're paying their respects to dead Quiripi."

The trail went along the rim of the cliff. The vista to the west became more and more expansive as the ridge steepened. The sun cast a warm glow over the forest. Here and there, like patches on a quilt, early-turning maple trees blazed orange and red. On any other day it would be a view to make one pause and marvel at New England's beauty.

Several miles on, the ridge had risen four hundred feet above the forest. Huncks said they must be near the southern rim. Still, Jones and Repent continued. If they were making for New Haven, this was a very circuitous route.

Through the trees ahead loomed a large and discrepant object. As they drew closer, they saw it was an irregular rock, a giant boulder that had cracked into three or four sections. There was something otherworldly to it. In ancient Greece, people might say it was the remnant of a battle fought at the dawn of time between the Titans—a sling stone shattered into pieces by a retaliatory lightning bolt.

Jones and the Indian dismounted in front of it. Balty and Huncks took cover behind trees.

Jones called out, as if addressing the rock itself: "General Whalley! It's William."

Two men, old, frail and filthy, clad in rags, emerged from a cleft in the rock, a pair of Lazaruses, rising from the tomb. They clasped hands with Jones.

"Well, old cock," Huncks said, "behold—your regicides."

Balty stared, incredulous. Was it possible that these . . . *trolls* were Edward Whalley and his son-in-law, William Goffe?

Whalley, hero of the Battle of Naseby, cousin to Oliver Cromwell, one of seven men summoned to his deathbed; King Charles's jailer at Hampton Court; signer of his death warrant?

Goffe, most radical of the Puritan commanders, who'd declared the King was Antichrist, with all heaven arrayed against him and the Second Coming at hand?

Was it *possible* these ragged creatures who'd crawled out from under a rock—literally—had only a few years ago been two of the most formidable men in England? Who'd wielded the ultimate power, decreeing that the monarch's head should be cut off?

Over the nine months since Downing had dispatched Balty over the sea, he'd had various images of the men he was hunting. Stout, hardy men, dashing figures, gleaming in armor, swords in hand, mounted on prancing steeds with flaring nostrils. Such was how England had known them. Balty had suspected the reality might turn out to be less impressive. Fugitives tend not to go about gleaming in armor on prancing steeds.

But—*this*?

Balty had made a fantasy for himself about the moment when he would run his prey to earth. The regicides would be on their backs on the ground. He'd stand over them, holding his sword. Conscious of the drama of the moment—the *history*!—he'd address them in a commanding voice, perhaps in iambic pentameter.

"In the name of his majesty Charles, King of England, I, Balthasar de St. Michel, arrest you for the crime of high treason and the odious sin of regicide!" Balty had rehearsed it a few times out loud, out of Huncks's hearing.

What grand oratory was appropriate to this shabby scene? "I say—you there, Whalley. You, Goffe, come along, then. Oh, *do* get up." Balty was so flummoxed he didn't even ask Huncks "What now?"

Jones was doing most of the speaking, Whalley and Goffe listening with long faces.

They couldn't hear what he was saying. Probably that a great force of English arms had arrived and soon these woods would teem with English soldiers. They were no longer safe here, even inside a rock atop a ridge thick with trees.

Daylight was fading. Repent left the white men to their talking and gathered wood. He assembled a pile in front of the cleft from which the regicides had emerged, struck shavings with a flint, crouched, and blew. The wood crackled and wisps of smoke rose.

Balty whispered, "All this time, they were *here*?"

Huncks seemed amused. "Ironic, eh? But these cliffs get their color from iron. So, what are your orders?"

"Orders? What are you talking about?"

"You're the judge hunter. My remit was to prepare the way for Colonel Nicholls. There are your judges. What do you propose?"

"They look more like beggars."

"Um. Fresh air seems not to have agreed with them. Still, preferable to the Reverend Davenport's root cellar."

"I thought we weren't after them."

"We weren't. We seem to have stumbled into a forest rich in game."

"I don't care about them, Huncks."

"What about your commission?"

"Damn my commission."

"And your knighthood?"

"Damn that."

"You're blithe. You used to preen at being made Sir Balthasar de St. Michel. What happened to him?"

"Seem to have lost him somewhere."

"You've gone native."

"What's that supposed to mean?"

"You came here to catch killers of a king. Now you care only to avenge the death of farmers."

"Yes, all right. But what now?"

"Thought you'd never ask." Huncks studied the scene. "I'll circle around right, see if there's a back way into that rock. Look for me to come out where the judges did."

"*Then* what?"

"Then we'll see."

"What kind of plan is *that*?"

"The only one I can think of at present."

"Well, it's pitiful. What am I supposed to do while you're spelunking?"

Huncks pointed to a thick tree. "Put yourself behind that and wait."

"Wait for what?"

"For things to happen. You've got two pistols, don't you?"

"Yes?"

"Well, use 'em." Huncks grinned. "If you decide after all you want the knighthood, shoot the judges."

Thankful opened her eyes, felt the throb of pain at the back of her head. Sitting up, she saw Huncks's pistol in her lap. She looked about for signs of a struggle. Nothing.

She stood, and saw the footprints in the rain-wet path. She followed them to the fork, where she saw the other foot- and hoofprints, and ran.

- *CHAPTER 49* -

Repent

Repent crouched over the fire, its heat inflaming the scar on his forehead, turning it livid. He put a fingertip to it and traced along it.

He was a boy then, proud that the white sachem So-Big-Study-Man took an interest in him, teaching him English and the Great Book, to make him a good Christian. He wanted in return to make a gift for So-Big-Study-Man. But what could he give him? Then one day in the graveyard of the New Heaven whites he saw on the stone the face with wings for ears and knew this would make a good gift, carved into his face.

But when he presented So-Big-Study-Man with his gift, he became angry and shouted at him and called him names from the Great Book, names of evildoers and devils. He said this was a great sinning, that God was angry. Images made God angry. God brought down thunder and lightning to destroy images. God might destroy *him* now.

He told So-Big-Study-Man that he did not understand. If God hated images, why did the whites put images on the stones of their dead, of angels, man-birds who carried the spirits of their dead into the sky three days after they were put into the earth?

So-Big-Study-Man became even more angry and struck him, again and again, on his face. The scar opened and bled. His eyes filled with blood so that he couldn't see. So-Big-Study-Man stopped hitting him and said he must have a new name, a name that would make God less angry. The name he would have from now on was Repent.

He remembered this name from the Great Book. It was what the sachem Moses of the long-ago time told his people when he saw them praising a cow. Moses told them they must repent or he would not bring them to the promised place. If they did not, he would leave them in the desert to die of hunger and thirst and be consumed by the flaming tree.

So he took up the new name, hoping that this would make So-Big-Study-Man happy with him again. But the whites looked at him in a strange way, and would laugh when he passed. He thought this was a good thing because they never laughed, these whites.

For a time it was better between him and So-Big-Study-Man.

Time passed. One day when he was no longer a boy he saw the girl with gold hair. She was kind to him. He wanted her, but she had a husband. So he became a friend of the husband's and took him on a hunt and put him with the snakes.

He went to the girl and said now they could be together. She cried and threw stones at him, which made him angry, after all he had done so that they could be together. So he took her and put his seed into her so that she would have to be his wife. But she ran away and went to the whites and tried to make trouble for him.

He went to So-Big-Study-Man and asked him to make her be his wife, but he would not do this. The woman was a Quaker, a Christian she-devil, and Repent must have nothing more to do with her. He said that there would be trouble with the whites because of the dead husband. Repent must go away from New Heaven and stay on the land the whites had given the Quiripi.

Then one day Jones came with gifts, two fathoms of black-eye wampum and pommy and jugs of burning water. He told Repent that two Owanux had come to steal from the graves of the Quiripi. The

Quiripi must kill them. But the Owanux escaped. The white farmer hid them and mocked him by making false graves. The white farmer and his woman and boy suffered for this.

Then Jones came again and said that So-Big-Study-Man and the New Heaven whites were not pleased by the suffering of the farmer and his family. Repent must now come with him.

They went through Siwanoy and Munsee land to the Island of the Hills where the Swannekens had made their settlement. Jones said the Owanux grave stealers had gone there to hide, and they must find them and finish killing them. This would please So-Big-Study-Man and the whites.

But he killed only the Swanneken soldier who would not give up the Owanux, and again they escaped. Then came great ships with many soldiers. Jones said these had come to make war on the Swannekens and take their land. He said that this was not a good thing, even though Swannekens were a bad people. The Owanux across the sea had a new king, an evil king who worshipped images. After his soldiers had killed the Swannekens and taken their land, they would come to New Heaven to make war on So-Big-Study-Man and all the whites, because they refused to worship images. So he and Repent must leave and warn them.

When they were almost to New Heaven, Jones said they must go up the red hill and warn the two holy Owanux who lived in the cave there. Repent asked Jones why they were holy. Jones said it was because they had killed the father of the new Owanux king who, like his son, was evil.

They would camp tonight by the cave with the holy Owanux. Tomorrow Jones would return to the whites in New Heaven and warn them, while Repent must return to the Quiripi land and stay there.

Repent told Jones he would help him fight the Owanux when they came to New Heaven. But Jones said no, he must stay with the Quiripi and not show himself again in New Heaven. This was what God wanted.

Repent stopped tracing the angel on his forehead and lowered his hand. As he did, he saw movement in the trees beyond the fire.

Huncks made a wide circle through the trees to the back of the rock, where he found a cleft. Great slabs of stone were at irregular angles, making passage difficult with one hand holding a pistol. Huncks made his way in.

Inside was pitch-black, with a rank, damp smell. The ground felt soft under his feet. He crouched to feel. Blankets. He continued groping his way forward. His boots slipped on the slick rock, and he caught himself.

Coming to the opening he drew back the hammer of his pistol, and eased himself out.

The regicides were facing away from him, at Jones, and didn't see him. Jones's eyes went wide. He went for his pistol.

"If you please, Mr. Fish."

Whalley and Goffe wheeled. Goffe started to bolt, but was restrained by his father-in-law.

"My business is not with you gentlemen," Huncks said. He addressed Jones: "The Indian—where is he?"

Jones made no reply. Huncks walked to him and put the muzzle to his forehead. With his other hand he removed Jones's pistol from his belt.

"Count of three, I'll make a cave of your head."

"Huncks!"

Balty was twenty feet away. Repent stood next to him, Balty's own pistol to his head.

"Sorry, old man. Didn't hear him."

Jones grinned and opened his mouth to speak. Huncks stuck the barrel of his pistol into his mouth.

"Pray, silence."

"Shoot him," Balty said. "Then shoot Repent. You've got two pistols. Repent's only got one."

Repent whacked Balty on his bandaged ear with his pistol. Balty recoiled in pain.

Huncks understood: Balty was telling him: *Repent only got one of my pistols.*

He said to Jones, "I shall remove this impediment to your speech. And you, sir, shall instruct your friend to lower his weapon. Agreed?"

Jones nodded, teeth clicking against the barrel.

"Put down the gun," Jones ordered.

Repent ignored him.

"Damn you! Do as I say!"

Repent lowered the pistol.

"There," Huncks said. "Much more congenial."

Huncks studied the way Repent held the pistol. Had he ever fired one? It was possible he hadn't. The one Bartholomew gave him as a peace offering—Huncks's own—was disabled. Unlike the Dutch, who'd sell anything to anyone for a price, the English enforced strict laws against providing Indians with firearms.

Might Repent miss at this distance? If he could provoke him to shoot, Balty would have a chance to get his other pistol.

Huncks turned his back on Repent and walked to Whalley and Goffe, to put more distance between himself and the Indian. He tensed for the shot. But Repent didn't fire. This told Huncks two things: he wasn't adept with a pistol, but was smart enough to know it.

Huncks addressed himself to the regicides.

"Lieutenant General Whalley. Major General Goffe. We've not been introduced. Hiram Huncks, Colonel, late of the Connecticut militia. At your service."

"He's not here to serve you," Jones said. "He's come to kill you. He and his mate over there."

"I beg to differ, sir," Huncks said. "We came to kill *you*. And your red friend."

It came to Huncks: *Goad him.*

He made a face of disgust. "*Christ*, but he stinks! I can smell him from here. How do you stand it?" Huncks laughed. "But then, you're no bouquet of roses, are you? We should have left you in that field covered with fish guts. You'd have made a fine dinner for the beasts. They'd still be gorging on you."

Huncks turned sideways to make a smaller target. He spoke to the regicides as if delivering a lecture on local customs and traditions.

"Of course, nothing stinks worse than a Quiripi. Filthy tribe. Mind you, that's not their worst quality. They're thieves. Cutthroats. Cowards. Skulkers. Not warriors. That one there, he buried a family alive. Father, mother, and young boy. Really, Jones, you have deplorable taste in catamites."

"How *dare* you!" Jones roared. "I'm no sodomite!"

"Come, Jones," Huncks tsk-tsked, "all Connecticut knows of your unnatural proclivities."

Huncks turned to the ashen-faced regicides as if adding a footnote.

"He buggered a *cow*. They hang you for that, here. Bribed the judge. *What* a scandal! I'm sure neither of you gentlemen would have been susceptible to bribes in your capacity as judges."

Jones was trembling with rage. Huncks resumed his lecture.

"Ask any of the tribes here. They all abominate the Quiripi. We've many noble tribes in New England. Respected, honored. Great warrior tribes. Mohawk. Pequot. A *very* great tribe, the Pequot. Siwanoy. Munsee. Narragansett. Wampanoag. Splendid, all. Ask any of *them* what they think of the Quiripi and they'll tell you the Quiripi are a tribe of dogs. Stinking, filthy, cowardly dogs. Who sell themselves to the white man, cheap. To be his slaves."

Balty realized what Huncks was up to. Repent's jaw muscles were grinding, eyes gleaming with hatred. Balty poised to lunge for his other pistol, on the ground.

The silence was broken by a thunder of hooves. Torches flickered through the trees. Whoever it was, was coming hard and fast, no thought for stealth.

Six armed riders burst from the trees into the clearing and reined in their mounts.

The man in front leaned forward in the saddle and took in the scene before him. He looked at Jones, at the judges, at Repent and Balty. His gaze settled on Huncks.

"*You?*"

"Well, well, the Dependable Feake," Huncks said. "A very great honor."

Huncks walked behind the two regicides and put his pistols to the back of their heads. He whispered, "Forgive me, sirs, but as you see, circumstances press. I shall not harm you. You have my word. In return, I ask that you give our visitors every impression that I might."

Thankful watched from behind a tree beyond the circle of firelight. Huncks's pistol felt alien in her hand. She had never held one.

Huncks said to Feake, "Do I gather the purpose of your visit is to inform the Generals that the English Navy has arrived?"

Feake signaled his men to dismount.

"You're outnumbered," Feake said.

"I disagree, sir. The Indian there may have Mr. St. Michel as hostage. But I have these fine gentlemen. Your hostage may be valuable, to be sure, *being* his majesty's commissioner. But mine are no small prizes. Indeed, it's a privilege to hold pistols to such distinguished heads."

Huncks called out to Balty, "No disrespect intended, old man. You're a lovely hostage. If they kill you, there'll be nothing left of New Haven but elm trees, and Magistrate Feake and his constables here hanging from them. Whereas if I shoot *my* hostages, his majesty's like to rename the town after me. New Huncks. Fine name. What say you, Dependable? Does it ring for you? New Huncks?"

"Shoot them both," Feake ordered his men.

The constables looked at each other. One said, "Sir, the judges— we might hit them."

Huncks recognized the voice. It was Bartlett, the young sergeant who'd come to arrest Thankful at the Cobbs' farm.

"Then shoot *that* one!" Feake pointed at Balty.

Still the men hesitated. Feake dismounted, muttering.

Huncks called out, "Sergeant Bartlett? That you?"

Bartlett said diffidently, "Yes, Colonel."

"Good to see you again, Amos."

Feake, apoplectic, shouted, "Bartlett! I gave you an order! *Shoot that man!*"

Huncks said to the constables, "Think it through, lads. He's walking you to the gallows. An English army's coming."

"You, Repent!" Feake screamed. "*Shoot that man!*"

Repent raised his pistol to Balty's head.

"No." A woman's voice, from the darkness.

Thankful stepped into the circle of firelight, just as Balty had first seen her that day at the worship house, only now her belly was protuberant with child.

No one moved.

She walked toward Repent. Repent's eyes fixed on her belly. She stopped ten feet from him.

"Repent," she said.

The Indian stared. She put her left hand to her belly.

"Here is your child, Repent."

A storm raged across his face.

Thankful brought her right hand from behind her back. In it was Huncks's pistol, hammer cocked. She put the muzzle to her belly.

"Let him go, Repent. Let him go or I will kill thy child."

Repent's eyes blazed.

"She'll do it!" Feake shouted. "She killed the Cobbs. She's mad!"

"No!" Huncks said. "He killed them. Lay down the gun, Repent. It's over."

But it wasn't.

Overwhelmed by exhaustion and the horror of what she had threatened but had no intention of carrying out, Thankful fainted and fell to the ground.

Repent fired. But his gaze fixed on Thankful, he failed to see that Balty had removed his head from the muzzle. Balty lunged for his other pistol.

Repent walked to Thankful. He picked her up and held her in his arms with tenderness.

Balty raised his pistol. "Put her down, Repent."

The Indian stood motionless, looking into Thankful's face. He turned and began to walk toward the nearby cliff.

Huncks shoved the regicides aside and bolted after him. Feake grabbed a constable's musket and fired. Huncks spun and staggered. Then righted himself and, turning to face his attacker, assumed the formal posture of a duelist, aimed, and fired. The ball opened a hole in Feake's forehead.

"The judges!" Jones shouted. "Protect the judges!" The constables ran to Whalley and Goffe and formed a cordon of musketry around them.

But there was nothing to protect the judges from. Huncks, clutching his side, stumbled after Repent.

Balty was right behind the Indian, who was now striding with deliberate, almost ceremonial steps.

Balty didn't shoot, fearful of hitting Thankful. Realizing Repent's intention, he ran ahead of him to block his way.

"Repent! Stop! Please!"

Repent was now twenty feet from the cliff. He kept coming, eyes blazing, scar livid in the moonlight. He bent forward to gather momentum.

Balty raised his pistol. "*Please, Repent!*"

The Indian quickened his pace, tilting forward, becoming a battering ram, Thankful limp in his arms.

Balty threw away his pistol and braced to intercept him.

In the next instant there was an explosion from behind. The angel burst from Repent's head, splattering Balty with brains. But the Indian's body still came at Balty, colliding, knocking him backward.

Balty teetered, flailing, trying to regain his balance. Then a hand grabbed him and another hand got Thankful, pulling them back from the abyss.

CHAPTER 50

Don't Be a Tit

As a doctor's wife, Mrs. Pell saw that Huncks's wound was likely mortal. She dispatched a message to her husband by fast rider: "Huncks dying. New Haven danger possible. Make haste."

Toward late afternoon, the King's Highway became a dust storm of hooves. Winthrop rode at the head of thirty of his Connecticut militia. Dr. Pell brought twenty of his Westchester Trained Band. Dr. Pell's house became a fortress an army would hesitate to attack.

Dr. Pell did what he could, but the ball had nicked Huncks's liver. Bile was emptying into the abdominal cavity, turning his water black.

Pell and Winthrop and Underhill kept vigil at Huncks's bedside. Thankful nursed him as she had at the Cobb farm. Balty, unable to govern his emotions, stood his own miserable watch alone in another room.

The delirium began. Huncks slipped in and out of consciousness. Winthrop left, hiding his face. He had to return to New York to attend to the hand-over. He took only a few of his militia with him.

*　　*　　*

Thankful nudged Balty, who'd dozed off.

"It's time," she said. They hugged. Balty went in alone to Huncks's room.

Huncks was propped on pillows, whisky jug cradled in his right arm. Balty sat on the bed and took his hand.

Huncks opened his eyes.

"Who's that?"

"It's me, old cock. Balty."

Huncks frowned. "Balty? We met?"

"I should hope so."

"We ... serve together?"

"I suppose you could call it that."

"Where?"

"Well, let's see. Boston. Hartford. New Haven. Here, in Fairfield. Oyster Bay. New Amsterdam. New York."

"New York? Where's that?"

"Not so far."

"Bird," Huncks said. "There was a bird."

"Mm. Parrot. Name of Johann. Frightful thing. Didn't much care for *you*. Look, old man, I wanted . . . I wanted to say thank you."

"For what?"

"Looking after me."

"Don't be a tit. Balty . . ."

"I'm here."

"No. *Balty.* Did he get his knighthood?"

"Oh. Yes. He did. He did. His majesty created him Baron . . . Baron New Huncks. Very grand title."

Huncks's lips moved. Balty leaned in.

"What is it, old man?"

"What . . . now? Balty always asking . . . what . . . now?"

"What a bother he must have been to you."

Huncks shook his head. "Brother Balty. What . . . now . . . ?"

"Get some rest, old man. I'll take first watch."

*   *   *

Huncks had told Thankful he wanted to be buried alongside the Cobbs. She told Winthrop, who smiled and said: "Just like Huncks to request burial behind enemy lines." Before returning to Breuckelen, he gave instructions to the captain of his militia.

The next day an unusual cortège made its way along the King's Highway from Fairfield to New Haven. At the head of it rode a captain of Connecticut militia. Behind him, a carriage drawn by four horses carried a coffin draped with the flag of the Connecticut Colony. Balty and Thankful followed behind, at the head of a troop of twenty mounted militia.

Word of the procession passed quickly up the highway.

They were met at the New Haven line by a dozen New Haven constables forming a barricade across the highway to deny them passage.

The Connecticut captain and the young New Haven sergeant each insisted on superior authority. Muskets were raised. But when the name of the man in the coffin was revealed, the New Haven sergeant ordered his men to stand down. The cortège was allowed to pass. As it did, the sergeant removed his hat.

Huncks was laid to rest beside Bartholomew and Amity and Micah, by the stream at the foot of the red cliff. A volley was fired in salute and a guard posted over the grave for one month, the period of mourning officially proclaimed by the Governor of the Connecticut Colony.

Over the years, people who'd heard versions of the story came to see the grave of the man whose name over time was lost, known only as The Judge Hunter.

– EPILOGUE –

November 24th, 1664. Today arrived from New England by one of Col. Nicholls's ships a letter from Brother Balty. Mirabile dictu.

No surprise—he reports lack of success in his endeavor. But joyous news! He intends to stay on in New England—says he has information as to the whereabouts of the regicide judges. Whalley and Goffe doubtless guaranteed to die of old age. God save New England.

Bro Balty's letter oddly full of "thees" and "thous."

My wife naturally in a grievous state and blaming me. Great haranguing. Boxed her ears.

To my barber, to arrange with him to keep my perriwig in good order at 20s. a year, which will make me go very spruce.

And so to bed.

Historical Notes

The bloodless seizure of New Amsterdam in 1664 by the English, cunningly plotted by **George, Lord Downing** and **Charles II's brother, the Duke of York**, led to a copious spillage of blood a year later, with the outbreak of the Second Anglo-Dutch War. It was during that conflict that the Dutch carried out their daring nighttime raid on the English fleet in the Medway, burning, among other ships, the *Royal Charles*, which had brought Charles II home to England after his exile (with Pepys aboard). That and other disasters on the English side brought Charles II's reputation low and weakened his rule. Downing, who had avidly fomented war with Holland, prospered. Land once his, on which he built and sold houses shoddily made on the cheap, still bears his name as the residence, since 1735, of British prime ministers—Number 10 Downing Street. The official Number Ten website acknowledges that Downing was "miserly and at times brutal."

In 1672, during the third war between England and Holland, **Richard Nicholls**, who took New Amsterdam without a shot fired, and **Edward Montagu, First Earl of Sandwich**, were both killed at the Battle of Solebay.

Barbara Palmer, Countess Castlemaine, principal mistress to King Charles II, bore him five illegitimate children. Seldom has the title "Lady of the Bedchamber" been more faithfully undertaken. Her descendants include Diana Spencer, erstwhile Princess of Wales; Sarah Ferguson, erstwhile Duchess of York; Mitford sisters Nancy, Pamela, Diana, Unity, Jessica, and Deborah; philosopher Bertrand Russell; and British prime minister Anthony Eden.* Many hated her. Pepys adored her.

The land **Dr. Thomas Pell** bought from **Wampage, chief of the Siwanoy**, is now Pelham, Pelham Manor, the eastern Bronx, and southern Westchester County. Pell died in 1669. His descendants include the U.S. senator from Rhode Island, Claiborne Pell.

Thirty years after cofounding the Colony of New Haven, the **Reverend John Davenport** found himself defeated—politically by the absorption of New Haven into the Connecticut Colony, and spiritually by the rise of Arminianism (the Dutch theology that rejected original sin and predestination). He returned to Boston and became pastor of the First Church there, dying of apoplexy on March 15, 1670, age seventy-two. His descendants include Watergate prosecutor Archibald Cox and Maxwell Perkins, the legendary editor of F. Scott Fitzgerald, Ernest Hemingway, and Thomas Wolfe. Yale University's Davenport College bears his name.

Captain John Underhill, warrior and Indian fighter, died in the Quaker faith on his farm at Oyster Bay in 1672. The plot of land he owned when he lived in New Amsterdam is the site of Trinity Church in lower Manhattan. His sister-in-law played an important role in the Flushing Remonstrance of 1657, which resulted in the Dutch West India Company granting rights to Quakers. The Remonstrance went on to influence the First Amendment of the Bill of Rights, establishing freedom of speech.

Following the British seizure of New Netherland, **Peter Stuyvesant** was recalled to Amsterdam in disgrace and blamed for the loss, by his neglectful and indifferent employers at the West India Company. He eventually returned to Manhatoes and lived out his life in tranquility at Bouwerie Number One. He died in 1672. Russell Shorto notes

* Per an unsourced entry in Wikipedia.

that his tombstone in St. Mark's Church-in-the-Bowery "manages to get both his age and his title wrong." His descendants include former New York governor, U.S. senator, and U.S. secretary of state Hamilton Fish; writer Loudon Wainwright Jr., under whom the present author studied journalism at college; and singer-songwriter Loudon Wainwright III.

John Winthrop (the Younger), Governor of the Connecticut Colony, was a man of abundant scientific curiosity. In England, he gazed at the heavens with Charles II through his majesty's "royal tube." Winthrop owned a three-and-a-half-foot telescope in Hartford. In 1664, the year of events related here, he observed a fifth moon of Jupiter. In 1892, the Lick Observatory in California confirmed its existence. Winthrop died of a severe cold in Boston in 1692. His direct descendants include former senator and secretary of state John F. Kerry.

Neither **Edward Whalley** nor his son-in-law **William Goffe** was ever apprehended. An incident during the conflict known as King Philip's War gave rise to the so-called legend of the Angel of Hadley. On Sunday, September 1, 1675, the Massachusetts town of Hadley came under Indian attack. The settlers, at pains to get themselves organized, were surprised by an aged man with white hair and military bearing, who appeared suddenly and rallied them to repel the attack. The old man, whom no one had seen before, disappeared and was never seen again. According to the legend, this was Goffe, who had been hiding for many years in the local pastor's house. Seeing the Indians approaching, the old soldier sprang into action. The episode furnished inspiration to Sir Walter Scott, James Fenimore Cooper, and Nathaniel Hawthorne.

Samuel Pepys was eyewitness to the execution of Charles I, the Restoration, the execution of the first of the men who condemned Charles I to death, the Great Plague and the Great Fire of London. (It was Pepys who informed the king and his brother, James, Duke of York, that the city was on fire.) He rose to be secretary of the admiralty. His career ended in 1688 after the Glorious Revolution deposed the Catholic James II who, as Duke of York and Lord High Admiral, had successfully schemed to seize New Amsterdam. Pepys died on May 26, 1703. Despite their stormy marriage, his myriad infidelities, and the importunings of his brother-in-law Balty, he remained devoted to **Elizabeth**. She died in 1669, leaving him grief-stricken. He never remarried. The six volumes of his diary, which he kept in his own shorthand, were deciphered and published in 1825. Pepys is considered by many to be the greatest diarist in the English language.

Balthasar de St. Michel came to his brother-in-law's defense in 1673 when Pepys was maliciously (and falsely) accused by his political enemies of "popery." He wrote a letter for the record, staunchly (and falsely) asserting his sister's Protestant bona fides. An elusive figure, Balty disappears from history as casually as he enters it.

The curious "glacial erratic" boulder atop West Rock Ridge State Park in New Haven, Connecticut, is known as Judges Cave. Here, in 1661 (and perhaps again in 1664), two of the men who signed the death warrant of King Charles I hid from their pursuers. Their first stay ended when they were surprised by the growl of a catamount and decided to seek refuge elsewhere. A plaque noting what took place here ends with a paraphrase of Benjamin Franklin's design for the Great Seal of the United States: "Opposition to tyrants is obedience to God."

Sources

The Diary of Samuel Pepys, which Sam kept from 1660 until 1669. Pepys laid down his quill for fear the diary might be ruining his eyes. Our loss—he lived until 1703. To him we owe much of what we know of life during that decade: the Restoration, the Great Fire of London, the Plague, royal gossip, executions galore. Historians tell us what happened. Pepys tells us what it looked, felt, sounded, and tasted like. The alert reader—that is, all of you—will recognize that all but the first diary entry and a few extracts are of the author's devising. It is most Earnestly and Prayerfully hoped that these pastiches will be seen as a token of Homage. For further reading, see Claire Tomalin's *Samuel Pepys: The Unequalled Self* (New York: Knopf, 2002).

Second, and no less indispensable, Russell Shorto's superb *The Island at the Center of the World. The Epic Story of Dutch Manhattan and the Forgotten Colony That Shaped America* (New York: Doubleday, 2004). It was in these pages that I learned, among a thousand other shimmery details, that grumpy old Peter Stuyvesant had a soft spot for tropical birds.

Research happily included rereading a book—by any measure, *the* book on our Puritan forefathers—by my college tutor, mentor, and friend Kai T. Erikson: *Wayward Puritans: A Study in the Sociology of Deviance* (New York: Wiley, 1966). It was in these pages, forty years ago, that I first learned of the unusual—indeed arresting—form of protest by Quaker women in old New England.

I'm in debt to the fine scholarship and narratives of the following authors and works.

Books

Ackroyd, Peter. *Civil War: The History of England*, Vol. III. New York: Macmillan, 2014.

Blue, Jon C. *The Case of the Piglet's Paternity: Trials from the New Haven Colony, 1639–1663*. Middletown, CT: Wesleyan University Press, 2015.

Daniels, Bruce C. *New England Nation: The Country the Puritans Built*. New York: Palgrave Macmillan, 2012.

Demos, John. *The Unredeemed Captive: A Family Story from Early America*. New York: Knopf, 1994.

Frasier, Antonia. *Royal Charles: Charles II and the Restoration*. New York: Knopf, 1979.

Gunn, Giles, ed. *Early American Writing*. New York: Penguin, 1994.

Hawke, David Freeman. *Everyday Life in Early America*. New York: Harper, 1988.

Jaffe, Eric. *The King's Best Highway: The Lost History of the Boston Post Road, the Route That Made America*. New York: Scribner, 2010.

Jordan, Don, and Michael Walsh. *The King's Revenge: Charles II and the Greatest Manhunt in British History*. New York: Pegasus, 2016.

Karr, Ronald Dale, ed. *Indian New England, 1524–1674: A Compendium of Eyewitness Accounts of Native American Life*. Pepperell, MA: Branch Line Press, 1999.

Lipman, Andrew. *The Saltwater Frontier: Indians and the Contest for the American Coast*. New Haven, CT: Yale University Press, 2015.

Malone, Patrick M. *The Skulking Way of War: Technology and Tactics Among the New England Indians*. Baltimore: Johns Hopkins University Press, 1993.

Nicolar, Joseph. *The Life and Traditions of the Red Man*. Durham, NC: Duke University Press, 2007.

Pagliuco, Christopher. *The Great Escape of Edward Whalley and William Goffe, Smuggled Through Connecticut.* Charleston, SC: History Press, 2012.

Shapiro, James. *The Year of Lear: Shakespeare in 1606.* New York: Simon & Schuster, 2015.

Shonnard, Frederic, and W. W. Spooner. *History of Westchester County, New York, from Its Earliest Settlement to the Year 1900.* New York: New York History Co., 1900.

Spencer, Charles. *Killers of the King: The Men Who Dared to Execute Charles I.* New York: Bloomsbury, 2014.

Ulrich, Laurel Thatcher. *Good Wives: Image and Reality in the Lives of Women in Northern New England, 1650–1750.* New York: Alfred A. Knopf, 1980. Reprint, New York: Oxford University Press, 1982.

Wilbur, C. Keith. *The New England Indians: An Illustrated Sourcebook of Authentic Details of Everyday Indian Life.* Guilford, CT: Globe Pequot Press, 1996.

Pamphlets

All of the following were addresses delivered at St. Olave Hart Street's annual Pepys Commemoration Service.

de la Bédoyère, Guy. *Pepys and Shorthand.* May 20, 2010.

Latham, Rt. Hon. Sir David. *The Convivial Pepys.* May 25, 2011.

May, Simon, Esq. *Pepys and St Paul's School.* May 27, 2009.

McCullough, Peter. *Pepys and Faith.* May 25, 2012.

Skeaping, Lucie. *Pepys's Musical World.* May 25, 2007.

Skipp, Matt. *Pepys and the Theatre.* May 26, 2005.

Walker, Rev. Andrew. *Pepys, Hooke and the Renaissance Spirit.* May 25, 2006.

Woodman, Captain Richard. *Pepys and Trinity House.* May 28, 2008.

Finally, my thanks to the indispensable Wikipedia. I endeavored to rely only on information whose source is certified by footnoted entries.

Acknowledgments

I'm indebted to John Tierney, for his valiant friendship and unstinting generosity as first responder. Greater love hath no man than he who reads draft after draft after draft, without complaining. LF.

Thanks and hats off to my good and dear friend, one of America's preeminent artists, William C. Matthews, for the inspired jacket of the book.

Greg Zorthian lent me his eagle eyes and caught many a typo and infelicity. He also told me that the final scene made *no* sense at all, as written. Thank you, Z.

My stepdaughter Kingsley Trotter, now embarking on a brilliant legal career, provided encouragement and diligent editing. Thank you, Kake.

A shout-out to my young friend Emmett Foxe.

In addition to being a source of support, my clever and loving wife, Dr. Katherine Close, provided her doppelgänger colleague Dr. DeVrootje (Chapter 19) with his insight into how Huncks might recover from his injury.

I'm thankful, too, to my agent Amanda Urban. What *would* her name have been if she lived in Puritan New England? Probably not "Binky." How about "Fabulous"?

At Simon & Schuster, thank you, Eloy Bleifuss, Martha Schwartz, Cynthia Merman, Larry "Dismas" Hughes, and Emily Simonson.

Finally, but never leastly, Jonathan Karp. This book is our twelfth together. I am the luckiest author in the world. Thank you, my very dear Mr. Karp.

ABOUT THE AUTHOR

Christopher Buckley is the author of seventeen previous books, including *Thank You for Smoking* and *Losing Mum and Pup*. This novel, set in the seventeenth century, is his second work of historical fiction, following *The Relic Master*, set in the sixteenth century. His aim, quixotic to be sure, is to write novels set in the eighteenth, nineteenth, and twentieth centuries and—Grim Reaper permitting—twenty-first. Good luck with that.